LIES

THAT

BIND

LIES THAT BIND

PENELOPE WILLIAMS

DUNDURN
TORONTO

This is a work of fiction. Characters, names, events, places, settings, and organizations are either used fictitiously or are the product of the author's imagination. Any similarity to persons, living or dead, is coincidental and not intended by the author.

Edna St. Vincent Millay, "Dirge Without Music" from Collected Poems. Copyright 1928, © 1955 by Edna St. Vincent Millay and Norma Millay Ellis. Reprinted with the permission of The Permissions Company, Inc., on behalf of Holly Peppe, Literary Executor, The Millay Society. www.millay.org.

Cover image: shutterstock.com/FCSCAFEINE
Printer: Webcom, a division of Marquis Book Printing Inc.

Library and Archives Canada Cataloguing in Publication

Title: Lies that bind / Penelope Williams.
Names: Williams, Penelope M., 1943- author.
Identifiers: Canadiana (print) 20190061391 | Canadiana (ebook) 20190061405 | ISBN 9781459745148 (softcover) | ISBN 9781459745155 (PDF) | ISBN 9781459745162 (EPUB)
Classification: LCC PS8645.I4555 L54 2019 | DDC C813/.6—dc23

2   3   4   5   23   22   21   20   19

 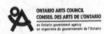

We acknowledge the support of the Canada Council for the Arts, which last year invested $153 million to bring the arts to Canadians throughout the country, and the Ontario Arts Council for our publishing program. We also acknowledge the financial support of the Government of Ontario, through the Ontario Book Publishing Tax Credit and Ontario Creates, and the Government of Canada.

Nous remercions le Conseil des arts du Canada de son soutien. L'an dernier, le Conseil a investi 153 millions de dollars pour mettre de l'art dans la vie des Canadiennes et des Canadiens de tout le pays.

Care has been taken to trace the ownership of copyright material used in this book. The author and the publisher welcome any information enabling them to rectify any references or credits in subsequent editions.

The publisher is not responsible for websites or their content unless they are owned by the publisher.

Printed and bound in Canada.

VISIT US AT

dundurn.com | @dundurnpress | dundurnpress | dundurnpress

Dundurn
3 Church Street, Suite 500
Toronto, Ontario, Canada
M5E 1M2

To Allen

What's past is prologue.

— William Shakespeare, *The Tempest*

PROLOGUE

SPRING WAS LATE that year in the town of Parnell, but the annual attack marking the end of winter still caught everyone off guard. Except Leo Harding, twelve years old, slight, dark-haired, and very quiet. He had learned to keep his counsel at a young age.

The snow was melting; rivulets of dirty water ran over the schoolyard, exposing the asphalt and dead grass — better than daffodils as heralds of the season, drawing the Parnell kids out after class to skip, play marbles, and fight. The usual.

"Saturday at five," Mikhail said. "Don't let anyone see you." The four friends — Leo Harding, Tulla Murphy, Mikhail Novak, and Kat Kominski — had moved their secret club to a construction site on Beecham Avenue when someone discovered the rules written on the underside of their table. After "No spitting, No swearing, No lying," the long arm of Parnell had stretched in and added "No fucking."

They arrived separately, sneaking into the basement under the cover of a misty March dusk, a safer venue since the older kids in the Hill Top Gang now met upstairs — the leaders, the protectors of the younger ones. But the subterfuge didn't work. Someone saw. This time Parnell came in person.

"I call this meeting to order." Mikhail banged the gavel on the newly "edited" table just as a barrage of clods hit the walls above them.

Footsteps clattered over their heads, and a voice yelled down the stairs, "Get up here quick! Valley Gang attacking!"

It was the opening salvo of a war whose battle lines had been drawn long before, but every generation answered to the atavistic need to carve them anew. Tulla's father, Warren Murphy, who'd grown up in Parnell, claimed that the animosity dated back to the earliest settlers who stumbled onto this rocky riverbank in the wilderness, saw the potential of the rapids boiling down out of the broad lake to the south, drove the Algonquin off the land, founded Parnell, and then turned on one another.

The cold had returned with the dusk, refreezing the construction detritus into the ground at odd angles. In the dark winter months, the Hill Top Gang, led by Tulla's sister, Bridget, had fashioned a fort out of what would eventually be the house's capacious living room, nailing boards across the window openings and building a makeshift table against one wall. Their war table, they called it, with a rudimentary map of the town sketched on its rough surface — a dark line dividing the town in half between the hill and valley territories.

Figures zigzagged across the site, hurled missiles, and scurried back out of range. The Valley Gang, the townies, the enemy, were on the move. Bridget peered through the cracks between the boards. "We're outnumbered. Where'd they all come from?"

"I'm here. Count me."

Bridget groaned. "Tulla, go home. Someone take her. She can't stay here."

Tulla stood her ground. "I'll just come back."

"I'll watch her," Leo said, stepping forward. Mikhail and Kat moved in closer.

Bridget hesitated. "Okay, no time left. Tulla, do exactly as you're told. I don't want to be the one carrying you home dead."

Tulla saluted, grinning from ear to ear. "Yes, sir."

Bridget turned to the others. "You four, go out from the back and draw the enemy fire. Give our guys a chance to get clods."

Instantly, Tulla imagined a pencil drawing flames in a fireplace and stood irresolute, not knowing what to do. Leo grabbed her hand and pulled her through an opening in the back wall. Mikhail and Kat followed. He hauled an old tarpaulin off a heap of earthen lumps. "I stockpiled some ammunition. Rosie warned me there might be an attack."

Mikhail stared at him. "Rosie, she's Valley."

"Sometimes." Leo handed clods to Mikhail and Kat. "Tulla, you stay under cover here."

As soon as the three disappeared around the corner of the house, Tulla trailed after them, exhilarated at being in her sister's army. That day of the Clod War she was ten years old, the enemy all around her in the waning light, not understanding why they were the enemy, but if her sister said they were, that was good enough for her.

Behind the swirling front line of Valley attackers, she could see a row of figures, motionless against the darkening sky, sticks thrust in front of them like rifles. On a shouted command, the line started slowly toward the house. Stone soldiers come to life, closing in. One seemed to break rank — she couldn't see where he'd come from — and ran straight at her. Leo yelled a warning. She scooped up a lump of frozen mud the size of a softball and hurled it. Her attacker went down without a sound, spread-eagled in the mud.

A tableau of frozen figures, her allies, turned toward her, not in admiration but in horror. Then she heard the voices.

"Holy crap, he's out cold."

"Look at the blood. His head's gushing blood."

"Who is it?"

"Jeez, it's Connolly, Bobby Connolly. His mouth's full of mud. He can't breathe."

"What the hell did you throw?" Bridget hissed as she ran past Tulla and knelt by the still figure. She pulled off her frozen mitts and squished them against the gaping wound, trying to staunch the blood.

"Is he dead?" whispered Kat.

Tulla stood rooted to the spot, shaking with the enormity of what she had done.

"Snake, get your father fast," Bridget ordered. "He needs a doctor."

Paul Skinner limped forward. "I can't. I … he's away, at a medical —"

Bridget peered over her shoulder. "Tulla, run. Go home and get help. If Mum isn't there, phone the operator to get the ambulance. Go, go!"

Tulla ran.

All heads jerked toward the scream as a figure hurtled out of the shadows and fell on Bridget, wrenching her backward into the mud. "Get away from him!"

Leo grabbed her. "She's trying to stop the bleeding!" he shouted. "She's not hurting him."

Spitting like a cat, Darla Connolly dragged her fingernails down his face as he pulled her away from her brother's motionless body. The two sides, enmity on hold, stood as silent as mourners at a gravesite, except for Darla. The mill siren suddenly whooped over her shrieks, not the long five o'clock wail indicating quitting time at the mill but an urgent staccato summons — two bursts for an ambulance crew, three for the volunteer fire brigade. Tulla had carried out her orders before racing back, terrified, to find out if Bobby was alive. Or, because of her, dead.

An eternity later headlights appeared, moved fast along the road, turned, and bounced across the darkened battlefield.

ONE

THE PEOPLE OF PARNELL knew a storm was brewing, even if the Weather Channel didn't. It was September 21, and the equinoctial winds had been blowing hard for two days, stripping the trees of their leaves and bending branches upward like arms beseeching calm.

The storm started in a sudden stillness, a hollow in the sky that sucked the air out of the town. Pedestrians peered uneasily skyward and walked faster toward home, leaving their chores for another day. Vehicle traffic thinned out. In a field at the edge of Parnell, a tractor stopped midway through cutting hay, its driver shading his eyes and studying the sky. Nothing but a dome of bright breathless blue, but he'd grown up in Parnell and knew the signs. He steered his tractor back to the barn. A single car sped up Crow Lake Road toward the ridge, shimmering in the brightness like a giant black beetle.

* * *

Harriet Deaver and Agatha Breeze stood at the window in the town library. "Still clear," Aggie said.

"Not for long. Way too still."

"It's the wrong time of year for the Fist."

"It's happened before. The *Farewell Belle* sank in a September storm on her last trip of the season."

"It was her last trip forever," Aggie said wistfully.

They leaned toward each other, their shoulders just touching, and studied the sky.

"Lock up now, Aggie. No one will be looking for books this afternoon. Come back with me before it hits."

Agatha Breeze, the town librarian for more than fifty years, and Harriet Deaver, a recently and reluctantly retired schoolteacher, were Parnell's unofficial Greek chorus. They observed, commented, and predicted, and as was often the way of close friends, rarely agreed on anything, including the cause of the coming storm. Agatha held that a particular photo had a part in it. Harriet said fiddlesticks, superstitious nonsense. They agreed, though, that the Fist of God was about to strike again.

By 8:00 p.m., the regional TV stations that still had power were running a crawl warning of a storm on its way "with gusts exceeding a hundred and seventy-five kilometres." For Parnell it wasn't a warning; it was old news. The storm had already struck.

When Bobby "Dominique" Connolly flew out his front window, most of Parnell thought it was simply his comeuppance; Toronto's *Globe and Mail* reported his death as a freak accident caused by a freak storm. Norbert "Nob" Tinsley, the police officer who was first on the scene, put it down to a direct punch by the Fist of God. And when Tulla Murphy phoned her father, he called it a by-blow of history. "Always look to the past for explanations, Tulla."

"History can't be held responsible for a tornado, Dad."

His voice, oddly subdued, came again. "Trust me on this, Tulla. That boy did not go out the window all by himself."

Which was true. "That boy," forty-nine at the time of his death, had shot through the plate-glass wall of his two-storey living room in the company of an Italian leather sofa, two end tables, and a Tiffany lamp.

"It must be a shock for you, darlin'," Tulla's father said. "One of your old gang to die so young."

She sighed. "Wrong on two counts. We're not so young, and Dom was never part of our gang."

"He wanted to be."

Their gang of four had been exclusive and impenetrable, a carapace of friendship protecting them through childhood and adolescence in schoolyards that were often more battlefields than playgrounds. Mikhail Novak, the oldest, was the unacknowledged leader by virtue of his apparent composure in all circumstances and his unshakable opinions about right and wrong. Tulla was the youngest, a dreamy kid, lost in her own world of imagining. In between were Leo Harding, shaped by early loss, and Kat Kominski, wise beyond her years, street smart, and vulnerable.

At the end of high school they had scattered. Now, after nearly thirty years, Mikhail and Tulla were back. Kat, who had never really left, ran the Koffee Klatch restaurant, and Leo was still among the missing.

When Tulla returned to Parnell, Kat had told her, "Don't know why you ever came back to this petri dish of a town. But thank God you did. I so need you here."

Just before eight the morning after the storm, Kat Kominski's cellphone rang.

"Hey, it's me," the voice at the other end said. "Are you okay? What's going on up there?"

"Hi, Tulla. We're fine, but what a night — wild. No power, lines down everywhere, trees uprooted, branches all over the place. One came through the roof of the garage next door. It sounded like a bomb."

"Anyone see the Fist?"

"We didn't, but the storm hit just after dark. Zero to one hundred and sixty in seconds. Like a freight train. The kids slept with me, though *slept* isn't the operative word. We've already had a visit from Elvie and her band of volunteers checking house-to-house in the worst-hit areas. Says we're not to go outside until they're sure there are no live wires down. So, no Klatch today."

Elvie Paterson worked at the police station and was occasionally assigned to tasks that didn't just include answering the phone. She was a bit younger than Tulla but already had reached six feet tall by grade ten.

She was the only kid back then who came to school with purple hair, for which she'd been suspended. Undeterred, she proceeded through the Goth and tattoo stages, the latter being fairly discreet, followed by a limited piercing phase until finally settling into adulthood and returning to her purple roots.

"The news report said someone was killed...."

"Bobby Connolly, a.k.a. Dom, of course. To quote Elvie — 'The storm targeted his house like a heat-seeking missile.'"

Tulla went silent, remembering. In grade three she'd played the lead in the school production of *The Princess and the Swineherd*, based on a Hans Christian Andersen fairy tale. Kat said she got the role because she already had the costume: a pink floor-length gown, stiffened with poplin, crackling with age, that had been her grandmother's. Her mother had curled her hair into fat ringlets, as stiff as her dress. Dominique — his name was Bobby then — played the swineherd. He was chosen not for his costume but for his beauty: glowing cheeks; eyes so brown they looked black, like his mother, Opal's; curly dark hair and long eyelashes, the envy of every girl in his class.

Tulla was required to kiss him in the last scene, an act necessary to turn him into a prince. Not enough magic in the universe to do that. She couldn't remember the plot — like so much of her early childhood, she was hazy on details — but she remembered the kiss with revulsion: the horror of his probing tongue, like a worm trying to get into her mouth, his knowing, adult eyes watching her. She'd jerked away as if scalded, wiping her mouth with the back of her hand, and ran from the stage. The audience erupted in laughter. The swineherd did not. And now the swineherd was dead. And all she could think of were those watchful eyes. And all she could feel was nothing. It had been shortly after the play that Bobby renamed himself Dominique and decked anyone who persisted in calling him anything else.

"Rosie was on ER duty when they brought him into the hospital," Kat said. "In bits. But she 'was cool with it.' Elvie again."

"Cool with her own brother in bits?"

"No love lost there. You okay? Was the funeral awful?"

"It was a memorial service. Not so bad. Would have been a lot harder if it had been a funeral right after Portland died. His parents were wise to delay it so long. I left Saratoga Springs right after. Got to Toronto last night. I'll fill you in when I get home. Should be there in a couple of days, as soon as I've sorted out things for Mother, who seems to have thoroughly spooked the staff again."

Tulla's mother, Sadie, lived in the Alzheimer's wing of the Walker Extended Care Facility, not far from Princess Amelia Women's Hospital in Toronto, where Tulla had done her medical school rotations in the years following the demise of her marriage. During that time, she watched her mother's deterioration with helpless sadness. Now, after months in the Bahamas witnessing her ex-husband's roller coaster ride from death's door to remission to rapid downward spiral into death, she was even more fearful of how she'd find her mother.

The room was in semi-darkness when she arrived, curtains pulled against the day. Sadie was curled up in bed, eyes half open.

"Hi, Mother."

"Oh, hi."

"It's me, Tulla."

"I know." Her fingers plucked at the bedspread. "Did you bring me anything?"

Tulla handed her an African violet, in deep purple bloom.

"Oh, good. I've just about finished the last one."

"Did it die?" Tulla rummaged in her bag for the peppermint patties her mother liked.

"No, I ate it. Come and see." Sadie stood shakily. "The staff gave it to me. It's for when I wake early and have to wait for breakfast. It takes care of the hunger pangs." She tottered into the bathroom and pointed to the denuded violet beside the basin. "It's quite tasty." She pulled a leaf off and handed it to Tulla. "Try it."

Tulla nibbled as instructed. "Tastes like velvet."

"How do you know what velvet tastes like?" Sadie asked with interest.

Oh, God, now she's going to eat the curtains. How did I get here in my life, standing in a bathroom eating a potted plant with my mother? Having wasted all those years in medical school trying to convince myself I wanted to be a doctor, then haring off on a fruitless odyssey with my ex-husband only to watch him die. And then maybe the stupidest decision of all, defying old Tom's counsel that you can't go home again by doing just that.

Her mother peered into her face. "Don't you like it? My father wouldn't even taste it. He was here last night." Her voice dropped to a whisper. "Of course, I know he's been dead for years, but it's nice of him to visit. Lots of dead visitors drop by. Ida was here, too. She's very sad. She said she never got over that child's death."

"What child?" Tulla waited for one of her mother's ghost stories, matter-of-fact reports of nightly visitors who floated through her room, summoned by voices from her bedside radio, which was kept unplugged by the spooked staff.

No stories today, though. Her eyes clouded over. "I wish they wouldn't tell me so many secrets. Thank you for coming, dear." She shuffled back to bed and turned to face the wall.

TWO

ROSIE WAS ONE of the few who knew that her brother, Dom, had been in temporary residence in his new house at Crow Lake before the storm hit. She was picking up a prescription in the town's only drugstore that advertised 24/7 service — as long as it was Friday — when her cellphone rang. It hung in a crocheted pouch around her neck, a tiny electronic albatross, ever since her husband, Stan, fell off the mill roof and nobody could find her. She'd been down by the river reading a Harlequin novel, her one secret vice, a whole other life.

She dug out the phone and frowned at the screen. "Stan? Just waiting for your prescript— Bobby?"

The phone squawked.

"I'm at the drugstore, Bob. Okay, okay, Dom, Dominique ..." Stupid name, she muttered. "No, I wasn't talking to you. I was talking to — oh, hell, I've lost the connection!" She held the phone aloft as if to prove it wasn't connected to anyone. "He wants me to pick him up at the Ottawa airport."

"That's a three-hour drive. Six there and back. Tell the selfish bastard to rent a car." A tall woman, made taller by a gelled purple mohawk and Doc Martens, stood behind her in the line.

Rosie grinned up at her. "Easy for you to say, Elvie. You were born brave. I wasn't."

"You were born good, Rosalie, and obviously into the wrong family." Her ridge of hair swayed at the shake of her head. "Never understood how you could be remotely related to that bunch."

Rosie sketched a wave and hurried out, digging her car keys out of a voluminous purse. The clerk held up the paper bag with a prescription stapled to it. "She forgot Stan's medicine."

"And there's another loser," Elvie said to the clerk in disgust. "You'd think Stan had broken every bone in his body falling off that roof. He broke his wrist for God's sake. Two years ago and he still apparently can only use that hand to operate the TV remote. Rosie's been doing everything around that house — she's better now with a screwdriver than he ever was."

"He's not a bad sort," the clerk said. "At least he's great with their kid. And he *is* still on heavy-duty pain meds — hydromorphone."

"After two years? Who's prescribing it? Old Doc Skinner?"

The clerk nodded.

"Figures," Elvie snapped.

* * *

Rosie and Dom got back to Parnell just before dawn. He'd slept all the way, rousing only to take over the driving and make a detour to his house, a huge cedar-and-glass chalet with a monstrous deck cantilevered over the rock face at the north end of Crow Lake, south of town. Parnell's citizens were vocal in their resentment of this house, not only because of who was building it, when they found out, but also where.

"Bobby, it's too late. I'll bring you out later."

He shook her hand off his arm and wheeled up Crow Lake Road and into his driveway. "The name's Dominique, for Christ's sake! Is that so hard for your pea brain to grasp? Did you tell anyone who owns this house?"

Rosie turned away from him. "This is Parnell, *Dominique.* Everyone knew from the beginning."

"You told." His tone was savage. "I warned you to keep your mouth shut until I was here."

"I didn't tell anyone." She was proud of herself. No flinching. No cowering. "Harriet Deaver found out from the land registry office."

"That meddling old bitch. I can't believe she's still alive."

Rosie smiled slightly. "Oh, she's very much alive. She's the one who bested your security guard."

He glanced back along the driveway. "Nice to look down from up here on this shithole of a town. It'll be my party palace. Starting with one hell of a housewarming." He rubbed his hands together. "I'll invite all the old 'gang.'" He made quotation marks with his fingers. "I hear Tulla Murphy's back. She'd love a housewarming."

"She would?"

"Damn right! I'll send a car for her." He grinned and looked sideways at her, laying a finger against the side of his nose.

Childhood memories flooded Rosie. When her brother did that, it meant someone was going to get hurt. Usually her, if she didn't do what he wanted.

"We have plans ..." he continued.

"You and Tulla?" She tried to keep the disbelief out of her voice. "You've seen her lately?"

"Oh, for fuck's sake, Rosie. You can be so dense."

"Then who's *we*?"

"None of your business." He lit a cigarette and blew smoke toward her. "Anyone else back I should know about?"

"Paul Skinner. Remember him? A doctor now, like his father."

"Yeah, I knew he was here. We'll probably have a beer or six before he goes back."

"He's not just visiting. He's moved back here."

Dom's mouth tightened. "Wonder what the fuck he's up to coming back to this friggin' piss-pot. I see I'll have to talk some sense into him."

Rosie frowned. "Why do you care?"

"I don't give a rat's ass, actually."

* * *

Forge Ridge cupped the north shore of Crow Lake, a granite crest of the Canadian Shield, ground smooth by glaciers millennia ago. Scree and crabgrass lapped up against islands of mossy bedrock, and at either end, fields of quack grass stretched down to a narrow scallop of beach. Generations of Parnellites had camped and picnicked on this Crown land until the previous spring when hikers discovered the gate blocking Crow Lake Road. The guard and little gatehouse suggested this was no temporary measure. Great consternation ensued.

Parnell's chief of police, Rock Roland, drove out to have a look, followed by a convoy of cars from town. Grasping the edge of the car roof to hoist his bulk out of the cruiser, he sauntered up to the guard, like a sheriff in an old western movie. He'd practised that walk. In his "I am chief of police and you are not" voice, Rock ordered the guard to open the gate. "This is a public road," he added.

The guard crossed his arms over his chest as if they were a pair of hams. "Not anymore."

The chief crossed *his* arms, but without the same effect, resting as they did on a flabby shelf of belly.

The guard stood immovable. Rock was flummoxed. If the land was still public, then who ordered the gate? If the land was now private, who owned it, and how come he didn't know about it? He sighed. Of course — Thurston.

Thurston Babbitt was Parnell's mayor, his father the mayor before him, and his grandfather before that. All of them were called Thurston, so their reigns tended to run together in the collective town memory. It wasn't a mayoralty; it was a monarchy, each Babbitt anointed by flagrant nepotism and accepted with resignation by most of the populace.

A small figure skirted the chief and waved a furled umbrella under the guard's nose. He grinned down at her. "Now, little lady, I don't want no trouble."

"You mean you don't want *any* trouble, not *no* trouble," Harriet Deaver said crisply. "Unless you mean you *do* want trouble, which I'm sure you don't. Now then, we've been coming here for generations and we intend to keep doing so. Stand aside, please."

She got back in her car, inched forward until the bumper rested against the gate, gunned the engine, and flattened it. She might have been driving a bulldozer instead of her old Lincoln, which did its job without suffering a scratch. Everyone cheered, piled back into their cars, and followed her through and down to the shore.

Her victory was short-lived, though. The new owner called in an Ontario Provincial Police special detail, strangers who could block the road without having to take on their own kin. The new owner was still a mystery, but not for long.

Harriet Deaver called Norm Buchanan, who headed up the Ontario land registry office. Norm had been one of her students in grade eight. The day he'd come to school with a black eye, bruised face, and cracked rib, Harriet had rejected his claim that he'd fallen down the stairs, paid his father a visit that evening, and he never laid a hand on Norm or Norm's mother again. Since that day, Norm had joined the ranks of her devoted students who would do anything for her.

Dom's secret was out.

"It would've been out soon, anyway, because what fun is it when you thumb your nose at a whole town and no one knows you're the one doing the thumbing?" Elvie Paterson said to her boss, Police Chief Rockin' Roland.

Five months later Dom stood gazing up at his splendid new edifice just as the first rays of sun transformed the huge windows into a golden glare. He slapped his knee. "Good omen, Rosie. The sun rises on my return. Come and look. Get out of the car, you lazy slob." His tone was jovial. It always was when he got his own way.

Rosie climbed out and stood with her eyes closed against the blinding rays. "Watch that you don't fly too close to the sun, like Icarus."

"Who the hell's Icarus?" He turned back to the house whose windows blazed down at them with eyes of fire. "Lookin' fine, lookin' fine. Furniture's in, right? You took care of that?"

She nodded tiredly. "Delivered last week."

"Who'd have thought, eh, Rosie, that Parnell's old punching bag would be so successful. I'm *sooo* rich, *sooo* rich, and it's going to be a fucking pleasure to rub everyone's nose in it." He tossed her the car keys. "You drive. I'm tired."

"Wait." She leaned against the car and crossed her arms to quell the shaking. "I came to get you, Bobby —"

He pushed his face up to hers. "Do … not … call … me … Bobby."

She raised a hand, palm facing him. "The reason I came for you —"

"It can wait. I need my bed. Now." He started to open the passenger door, but she held it shut. "What the fuck?" He turned toward her, face flushed with anger.

Rosie stood straight. "When you come here to party, to hide out, whatever, I don't want to see you. I don't want you to come to my house. When you visit Mother at the Manor, I'll make sure not to be there."

"What … are … you … talking … about?"

The signs were clear. When Dom spaced his words so deliberately, his rage was building and would culminate in an unrestrained fury. Dom had never liked surprises, and this was surely one. Rosie never defied him, never told him what to do. It was always the other way around.

"We're family, remember?" he snarled. "Family stick together. And you have a little girl. Mother tells me she's a pretty little thing. I haven't even met her yet, and she must be what, four, five?"

Rosie hit him. A sideways, close-fisted punch that caught him below the eye. She ran around the car and into the driver's seat, slammed the door lock down, and jammed the key into the ignition.

Dom pounded on the side window. "Unlock this door, you stupid bitch! Unlock it *now*!"

Blood poured down his cheek where her keys had caught him. She stared into his face, locking eyes, and stamped on the accelerator.

THREE

ANOTHER RIVER BESIDES the Farewell flowed through Parnell, population fifty-nine hundred. Gossip, the town's lifeblood, moved through the streets like fog, whispering over the phone lines, across backyard fences, thickening with details as it swirled through conversations at the post office, at street corners, culminating in Kat's Koffee Klatch. The tiniest hint of something afoot swelled with each telling until a Terrible Beauty was born. Parnell, like most small towns, was full of Terrible Beauties slouching the streets, mostly phantom, a few real, all with the power to hurt, even kill.

When the Klatch reopened three days after the storm, the hum of conversation sounded as if the café were preparing for liftoff. Before Kat's mother turned the Klatch over to her daughter several years earlier, her one stipulation was to retain the alliterative name, compounded by the addition of "Kat." Preserving much more than the name, Kat had kept the look of a 1950s diner: stools, chairs, and booths upholstered in vinyl, a linoleum floor, but with one quirky change. The pressed tin ceiling was not tin at all but felting stamped to look like tin, absorbing the echoing voices and thus enabling the aging clientele to hear not only each other but most of the conversations around them, as well. It was a feature that, along with the good, old-fashioned food, ensured loyalty even when a new Tim Hortons opened at the highway turnoff.

The details of Dom's "defenestration," as Norbert "Nob" Tinsley called it, had shifted from speculation to facts within hours of the reopening. Nob was holding court, describing how he had seen the Fist of God in the sky over Forge Ridge just before the storm struck, a tower of boiling black air against the deepening dusk, topped by a thunderhead like a fist, knuckles pointing downward over the town. Winds later gusting to nearly two hundred kilometres per hour spat out a tornado that tore apart Dom's proud house perched in its path.

Nob was a happy man; Police Chief Rockin' Roland was not. The latter sulked at a back table, out of the loop since he'd been at a workshop at OPP headquarters in Orillia when the Fist struck. Second-in-command of a two-person force didn't often bring much glory to Nob, three counting Elvie, who answered the phones at the police station and could be sworn in as a temporary deputy if, say, Parnell ever had another riot. The last one had been in 1836, but one could never be too careful. And when the phones didn't ring, which was most of the time, Elvie monitored the gossip and trolled the

Internet, searching for an exorcist who might rid her, legally, of her father. She told Nob she couldn't afford a hit man. For a minute he'd believed her.

Now, through a mouthful of pancake, Nob said, "Elvie claimed he came outta that window like a ... quiver."

Harriet Deaver and Agatha Breeze, at their usual table for two, exchanged glances.

"A quiver? Did that child learn anything in your class, Harriet?"

"Did you actually see him come out the window?" Kat asked, setting Elvie's usual order of dry toast and a raw egg in tomato juice in front of her. Elvie told everyone that this breakfast was her father's secret to longevity and that she was determined the old bastard wasn't going to outlast her. The two coexisted in a century-old brick farmhouse on the ridge beside Dom, its small windows and sturdy walls withstanding even a Fist's blow. "Was he still alive?"

The conversation died down, patrons waiting for the answer. "Since I'm not dumb enough to stand in front of a window looking out at a tornado," Elvie said, "I don't know. I was in the root cellar, but my father, who *is* dumb enough, claimed he saw Dom fly out with the furniture. All I know is the wind was screaming like a banshee, and when it died down, Dom was hanging on the end of a rope like a fish on a line. My father says it was one of Dom's own skipping ropes." She rolled her eyes.

* * *

When Tulla came through the door, the café was loud with excited chatter, like a theatre before the curtain rises. Her hand flew to her ear, and she swayed as the wave of voices engulfed her, not just from the noise but from obvious exhaustion. It had been a long, rainy drive from Toronto after the unsettling visit with her mother.

"You okay, Auntie Tulla?" Melissa, Kat's fifteen-year-old daughter, stood at her elbow hugging an armful of menus. She was a pint-sized version of her mother, with one small difference. Kat was white, Mel was not.

She had inherited her darker skin from her father and not much else. He'd been a great guy when he was Joe at university with Kat, both of them mature students in a continuing education course; not so great when they'd gone to Saudi Arabia to tell his family they were getting married — omitting that a baby was on the way — and he reverted to Mohammad. Kat wasted no time in getting out of the country. Joe/Mohammad stayed there.

Melissa looked so much like Kat at the same age: short, curvy, and so pretty, bright-blue eyes, a small turned-up nose. Tulla had envied that identical nose on Kat when they were teenagers. Mel even had Kat's mop of unruly curls, the only difference being that her hair was black, Kat's blond. Tulla watched her tucking the wayward strands behind her ears, just as Kat did. Never worked. The curls flew out again with a mind of their own. Just like their owners.

"I'll find you a quiet table," Mel said, leading Tulla toward the back.

Tulla caught her arm. "Not with Rockin' Roland, if that's where you're heading."

Melissa's eyes opened wide and innocent. "Aren't you old friends? Mum says he was a big football star in high school. All the girls were after him."

"Not this girl."

Melissa looked over at him. "Hard to believe he was ever a star. He's kind of pathetic now, isn't he? That comb-over? Ought to be illegal, and he's *soooo* fat. Mum says he used to be fit and quite good-looking."

"We all were … in high school. Keep that in mind."

"Yeah, but the rest of you aren't fat and … grey. He looks so beaten-down."

Tulla pointed to two empty seats at the counter. "Those would be good. I'm meeting someone."

Melissa veered toward them, neatly cutting off a stubby couple lumbering in the same direction. They wore matching hand-knit sweaters, each sporting a moose with button eyes and antlers that twined over their backs like ivy. The woman's moose was pink, the man's blue. Their baseball caps said STAY CALM. KEEP HUNTING.

"Last time those guys came in they had their rifles with them!" Melissa shouted over the din when she saw Tulla cup her ear. "Loaded. When Mum told them they couldn't have them in here, they said, 'Why not? They're not smoking.'"

Tulla snorted. "You made that up."

Mel glanced over at the entrance. "Your date's here."

Tulla sighed. "Parnell, the ultimate secret-free zone."

Mikhail reached over Tulla's shoulder for a napkin and wiped off the stool beside her. "Those are flecks in the vinyl, Mikhail. They don't come off. Hi." Tulla smiled at him.

"Seen this yet?" He handed her his newspaper. "Connolly made the front page."

Skipping Rope Tycoon Dies in Freak Accident

Hillside House Demolished by Tornado in Eastern Ontario

PARNELL, Ont. — A freak storm that swept through part of the Upper Ottawa Valley late Thursday evening claimed one victim: Dominique Connolly, age 49, was confirmed dead by police, who said his house was shattered by tornado-force winds. There were no other occupants in the luxury house that sat on a bluff near the town of Parnell where Connolly grew up.

Both Connolly and his home have been shrouded in controversy. A police spokesperson from OPP Regional Headquarters in Orillia said that Connolly was known to them. He had only recently returned to Parnell where he bought and barricaded a popular park area long used by local residents. The area has been sealed off and further questions to both the local police chief and OPP have been deferred to a press conference to be held later this week.

A well-known figure in the fitness industry, Connolly had until recently lived in Las Vegas. His runaway bestseller, *Skipping to Success*, was the launch pad for a highly lucrative chain of skipping centres, a TV show, and several videos.

Parnell police officer Norbert Tinsley would not confirm an eyewitness account that Connolly's body was found hanging from a skipping rope tangled around the balcony railing. He said that foul play was not suspected at this point.

Katarina Kominski, proprietor of a popular coffee shop in Parnell, said that some residents reported seeing a funnel-shaped cloud near the bluff at the height of the storm.

"They call it the Fist of God," she said.

Tulla put the newspaper on the counter. "You know, I'd like to feel even a little bit sad for him. Not happening, though. I haven't seen the guy for what, thirty years or more, and I still have the occasional nightmare about him. Remember that play I was in and I had to kiss him? Scarred me for life."

"I think it might have scarred him for life, too," Mikhail said. "To be so publicly humiliated by you. And then you did it again."

Tulla shrugged. "You mean when I clocked him in the Clod War? Then after nearly killing him that day, apparently, I had to pretend to like him, Father's orders, but I never did. You didn't, either. The only people who had any time for him were his mother and my father, and that's still a mystery. His scary mother lives at the Manor now, right?"

"She and his father. Daniel's in the early stages of Alzheimer's, and Opal is so obese she can hardly walk, but her mind's as sharp as ever."

"Yuck. Imagine those two living in our old home."

He raised an eyebrow.

"It was your home, too, Mikhail. Don't get all defensive. And Darla? God, she was a piece of work. Is she still around?"

He shook his head. "Not sure anyone knows where she is. I see Rosie, though. She works at the Manor as well as the hospital. Brings her little girl in sometimes. Nice little kid. Looks just like Rosie did at that age. Only happier."

"Hard to believe Rosie and Darla are sisters."

Mikhail had been a behavioural psychologist with the OPP for several years before abruptly returning to Parnell a few months earlier to work on a research project involving Alzheimer's patients living at the Manor. When Tulla asked him why, his answer had astonished her. "I got tired of working with the criminal mind — profiling the same type every day. A psychopath, a sociopath — whatever the label — is usually a very bad person." She'd laughed before she realized he wasn't making a joke. Mikhail rarely did.

Tulla studied him now, the broad planes of a Slavic face, flat cheekbones, wide mouth, brown eyes, a face that in repose looked calm and trouble-free. "You and Paul Skinner have something in common. Remember him? He's back here too. You both left successful careers to —"

His nostrils flared. "Skinner and I have nothing in common." His face wasn't in repose now. She caught sight of the anger before he smiled at her. "I left my successful career, as you call it, because I no longer cared what formed the psychopaths I was assessing. Genetics or environment, childhood trauma or brain malfunction, chemical imbalance or … an allergy to peanut butter. The bottom line is they were evil."

Tulla blinked. "As in Devil evil?"

He nodded. "Found myself thinking these people should all be locked up for good. Or put down." He tented his fingers and flexed them.

She grinned. "Spider doing push-ups on a mirror. Our secret code. Meant *help*."

Mikhail clasped his coffee mug with both hands. "My research before specializing was genetics, so the change isn't such a stretch. I did my doctorate on the possible genetic components in psychopathy. Now I'm looking at the possible genetic components in Alzheimer's." He swung his arm to encompass the still-busy café. "Look out there. What do you see?"

"Uh, a bunch of people gabbling and gobbling?"

"A bunch of people related to one another. This town is fertile ground for genetic research."

"Kat calls it a petri dish."

Mikhail gave a surprised laugh. "She's absolutely right. A petri dish holding a very shallow gene pool."

She narrowed her eyes. "You talking about incest among our ancestors?"

"Yours. I wasn't born here. But, yes, the earliest settlers here, not counting an earlier Scottish influx to the north, were two Irish Catholic families, maybe eight or ten individuals. Bog Irish. A larger group followed a few years later, fleeing the potato famine, so for a few decades their choices of mates were limited to each other basically. So here we have the Manor with a full complement of Alzheimer's patients, all from around here. Correlation? Doubt it. It appears that among all the other problems arising from such entanglement might be a mutated gene that plays a role in the disease."

"And a role in psychopaths?"

He smiled. "Not the same gene."

Kat appeared from the kitchen, scooted around the end of the counter, and grabbed Tulla off her stool in a bear hug. "Hey, kiddo. Mel said you were here."

Mikhail picked up his briefcase and stood. "I'm just off. Interviewing Daniel Connolly at ten."

"Poor bugger. Rosie told me last week she had to dig a battery out of his ear. He forgot to put it into his hearing aid first. Does he know about Dom?"

"Nob told him," Mikhail said. "Apparently, his response was, 'I don't have a son.'"

"Was that Alzheimer's talking?"

"I don't know ..." His pocket suddenly broke into a tinny rendition of "Ode to Joy," and he headed for the door, phone to his ear.

"Leo?"

"Yeah."

"Where are you?"

"Orillia, but on my way to Toronto. On a re-entry assignment. So tell me, how did that SOB manage to die a natural death?"

"Hang on. Can't hear you." Mikhail pushed through the café door and walked a few steps down the street. "I think the insurance companies call it an act of God."

"Good for God. Honed sense of irony to tie a skipping rope around the bastard's neck and throw him off the balcony. Must be true, though, if the *Toronto Sun* says so."

"That your only source?" Mikhail asked.

"Yup. So far HQ is mum on the subject. You know anything more?"

"Only what Elvie tells me. So how's it going?"

"Life in general or —"

"That, too, but I meant the trial." The line hummed between them. "Any progress?"

"Of a sort. Still some gaps, but a few are beginning to fill now. Enough, anyway, that I've been cleared to go back on active duty. Homicide again."

Mikhail glanced into the branches above his head as

a single leaf pulled free of its moorings and floated to the sidewalk. "Right back into the deep end."

"You don't approve?"

"You're the only one who knows …"

"If I can still swim?"

Mikhail didn't answer.

"Enough with the metaphors. So far I've been on ob-server status. A couple of raids, an investigation of a drive-by shooting at Jane and Finch. I've been back and forth like a yo-yo between Toronto and Orillia. They're keeping me on a short leash, a close eye for the moment. Last test assignment tonight, with a SWAT team at this big evangelical rally back in Toronto. So if I don't do anything stupid, like stand in front of a sniper, I'll be cleared for full duty by the end of the week."

"Snipers? At a religious rally?"

"At this one, anyway. CBC got an email from some-body saying he'd planted a bomb. No one knows if it's a hoax, if it's part of a gang war, or what the hell it is. We've had word there'll be some cults mixed in with the bona fide church groups at this rally, with gang con-nections — the Angels, apparently, Bandidos from the States, Rock Machine from Quebec. The arena's been swept seven ways to Sunday and we found not so much as a peanut, but the security guys are still jumpy as cats. Hard event to police properly, and Langtry won't cancel."

"Who's Langtry?"

"The Main Guy. Wears a sparkly powder-blue suit, races around the stage with a mike and yells a lot. He heals people. By thumping them on the forehead, apparently. They fall down, jump up, and are all healthy. Wish it were that easy."

"Hadn't heard a thing about this."

"The email went to the morning radio show *The Current*, addressed to Anna Maria Tremonti personally. No other media got it, so the network was persuaded to keep it under wraps until tomorrow."

"Gag order?"

"Langtry has a lot of pull. Tonight's the last night — a mass choir, leaders of all the organizations onstage. Wouldn't mind blowing some of them up myself."

"You might want to keep that thought to yourself, Leo. Where are you phoning from?"

"A street corner … on my new cellphone. Police issue. First time I've been able to figure out how to make a call. Let me know what transpires re: Connolly."

"That Mik's a real study," Kat said, leaning on the counter in front of Tulla, watching the door for new arrivals. "So controlled. He sure doesn't give away much."

"You know what he said just now?" Tulla asked. "That he no longer cared what made a person a psychopath. If they did bad things, they should be 'put down.'"

"Missed his calling. He should have been a vet."

"I think he's just reverting to type. Remember how judgmental he was when we were in high school? Really knew his own mind about things, what was right and wrong. No greys."

Melissa came through the swing door from the kitchen carrying a tray laden with breakfast orders. Kat watched her approvingly. "She's doing fine, that kid. But she does put on airs. Told me trays were tacky. Only short-order fast-food joints use them. Which, of course, is what we are. But she's bent on raising the tone."

"She's also bent on mischief. Tried to put me at Rockin' Roland's table."

"Of course she did, because she's Emma at the moment. She's reading her way through Jane Austen. It's like living with — what's that woman's name who had twenty different personalities? In the past six months, Mel's been, let's see, Elizabeth, Fanny, Anne — she even branched out into Catherine for a brief moment."

"After you?"

"No fear. A fifteen-year-old daughter calling herself after her mother? She'd just finished *Wuthering Heights*. She's so like my grandmother, Nana Anna. It's amazing. Mel never knew her, but she does so many similar things, so maybe she's channelling her. I remember your father saying you could always tell what novel Nana Anna was reading by the way she spoke that week. Same with Melissa."

"Just don't let her read *Lolita*, okay?"

"It's the only book I've banned. I even told Aggie Breeze not to let her take it out of the library. And, boy, Tulla, you'd better not let her buy it from you when you open your bookstore."

"My bet is she read it the day after you told her not to. My goodness, she's a beautiful girl. You're going to have to put her under lock and key."

They watched her weave through the tables, delivering orders, smiling, a bright gleam of youth among the "wrinklies," as she called the Klatch regulars.

Kat looked around the still-crowded café. "Back in a sec." She hurried over to the cash register where the moose hunters were waiting. "Enjoy your breakfast?"

"Not bad … for pig," the man said. "You ever want groundhog, let us know. Tastes like chicken."

Kat came back, shaking her head.

"They look familiar," Tulla said. "Who are they?"

"They look familiar because they're related to half of Parnell, as well as to each other."

"Mikhail was just talking about that. He called it entanglement."

Melissa appeared at their side. "Look who just came in." She pointed with her chin to the door. Kat's eyes narrowed when she saw a very short man with a head as round and big as a basketball take tiny strides toward her. Two men followed him like a not-so-secret-service team. They both wore earpieces.

Melissa giggled. "Crabbe and Goyle. See those wires? They go to iPods in their shirt pockets. They're listening to tunes. Pathetic." She reached for the menus stacked next to the cash register.

Kat put a hand on her arm. "I'll deal with this, Mel."

The short man watched her coming. So did half the people in the restaurant. "Ah, the lovely Katarina." Kat gazed at him silently.

Tulla whispered to Mel, "That's her Medusa stare. Perfected in grade ten."

"You're busy in here today," the short man said, "but I'm sure you can find room for three more?"

"For you, Thurston, of course. You don't take up much space."

Mel gasped. "What's she doing?"

Kat led the trio through the tables toward the booth where Rock Roland sat alone, sulking. "Okay if these three join you, Chief?"

As she put down the menus, Thurston slid an arm around her waist. "You're getting a little plump there, Ms. Koffee Klatch. Another baby on the way or just enjoying your own cooking too much?"

Kat glared down at the hand resting on her hip, raised her eyes to his, and spoke in a clear, carrying voice. "Will you be needing a booster seat, Thurston?"

"Oh. My. God," Mel whispered into the silence.

His hand shot up and gripped her arm. "You got a smart mouth, Kat. It's going to get you into real trouble one day."

"Oh, dear, perhaps you haven't yet grasped the detrimental impact of Dom's demise on your teeny tiny fiefdom, Mr. Mayor. *Detrimental* — long word, look it up."

He squeezed her arm hard, face mottled with fury.

"Might this constitute physical harassment, Chief Roland?" Kat asked, wrenching away.

"Thurston ..." Roland's tone was part plea, part warning. He stood and lumbered after Kat. "Don't cross him, Kat. He'll get back at you. You know that. What's got into you?"

Tulla watched her friend with consternation. She'd heard enough of the exchange to know Kat was courting trouble. Ridiculing the mayor was dangerous. But the oddest thing of all was that Kat had always defended Thurston. She'd often said, "Not his fault he was born with a head the size of a pumpkin and tiny little sprigs for legs. He probably wasn't born a jerk, just became one to protect himself from the bully boys."

Kat stomped back to them. "Melissa, love, tell Einstein in there we need three breakfast specials, and I don't care if he spits on the eggs." She sloshed coffee into mugs, stood spoons in each of them, and shoved a handful of creamers into her pocket.

"Mum, you tell me never to do that ..." Her voice trailed off under her mother's glare.

Kat hooked her fingers into the mug handles and delivered them to the back table, slapped them down, and when the coffee splashed over, shook her head as if the mess had been caused by someone else entirely.

"I've never seen her do that before," Mel said. "I mean, I know she can be tough, but, God, I've never seen her make fun of someone's looks, or you know, physical —"

Tulla leaned toward Mel in the sudden silence. "Shortcomings? Me, neither. She always used to cut him a lot of slack. That he couldn't help looking like Chucky the Clown. What's going on with her?"

Mel shrugged. "Maybe it's just existential rage at the female existence." She laughed at Tulla's expression. "Medusa. She represents female rage." She closed her eyes and quoted: "Medusa 'guides women through their anger to the sources of the power we have as women.' Just finished an essay on feminist movements for my social history class." She twisted around as a big group came through the door. "Okay, back to work. Can you make sure she doesn't draw blood?"

There was no blood. Tulla caught Kat's hand as she headed into the kitchen. "Before you get yourself into real trouble, you're going to come for dinner and explain this outburst of existential female rage."

"That would be Mel-talk, I believe. But it sounds like a plan."

FOUR

LANGTRY WASN'T DUE for half an hour, but already the arena was almost full. A steady stream of people were still filing in, jostling one another for aisle seats. A worship group belted revival hymns into a line of microphones at the front of the stage, revving up the crowd. Many stood singing and swaying with the music, hands extended, palms up to receive the Lord. The parking lot was packed with the overflow watching the proceedings on giant videotrons.

The place was also crawling with police. Snipers stayed out of sight on the roof and on the catwalks, many of the stage technicians were undercover cops, and the officers now circulating on the floor had been posing as church representatives for the three-day event. The first two nights had been uneventful, but no one was resting easy yet. This was the big one — Langtry wasn't just saving individual souls tonight. With the help of a huge mass choir, already assembling on the risers behind the worship group, and a team of charismatic pastors waiting to urge people to come forward, he planned to save multitudes.

There was a stirring at the back of the centre aisle, and some of the crowd turned in excitement. It was starting. A parade of dignitaries moved toward the stage, solemn and slow at first, but as the music swelled, they walked faster and faster, their gold robes flashing in the spotlights raking over the audience. A golf cart shot out below the apron of the stage, and the crowd roared as Langtry stepped out, his arms raised in welcome. The show was on.

Leo concentrated on the scene below him. He wore a flak jacket, a handgun on his hip, and an earbud ran down into a two-way radio that was silent. Beside him, the SWAT team commander, with the unfortunate name of Nemo, leaned on the catwalk railing scanning the crowd through binoculars. Unfortunate because, with bulging eyes and a slightly receding chin, he looked like a fish.

"If this was a rock concert," Nemo said, "that area at the front would be the mosh pit." He shook his head. "They're packed in so tight, even if just a smoke bomb goes off, there'll be a stampede. And if there's a real bomb, it'll be carnage." He handed Leo the binoculars. "Langtry wouldn't cancel because he said too many people would be disappointed. Crap. It's an ego trip. My way of thinking, being disappointed is better than being dead."

Leo studied the seething mass of humanity in front of the stage, then swung the binoculars gradually over the choir members filing in from a side door. He refocused on the stage, where a technician was trying to shift one of the giant speakers. "That's Anderson, right? On the stage? He was in my old unit. Isn't he a bit over the hill for this kind of caper?"

Nemo peered down. "He asked to be assigned. He's on a mission of his own — dyed-in-the-wool Presbyterian, hates this kind of over-the-top stuff. I think his plan is to arrest Langtry for giving Christianity a bad name."

Leo swung the binoculars back to the line of choir members and stopped breathing. "Who's on the floor by the stage where the choir's coming in? What's his call number? Quick."

"Can't call him. They're under radio silence."

"Damn it, Nemo, give me his number or I'll broadcast the call."

"Jesus, Leo, you're going to get canned before you even get back on strength."

"Just give me his number." He wasn't whispering anymore. The two SWAT cops on the same catwalk eyed him with curiosity.

"It's 224, but —"

Leo growled into his shoulder mike, while slowly tracking the procession onto the stage. "Come in, 224, urgent."

The officer on the floor put his hand over his ear and glanced around in surprise, then mumbled, "Copy."

"Just passing in front of you, woman in the choir, grab her."

The officer moved forward toward the line. "Copy, but who the hell is this? Orders are that we make no move to —"

"Just do it!"

Nemo grabbed Leo's mike and barked into it, "This is Nemo. I don't know what the hell Leo Harding thinks he sees, but grab her if you can do it without stampeding the whole goddamn choir. If not, just follow. Over." He clipped the mike back onto Leo's shoulder. "This better be a good collar, Harding. I've just stepped way out on a limb for you."

Leo held the binoculars steady on his quarry. She had sensed something and was moving faster, pushing past the people in front of her. "He's going to lose her. She's on the move."

His radio crackled. "Suspect out of sight. At this level, can't pick her out from all the other hoods and gowns."

"They've lost her." Leo thrust the binoculars back to Nemo. "I'm going down. See if you can pick her out from here."

"Pick who out?" Nemo growled. "All I see is a line of Death Eaters." He jerked the binoculars around. "What the hell's happening on the stage?"

Leo ran along the catwalk and down the metal stairs two at a time. On the stage, a technician was scrambling away from one of the giant speakers, and the undercover cops in the mosh pit were moving swiftly through the crowd toward the apron. The procession of choir members faltered, some throwing back their hoods to see what the holdup was. Leo slowed to a quick walk, studying faces, unaware of anything but his own pursuit. In front of the stage, the crowd had gone silent, sensing something was amiss, the people at the back still swaying and swinging in oblivious ecstasy.

Leo searched every hooded face, but the woman was gone. Faded back into the weeds. He radioed to Nemo. "Lost her."

"Copy, damn it! Whoever the hell *she* is, the broad is the least of our worries. Get back to the stage fast. We've got a big problem."

The videotrons in the parking lot had picked up the flurry around the speaker before the cameras were hastily switched to pan the outside audience and then to the commentator whose smooth voice spread calmness like syrup over the crowd. "All right, folks, Reverend Langtry will be ready to welcome you in just a few minutes. Soon as they get that speaker sorted out and the choir in place. What a night, what a night! Just received the attendance figures, almost thirty thousand people here tonight. More than for a hockey game, folks. Have to go to commercials now. Mammon still has to be served, it seems." He chuckled unctuously. "Then we'll be back for the opening hymn. It's going to lift the roof off this place. Be patient." He kept his smile pasted on until the red light blinked off, then whirled around to his crew. "What's going on down there?"

His producer held up a hand, listening intently to a voice in her headphones, her eyes round with dismay. "Okay, this is going to be a tough one. I'll tell him now." She pulled the headphones off. "It might not be a hymn that blows the roof off. When a technician shifted one of the speakers, it sparked and a little flag shot out of it with a pop. You saw him on the monitor. He nearly fainted. It happened again from the podium where Langtry will speak from. I so do not like this stuff. Now I'm hating it."

"I don't get it. A prank?"

"The guy in charge of the cops — did you know the place is crawling with them? — doesn't know or won't say."

The commentator looked around uneasily. "So now what?"

"They're deciding whether to try to clear the place without causing full-on panic, or —" She held up a finger and slid her headphones back over her ears.

"What?"

"They're going ahead. I can't believe it. Langtry insists. Says God won't let anything happen to his flock. The guy's a nutbar."

"But no bomb," Mikhail said when Leo phoned him the following day.

"Nope."

"Gutsy decision on the part of the chief not to clear the place."

"Going nose to nose with Langtry would have taken more guts. He's one powerful man. And he has God on his side, which helps. The pop guns were a distraction for something else going down."

"Trolling," Mikhail said flatly.

"For sure. The Bluebird folks were there front and centre. Had their own reps on the stage, a prayer tent in the parking lot, even had a couple of phonies handing out brochures about their school."

"Hasn't that place been busted yet?" Mikhail asked. "It's still operational? That's unconscionable."

"It's under surveillance, but we still can't touch it. Not enough evidence."

"It should be shut down, anyway," Mikhail said bitterly. "Then find the evidence. Because in the meantime —"

"Yeah, I know. Kids are getting scooped up. Someone there's pretty damn cocky, though. They're sure of their cover, having such an obvious presence at an event like that. But it worked. They came out scot-free and we missed the action entirely."

"You didn't. You spotted Darla."

"Yeah, but I lost her. Besides, I have no proof she's mixed up with the cults."

"Of course she is," Mikhail said savagely. "Trolling is what she does best, or used to. She and Dom are bottom-feeders from way back. This mission thing, what an ideal hunting ground to find their prey — vulnerable lost kids searching for something to make sense of their lives."

"Well, at least Dom's hunting days are over."

FIVE

STORM DEBRIS BLANKETED Crow Lake Road. Along the verges, trees lay like giant pickup sticks, their branches chainsawed by hydro crews. Tulla drove slowly, searching for wires. Her recently acquired dog, Clancy, watched for squirrels. His previous owner had said he was a sweet-tempered, well-behaved, docile little fellow. The woman had lied on all three counts. Clancy came with a bipolar personality, an enormous sense of entitlement, and answered only to himself. Nevertheless, Tulla had grown inexplicably fond of the little wretch.

Half buried under the arm of a giant poplar snapped off at the shoulder was a large wooden sign: CROW'S NEST in gilt letters a foot high. *Cute*, she thought. Underneath in black: PRIVATE PROPERTY. TRESPASSERS WILL BE PROSECUTED TO THE FULLEST EXTENT OF THE LAW. She drove through the open security gate and parked by the guard hut, now lying on its side.

When she was young and her family still intact, they'd driven this road every summer to their cottage at the far end of the lake. Now asphalt, it had been gravel and washboard then, potholed and weedy. It was an ancient road, originally an animal track, then a First Nations trail that wound its way down to the water's edge.

Tulla remembered her father, Warren's, stories about the Algonquin on those long-ago nights around the campfire, the black sky glittering with sparks and fireflies, and truths stretched thin. Warren refashioned the history of Parnell into a gentle retelling to match the velvet darkness, the cherry brandy, and the contentment of the family before it cracked apart. It appalled her now to think how he colluded in the retelling of such an ugly history. Even as a child she knew he was falsifying the record, but she still loved to hear his tales of those olden days.

He recounted how the Algonquin had been pushed gently off the land by the earliest white settlers of the townsite that became Parnell without shedding a drop of blood — a fair settlement with no angry words. Warren told of an early homesteader who lived by a beaver meadow where the Algonquin came to trap and occasionally walked silently into his house, lit their pipes from the fire, and just as quietly strolled out again. Then there was Edmond, an accomplished violinist whom the Algonquin loved to hear play. They even, so the story went, took lessons from him. "Edmond was always on good terms with the Indians," Warren would say, gazing into the fire.

"How good?" Tulla would ask obediently.

"Well, he once shot a deer while watching a flock of ducks," her father replied. It turned out that an Indigenous man had been tracking the deer and was disappointed that he'd lost his game and there would be no meat for his family. But the matter of the deer was settled "justly for both and established a rule to govern in like cases." Her father's stories were Tulla's first inkling that Parnellites had their own way with truth.

Her favourite, and the one she never questioned was about the first Algonquin encounter at Crow Lake. While exploring land to clear for grazing, an early settler heard rushing water. He fought toward the sound through dense bush latticed with fallen trees. "After infinite toil" — she loved that phrase, repeated at every telling — he struck the river just at the gorge where it poured into a broad, rock-bound lake. When he emerged from the forest, an Algonquin woman rose from the riverbank, plunged into the water above the gorge, and swam across to the other side. It was the image of this powerful woman she loved: strong and fearless, turning to look at this strange, pale creature before diving into the current, risking going into the chute, but confident in her own strength to get to the other bank. Tulla wanted to be that woman — strong and fearless.

Now, she followed the asphalt until she caught sight of Dom's house in all its broken splendour through the skeletal branches jagged and snapped by the storm. Teeth of glass edged the blown-out window frames, a tongue of curtain swung in the breeze. All that remained of the deck was a bone of splintered railing.

A van was parked close to the front door inside a loop of yellow police tape across the driveway. Nob Tinsley leaned against the ground-floor entrance, head cocked toward the scratchy voice issuing from his shoulder.

"Tulla. Hey. How's things?" He glanced down at Clancy and shook his head. "Don't mean to be rude, but that's one sorry excuse for a dog." Clancy stared at him, appraisingly. "Can't come in here, Tulla. I've been tasked to keep everyone out." He drew himself up to full height, which wasn't much more than a metre and a half, but what he lacked in height he made up in muscle. Nob had grown up in Parnell, a couple of years behind Tulla in school. She didn't remember him from back then, but liked him now as she'd gotten to know him these past few weeks: his lack of pretention, his simple honesty, and as a bonus, his loud, clear voice.

"Actually, I'm just going on up the shore," Tulla told him. "Our cottage used to be farther along —"

"Can't do that. You'd have to walk through the crime scene." He bent toward the radio squawking like an irate parrot on his shoulder. "Can't make out a dang word," he muttered and slapped it into silence.

"Crime scene?"

Nob shrugged. "All I know is no one's allowed on the premises."

Clancy scampered past him through the open door and up the stairs. A shout came from inside the house, and a minute later Clancy shot out the door, pursued by a young woman wearing white overalls, booties, rubber gloves, and what appeared to be a shower cap. She faced

Tulla. "This your dog? He's just run off with a chunk of evidence."

Nob made a grab for Clancy and missed. "Dang it! I'm sorry, ma'am. He's contaminated the crime scene."

"Not a problem. The storm's already done that — in spades. The front of the house is scoured clean, the back's heaped with rubble." She turned back to Tulla. "I'm part of the forensic team. "We're not finding much, but I think the dog has. Here, boy."

She knelt in front of Clancy, who growled deep in his throat. Tulla put out a cautionary hand. "Watch it. He's a biter. And he certainly won't let go. He's a cairn terrier, and they're tenacious."

The forensic woman nodded. "I know cairns. Looks like he's got a rock, which fits. Drop it, boy. Drop it." She held her hand beneath his chin. He growled louder.

Nob patted his pockets and pulled out a stick of beef jerky. "Maybe he'll trade?"

The technician waved the treat in front of Clancy. The dog eyed it closely, dropped the rock into her open palm, and took the jerky between his teeth like a cigar.

Nob peered over her shoulder. "Holy crap! Looks like an eyelid stuck to it."

Tulla took a step backward. The technician raised the rock into the sunlight. "Does look like a piece of flesh. Don't think it's an eyelid, though. Those lashes are bits of wool." She pulled a Ziploc bag from her pocket and dropped the rock and its attachment into it. "The vic apparently came into Emergency in pieces, probably his."

Nob's face shaded into green.

The technician took a marker out of her breast pocket and wrote across the plastic bag: "Evidence retrieved by dog." She added the date and approximate location, got to her feet, and glanced at Clancy. "Think he'd like a job in forensics? He's already found more than we have. Why are you still growling, dog? It was a fair trade."

Tulla snapped the leash on Clancy's collar and cocked her head, listening. "That's not him. The ground's vibrating."

Nob peered skyward. "Thunder?"

Clancy whimpered and leaned hard against Tulla's leg. The rumbling grew louder, and a line of motorcycles roared up the driveway toward them, their riders slouched back, handlebars at shoulder height. Instead of the raggle-taggle of neckerchiefs and do-rags, jeans, and fancy shirts, there was sombre uniformity to their dress. All wore German army helmets painted black, and shiny black leathers, some with fringed jackets, some in sleeveless vests showing beefy arms, tattooed from wrist to shoulder. Each biker wore his jacket or vest open to reveal a red-and-white insignia emblazoned on a T-shirt beneath.

"Angels," Nob breathed, not moving.

The riders wheeled in formation around the pond where a pre-storm fountain had squirted water from a snake's mouth, the snake being wrestled to submission by a muscle-bound figure who, Harriet Deaver had pointed out, was supposed to be the famous Trojan priest and seer Laocoön, but who had borne a passing resemblance to Dom. Now, all that was left of the statue was a single coil of reptile and a sandalled foot sticking out of the murky, leaf-filled water.

The motorcycles thundered back down the driveway, leaving the air shimmering with silence. "What was *that* about?" Tulla whispered.

"I'd better call it in." Nob plucked the two-way radio from his shoulder belt and yelled into it, "Remote to base! Remote to base! You hear me? Ten-four."

Tulla waved a goodbye and turned to go. Clancy followed close, panting with fright, his tongue hanging out like strawberry fruit leather.

SIX

ON THE WAY BACK from Crow Lake, Tulla stopped at the farmers' market, bustling with people, bursting with produce. There were boxes of early McIntoshes, pyramids of pumpkins and squashes, and the last of the zucchini and pepper crops spilling out of bushel baskets. Heaps of gently rotting tomatoes sported marked-down prices. But more tempting were the buckets of fall flowers, the deep golds and purples of the dahlias, sunflowers bent almost double with the weight of their seedy heads, and giant marigolds so festive if one didn't get close enough to smell them. Several stands displayed small expensive selections of organic fruit and vegetables, a butcher advertised hormone-free beef, and the local bakery had set up an outdoor café.

Tulla drove into the parking lot, and Clancy exploded into frenzied barking at a Great Dane the size of a small horse passing in front of the car. Doc Skinner tugged the dog's leash. His son, Paul, limped at his side. The two men looked as if they'd stepped straight from the pages of an L.L.Bean catalogue in hunting jackets and riding boots that gleamed in the sunlight.

Clancy scrabbled around on the sill to get a better look, his growling and barking undiminished. "Shut up, shut up, shut up, they'll hear you," Tulla whispered, waving an arm back at him while keeping her head down. Too late. As they approached her car, Paul's nickname jumped into her memory: Snake. It was his father's nickname, transferred to him because of his odd gait, the legacy of a bout with polio when he was a toddler. Paul appeared to slither slightly, and Dom had cemented the nickname by saying Paul moved like a sidewinder as he slid through school hallways, eyes down, charming teachers with his eagerness to please.

He'd been a handsome teenager. Not a single zit ever appeared on his smooth, tanned face, and his blond hair flopped over a broad forehead when it wasn't being held back by a pair of Ray-Bans, a style he practically invented in Parnell. And his teeth, straight and white, never bore the jagged smile of braces. But Tulla's memory was of a lost boy hiding his insecurities inside this shell of physical perfection only accentuated by his withered leg. He was amiable, easygoing, and very, very watchful.

"Hello, stranger," Paul said. "I saw you this morning at the Klatch. But you were so deep in conversation with Mikhail, I didn't want to interrupt the tête-à-tête."

Oh, for God's sake. Tulla leaned away from the window and stared pointedly at her watch. "Hello, Dr. Skinner. Nice to see you again, Paul." *Liar, liar, pants on fire …*

Dr. Skinner grunted a greeting. "Can't you keep that dog quiet? He's upsetting Gibson." The doctor jerked the leash as the enormous dog reared up and pawed at the open window. Clancy unleashed a paroxysm of yelping from the safety of the back window ledge.

Paul smiled. "The last time I saw you was with your husband … ex-husband, am I correct? Patrick, right?"

"Portland."

"Of course, Portland. You two were on a quest for the Holy Grail. Searching for a miracle, the elusive cure for breast cancer, if I remember …"

"How'd you know that?" Dr. Skinner sounded petulant.

"They came to see me for a consultation, Dad."

"I didn't know you have breast cancer, Tulla," Skinner said, his rheumy eyes brightening with interest. Or malice.

"Not me. Portland."

"A man with breast cancer? I still don't believe that's possible. Misdiagnoses."

"He can also die of it," Tulla snapped.

Paul's voice oozed sympathy. "I'm not surprised. 'The road less travelled' rarely works out. And, of course, he was at the end of the road when I met him, but I'm sorry nevertheless." He squeezed her arm, leaving his hand on her a little too long.

She took a deep breath and removed her arm from the windowsill. "You've given up your practice in Toronto?"

"I have. I came back to help Dad out." He smiled fondly at his father. "He's due for a well-earned rest."

"I'm not retiring, Paul. I'll be here to show you how a good GP works. And don't forget that I'm still the coroner in this district. "

Tulla's hand crept up to her ear. Another burst of growls and barks from Clancy and Gibson masked her snort of disbelief. She threw the car into gear and shouted over the dogs' racket, "Gotta go! See you later!"

The telephone message light was flashing when Tulla and Clancy got home. "Call me. Urgent."

Tulla pushed the speed-dial number for Kat. "Hi. What's —"

"I have an exciting business opportunity related to your bookstore. Ready?"

"*Okaaay.*" Tulla tried to keep the doubt out of her voice.

"Mose Cohen called me this afternoon."

"He can't still be alive. He was old as Methuselah when we were kids."

"This is that Mose's grandson. He lives in Montreal, inherited the old Cohen store from his father, and wants to sell. He just phoned me and wondered if I'd be interested, being right next door. Fat chance. I said I'd ask around before he lists it. I'm asking. Don't know what his price is. Probably pretty reasonable, since he really wants to be rid of it."

"Wait. Is it empty now?"

"Has been for years. Ever since middle Mose died. The third Mose told me —"

"This is sounding extremely biblical. Does he speak to you from a burning bush?"

"You need to brush up on your Bible, Murphy. That was God lurking in the underbrush, but would you shut up and listen? Here's my idea. You buy it for your bookstore, we punch a door through the common wall between it and the Klatch, and we have an Indigo/Starbucks setup ready-made."

Tulla paced the kitchen with the phone caught between shoulder and cheek, hands tucked into her armpits to warm them. "What common wall? There's an alley between those buildings."

"Not at the very back end. They each have a back kitchen with a shared wall. So?"

"*Shush*, I'm thinking."

"What's to think? It's a slam dunk."

"But you know what they say about friends going into business together. End of friendship."

"What do you mean? We wouldn't be a business partnership. This would be a symbiotic partnership. No shared income or expenses, just mutually beneficial. You get free coffee, I get free books."

Tulla laughed. "Like hell you do. When can I see it?"

"Anytime. I have the key. Being a good neighbour, I offered to keep an eye on it. When I come for dinner we can discuss it. I'll bring a bottle of wine."

* * *

The raised ceilings and yellow rough-plaster walls of Tulla's living room seemed to hold the sunlight, storing the warmth for winter. Kat turned slowly in the middle of the room, nodding with approval. "The Santa Fe look. Now you have to find furniture that'll work in here. This stuff" — she waved her hand to take in the heavy oak pieces crammed into the room — "is from your old house, right?"

Tulla nodded. "Been in storage for years."

"My advice? Sell all of it. You'd make enough money to furnish this place with lovely light pine stuff and then you could buy a Georgia O'Keeffe for over the fireplace, if you had one."

"I do. It's in the den."

"A Georgia O'Keeffe?"

"No, a fireplace. I hate Georgia O'Keeffe. But come see the bathroom." She led the way down the hall, through her bedroom, and into the ensuite bathroom. An angle pose lamp stretched from the wall out over a slant-backed tub, long and deep as a coffin. A movable shelf ran across it bearing a cup holder, a candlestick, and a bookrest.

Kat burst out laughing. "Perfect!" She cocked her head. "What's buzzing?"

Tulla looked around. "I don't hear anything."

"Sounds like a trapped bumblebee." Kat followed the sound to the vanity and picked up an electric toothbrush, which vibrated in her hand. "This is on."

Tulla grinned sheepishly. "Sometimes I do that with the car, too."

"Reassuring," Kat said.

They retraced their steps and went out through the patio doors onto the deck. Below them the water glinted copper in the setting sun. Kat turned to Tulla. "'What's water but the generated soul ...'"

"Yeats, 'Coole Park and Ballylee.'"

"Yeah. Thought I might have you on that one. Gosh, this is a lovely spot."

At the end of a normal summer the river below would have been shallow rapids, no more than ankle-deep, an occasional swirl of white water in the crevasses the only indication of the slumbering power of the current. The rock outcrops below the mill would be dotted with picnickers, and the river loud with splashing kids. But this was no ordinary September. The water, so high this year after months of rain, flowed dark and smooth as syrup, boiling against the sluice gates clogged now with storm debris.

Tulla leaned her elbows on the railing and gazed down into the river. "The river's why I bought the place. And the neighbours, of course."

"Mikhail?"

"An unexpected perk. Like old times — him living upstairs. But come and see what I found in one of the boxes from storage."

She led the way back down the hall to narrow double doors, tongue-and-groove pine inset with stained-glass panels. Prisms of colour scattered across the floor as she swung them open into an octagon-shaped room. A limestone fireplace opposite was flanked by half-windows, their deep pine sills covered with floor cushions. Floor-to-ceiling shelves bracketed a desk built into another of the room's angles. Boxes stood six high against one of the bookshelves. She picked up a stack of coil binders from the windowsill.

Kat's eyes widened. "My God, are those slam books? Why would you ever have kept those? Hate literature. Burn the bloody things."

Tulla handed her one. "Grade ten."

Kat flicked through the first pages where the unwritten rule had been that you had to sign your comments. The category lists were boyfriends, girlfriends, favourite sports, teachers, and clothes, and the observations were mostly benign or gushy: "You look so cute in pink!!!" or "How come you're so smart!!!!" But the back pages of anonymous notes weren't so kind.

"This stuff is so cruel," Kat said, shaking her head. "It's a low-tech version of cyberbullying, but just as effective." She read aloud. "'You know what you're called behind your back? Miss Boosy Bitch. You're so full of yourself.'"

"And I didn't even drink in high school," Tulla protested.

"Not *boozy* — *bossy*. Whoever wrote that still couldn't spell even by grade ten."

Tulla leaned over her shoulder and pointed. "There's you, Kat."

Kat's distinctive writing jumped off the page, big, looping letters in purple ink: "To my best friend, Tulla M. Who lives in her own world. Because it's safer."

Below, in an almost indecipherable scrawl: "Own world to keep out Valley kids, you stuck-up cu—" The last two letters had been scratched out. No signature.

"Bobby," Kat said.

"Dom, by then."

Kat pointed at the line below in block caps: "Don't let the turkey get you down," with an arrow pointing to the comment above. "That would be Leo." She sat back on her heels and peered up at Tulla. "You sure had a thing going, you two."

"My mother called it puppy love. Dismissive. Imagine me, her daughter, linked with a Valley boy. Horrors!"

"She should've been more understanding. *She* linked up with a Valley boy."

"That's why she was so against Leo. Look what happened to her and Dad."

Kat riffled through the pages. "Nothing here from Mikhail."

"He didn't approve of slam books. Said they were 'cruel and unusual punishment,' a phrase I thought was his own. Look what else I found." She pulled a folding card table away from the wall. "Our membership and club rules are still written on the bottom. The Core Four — plus one. You, me, Leo, Mikhail, and the long, nasty hand of Parnell, probably Bobby, which finished us."

"It wasn't Parnell that dealt the death blow. It was the Clod War."

"Same thing."

Tulla had a theory that memories from childhood were divided by degree of intensity, ranging from vague feelings to a series of snapshots from a particular location, to the primary colours and emotions of a seminal event. The Clod War fell into the final category.

When she explained her theory, Kat nodded. "I can understand that. At a young age you almost murdered someone. Hard to forget."

"It's not a joke. Besides, I wasn't the one who killed someone."

"The day of the Clod War? No one killed anyone that day."

Tulla leaned back on the window seat and clasped her knees. "Do you remember a book by John Buchan? It's called *Memory Hold-the-Door*. It's a kind of memoir. I don't remember much about it except the title. Because here's the thing. The title can mean two entirely different things. Did he mean memory holds the door shut on the past, at least certain events that your subconscious doesn't want you to remember? Or does it mean memory holds the door open to your past, events you have no conscious recollection of that suddenly, out of nowhere, pop into your head?"

"No idea. Give me an example."

"Okay. What do you remember about the Clod War? Don't think about it, just what comes into your mind immediately."

"Sounds," Kat said. "The thump of the clods hitting the wall when the Valley kids attacked."

"What else?"

"The factory siren calling the ambulance, the whoops — so different from the five o'clock end-of-workday whistle. Darla screaming ... and then the sudden hush. I'm not sure this is accurate, but I remember suddenly all the voices going quiet. We were standing in a circle around Dom, and no one said a word. Do you remember that?"

"No. I'm not sure I was in the circle. I think by then I was hiding under this —" she put her hand on the club card table "— thinking I was going to jail for killing Dom."

"What *do* you remember?"

Tulla said slowly, "Up until a few weeks ago, if I thought about it at all, I remembered how cold it was, the slush and mud. I remembered the fright when the opening salvo of clods hit the wall. I remembered Bridget ordering everyone about and being so delighted that she, my bossy big sister, for once wasn't sending me home. Funny, you remember the sounds, I remember the feelings. The bewilderment when everyone looked at me as if I'd done something terrible when I thought I'd be a hero. The misery of hiding. Dad being so mad at me when he heard —"

"So what happened a few weeks ago?"

"I think memory suddenly threw the door wide, triggered by an image. When Portland and I were on our way to the cancer clinic in the Bahamas about six months ago — seems like a lifetime now — we stopped in Washington, D.C., to see an oncologist who specialized in male breast cancer. While we were there Port wanted to do the tourist thing, even though he could barely totter, he was so sick. Said it was probably his last chance, which it was."

Tulla turned her head and gazed upward, as if her memory was unspooling on the ceiling like a film. "We went to the Korean War Veterans Memorial. Ever seen it?"

Kat shook her head.

"Google it. It's amazing. A group of oversized sculptures of soldiers creeping across a field, rifles in hand. We saw it at dusk. The statues were lit from the ground, all shadowy. And all of a sudden — *wham!* — I'm back on that building site in the Clod War. I'm me that day, scared, excited to be included with the big kids, and then I see two figures with sticks, baseball bats, I think, like rifles stocks. In the dusk, out on the road. And they're beating someone, a child crouched down. And one of those figures is Dom."

"And the other?"

"Couldn't see well enough."

"Then how did you know it was Dom?"

"Because he was the one who broke away and ran at me, and that's when I got him with the rock. And I remembered trying to tell Bridget and Mother, but they didn't believe me. No one else saw it, no one heard of any little kid being hurt. And since I was prone to making things up, they said —"

"You? Make things up? Just because you had imaginary friends living in half the trees along your driveway and you saw two-metre-tall, pointy-headed Martians in your back lane? Never!"

"Well, I didn't make it up. But I did forget it. I buried the memory. And after all these years it resurfaced when I saw those soldier statues. Funny thing, memory."

SEVEN

SINCE THE VISIT to the memorial, Tulla had thought often of the Clod War, replaying it like a silent black-and-white film, feeding back into it the frames her memory had edited out.

She remembered the thumps of the first volley of clods hitting the plywood walls of the half-built house, remembered Bridget issuing orders, and remembered Leo taking her hand. She recalled the feeling of exultation at being part of the group, and the sensation that she could do anything. She was strong and fearless like the Indigenous woman diving into the current at the top of the gorge, felt invincible, protected by her friends and doing the bidding of her sister. She remembered her surge of rage at the sight of the two boys beating the child, then scrambling to find not just a clod of snow and mud but a rock to throw at Bobby. She wanted to hurt him for his cruelty.

Bobby was in the hospital for eleven days, two of them in intensive care. It was nearly twelve hours before he regained consciousness to find himself with a shaved head, thirty stitches closing a leering slice of skull, and a severe concussion.

"Whatever possessed you?" Bridget demanded, storming into Tulla's room that night after returning from the hospital.

"Leave her be," their mother, Sadie, snapped. "I've only just got her home and calmed down. She's still shivering even after a hot bath."

"Where's she been?"

"After the ambulance left, that young hooligan, Leo, found her hiding in the freezing dark under a table in the basement of that house. Someone told her she'd killed the boy, that she was a murderer."

"Well, she nearly did. The rock she threw was like an axe head."

"I didn't know it was a rock," Tulla said through chattering teeth. But she did. She remembered now. She knew.

Bridget grinned slowly. "You'll really have to watch your back now, Tulla Bean. Nice shot, though."

Tulla gazed at her miserably. *How can you watch your own back?*

Bridget had been right. One afternoon in mid-June, the golden light heavy with the scent of lilac, Tulla was biking home from school, counting the days to the summer holidays. A rock whistled out of nowhere, catching her on the side of her head and sending her crashing into the ditch, winded and disoriented.

"Gotcha, bitch!" Bobby yelled, firing another missile, this time hitting her arm. As he took aim again, a car turned the corner and stopped. Before the driver got out, Bobby had vanished between the houses.

Harriet Deaver bent over her. "What happened, child? Your head's bleeding."

Tulla gulped for breath, unable to speak.

Harriet pulled her to her feet and brushed the dirt off her clothes. "You need that ear looked after. It's cut badly, will need stitches. We'll put your bike in the trunk."

Thus began a wonderful friendship — the first time Tulla understood that you could actually be friends with an adult.

"So, we're agreed?" Kat said. "Get rid of the slam books. Throw them on the fire."

"Good idea. Except it's propane and would probably explode."

"If it's propane, why have you got a poker? You don't need a poker for a fake fireplace."

"Because my grandfather made it. It came from the old house. So, Bossy Boots, let's get drinks."

"Don't you mean Boozy Boots?" Kat stopped short in the doorway of the kitchen. "What's that?"

"My dog. Meet Clancy." Two bright eyes peered up through a fringe of grey hair. His paws cradled a large rock like a treasure.

"Why do you have a dog? You don't even like dogs."

"Sure I do. And a woman living alone needs a guard dog, or so everyone tells me."

"I think they meant one that's more than twenty centimetres high." She bent to pat him, and Clancy let out a ferocious growl. She jumped back. "Jeez, is he part pit bull?"

"Nah, he's actually a sweetie pie. All bluster … most of the time. He just thinks you're trying to steal his rock, which would be a seriously bad idea with a cairn. He had a tough start in life. He was taken away from his mother way too young. Poppy had to feed him with an eyedropper."

"Poppy? Portland's wife, your successor? She gave you her dog?"

"She was going to have him put down if no one took him."

Kat gazed down at Clancy, who gave her a baleful glare. "Your point?"

They had their dinner at the kitchen counter, Kat with her feet propped on a rung out of reach of a stealth attack, then took their drinks into the den to sit in front of the fire.

Kat waved her glass of wine to take in the surroundings. "If it's not too crass a question, may I ask how you can afford this condo, and whatever house you're buying for your bookstore, and who can make any money running a bookstore so you must be rich …?"

"Well, I sort of am. Portland gave me a bunch of money when we split, I think to assuage his guilt about his mother's behaviour. He insisted on paying my medical school fees — you knew that — and now, well, now I'm inheriting half his estate, split with Poppy."

"No wonder she gave you that vicious dog."

"It wasn't Poppy who minded. She told me she's stinking rich in her own right. Portland's mother, Lilly, wasn't too pleased, though."

"Just because you nearly killed her?"

"Not on purpose. I didn't hear her damn horse."

Tulla remembered the accident so clearly. She and Portland were still married, but already struggling. She'd taken up running, a distraction that had become an addiction. That morning there had been fog when she set out on her usual route through the park in Saratoga Springs, lost in the silence of the trees and her own muffled world. She ran easily, up over a slight rise and down to join the riding track lined by a hedge of tamaracks, yellow as flame against the evergreens. Her world exploded into the high-pitched whinny of a rearing horse, the piercing scream of her mother-in-law thrown from her saddle, and the thrashing of limbs as the horse fell backward onto Lilly's leg.

Late that afternoon she went to the hospital to apologize. Lilly's shattered leg had been set; her horse hadn't been so lucky. The fall had broken his neck. When Tulla crept into the surgical recovery room, Lilly was still dozy with the anesthetic and morphine. Neither drug was strong enough to quell her rage or her tongue. Lilly accused Tulla of spooking her horse on purpose, of making her son's life a living hell, and suggested she leave before she caused the family any more grief.

Something snapped that day, and not just Lilly's leg.

"Before that day I already knew our marriage, Portland's and mine, was doomed," Tulla said to Kat. "I felt like I was walking a tightrope I couldn't see. When

Lilly shredded me that afternoon, that tightrope broke. I could nearly hear it snap."

"You're being very fanciful. You can't hear anything."

"I heard that. It was like a starting pistol shot. I was gone that same day."

Tulla recalled arriving at the Canadian border, just barely holding it together, handing the border agent her passport, and bursting into tears.

"You all right, ma'am?" he asked, leaning out from the checkpoint booth, visibly alarmed.

She grabbed a handful of tissues from the glove compartment and mopped her face, but the tears kept coming. "Allergies." And then she was overcome with giggles.

The officer glanced at her passport. "Ms. Cole, do you need help? Are you ill?"

She hiccupped into silence, straightened, and for the first time in months, her face didn't hurt when she smiled. "No, I'm not ill. Thank you for asking. I'm actually fine. Really and truly fine."

He waved her through. "You might want to stop for a coffee before you drive much farther. There's a Tim Hortons about a kilometre on before the entrance to the 401."

At that point she knew for sure that she was home safe.

"Why did you split up, though?" Kat asked. "It couldn't have just been Lilly."

"No. Portland and I did have fun for a while. And then we didn't. He just … well, he kind of turned into his mother. He was fossilizing before my very eyes. Remember how we used to discuss that for hours —

were we like our parents because they grew us that way or because we were born that way? In Port's case it was both. He never had a chance."

Kat laughed. "Nurture or nature — heavy stuff for twelve-year-olds. But I can say this now. He was never right for you. I knew that even on your wedding day."

"You did not. That's hindsight speaking."

"Well, actually it was you speaking. After the rehearsal dinner and a couple of bottles of wine we nicked from Mr. Cole's wine cellar."

"I remember that … up to a point."

"Probably the point where you told me you were making a mistake, then started to reminisce about Leo …"

"Oh, God, I don't remember that." Tulla's voice trembled with laughter. "But since we're on the subject of ex-husbands, why did you marry Shug Bassett? Big bully in school, one of Dom's henchmen …"

Kat raised a weary hand. "I know, I know. Worst decision of my life to marry that jerk."

"Lapse of judgment?"

"Colossal."

"So why did you?"

"All I can think now is that maybe it was for the same reason Celia married Dom. I mean, she basically abandoned her beloved little brother, Leo, for a complete loser, and I bet she kind of knew that. But I guess she thought she could change him. Hah! Same for me. For a brief and misguided moment, I thought there was a tiny ember of humanity in Shug that I could fan into a flame. I was wrong. Nothing but clinkers there."

"But you're out of the whole mess now, aren't you?"

"No, but at least I've got him out of the house. And I doubt he'll try to beat me up again." Her smile was bleak. "I don't think he suspected I was such a dirty fighter. He should have, though. We studied at the same fight school — Parnell Public."

"He hit you?"

She looked up at Tulla's indrawn breath. "Want to know why? You'll love this. I corrected his grammar, which was the least of his peccadilloes, but for some reason that bugged the hell out of me."

"No doubt." Tulla's mouth twitched despite herself. It wasn't funny, but Kat was doing what she always did to keep questions at bay: rewriting grim reality into a joke.

"It wasn't so much *what* I said as *when*."

"Bad timing?"

"Very."

They were falling into the rhythm of their old conversations.

"How bad?"

"The worst. We were in bed. Me very reluctantly, him drunk and randy as a bull. He was shouting, 'Lay still! Lay still!' And I pointed out that he meant *lie* still, that the verb *to lay* is transitive and has to have an object." Her smile faded. "That's when he belted me, and I belted him right back, which was an even bigger mistake than the grammar lesson. The next day he was all contrite, promised it would never happen again, but really it was my fault that he hit me. I'd made him feel stupid, which, of course, he is. I'd demeaned him, threatened his manhood. God, it was all so trailer park trash-y. I told him to leave. He wouldn't. I said I was going to then. He said he wouldn't let me. That he had friends in high places who could make my life miserable and I would lose the kids. So I stayed."

"After he beat you up?"

Kat's eyes flashed. "You ever been there? I don't think so. Ever been physically terrified of someone bigger, stupider, and drunker, not to mention with friends in high places?"

"Kat, I'm not judging ..."

"Like hell you weren't."

"No, I just can't fathom *you* taking that abuse. I don't know anyone stronger than you. When we were kids, and you were the shortest of us all, you always stood up to anyone who tried to bully you or anyone else. You even took on Dom on my behalf when he kept coming for me after the Clod War."

"That was then, this is now." She leaned her head back on the pillowed chair top and gazed at the fire. "Difference is I have too much to lose now. The one upside to this unfortunate union, Liam, is also the downside. My hostage to fortune." She gripped the arms of her chair and pulled herself forward. "Enough of this. Time to go, morning comes early for a working girl."

"You're not going anywhere until you tell me what this is about. Is Thurston one of the friends in high places? Was that what was going on in the Klatch the other morning?"

"Thurston's a pipsqueak, but dangerous because he squeaks at the bidding of others. I didn't know that before. He serves his handlers well. Or he did, since one of them isn't doing too much handling anymore."

"Dom?"

"Yup. Thurston was one of Dom's puppets."

"How do you know all this, Kat?"

"Shug. Apparently, before his house was built, Dom used to stay at the Russell and hold meetings with his gang of lackeys, including Thurston. That's why I've had to go very slowly and very carefully. I managed to get him out of my house ..." she paused. "But the negotiations are ongoing." She rubbed her face. "I had to agree to share custody of Liam with Shug — a court order issued by a judge owned by Dom."

"But, Kat, why would Dom care? I don't understand."

Kat wriggled her shoulders, tilted her head from side to side, and yawned. But Tulla saw the fear in her eyes. "Neither do I. There was something between them from way back ... a sick bond. I know it sounds bad, but I'm glad Dom's dead because I can petition for full custody, no visiting rights, and win. I know I can. I have to. Because every minute Liam's with Shug I'm on tenterhooks. But enough of all this. I'm going home."

Tulla picked up the wine bottle and shook it. "Empty."

Kat squinted. "Did I drink all that?"

"I helped. And the one before."

Kat let go of the back of the chair and swayed slightly.

"I'll walk you home," Tulla said.

"No way. Then I'd have to walk you back. We'd be out there all night." She headed to the front entry, got her coat on with some difficulty, pulled the door open, and turned back, eyes flooded with tears. "Tulla, I'm not closing you out. You have to trust me. Okay?"

"For now …" Tulla hugged her hard. "But, Kat, the two of us will deal with Shug and all his friends in high places, the ones still left that is. They won't have a chance."

"Yeah, we'll really scare them …"

Tulla watched her walk to the corner with careful gait, vanishing in the shadows and reappearing under the street lights like a wraith. Clancy shot down the steps and through the hedge to the riverbank. She took the walkway after him and leaned against the stone wall, gazing at the river as it slid past in the moonlight. An owl hooted from the opposite bank; a breeze whispered like a conversation in the trees. Clancy lifted his head and growled. She scooped him up. "Want to sleep in my room tonight, dog?"

Clancy came, but sleep didn't. She laced her fingers behind her head and stared at the ceiling where moonlight danced in reflection off the river. Tulla couldn't shake the image of Kat cowering beneath the fist of Shug Bassett, one of the lowest of low-lifes in Parnell. She must have been out of her mind to have married him. Just like Celia, Leo's beloved older sister, marrying Dom — good women so eager to throw themselves under the bus for bad men.

What was it with this town? It was poisonous, and she wondered now how she'd ended up back here. She'd been on another path entirely. When her marriage disintegrated, she was surprised to find that the emotion she felt wasn't grief or despair; it was elation. Relief to have her old self back after pretending to be someone else for all those years. The years in medical school had been exhausting but exhilarating until the reality had set in — how could she ever be a doctor when she couldn't hear what her patients were telling her? She had just about accepted that if she were to stay in medicine it would be in research or lab work when she was launched on the gut-wrenching journey by the midnight telephone call from Portland's father — Portland was sick and needed her — and now here she was back in Parnell. She didn't feel it was her choice at all, but if not, who had made it?

Tulla flipped onto her stomach. And who said you had a choice in this life, anyway? If we had choices, we'd all be kids again, pre–Clod War kids when at least in hindsight life was simple and the gods kept their distance, busy pulling wings off other flies. Kat would never have married Shug, Celia would never have married Dom, and she would never have married Portland. Not that Port was bad; he'd just been a detour.

EIGHT

AFTER THE EVANGELICAL rally, Leo Harding was approved for full working status and assigned to his own investigation. His flight was the last to leave Toronto's Pearson Airport before fog shut it down for the night. It had been two hours late taking off for the short flight to Ottawa, another hour in a holding pattern waiting to land. Passengers hurried into the airport, cellphones glued to their ears, remaking reservations, jostling to get to the baggage carousels.

Leo waited for a break in the stream of humanity and made his way to the express exit from the arrivals level. He could see the snarl of traffic through the glass doors, security guards hustling cars out of the drop-off zones. In the darkness, a blue light flashed from the dash of a vintage Marquis parked halfway up on the sidewalk. The driver leaned against the dented side door, arms folded, staring at the ground, lost in thought. Leo studied him through the glass.

It had been six years before, September, and this same man had been waiting for him then, leaning just like tonight, against the side of a battered old car, ankles crossed, head down. But at a jail, not an airport …

"Release papers are here." The guard unlocked the cell door for Leo and held it wide. "Glad you won, Harding. Your first case was a bloody travesty. You packed?"

Leo held up two books and a toothbrush.

The guard eyed the books. "Are those from the prison library?"

"Yes."

"Be my guest. The system owes you something."

Leo stood on the prison steps and took a deep breath. Everything shone: the leaves on the trees, the cars in the lot except one, the grass verges, the windows of the buildings, the barbed-wire coils along the top of the walls now behind him. He'd only been in prison a few weeks, but it had felt like a lifetime. And he was out because of the man who leaned against the dusty, battered car waiting for him.

He strode across the parking lot and held out his hand. "Mikhail."

Mikhail shook hands quickly. "Everything go okay in there? Did you get your papers?"

"The ones that say all of this never happened? Yeah. Let's get out of here."

"Where to?"

Leo shrugged. "As far away as possible. From here on in, it's one day at a time."

"You know you can stay with me as long as it takes," Mikhail said.

By early evening they were sitting at the kitchen table in Mikhail's Orillia apartment, an extra-large, all-dressed pizza in front of them. Mik opened two bottles of beer, poured one carefully into a glass for himself, and handed the other bottle to Leo. They saluted each other and drank.

"Nectar." Leo held his bottle up to read the label and began peeling it with his thumb. Mikhail eyed the bits of paper falling onto the table as if they were mouse dirt. "So, any word from Celia?"

"No." Mikhail watched him closely. "No one seems to know where she and Dom are. They've been out of the country for several months. Dom must have gotten word that your appeal was going to be successful."

"Then Celia must have known, too."

"I don't think so, Leo. I don't think she knew anything. Dom controls her. You know that."

"How's that possible? She used to be the strongest person we knew. She ..." Leo's thumb scraped faster, bits of label curling off the bottle like wood shavings. There was a long silence. Finally he spoke again. "So, my friend, you demolished them." He tilted his beer in tribute.

"The first case was a travesty."

"Funny. That's just what the guard said today."

"A perfect example of another colossal screw-up in a system where the domino effect carries the day. Starts with a wrong assumption and snowballs."

Leo tilted his chair back on two legs and sipped his beer. "What's the story on Dom? Will he be charged with contempt?"

"Unlikely. He's got influence in high places."

"And Darla was exonerated. Hard to believe."

"She wasn't exonerated. She was put on probation for two years which, by the way, she's already broken. Got across the border within days. But the judge seemed to believe her newfound piety and took compassion on her because of the death of her child."

Leo's head shot up. "She died?"

Mikhail nodded. "And the other child would've had to go into care if Darla had been given a prison term."

Leo had stopped listening, his eyes bleak with grief. He slammed his chair back onto the floor and leaned toward Mikhail, nostrils flaring. "How did she die?"

Mikhail regarded him steadily. "Word was spinal meningitis."

"Whose word?"

"Dom's."

Leo gripped his beer bottle until his knuckles turned white.

Mikhail pulled it away from him. "You're going to break that."

Now, the sight of Mikhail leaning on his car, arms folded, staring at the pavement, swamped Leo with the memory of Mik waiting outside the jail all those years ago. Their friendship had only strengthened during Leo's nightmare. He pushed through the airport terminal doors, and strode across the pavement toward the car with the blue light on the dash.

"Sorry about the delay, Mikhail. Fog in Toronto, and half the planes were rerouted here. We've been flying in circles over your head for the past hour." He pointed at the revolving blue light. "Nice touch. Illegal, but nice touch."

Mikhail smiled and held up a hand in thanks to the security cop standing near the car. "Knew him in Orillia. He used to be with the narc squad. Took early retirement and hired on with the airport police."

Leo opened the back door and threw his bag onto the seat. "Want me to drive?"

"Ah, no. This car has a bit of a death wish — keeps heading for the ditch. Moody creature." He patted the roof fondly. "But I'm used to her moods. Hop in."

Mikhail manhandled the big car down the ramp and out onto the parkway, ignoring a yield sign and the cacophony of honks from the vehicles he'd cut off. It was past midnight by the time they reached Parnell. Mikhail pulled up in front of the hotel. "Welcome home?"

"I guess ..." Leo raised an eyebrow. "Home." His tone was flat.

NINE

IT WAS A GREY and windy day. From her bed, Tulla watched birds stream past the window along with litter and leaves, helpless in the gale. She lowered her feet gingerly to the floor and headed for the kitchen.

"Come on, Clancy, out you go." She pushed the door shut behind him against the wind.

"No more booze. No more. Ever." She massaged the bridge of her nose where a headache had settled like a stone, willing the coffee maker to finish its steaming and wheezing. Too impatient to wait, she filled a mug and slammed the pot back onto the hot plate to catch the stream of coffee puddling over the counter. The filter flew across the kitchen, scattering soggy grounds in a perfect arc over the tiles.

She studied the mess, shrugged, picked up her book, and headed for the den. In response to a nudge of the thermostat, the gas fireplace flickered into life, and she marvelled again at its easy, instant warmth. *Okay, so it doesn't have that lovely woodsmoke smell, and the grate does look a little fake.*

As she curled into her chair, she totted up the stove's advantages, an exercise she hadn't tired of yet: no wood to buy, chop, and carry; no mess; no sulky fire on low-pressure days; no soot-filled room after a downdraft; no starlings flying down the chimney and out into the room, leaving black smudges all over the ceiling; no more —

A ferocious thumping on her front door interrupted her reverie. Faintly, she could hear yelling. Something about a dog? *Can't be Clancy. He's in the back garden.*

She scurried down the hall and pulled open the door, ready for a fight. "My dog's in the back garden," she snapped. Her heart lurched.

A man wearing baggy shorts, a long-sleeved T-shirt, and a baseball cap pulled low over aviator sunglasses stood on the porch, fist raised to pound the door again. He held up his foot, blood dripping from his ankle. "That's your dog, right?" He pointed down the steps.

Clancy sat on the path, grinning. Bits of cedar hedge were stuck in his coat, and what appeared to be a snag of white sock hung from the corner of his mouth. He stood up and scampered down the street.

"Oh, shit! Yes, it is. I'm so sorry. You'd better come in." Tulla's heart was beating like a trip-hammer. "Did you antagonize him?"

"I was running past. Does that constitute antagonism? Listening to my music and he just ran out and attached himself to my ankle."

Tulla looked at him. "Say again?"

He touched the earbud running to an iPod in the pocket of his T-shirt. "Tunes."

"What tunes?"

"It makes a difference? Neil Young."

Tulla shook her head. "Knew it. Clancy *hates* Neil Young. Leo? Take off those stupid glasses."

He removed his cap, pushed the glasses up onto his forehead, and smiled hugely. She grabbed him in a hug that sent him staggering into the door frame.

Leo held her away to study her. "You look good, Tulla, for an old broad."

"You don't look so bad yourself." But he did. He hadn't so much aged as hardened. He appeared worn and thin and stringy. She had a sudden memory of Paul Newman in *Hud*, a film she'd seen with Leo at a drive-in years ago in a blizzard. Snow had blown across the screen, obliterating the hot, dusty farmland full of dead cows. Sexy Patricia Neal, leaning against the door frame, drawling, "You're an unprincipled man, Hud," and that was Leo in those days.

She studied him now. He was still a handsome man, in an old cowboy way, with chiselled features, a wide, straight mouth, but now he resembled … who? A slightly younger Gordon Lightfoot, that was who. Gord before his illness. Or maybe after. Wherever he'd been these past few years, it seemed as if life hadn't been too good to Leo.

"What brings you back to Parnell?" she asked.

"On assignment." He gazed at his foot. "Didn't realize it was going to be so dangerous, though. Maybe you have a tourniquet before I bleed to death?"

Tulla knelt to examine his ankle. "There's a first-aid kit on the shelf under the sink in the kitchen. A Band-Aid should cover it. And there's coffee. I'm going to get Clancy."

As Leo limped heavily down the hall, Tulla grabbed a jacket, shoved her bare feet into her running shoes, and stepped outside, peering up and down the street. She jogged to the end of the block and back, tripping on her laces when Leo called from the steps. "He's on your back deck." He'd bandaged his ankle, a big muslin pad taped over the wound.

"Oh, good, that'll probably prevent gangrene until Monday. I don't think they do amputations on Saturdays." She pushed past him, trying to control a gurgle of laughter, not wanting to show how crazy glad she was to see him again.

He sat at the kitchen table, tilted back, and propped his injured foot on a chair.

"Don't do that," Tulla said. "Did you get coffee?"

"Yeah." He held up his mug. "Although most of it seems to be on the floor."

She opened the cupboard under the sink to find the floor cloth. "Don't do that, Leo."

"Don't do what?"

"Rock back in your chair. You'll fall over backward."

He smiled. "That would be your mother speaking. How is she?"

"Not so great. She has Alzheimer's."

"I'd heard. I'm sorry."

"And then you probably know Dad's remarried?"

Leo made a noncommittal noise.

"Lives happily in the Bahamas with a very nice wealthy wife and wears emerald-green suits to church where he's an elder, if you can believe it. Plays golf, swims every day, drinks too much, and loves his life."

She slid into the chair opposite and studied him over the rim of her coffee mug. God, how she'd missed him, hadn't realized how much until now, seeing his face, his hooded eyes, his smile that had been so rare.

Leo clasped his hands behind his head. "Can't believe you didn't recognize me."

"I did recognize you, despite your disguise. I also thought what kind of jerk would wear shades on a day like this, especially those mirrored things that cops wear to intimidate people."

"Could be because I *am* a cop."

She blinked. "You?"

"Detective. With the OPP. That would be the Ontario Provincial Pol—"

"I know what the OPP is. So your assignment's a cop assignment?"

"Yup. Your dog wants in."

When she pulled the door open, Clancy scrabbled across the tiles in a beeline for Leo, tail wagging in a suspiciously friendly fashion. Leo reached down and scratched his ears.

"He didn't bite you, did he?" Tulla said. "You faked the whole thing."

Leo grinned.

"Where did the blood come from? Unless, of course, you planned this, which is just plain creepy."

"The blood was real. I ran through the swamp on my way here and tripped over some brambles. When I saw this guy wiggling through the hedge, looking as if he'd *like* to bite someone, I came up with the plan."

Tulla watched Clancy gaze adoringly up at Leo. *You, too, eh?* She stood up to reach the coffee pot, tripped on the belt of her robe, and stumbled across the kitchen.

Leo smiled. "Remind me, Murph, did you ever make it onto the cheerleading squad?"

She could tell he was assessing her. What did he see? Tall, chestnut hair sun-streaked and tousled, feather-cut to well below her jawline, bare legs and feet brown from the Bahamian sun, a woman who moved with the same coltish awkwardness he likely remembered from high school, as if she never actually got her long legs under control. A lack of awareness of the effect she had on people, so much part of her personality — an unusual combination of unselfconsciousness and shyness.

Tulla gazed up at him over her shoulder. "What?"

"Nothing. Not a thing." He checked his watch. "I'd better go. My unit will be arriving anytime, and I want to make sure they don't check in with Roland before I do."

"Not before you tell me what you've been up to all these years." *Worth a try.* "Like, where do you live now? Are you married? If not, why not?" Tulla counted the questions off on her fingers. "Have you seen any of the old crowd?"

Leo held up a hand. "Number one, right now at the Russell. Number two, no. Number three, none of your business. Number four, Mikhail."

"Can't do the math. At least tell me what your assignment is here. Or is that a secret, too?"

"I'm investigating a suspicious death. Dom Connolly's."

"What's suspicious about being blown out of your house by a tornado?"

Leo's face was still as granite. "Leo's lockdowns," she used to call them.

"Preliminary autopsy report says he was dead before the storm hit. This is classified, by the way, until Orillia tells the local force." He jumped and dug a cellphone from his back pocket. "Hate this thing. First time it vibrated I thought a mouse had climbed into my pocket."

He pushed a button. "Hey, it worked." He grinned at Tulla and spoke into the phone. "Harding." A pause. "No, not to the police station. Go to the hotel, the Russell on Main Street, and I'll meet you —" he checked his watch "— in ten. Stay under the radar. The chief of police here doesn't know we're on his turf yet." He snapped the phone case shut and stood.

"How come Roland doesn't know about this?" Tulla asked.

"Because OPP HQ in Orillia can't raise him. Hard to believe, isn't it?"

"Not really. They're dealing with the ultimate gatekeeper — Elvie. Give me two minutes while I get dressed and I'll come with you. Have to get some groceries." She ran down the hallway, pulled on jeans and a turtleneck, scraped her hair into a ponytail, and hurried back to the entry.

They walked to her car together, and she opened the door for Clancy, who hopped in and up onto the back windowsill.

"That's a dangerous place for him to travel," Leo said. "If you have to brake suddenly, he turns into a missile."

"More dangerous to not let him sit up on the ledge. I tried to put a dog-restraining harness on him, but he attacked it, almost bit me, and finally threw up all over the back of the car as soon as I started the engine. So he won, I lost, and he travels on the windowsill. Want a lift to the Russell?"

"No thanks. Too dangerous." Leo adjusted his cap against the wind, gave a brief wave, and set off up the street at a brisk pace.

Tulla rested her chin on her forearms on the steering wheel, watching until he turned the corner, then climbed back out of the car. "C'mon, Clancy, grocery run's aborted."

TEN

MIKHAIL OPENED THE DOOR to Tulla's knock. She tilted her head to read the title of the journal in his hand: *Nature Neuroscience*.

"Good plot?"

Clancy shot past her, heading for the hearth.

Tulla heeled off her shoes before going through to the living room. She loved this room: cozy, inviting, and regimented to the extreme. Every wall was lined with bookshelves, the volumes standing like soldiers on a parade ground, their detachments organized by height and colour rather than author or subject. Pillars of carefully aligned books stood on either side of the glass doors onto the deck. A Queen Anne armchair angled toward the fireplace, a matching footstool in front of it. On an antique wine table, cherrywood inlaid with ivory, a crystal glass glowed amber in the firelight.

Mikhail pulled a twin armchair forward, positioning it precisely to reflect the angle of the chair he had just vacated. "Coffee? Tea?" He gestured to his own glass. "Too early for a whisky?"

"Don't suppose you have herbal tea?"

Tulla followed him into a gleaming kitchen. Mottled black-and-ruby granite counters were showroom-bare — not a crumb, not a streak, not a toaster, not even a coffee maker marred their pristine expanse.

The tea was arranged alphabetically. Tulla shook her head in wonderment, noticing that for the first time today it didn't hurt. She chose Tension Tamer just in case.

They took their drinks to the living room and the fire where Clancy was curled like a cat in front of the real flames.

"So, how about I take you out for dinner tonight at that restaurant your friend owns and you can tell me all about Leo? Why didn't you tell me he was here?"

"He asked me not to."

"Where's he been all these years, Mik? He was totally elusive when I asked him more than the time of day. You seem to be the only person he's kept up with."

Mikhail turned his glass to catch the firelight, took a small sip, and put the glass back precisely in the middle of the inlay pattern on a coaster. He stood and pulled a log from the woodbox, a carefully cut chunk of hard maple so clean it looked dusted. After wiping his hands on a towel hanging from the pine mantelpiece, he sat down again. She waited.

"There are gaps. He had some bad years — he called that time his personal perfect storm, full of rage, guilt, and regret."

When Mik stopped speaking, Tulla leaned forward, peering into his face. "What happened to him those years?"

He shook his head. "We lost touch for a while, but we both ended up working for the OPP in Orillia. I was in the Behavioural Sciences and Analysis section, and he was on the international side investigating criminal enterprises and organized crime, usually away on assignment. One was to Afghanistan, military police, a wretched job in a wretched country in a wretched situation. When he came back, he went on medical leave. And now he's in the homicide division." Mikhail sipped his whisky.

Tulla waited. "That's it?"

"Pretty much." He glanced at his watch.

Tulla sighed. "Okay, I'll pursue this at dinner." She stood up. "I have to drop a couple of books at the library on the way."

The town hall stood at the northeast corner of the square marking the heart of Parnell. Built in 1900 of local limestone, it was a whimsical version of the Gothic Revival style of the Parliament Buildings in Ottawa, including a verdigris copper roof, a bell tower with a fake clock set into one side, and gargoyles on every corner. The council chamber and municipal offices were on the ground floor, the second floor housed the library, and the third floor was mainly home to bats. At dusk they could be seen flying out of the bell tower like smoke.

Tulla and Mikhail walked across the square, skirting the boards already erected in readiness for the hockey rink. A small crowd hovered around the entrance to the hall.

"They must be here for the council meeting tonight," Tulla said. "Probably hoping to hear more about Dom's death."

The bikers' appearance in town had turned the river of gossip into a flood. Dom's death was no accident; it was a Mafia hit, execution by skipping rope warning anyone else who might be considering an end run around the Family's chokehold on the fitness industry. Or Dom had been murdered by the lover of his third wife; several residents reported sightings of a stranger in town the day of the storm, a tall man with a scarred face. Of course, no one knew what the lover looked like, or even if there was one, but no matter. The current of gossip carried the flotsam of other theories: a childhood enemy, a man he'd crossed in prison, a woman he'd scorned. The one thing the town was fully in agreement about was that it wasn't the Fist of God that had felled Dom.

"I'll just take my books up to the library," Tulla said. "Back in a sec." She ran up the broad, curving staircase to the second floor. When she got back, Mikhail was standing in the council chamber doorway, finger to lips.

"This might get interesting," he said. "Thurston's gearing up for an eruption."

The council chamber was packed. Thurston's squeaky voice penetrated the chatter. "This meeting will come to order." He whacked the table with his gavel.

Tulla winced at the crack — like a pistol shot.

The mayor rapped his gavel again. "Environment Canada has confirmed that a tornado touched down in the vicinity of Crow Lake, and it is with great sadness that I have to report that Dominique Connolly was killed when his house on Forge Ridge was hit."

Nob heaved to his feet. He was fizzing with excitement. "Mayor —"

"Sit down. You're not on the agenda."

Nob couldn't be stopped. "The preliminary autopsy results indicate he was dead before the storm —"

"That's privileged information, you fool!" Thurston roared.

"Look at Roland," Mikhail whispered. "He's probably the only one here who didn't know." The chief's face was a mask of fury.

Thurston banged the gavel so hard the end broke off and flew into the tiered seats. "Shut up!" He thumped the table with his fist. "The OPP is sending investigators. Now that Dom's death has been ruled suspicious, an investigation is well beyond the capabilities of our local police force." He fixed his gaze on the chief.

Mikhail spoke in Tulla's ear. "The Criminal Investigation Unit would be called in, anyway. It has nothing to do with the capabilities of the local force. Thurston knows that."

Chief Roland sat bolt upright at the council table, nodding as if he'd been the one to call in the reinforcements. He rapped the table mike to get attention. "*Listen up!* Connolly's house is officially a crime scene now, so anyone caught trespassing up there will be charged with evidence tampering, a serious offence."

"Oh, great," Tulla whispered, reaching for her jacket. "They'll find dog hair and arrest Clancy. Let's get out of here."

ELEVEN

THE WIND WHISTLED through the oak tree at the edge of the town hall steps, a tree that had figured large in Tulla's childhood nightmares: the howling face in its bark rent the air with screams only she could hear, its branches thrashing like huge fingers reaching for her. Old-timers insisted it was "first growth" and had been a hanging tree in Parnell's early days, that criminals had been strung up from its lower limbs after the travelling magistrate passed through town. Her father had told her that was rubbish, but the image of rotting bodies turning in the wind in a dance of death had stuck in her mind.

"An Ichabod Crane night," she said, shrugging into her sheepskin jacket. "Mikhail, you must be freezing."

He wore no jacket, impervious to the cold, a legacy from his mother who had kept him in shorts in the winter and dressed him in wool on the hottest summer days. A particular summer memory never faded. They were waiting on the stone patio for her father to take them to the ice-cream wagon. It was a scorcher, the air shimmering with heat, the birds stunned into silence. And Mikhail had taken off his sweater. His mother came out of nowhere, grabbed him by the arm while he was still struggling to get it back on, dragged him across the flagstones, and threw him down the concrete steps to the root cellar. A whole lot of screaming had ensued. From Mikhail's mother — "You bad boy, you not take off clothes!" From Tulla, who clung to her leg scratching and biting. But not a sound from Mikhail.

"The Priest Hole Steak House, right? You sure I can go dressed like this?" Tulla asked.

"Designer jeans, cashmere sweater, and high-heeled boots? You'd be allowed in anywhere."

"You might be the only man I know who would know cashmere from cotton." She took his arm as they descended the steps but dropped it when she felt him stiffen. "One of the reasons, the many reasons, I love fall is you get to wear great boots." She held out one foot, the leather gleaming under the street lamp. "Nice, eh?"

The restaurant was in a stone cottage on a point thrust into the river just north of town. The front door, studded with brass nails the size of hockey pucks, opened into a low-ceilinged room lit only by the lamps on the tables, many of which were old Singer sewing machine stands, their iron treadles still in place. Forming the back wall, a huge stone fireplace included an inglenook big enough to park a small car in. A fire crackled with a blue flame, smelling of cedar.

A handsome woman came through a swing door under the stairs, loosening the strings of a chef's apron tied around her ample middle. Her auburn hair gleamed in the lamplight. "Sorry, folks, we're just closing. Oh, is that you, Mikhail? Come on in, and your friend?"

"This is Tulla Murphy, Maureen."

"Warren's daughter." Maureen smiled broadly and held out her hand. "I'm glad to finally meet you."

"We used to play here when we were kids." Tulla looked around her with pleasure. "It was pretty much a ruin then. You've made it into a beautiful space."

"Thank you. Let's find a table for you." She glanced around the empty restaurant as if it was full of patrons. "It's a night for this one — here by the fireplace. Actually, in the fireplace." She pulled out a chair from a small table tucked into the inglenook. "Now, I'm going to choose your dinner, since the kitchen is pretty much closed down. You aren't a vegetarian, are you, Tulla?"

Tulla shook her head.

"Good." She hurried back into the kitchen yelling, "Fire things back up, Andy. The night isn't over yet."

Mikhail stood up. "I'll get the wine and save Maureen the bother. That way I get to choose." He returned with a bottle in one hand and a basket of bread in the other. They sipped in companionable silence, feet stretched to the warmth of the fire.

Andy appeared with their plates balanced along his arms like turtles on a log. Perfectly grilled filets mignons, pommes frites with aioli, tomato salads with fresh basil and olive oil. Another basket of bread, a sauce boat. And another bottle of Beaujolais. "Maureen says she'll be out later to help you drink that," he said, sliding the plates in front of them and placing the open bottle on the next table. "She said to put it there out of your reach until she gets here. Just quoting." He loped back to the kitchen.

Maureen came to the table, untying her apron. "Sixty-four-year-old bones are beginning to wear out. Mikhail, be a love and pour me some of that wine." She held out a tumbler. "So were you at the council meeting? Anything interesting, or just the same old Thurston palaver?"

Tulla told her about Nob's announcement. "Poor Rockin' Roland was gobsmacked — only one who didn't seem to know."

"*Gobsmacked.* Now there's a word I haven't heard since back home. You been to Newfoundland?"

"You're from Newfoundland and you opened a *steak* house?"

"Can't stand fish. Hate cods' cheeks. Can you imagine?"

"How in the world did you end up here?"

"Your father. He used to come to my little restaurant in Ottawa. It was so small, I called it the Telephone Booth. Six tables and me." She patted her girth. "Tight squeeze. He told me about a building in a town far, far away. Made it sound as if it was in another galaxy. I half expected the clientele would be bounty hunters and mythical monsters. Your father's such a romantic soul." She threw out an arm in a sweeping gesture. "It had me from the front door. Did you see the brochure?" She pushed herself up from the table with a little groan and went to the table by the front door.

Tulla leaned forward and whispered, "Did I hear her right? Did she say my father's a romantic soul?"

Maureen sat back at the table and handed the brochure to Tulla. "Heard you. Here's the evidence. He wrote this."

The Ballygiblin Riots, 1824

In 1824 fighting broke out at a stagecoach inn near what is now Parnell between a group of established Scottish Protestant settlers and a gang of newly arrived Irish Catholic immigrants. The religious animosity, which had obviously had a successful Atlantic crossing, was exacerbated by the rumour that the new Irish settlers were being given more assistance than the Protestant groups had enjoyed on their arrival a few years earlier. Indeed, the newcomers were not only provided with cash and provisions but each family was the recipient of a cow. This proved not only to be a valuable staple but the last straw. Tempers flared, fists flew, and the militia arrived in time to shoot a few fleeing Irish. The fighting intensified over the next two or three days because, as one onlooker put it, "Them Bog Irish was born fightin'. Kept their minds off The Hunger." One of the companies of the 3rd Lanark Regiment Militia was led by Captain Thomas Glendinning. His zeal in quelling the "small civil war," as he later described it at the military inquiry, made him into a marked man. The Irish hunted him across the county, hallooing like John Peel at every fence and ditch. The captain ran for cover. Legend has it that he was lucky enough to find an ally at this very house where you are enjoying a quiet meal. The landlord, a retired British magistrate, tamped down the fire, hid Glendinning in the priest hole, sat in his rocker with a noggin of whisky, and expressed great surprise when the Irish burst through his door in search of the hapless captain who was quietly roasting in the chimney above them. The landlord allayed their suspicions with pints all around, and by the time he'd sent them on their way, the captain was about medium rare but survived his ordeal.

Enjoy your steak!

Tulla looked up at the fireplace. "Is the hole still there?"

"Yup. The fireplace was just a pile of rubble when I bought the place, but I had it rebuilt with the hole restored." Maureen leaned back in her chair and gazed up at the chimney, flickering in the lamplight. "I've never told anyone this, but I'll tell you because you're Warren's daughter, and Mikhail, you're my friend, and because this wine's gone straight to my tongue. Sometimes late at night, after the restaurant's closed, I swear I can hear someone up there breathing ..."

"You chose the right people to tell your secret," Mikhail said. "Tulla and I grew up in a house full of sad breathing sounds."

"Not to mention howls and shrieks and —"

"You two grew up in the same house?"

"My mother was a DP," he said. "Displaced person. Tulla's parents hired her as a maid when she came to Canada a few years after the war with me in tow. She was born in a camp in Albania where her parents were deported in 1943 when the Germans occupied the country."

"Because they were Jews?"

"Because they were Serbs. The local Albanians hated the Serbs, and the Germans gave them free rein. Thousands were killed or put into camps. My grandparents died there."

Tulla listened to him speaking easily to Maureen about a subject he rarely mentioned. "We had a DP club when we were kids," she said. "There were four of us — me, Mik, Kat Kominski. You know her? She owns —"

Maureen nodded.

"And Leo Harding."

Maureen nodded again. "Met him, too. Mik brought him here a couple of weeks ago. Liked him. Very quiet."

Tulla turned to Mik, puzzled. "He was here?"

"We had to redefine the term *DP* to allow you in," Mikhail said.

"That club was a safe haven," Tulla said. "When I think back, it was the one spot I felt in the *right* place, with you three."

Kat claimed she was a legitimate DP because her Nana Anna had arrived in Parnell from war-torn Europe and worked for Nell, Tulla's great-aunt. They became fast friends, much to the disapproval of Nell's bridge club. When Kat was ten, Nana Anna taught her how to roll her own cigarettes. Kat adored her.

Leo never tried to explain his DP status but didn't deny it, either. Tulla and Kat were certain it stemmed from his mother's early death. He'd been displaced so suddenly and violently from her love and protection.

"So you all went out into the world, but here you are, all back again," Maureen said wistfully. "You're lucky. Not many people could claim friendships that have lasted that long."

TWELVE

THE NEXT MORNING Tulla phoned her father with the news that Dom's death might not have been accidental. He'd already heard. And that Leo was in charge of the investigation. "Such a coincidence, that's two of your old gang — one who might have been murdered and the other investigating his death," he said.

"Dad, Bobby/Dom was *never* part of — oh, never mind."

After she hung up, she thought about what Warren had said. *Coincidence?* Grey shadows edged the kitchen blind. She turned the overhead light off and watched the dawn creep in. *On cat's paws. What's that from? Eliot? No, Sandburg. Cat's feet, and not dawn, fog. Coincidence? Maybe.*

She took her coffee out on the deck and watched Clancy nosing around on the riverbank. Leaves swirled in the back current along the shore, and the water, pewter from the reflected sky, appeared solid enough to walk on. She whistled, and he came like a shot up the steps, dancing on cold feet.

Her plan for the morning was to check out the fitness centre. "It's in our old church," Kat had said. "If you join, I will."

Clouds scudded behind the steeple, the cross replaced with a snapping banner of cartoon figures gyrating in the wind. A ladder of neon flashed the words *pump* and *skip* like a traffic light on speed. Leo stood on the front step.

She ran up the stairs. "Thinking of joining?"

He stubbed out his cigarette. "Police business."

"Can I join you?"

"No."

Tulla walked in behind him, staying close.

The man behind the reception desk had no neck, his head apparently rising directly out of a plinth of muscle-bound shoulders. Lank hair, starting at mid-skull, hung in a thin ponytail down his back, and both ears sported diamond studs as big as cufflinks.

"Hello, folks. Name's Leroy, manager here." His voice was high and light, startling given the beefy throat it came from. The phone on the reception counter rang, and as he reached for it, a snake curled across his shoulder, disappearing under his muscle shirt, scales rippling. "Not on the phone, you idiot. I got it covered." Leroy slammed the receiver down, rolled out from behind the desk, and extended a hand the size of a ham. "What can I do you for? Lookin' to join?"

"That's some tattoo, Leroy," Leo said. "Get it inside?"

Leroy's face closed like a clam.

"Detective Sergeant Harding, OPP." Leo flipped open his badge. "Got a few questions about Dom Connolly."

"And the broad?" Leroy eyed Tulla up and down. A tip of tongue appeared between fleshy lips, and Tulla imagined it unfurling to catch lunch.

"She's not with —"

"Murphy," she growled, flashing her wallet in a blur.

Leo shot her a look.

"So what d'ya want from me? Hardly knew the guy."

"He owned this place, right?"

"Yeah."

"You met him in prison, right?"

"So what?"

Leo scrutinized the lobby of steel and glass, a reception desk papered in red foil. "Remember this in its church days, Tulla? Sad."

Through glass walls they could see the gym, its sprung hardwood floor bouncing with sweaty bodies skipping rope in time to a techno beat blasting from oversized speakers. A second wall of windows opened onto the pool, including an underwater view of what could have been an aquarium of giant slugs but was actually the flabby white legs of an aquatic aerobics class for seniors.

"Look. The original stained-glass windows." Tulla pointed at Jesus and his disciples looking askance from the end wall.

Leo eyed the spandex parade behind the glass. "And people actually pay money for this?"

"What d'ya think — they come in here for free?"

"And that contraption there? You just walk on it. That's it?"

"Leo … Detective, that's a treadmill," Tulla said.

She caught his blank expression before he turned away. *What is going on? How much has he changed?* Certainly not his body language — head thrown back, chin jutting — which said in any dialect, "Don't mess with me." High, sharp cheekbones and unsmiling mouth, but that hadn't changed, either. Leo had never smiled a lot. Probably one of the reasons why, as a teenager, he had every girl in town aching after him. The James Dean of Parnell High. The work it took to get a smile out of him. And when you managed, *whoo* boy, you were rewarded with radiance, brief as a star flash. And she'd been one of those girls.

Tulla saw something now that she hadn't ever remembered seeing in Leo. The wariness was there, as always, the stillness, but with it … what? Confusion? Uncertainty. No, not in Leo. Never.

"I don't have time for this shit," Leroy snarled. "Even a *deeeeetective sergeant* big shot like you must watch TV occasionally. Those babes with their perfect little asses hanging out of their shorts selling the latest exercise machine." He glared at Leo. "Just where the fuck you been for the past century. In a monastery?"

Leo's face remained impassive. "How did Dom get started in this business?"

"Had a martial arts setup out west. You do know what a martial arts studio is, *Deeeetective*?"

"And then?"

"Word was he set up in tong territory or something. He got a going-away party." Leroy screwed his mouth into a mean line.

"And then?"

"Jesus H. Christ. Do you think I held his hand all those years?"

Leo waited.

Leroy sighed. "Okay, so when he got out of jail —"

"What was he in for?" Tulla asked. "Oops, sorry, Detective."

"He beat up some big-shot businessman bad. The guy survived, or Dom woulda been dead meat. Although maybe not. He had pull, even back then. When he got out, he became a personal fitness trainer. Worked out like about twenty hours a day inside. Built like Arnold. And a couple of his celebrity clients backed him in a franchise deal with Starwalker."

"The trade name for a version of StairMaster," Tulla said hastily.

"And then?" Leo pressed.

"For fuck's sake! Okay, street says he broke his contract, moved to Toronto, and launched all this skipping rope shit. Yuh heard of skipping ropes, dude? They're those things with handles on the ends and people —"

Leo shot out his hand and twisted the muscle shirt into a knot against Leroy's Adam's apple. "You going to stop dicking around and answer the questions here, or do we go down to the station?"

Leroy frantically pointed to the floor, unable to talk.

"Here?"

Leroy tried to nod.

"Good. Now turn down the music so we can hear each other. Don't want to miss a thing you're going to tell me." Leo let go of the shirt and patted him once on the cheek. Leroy bent over, hands on knees, trying to catch his breath, then leaned across the desk and fiddled with a switch. The music faded, leaving only the vibration of the throbbing bass notes.

Leo pulled a notebook from his hip pocket and riffled the pages. "Let's back up. And let up on the profanity. You met Dom in jail."

"He hated that name," Leroy rasped, rubbing his neck, clearing his throat. "Had to call him Dominique in those days. No short forms. He sliced a guy once for calling him Dom. Just *whoosh*, outta nowhere. He made a shiv out of God knows what. Guards just looked the other way. Guy nearly bled to death."

"That would be Jack?"

"You know him?"

Leo nodded. "When did you see Dom again?"

"When I got out, he'd already been released on early parole. Amazing what a mob-connected lawyer can do. He was well in with the Family. Seems he took the fall for one of the lieutenants since he was facing jail time, anyway. Smart career move. I heard he was hiring ex-cons, and about a year ago I opened this place for him."

Nobody spoke for a moment. Tulla was still processing Leo's sudden outburst, her heart beating like a trapped bird.

"Was he in here lately?" Leo asked.

"Couple of times."

"With anyone?"

"Babbitt, that freaky mayor."

"Anyone else?"

Leroy's eyes shifted. "Uh, that manager from the Russell, a coupla times."

Tulla looked at Leo. "Kat said Dom had been holding court at the hotel bar, drawing his old gang like a magnet, all under his sway again, including Shug."

Leroy frowned at her. "You from here?"

"Know anyone who might have wanted him dead?" Leo asked.

"How the fu ... frig should I know?" His belligerence faded under Leo's gaze. "Well, *sheeeeit*." He spat a lump of phlegm onto the floor. "What I think, he went on them talk shows and mouthed off about all this fitness equipment stuff being useless and expensive. You'd get thinner and fitter just skipping, even though his ropes had some fancy computer gizmo counting steps and checking heart rate and all. Basically, they're just skipping ropes. So what I'm thinking, bad idea, the business bozos got pissed. He'd built up a big following with his book and videos and all, and when he dissed the Neptune all-in-one home gyms —"

"Neptune?"

Leroy backed up, careful not to take his eyes off Leo. "Man, you're wastin' my time. Want anything more, see my lawyer."

When they were back out on the street, Tulla said with disgust, "What a scumbag. Think he knows anything?"

Leo shook his head. "Doubt it. But he'll put the word out there's an investigation and that it's not just focused on Parnell. Might flush out some tips. He certainly wasn't offering much, like what Dom's main line of business was."

"Which was?"

"He ran the Angels' drug trade, was involved for years, worked his way up, started in Vancouver. When he died, he was at the Family level — very senior, delegated mostly, ran a very tight ship."

"Which explains the bikers in town," Tulla said.

"I guess."

"Who's Jack?"

"Jack Nicholson …" He watched her make the connection.

"*Chinatown*?"

Leo raised an eyebrow. "Nice one. Not everyone would get the connection."

"Easy. Did you forget I saw the movie with you? So what happened to Jack? Your Jack, I mean."

"When he got out of jail, he went back to university, studied law, and he's now a very successful consultant to some of the top law firms. He brought in a couple of partners, the guys he grew up with who also ended up with prison terms. Not allowed to be an actual lawyer, though. His focus, ever since they crossed paths in jail, was Dom. He's a good guy. You'd want him on your side. Not to mention he's a distant relation of Harriet Deaver's. Jail toughened him, but in a good way."

"What was he in for?"

"Kidnapping."

"And he's a good guy?"

"A college prank gone horribly wrong. The supposed victim was in on it, but something happened. Can't remember the details. She nearly suffocated in the trunk of the car. Jack says he learned a lot of things in jail, one of them being revenge." Leo lit a cigarette and blew smoke toward the sky. "You do know it's a criminal offence to impersonate a police officer?"

Tulla grinned. "We're a team. Good cop, bad cop."

THIRTEEN

PARNELL'S ONLY CATHOLIC church, across the square from the town hall, was massive, squat, and unmistakably male in contrast to the whimsical confection of the municipal building. Its belfry had sat empty since the Ballygiblin Riots when the bell was smashed from its moorings and fell rolling and tolling into the square below. Framed by stone ladders with figures climbing both ways — angels up, devils down — the enormous wooden doors, rarely unlocked, were flung wide open this morning.

"Fine day for a funeral," Kat said, squinting at the black clouds sailing across the sun. "For your day, Tulla, what weather would you want? A Brontë one, howling wind and a cold rain sweeping off the moors? Or all sunny and bright?"

"A Brontë one, for sure. On the day of Portland's service, the sun shone like a gong, first time Saratoga had seen a rainless day for months. The birds sang like fools, and the whole event turned into a garden party. I don't want that. I want people to be properly grief stricken and then go and get plastered."

The church steps were thronged, and a line of people snaked along the sidewalk and down the street.

Tulla pointed. "Mikhail … there, just inside the entrance. Let's go."

Nob bore down on them. "Off the street, ladies. The procession's coming."

The crowd went silent as rank upon rank of Harleys wheeled into the square with a throaty roar, the fitful sunlight winking off their shiny black flanks.

"Hells Angels!" Tulla shouted into a sudden lull in the wind. Several drivers turned their heads slowly in her direction, their tinted face masks like giant bug eyes. "I saw them up at Dom's house. They weren't wearing face masks then. Maybe they don't want to be caught on camera." Tulla pointed at the TV truck opposite the church, a camera mounted on its roof. "Looks like we're going to be on the national news."

The motorcycles wheeled at the end of the block and lined up on the other side of the church entrance as a pair of police outriders thundered around the corner followed by a line of black limousines, moving fast. The hearse, grey with chrome tracery along the sides, brought up the rear. The liveried driver jumped out of the lead limo, pulled a folded wheelchair out of the trunk, and snapped it open. Two enormous legs, ending in feet bulging over black oxfords, extended from the back seat. The driver bent to help, but two fat hands waved him away.

"Opal," breathed Tulla.

"Jabba the Hutt," Kat breathed back.

They watched as she squished herself into the double-wide chair, flesh rising like dough over the arms. Her face, with its serried chins, glistened with sweat and tears. The funeral parlour staff pulled a baby-blue coffin out of its nest of red roses just as a shaft of sunlight blazed down like a klieg light. DOMINIQUE written in rhinestones across the lid flashed like an old-time movie marquee.

"You think Opal even controls the sun in this town?" Kat whispered.

They followed the coffin into the church at a discreet distance and slipped in beside Mikhail, sitting close to the front.

"How did you manage to hold these seats?" Kat asked.

"Bribery." He pointed down the row where a little boy counted out some coins, a blond lock of hair falling over his forehead.

"Liam!" Kat hissed. "What are you doing here? Where's Mel?"

Liam tried to make himself smaller. "Dad told her you said I was to go with him to meet you at the funeral. He's gone out for a cigarette."

The organ soared into a soulful rendition of "Love Me Tender."

Kat reached past Mikhail and took Liam's arm just as Shug headed into the pew from the other end. "Something wrong?" he asked.

People around them craned to see what the disturbance was, their faces avid for more drama.

"Thought this would be an 'educational moment' for Liam." He made air quotes with his nicotine-stained fingers and smirked at his audience.

Kat said very quietly, "I don't know what you told Mel to get her to let Liam go with you, but I'll find out. Going straight at me, I can handle that. Going through Liam to get at me? Never going to happen again." She gestured at the coffin. "Your custody rights are toast, gone with Dom." She took Liam's hand. "C'mon, hon, we're outta here."

"Don't be too fucking sure," Shug snapped. "There are other ways, other people to skin a ... Kat. You get out of line and you might just never see him again."

"Shug Bassett! This is no place for your shenanigans." A voice honed to the clarity of steel by a lifetime in the classroom pierced the saccharine music. "Either sit down and be quiet or leave."

Tulla turned to see Harriet Deaver and Aggie Breeze sitting in the row behind, bookending an imposing figure who towered over both of them. A long braid of hair fell over one shoulder partially hiding the red-and-white insignia of the Hells Angels. He pulled the knotted bandana off his head in response to a whispered instruction from Miss Deaver, who had her hand tucked into his elbow. The Angel cupped his hand over hers and smiled sheepishly down at her.

Shug slammed his fist into the back of the pew and strode to the door.

The service included Communion — a model of diversity with tattooed bikers and elderly Presbyterians standing side by side, tongues out to receive the flesh of Christ. A glint of green caught Tulla's eye. "Dad," she whispered to Mikhail. "He said he'd try to come."

To the strains of "Crying in the Chapel," the pall-bearers wheeled Dom's coffin down the centre aisle, and, close behind, a dry-eyed Rosalie wheeled a weeping Opal.

FOURTEEN

SHUG BURST INTO the hotel lobby and stopped short at the closed door into the bar. A surly young man with a serious case of acne and a tattoo of a snake encircling his scrawny bicep spoke from behind the reception desk. "Funeral over?"

Shug pointed to the sign on the bar door. "What's that about?"

"Neil's orders. Out of respect for Mr. Connolly."

Shug puffed out his lips. "Well, let's you and me have a *drink* out of respect for *Mister* Connolly."

The clerk glanced around nervously. "I dunno …"

"Well, I do, Tim. Open the goddamn door. Neil's not going to be back for at least an hour."

"What about his wife? If she catches us —"

"She and that dozy cow of a daughter are at the funeral with him, making like a happy family. For sure they'll go to the bean fest afterward." He gave the door a kick.

Tim crossed the lobby with a key in his hand. "What's with you, man?"

Shug pushed past him. "Does he count the bottles?"

"Probably. What d'ya want. I'll get it."

"Single malt — double. On the rocks." Shug hauled himself up onto a stool and loosened his tie. Tim put ice in a tumbler, filled it with whisky, and slid it across the bar.

"And one for yourself, me man, 'cause neither of us is paying." Shug took a long drink and wiped his mouth.

Tim poured a draft beer and leaned on the bar. "Why'd you leave the funeral early?"

"None of your friggin' business."

They drank in silence. Tim kept an eye on the door and tried again. "What d'ya think the story is on Dom?"

"Seems clear someone wanted him dead, I'd say, seeing as how he's out there in a coffin."

"But who?"

"I have no idea, and if I did, I sure as hell wouldn't be sayin'. This town is nothin' but ears. What I'd like to know is, who's takin' over?"

"Neil."

"You're joking, right? That string-bean creep? You think he has the balls?"

"I don't. He does. I already heard him on the phone setting up a meeting with that guy at Bluebird."

"Well, if he's the new Mr. Big, I'm outta here. He's a cruel bastard. Dom was a businessman. Ran the whole setup like Apple. I'm tired of everything, anyway. The kids, especially. They're getting to me." He pushed his glass across the bar. "Empty."

Tim started to measure the whisky. Shug grabbed the bottle and filled the glass.

"You drink all that, you'll be on your ass. That's it, Shug. I'm locking up again. I'd lose my job if Neil came in now."

"You think?" Shug chugged the alcohol as if it were water. "With what you know about him, he'd fire you? That *would* take balls. And stupidity. The times are a changin', my friend. You and me, we could be sitting pretty if we play our cards right." He pretended to hold a card hand close to his chest. "Yuh know" — his words were running together now — "I won't miss Dom, at least not the new one. Ever since he started spending more time in Parnell, he sure was getting ugly. Uglier." He lurched sideways and grabbed the bar for balance. "Okay, Timmy, one more for the road."

"No way. You've already had nearly half a bottle. You won't be able to walk." He checked his watch again, eyes flicking to the door. "Get out of here before Neil comes back. You don't want to rile him. He's mean when he's riled. Just ask his wife. Out."

When Tim turned to wash the glass, Shug grabbed the half-empty bottle and stumbled across to the door. "Takeout." He giggled and was gone.

Leo stood on the top step, watching the church empty.

"Harding?"

"Jack." They shook hands. "Didn't see you in there."

Jack raised an eyebrow. "I am a hard man to miss." His lopsided smile, the result of Dom's handiwork, gave his face an unexpected charm. He was an imposing figure, his slim height emphasized by military posture and a beautifully tailored bespoke overcoat of grey wool. "What do you think?" He gestured to the hearse slowly pulling away from the church. "Could have been either one of us, right?"

"In that box?"

"Either one of us who put him there."

"Well, neither of us was lacking in motive."

"Or opportunity. You were in Parnell before the storm."

Leo gazed at him steadily. "Not common knowledge. How do you know that?"

"Because I saw you." He pulled on a pair of soft leather gloves and scanned the sky. "Seems we were beaten to the punch. Pity. If there was ever a man who deserved to die at the hands of an enemy …" He paused as Mikhail joined them. "Hello, Mik. Good to see you again. I was just saying that it was a fine but overdue funeral, would you not agree? Although I hear there is some confusion about how he actually met his demise. That God might have had help."

Leo smiled. "You have good sources, Jack. You probably know more than I do. Preliminary yet, but it looks like a drug overdose."

"Interesting. Did you see the body?"

"I did. Rest assured, he's dead."

"Good to know. Wondered, though. I had heard he didn't use."

"Didn't know that," Leo said slowly. "What's the street say?"

"That he was an addict. Sampled too much of his own product. Common knowledge in the trade. But uncommon knowledge — a very good source from the higher echelons of the Angels — told me he never touched the stuff."

"Well, needle tracks up both arms suggest differently. Final toxicity screen results aren't in yet, but if you're brimming with heroin, sort of hard to miss."

"True, but question is, how did it get there?"

"What'll you do now, Jack? Now that your main … focus is no longer —"

"I will find another mission. There are many out there, people who might evade the law, but not —"

"You?"

Jack shrugged. "We will see each other again, Harding, at least I hope so. We have much in common. You are a good man … and I am not a bad one." He touched his mouth with a gloved finger, the scarred smile broad and crooked behind it.

FIFTEEN

MAUREEN LIFTED WARREN off his feet in a hug. "For such a little shrimp, how could you be the father of such a tall, beautiful daughter. She must be a changeling."

"Half the population of Parnell are changelings, but they like to keep it a secret."

"Well, you can tell all the secrets you want in here." She led Warren and Tulla through the crowded restaurant to the table in the inglenook. "It's out of reach of Parnell Ears. It's pretty much out of reach of Parnell Eyes, too, at least those still in focus. There's a good deal of drinking going on here tonight. Funerals tend to bring out the Irish in all of us, whether we're Irish or not. I take it Brenda didn't come with you?"

"Brenda and Parnell don't mix. Maybe next time."

Tulla studied Maureen curiously. "You know Brenda?"

"We go way back. In fact, I introduced her to your father. She lived in St. John's with her first husband, a Brit, big shot in the oil business. He died there — heart attack on a visit to one of the rigs." She leaned in to straighten the silverware in front of Warren. "Quit fiddling. Looks like you're playing pickup sticks. Now, drinks first. I have a new single malt you'll like, Warren." She smiled down at Tulla. "And for you, my dear, I have a Pinot Grigio from Graham Greene's vineyard in Italy. Thought you'd enjoy its literary provenance." She took the menu out of Warren's hands. "I'll take care of that, too."

"Bossy, isn't she?" Warren smiled after her. He reached across the table and took Tulla's hand. "Now, are you okay, darlin'? How was the funeral? Awful for you? Did Lilly behave herself?"

Until she heard "Lilly," Tulla thought he was talking about Dom's funeral. She smiled wearily to herself. She'd learned the hard way — mistake after mistake in conversations — that context was everything, and it was crucial to wait until she had it.

"It was all right, a bit of a cocktail party, actually. How about you? Long way to come today for the funeral of … guess I don't really know why you came."

He waited as Andy, the waiter, set their drinks down. "A toast," he said, picking up his glass. "To Bobby, or Dominique as he preferred. Poor lad."

"So do you think he was murdered?"

Warren put his finger to his lips. "Not an ideal place for this conversation."

"Or do you think he died naturally?"

"You believe that?"

"No. But it's equally hard to believe he was murdered."

"I don't think it is, Tulla. I just think you don't want him to have been murdered because then you have to start thinking about who murdered him."

"And you think it's someone we know? Not the Mafia or the bikers or even the fitness industry moguls, which is Leroy's theory, the creepy manager of the Pump and Skip?"

Warren dropped his voice and leaned in close. "No, I don't think so. Dom had a lot of enemies, but apparently not the bikers, judging from their attendance at his funeral. That was an honour guard, and I don't think they honour people they've just bumped off."

"Who then?"

"I don't know. Harriet has her suspicions, but all I can say is if you suspect anyone, keep very quiet about it. Not a word to anyone."

"Not even to my *gang*?"

"Not even them. This town has a history, Tulla."

"Every town has a history."

"Not necessarily like Parnell's. Talk to Harriet. As she loves to tell anyone who will listen, she knows where the bodies are buried. She might fill you in on Parnell's seamier side. And warn her to be careful, too. Dom's death has set something in motion. I tried to tell her after the funeral, but she just called me a 'fretful old man.' And damn it, she's at least five years older than me."

Tulla murmured, "She says two."

He smiled slightly, then glanced around the room. "This wretched town is celebrating, not mourning, however he died. Not a lot of human kindness here." He leaned forward, chin in hand, elbow resting on the small table. "I was surprised that you chose to come back here, Tulla Bean. Think it was a good decision?"

"Probably not. But in the end, it is home, isn't it? I'm finding out, though, that I don't know as much about home as I'd thought."

His face took on what she and Bridget used to call his "got gossip" face. His eyes sparkled, and he hunched forward like a writer at a keyboard, eager to launch into a story. "What would you like to know?"

"Hard to know where to start ..." She jerked her head up as the restaurant fell quiet, not because everyone wanted to hear Warren's history lesson but because all eyes were riveted on the head bobbing and weaving toward them. Tulla pointed with her chin. "Incoming. Thurston has us locked in his beady sights."

The head stopped at their table. "Welcome back, Warren. Staying long?" He ignored Tulla.

"Ah, Mr. Mayor. 'Fraid not. Flying out tomorrow."

"I'll just join you for a moment then." Thurston looked around for a chair.

"Not enough room for three at this little table. You'd have to sit in the fire." Warren snapped his napkin across his knee. "Right now I'm just enjoying a visit with my daughter. Another time."

"Too bad." Thurston leaned on the table, his head level with theirs. "Thought you'd like to share your insights on Dom's 'suspicious' death. The authorities are being rather coy, don't you think, when it seems obvious he was killed by person or persons unknown?" His smile was an up-and-down jerk of the mouth, like a wooden soldier nutcracker biting down on a nut. "Wondered if you thought it a tad strange that Harding's in charge of the investigation. There's been some talk in town —"

"Talk is the lifeblood of this town, Thurston," Warren said, all pretense of affability gone. "Always cruel and almost always wrong. Never worth repeating."

The big head swung around to ensure its audience. "Some say making Harding chief investigator is like putting the fox in charge of the henhouse." He gave a squeaky laugh. "I mean, it's no secret that Leo and Dom have always been enemies and —"

"Guess that makes us all suspects, wouldn't you think?" Tulla felt the heat rising in her cheeks. "You even had your moments. He was a cruel kid … and seems to have been a cruel man."

"I'm not talking about childish squabbles, Tulla. Dom testified against Leo at his trial, which to some might appear to be a motive if, of course, there was foul play. Or at least it's a reason for recusing himself."

Warren's voice was a whiplash across the table. "You're a tiresome little man, Babbitt. Until there's any further information released from the coroner's office, it's spiteful and damaging to the extreme to be pointing fingers. You're simply stirring up trouble, as is your wont." The only sound in the restaurant now was the crackling of the burning logs and a low murmur of conversation from the kitchen.

"Ah, Warren, you know as well as I do what's what, even though there was a publication ban," Thurston said, the skin around his small eyes crinkling as he bit out a smile. "Dom testified that Leo was drunk. He'd seen him in the bar all over —"

"Enough!" Warren roared, leaping to his feet. "We're not interested in your trash talk, Babbitt. Go!"

Thurston backed away, his expression stormy. Before the door swung closed behind him, the chatter had resumed to a gleeful pitch.

Tulla leaned across the table. "What's he talking about?"

"You did know about Leo's trial?" Warren watched her closely.

Tulla nodded. "That was years ago. What did Dom have to do with it? I don't even know what Leo was charged with. Drunk and disorderly or something?"

Warren's mouth twisted as if trying not to let the word "rape" escape.

"What did you say?"

Warren regarded her miserably. "You heard me, Tulla. You just don't want to hear."

"Leo rape someone? Never, never, never."

"Of course he didn't. It should never have gone to trial. Darla brought charges against him more than three years after the alleged … attack." Warren took her hand.

"Darla Connolly?" Tulla threw herself back in the chair. "But Darla and Leo, they hated each other. When would they ever —"

"There was an appeal. New judge who had the sense to know Darla was lying. And it must have helped that

Rosalie, her own sister, said so when she gave testimony. The case was thrown out, all charges withdrawn. As if it never happened."

As if it never happened. It just doesn't work that way. How could he have stood yet another injury from another Connolly? Dom taking part of his life away from him when he eloped with Celia, Darla taking another part of his life away from him with this accusation.

"What an evil family ... except for Rosie," she said. "How could those two even be sisters?"

Warren's eyes shifted. "Probably half-sisters. Same mother, different father. Opal's modus operandi."

Maureen stood by the table holding two plates. "You talking in Latin? Good idea, since half the Big Ears in here are practically falling off heads trying to hear what you're saying. Here you are — Wellingtons. Not the rubber-boot kind. Warren, yours is beef. Tulla, yours is salmon." She put the plates down in front of them and took a bottle of red wine from the mantelpiece over their head. "Took the liberty of opening this earlier to let it breathe, Warren. A wonderful Malbec, and more Pinot for you, Tulla." She filled their glasses, put the white wine back in the ice bucket, the red on the mantelpiece, and vanished again.

Their table was an island of silence in a sea of voices and clattering silverware. Tulla took one bite and put her fork down. "Opal. She's like a fat black spider in the web of that family, jerking strands. Did she put Darla up to this? Is that what you mean about her modus operandi?"

"You haven't finished your salmon."

"Yes, I have." She pushed her plate away.

"Tulla." He put his napkin to his mouth as if to wipe away any more words. "You'll have to ask Leo. It's his story to tell. Let's talk about something else."

Her hands gripped the table edge. "Okay." Her voice was harsh. "So let's talk about your story then. I'm curious, Dad. How come you travelled all this way for Dom's funeral?"

Warren bowed his head and circled the rim of his wineglass with a finger. "I think you know why." He gestured at the raucous tables. "Some of them think they know why. Amazes me they actually still care. Parnell with its long memory and longer knives. If Bridget and your mother were here, they'd know why." He peered at his hands, now cupped around a snifter of brandy. "Where did that come from?"

"Maureen brought it."

"Didn't she bring you one, too?"

Tulla pointed to her brimming wineglass. "Can't do brandy. Gives me the heebie-jeebies in the night." Suddenly, she smacked the table. The cutlery jumped. So did Warren. "For years it's been the elephant in the living room, Dad. I've never had the courage to ask you straight out before."

"And I've never had the courage to answer straight out before."

"Courage?"

"Of course, Tulla Bean. It takes courage to tell your children about the mistakes you've made in your life. Much harder than telling your wife. I was afraid of losing you. I had already lost Bridget." His eyes filled with sadness. "Dom isn't my son, Tulla. That's your question, am I right? Before today I couldn't answer that question because I didn't know. Pretty Gothic, wouldn't you say, to discover on the day of your son's funeral — a son you never publicly acknowledged — that he wasn't your son. Now you know. Now we both know." He leaned back in his chair, his face pale even in the firelight.

"How did you find out?" Tulla whispered.

"Opal. But, Tulla, whether Dom was my biological son or not doesn't change the fact, the sin as your mother called it."

"Does Brenda know about all this ... about Dom?" Tulla asked.

"I told her years ago about the possibility of Dom being mine, but I called her this morning to say it wasn't so. I even included the humbling detail of me not knowing just how many other, uh, suitors, were possible fathers. She was quite understanding and said a very generous thing — that if I had a by-blow out there somewhere, she rather hoped it could've been Leo."

"Brenda's met Leo? She seems to know everybody."

Tulla watched her father gearing up to lie. His eyes slid back and forth like tiny trapped animals, then the final tell — suddenly locking onto her in his version of an open, honest gaze. "I must have told her about him. Can't think when she might have met him."

"Brenda's never been to Parnell, you said, which means Leo must have been in the Bahamas. When was this?"

She leaned forward, cupping her ear against the sudden racket. A toast was being proposed at a nearby table for eight, yelling and banging their glasses with their knives.

"I really can't remember ..."

"Why was he there?"

"Well, you know Leo. Or at least you used to know Leo. He wouldn't have said, would he? Brenda and I thought it might have been a drug investigation of some sort. Grand Bahama Island was awash with drugs then. It was the gateway into Florida for some of the big cartels."

Tulla glared at him. "You know, Dad, I'm not a child anymore. I can handle truths. Try me. At least tell me yours if you won't tell me Leo's."

He reached for her hand, tracing each finger in a game he'd played with her when she was a baby. When he finally spoke, it was as if he were talking not about himself but about a stranger, someone from the past he barely knew. "It's hard to credit this now, especially after seeing her today, but Opal, when she was young, was very, very beautiful, like Darla actually — slim, long black hair, eyes almost black, dark skin that went even darker in the summer. She had such a laugh. I called it a butterscotch laugh, but really it was tar. I was blinded by lust."

Tulla held up both palms. "Okay, maybe the truth without the details."

"So, Opal got pregnant, and, of course, I thought I was the father. And, of course, so did Daniel. Understandable in most families, since he was her husband, but so did a number of others about whom I knew nothing. Her modus operandi ..."

"No more." Tulla tilted her head toward the ceiling where the axe-hewn beams above her trembled in the lamplight. As if a dam had broken, tears poured down her cheeks. She grabbed her table napkin, starched to a board, but before she could use it, her father snatched it from her.

"Not Maureen's lovely linen. Here, use my handkerchief. Oh, come here, darlin'." He stood and pulled her up into what in a bigger man would have been a bear hug.

"Oh, sorry, sorry, sorry." Maureen veered away from their table. "Always had lousy timing."

Warren stretched to peer over Tulla's head buried in his shoulder. "It's been a tough day for everyone. A lot of old memories stirred up."

Tulla raised her head, scrubbing her dripping nose and wet cheeks with his handkerchief. "Bloody memories I never knew I had. And let's be clear, Dad, I'm not crying for Dom. I'm not crying for you. I'm crying for —" She caught herself before saying, *Leo. My heart is crying for Leo.*

SIXTEEN

AT THE POLICE STATION the investigation unit was setting up shop in the jail cell area, since the interrogation room was reserved for interviews and the lunchroom was needed for Nob and Elvie. Chief Roland never joined them for lunch. Leo's crew was off rounding up more desks and chairs, and a technician sat under a table working on the feeds to the computers.

When Nob came through the front door carrying sandwiches, Elvie beckoned to him, finger to lips. "Thurston's in with the chief," she whispered. "There's something nasty afoot. I heard him say something about knowing a way to stop Harding, then he shut the door."

Nob tiptoed over and put his ear to the crack between the frame and the door. "Can't hear them," he whispered.

"Try this." She dumped the pens out of a glass on her desk and handed it to him. "They do this in the movies."

Nob pressed the glass to the door, and his ear to the glass. He shook his head.

"This might help."

They whirled around, guilt stamped across their faces.

The young technician stood in the situation room doorway, grinning. He wore a baseball cap, a uniform shirt, wire-rimmed glasses, and a diamond-stud earring the size of a hazelnut. He looked not a day over sixteen. This was his first real job; he'd been hired by his uncle, Norbert, through the school intern program and would do anything for him, including never calling him Nob.

Elvie patted her chest. "Shaun, you almost gave me a heart attack. I didn't know you were still in there."

He held up a small electronic box and headphones. "Works better than a glass." He eyed her mohawk, stiff as a comb, and turned to his uncle. "Put these on." Nob fitted the headphones over his bald head. "Tell me when you can hear." Shaun fiddled with a tiny switch on the box.

Nob jumped. "Too loud, too loud, they'll hear it," he whispered frantically. Shaun adjusted the dial until Nob held up a hand and nodded. His face went blank, then he frowned, then a flush spread over his cheeks. "They can't do that!" he said indignantly, forgetting to keep his voice down.

"*Shh!*" Elvie hissed, then tugged his arm. "What are they saying?"

Nob held up a finger, concentrating. His eyes widened, and he darted into the situation room, pulling the earphones off just as the chief's door swung open.

Thurston came out, saying over his shoulder, "Get on it, Rock. We won't have another chance like this. Meeting's at my office in fifteen minutes. Don't be late."

Elvie watched him leave, then stuck her head into the situation room where Nob was pretending to connect the headphones to one of the computers. "What did you hear?"

"Thurston told the chief to send a message to OPP headquarters, saying they have evidence that could incriminate Leo in Dom's death."

"They do?" Elvie was thunderstruck.

"I don't think so. It sounds as if they're making it up."

"The bastards! Why would they do that?" Elvie turned to Shaun. "Can we stop that message from going through without the chief knowing? But I don't want you to do anything that would get you into trouble."

Shaun smiled with delight. "No problem." He hurried into the jail cell and sat on the cot in front of one of the computers.

A minute later, Chief Roland appeared in the doorway to his office. "I can't get onto the Internet. Are you having problems with it?"

Elvie's fingers flew over her keyboard. She nodded slowly. "Yeah, system's down. The technician's in there working on it right now."

Roland waved his hands as if swatting flies. "I have to get an urgent message out."

Shaun appeared in the doorway. "I heard you, sir. Sorry, I had to take the station off-line while I get the secure intranet hookup done with Orillia. It'll be a few minutes."

"Not good enough." Roland stared at his watch, beads of sweat standing out on his forehead. "I have to go to a meeting ..."

"I'll send it for you, Chief," Elvie said. "Just leave it up on your email."

Alarm in his voice, Roland said, "It's confidential police business."

Shaun spoke again. "Leave it in your draft folder and close down your system. As soon as I have you up and running again, I can make sure it goes without anyone having to go back into your email."

Roland glared at the young man with suspicion. He checked his watch again, hurried into his office, and a minute later rushed back with his coat and was out the door.

"Now, ma'am," Shaun said, "you want to see his message?"

She beamed at him. "Could I adopt you?"

"Think I might have a future in the police force?"

"Without a doubt."

SEVENTEEN

ALL WEEK IT RAINED. Day after day, grey, cheerless, and increasingly colder. Except for an emergency run to the Church Bakery, Tulla and Clancy spent most of the time in front of the fire, Clancy snoozing, Tulla brooding. Leo's story haunted her. She swung between not wanting to know anything more about the rape charges and then wanting the details because of the possible connection with Dom's death, which her father was treating as a lit fuse. He seemed genuinely fearful. And he'd passed the buck, which surprised her. She had followed his instructions and invited Miss Deaver for tea. It would perhaps become clear then, but she doubted it. Miss D.'s tendency to wander into irrelevancies was becoming more marked.

The doorbell sent Clancy into a paroxysm of barking and Tulla scurrying down the hall. A polka-dot mushroom stood on the step, streaming with rain. Miss Deaver's small face, like a dried apple, poked out from under a dripping hood. She stepped out of her welling-tons and trotted down the hallway to the kitchen, eyes darting in every direction. "I was curious to see your apartment, Tulla. I've seen Mikhail's, and it's very nice."

"This one is pretty much the same," Tulla said.

"Not exactly," Miss Deaver said, eyeing the cluttered counters and the sink filled with dishes. "Have you baked something delicious?"

"No, but I *bought* something delicious." She opened the flaps of a white box on the table.

Harriet peered in. "A lemon drizzle cake! The bakery makes these now?"

"Sort of. I found an old recipe book of my mother's with the stuff in storage, and Phyllis at the bakery is working through the cake recipes for me."

"I'd be interested in seeing that book, since your mother never baked a thing in her life. Maybe Aggie's recipe for her wonderful peach upside-down cake is in there. She says it was her mother's secret recipe and she won't give it to me. I suspect she laces it with liquor and doesn't want me to know. How is your mother, dear? Bless her, it must be a lonely life for her in that place."

"She does have lots of visitors, apparently. In the mid-dle of the night. Her father comes often. Her old friend, Ida Larson …"

Harriet narrowed her eyes. "Both of whom have been dead for years."

"Well, according to Mother they visit and tell her se-crets. It's odd, because she knows they're dead, but it doesn't seem to matter. I'll get the book for you before you go. And Miss D.? Keep in mind, I've only just moved in, so things are still in a bit of a mess. Mikhail's been in his place for months."

"Wouldn't matter if he'd moved in yesterday. It would already be pristine. Do you remember his mother? She was the neatest housekeeper I ever knew. Kept your house like a new pin."

"Might have been a good maid but one horror of a mother."

"Perhaps she was. You must remember, though, that she survived through terrible times we can't imagine. A young child on her own in those camps. She must have had terrible memories. It made her hard."

"And cruel and mean."

"Does Mikhail ever talk about her?"

Tulla felt Miss D.'s inquisitive eyes on her face. "Only to defend her."

Harriet nodded. "I used to see that in the classroom. Any child who was having a hard time at home would deny anything was going on. Give me a knife, dear."

Tulla blinked.

"Poor tykes. I could see their shame, their over-compensating loyalty to the parent who was abusing them. I could see their fear. I need a plate now."

Tulla handed her one from the cupboard.

"I recognize that," Harriet said. "Your mother used it for her special teas. Lovely."

"Did you do anything?"

"Well, of course, I used to help her sometimes at the bridge teas. That's how I know she never baked anything."

"No. I mean the children in your classes."

"Sometimes I confronted the parents. With only occasional success. In fact, it's possible I just made it worse for some. But I couldn't stand by and do nothing. I went to the police once, but that was a mistake. This was before Parnell had anything resembling Children's Aid and the police force consisted of one very untrustworthy man."

"Do you know how any of those kids fared as adults? I mean, besides Mikhail?"

"Some are fine. Some aren't. Hard to predict which child will break the pattern, which will repeat it. One boy in my grade eight class ended up in reform school for attacking his brute of a father. Put him in the hospital. It should have been the father who was jailed. That boy is now a judge, and woe betide an abuser who finds himself in his courtroom. And I just saw another of my old students who suffered at the hands of both parents. He was at Dom's funeral. Successful, too, in his own way. Very senior in the Hells Angels."

Tulla laughed. "Was he sitting with you and Aggie?"

"Hard to miss, wasn't he? Now there's a boy who broke the cycle. Eddy is like a big gentle teddy bear. Gives the Angels a good name." She chuckled at her own joke. "Although he tells me he's known as Eddy the Enforcer, so he can't be all that gentle. He knew Bobby, or Dominique — what a silly name for him to have chosen for himself. So pretentious ..." She stopped speaking, then found her place. "Not just when they were children, but in their later ... careers."

"You mean in jail?"

"And afterward. He told me an interesting thing about Bobby." She faltered, seemed confused. "Oh, dear, this is happening more and more. I've forgotten … does that ever happen to you? Just lose the thread …" She shook her head. "It will come back to me. Memories eventually do come back, even at my age. And those adults who've suppressed their recollection of bad things that happened to them as children, their memories usually surface eventually."

Tulla watched the expressions flit across Harriet's face. *She looks as if she's rifling through files, searching, seeking memories that are starting to fade. I so love this woman.* From that long-ago June after the Clod War, Harriet Deaver had been the unwavering centre for Tulla when things slowly fell apart, when her parents sank into a permanent state of attrition and bickering, when Bridget flipped from a friendly, funny, outgoing sister to a sullen stranger, withdrawing from everyone except Celia and leaving Parnell for good in the wake of Celia's betrayal when she eloped with Dom. When Warren left, Harriet was the one adult always there for Tulla, the centre that did hold in the ever-widening gyre.

"Don't look so worried, dear. When you get to my age, your brain is so full of memories it has to start shedding some to make room for more. At least that's what Aggie and I think."

They took the tea tray to the den, cozy in the firelight, curtains pulled across the windows rattling with the driving rain. Harriet looked around appreciatively. "I considered moving into this building, but I couldn't imagine trying to deal with a lifetime's accumulation of things. Not just mine but my parents', my grand-parents' … Aggie will have that job." Harriet grinned like a mischievous child. "She's my executor."

Tulla pushed aside the papers and books piled on the ottoman and put the tray down. Clancy lay on the hearth, close to the glass front, his wet coat steaming in the heat.

"Miss D. …"

"Call me Harriet, dear. Miss D. is a teacher's nickname, and I'm no longer a teacher. I notice you call Aggie by her first name. Perhaps because she's still a librarian." There was a touch of acid in her tone.

"Okay … Harriet. Dad told me to —"

Harriet put up her hand. "First tea and cake. Then I'll be strong enough to hear what your fuss-budget father said."

"It's a short message. He's worried that Dom's death has stirred up something out of Parnell's past. That you would know more about it than he does."

"This is a first. That he admits I know more than he does about anything." She smiled up at Tulla. "He's a good man, your father. I'm glad he's happy now. He's well out of Parnell. It was never good to him. Or indeed *for* him. Such delicious cake."

Harriet wriggled comfortably back into the chair, her feet nowhere near the floor. The rain continued to drill against the curtained windows while the fireplace fan filled the room with its low whisper.

She sat up suddenly. "I've remembered. I told you it would come back. Eddy the Angel told me that Dom never took drugs at all, not even so much as marijuana, but pretended he did to fool his enemies. He said that it was a power strategy, that he'd launched the rumour himself. She leaned back again, smiling happily, and continued without pause, "Nothing better than a hot cup of tea on a day like this. Never could understand the Americans' love of iced tea. An abomination."

"A what?"

"Sorry, dear, I was muttering. You seem to be managing better now, much better than a few months ago."

"When you warned me about the trap of self-pity? You really told me my fortune that day."

"That's an interesting expression, isn't it?" Harriet said dreamily. "The context in which you just used it changes its literal meaning entirely. To tell someone off, to scold ... I wonder where that usage originated."

"Harriet ...?"

She sat up straight and held her hands to the warmth of the fire. "Your father's right, Tulla." She turned her hands palm upright, fingers and thumbs gnarled with arthritis. "Do you remember the lines in Shakespeare's *Macbeth*, 'By the pricking of my thumbs, something wicked this way comes ...'? Well, dear, my thumbs are pricking. Evil often goes in cycles — evildoings, evil people ..."

"This evil thing — first Mikhail talking about it, now you. Harriet, Parnell isn't Derry."

"Hah, you've read *IT*. Scared me silly. Aggie won't let anyone under the age of twenty-one take it out of the library, and for once I think she has a point."

"Is there any book you haven't read?" Before Harriet could list them, Tulla added quickly, "Rhetorical question. Evil people? You mean like Arn Connolly? Every town has someone like him. The town pervert."

"No, not Arnold. In the overall scheme of things, he's fairly harmless."

Tulla disagreed. "Uncle" Arn sitting outside the pool hall, his belly folded over his knees like an apron, chair tilted back in the sun, toothpick zipping back and forth across his fat, wet lips. And the goitre, at least that was what the kids called it, hanging down his inner thigh. His eyes tracking every child who passed. Boy or girl, made no difference to Uncle Arn. *He lusted after us all*, she thought.

"Harmless if you could run fast enough," she said to Harriet.

One of Arn's stalking grounds had been Fortune Beach, not a beach at all but a clearing on the river shore with a bed of wide, flat rocks leading through the reeds to the water, their swimming place of choice because so few adults came to enforce rules. A day, late spring, it was still too cold to swim, but the sun was warm and golden. Some older kids were playing baseball, and Tulla remembered her excitement at being included because they needed more players to make up the teams. Her turn up to bat, and the hardball came whistling right at her, pitched by the bully arm of Dom. She'd had the sense to duck.

"Get that ball, brat," snarled the catcher, who also had the sense not to try for it with his bare hands. The catcalls of the other kids followed her into a stand of scrub poplar and pine. Scrambling through the undergrowth, she spotted the ball and Arn at the same time. He was on his hands and knees, rocking back and forth in a patch of sunlight filtering through the branches. What she thought was his famous goitre hung down between his naked thighs, a low humming sound coming from his throat.

Tulla ran. Through the scatter of kids waiting for her to fetch the ball, up the lane overhung with birches and aspen, through the back pasture and home.

Now Harriet said, "You children all knew to keep away from him because his proclivities weren't a secret."

"Not all of us," Tulla said, thinking of the little leg pinned beneath Arn that sunny spring day.

"Arn wasn't in the same league as those who hid their evil ways behind their town faces, pillars of society, benign and smiling on the outside. They were the ones who used their power over the vulnerable. They *were* evil. It was a long time ago. But such evil has a way of resurfacing, like a snake coming out of its lair. I've always been afraid of snakes. The real ones, I mean. I've never been afraid of the human kind. They usually slither away when confronted. Cowards mainly." Tulla waited as Harriet struggled to find her way back to her story. She looked up, eyes bright again. "What I do now, and it does help, I write reminder notes to myself and leave them everywhere. On those sticky things."

"Post-its?"

"That's it. I'm eternally grateful to their inventor. Too bad they can't be used in a conversation. What *was* I talking about?"

"Snakes," Tulla said faintly.

"No, no, dear … before that." She waved her hand in a backward circle.

"Arn? Stephen King?"

Harriet nodded. "Of course, Parnell isn't Derry. But there were some shocking similarities — not the crazy paranormal stuff but the mood, the sense of fear that permeated the town. Two youngsters disappeared, a brother and sister. Their parents were suspected at first, of course, but they were cleared. They moved away from Parnell, and I don't know if the children were ever found. You don't remember any of this probably. You were so young, maybe not even born yet. But that doesn't seem to matter in Parnell. The collective memory of this town keeps the past alive for all of us, whether we lived through the actual events or not."

"A little while ago I recalled one thing from way back, at least way back for me," Tulla said slowly. "In the infamous Clod War, I suddenly remembered two bigger boys beating a small child with sticks. The child was crouched down trying to protect himself. No one else remembers. Either the child or the incident."

"Who were the boys?"

"One was Dom. I don't know who the other was."

Tulla pulled her feet up onto the chair, hugged her knees, and rested her chin, thinking of more recent vulnerable children. She thought of Kat saying that Liam was her hostage to fortune … so much to lose.

Harriet continued. "When I told Aggie that something evil was slouching toward Parnell to be born again, for once she agreed with me. But she pointed out I was misquoting Yeats." She gazed into the flames. "He's another survivor, isn't he?"

"Yeats?"

"No, dear. Pay attention. Leo."

Tulla took a deep breath.

"Mikhail survived a physically abusive, unstable mother," Harriet continued, "but Leo survived so many losses. His mother dying when he was just a tyke, then Celia when she went off with Dom, then the false charges against him, and then Celia's death. He's a strong man, Tulla, but how strong? When you think of it, so many of his losses were because of Dom and Darla. Not the death of his mother, of course. Nor Celia's death, even though he believes —" She shook her head. "But the rest …" She studied Tulla over the rim of her mug. "You were so close as children. How good you all were for each other, you four — Katarina and you, Mikhail and Leo."

Tulla dropped her feet to the floor and leaned forward, studying Harriet's face for truths. "You've heard these stupid rumours? Thurston sought Dad and me out for the sole reason of telling us that putting Leo in charge of the investigation was like —"

"Putting the fox in charge of the henhouse? Thurston. Yes. That seems to be his favourite line. Or perhaps that was the one he was issued. There are others. I think each of those lost boys was given one to broadcast."

"What lost boys? And who's doing the issuing?"

"Those ones who didn't break the cycle, like dragons in amber. Well, not so much dragons. More like … little insects caught in their pasts forever. And the issuer? The ringleader? Dom was, I believe, but he'll have a successor now, someone perhaps more dangerous."

"And they expect people to believe that Leo killed Dom because he lied at his trial years ago? What took him so long? This is ridiculous."

"Well, dear, Aggie and I believe that he certainly had reason to —"

"What are you saying?" Tulla stared at the wrinkled apple face gazing serenely back at her. Her voice had lost its warmth.

"I believe you mean, what am I *implying*. And what have Aggie and I *inferred* from the rumours."

"Please, no grammar lessons, not now. I know that Leo wouldn't kill anyone, not even Dom."

"No, actually, you don't, Tulla. Your loyalty's commendable. I think you four would lie and die for each other whatever the circumstances. But it is possible, you know." She was matter-of-fact. "You don't know all that Leo's been through, where he's been, how he's changed, ergo you can't *know* anything about him for sure."

She leaned forward and whispered conspiratorially, "Of course, I happen to agree with you. I do have a suspicion and I intend to follow it up. Aggie will help me, though she doesn't know it yet. She'll be my memory bank. Because of our age ... well, she's a year older, and much as it pains me, she does remember some things better, but I'm the one people confide in. We make a good team, don't you think?" Her eyes sparkled, her voice gleeful. "Now then, off I go before it gets dark." She looked down at Clancy. "You should keep an eye on that dog, Tulla."

"What? Now *you're* telling me he's a dangerous animal, too?"

"No. But Aggie had a cairn terrier when she was a girl. Adored it. I think she has designs on your little fellow." Harriet squeezed Tulla's hand between her nobbled fingers. "Tulla, dear, don't worry about all this. Worry never solved one thing, as the Bible says more poetically. Now I do remember you telling me you'd lend me your mother's recipe book?"

"Yes, of course, and I'll drive you home. It's still raining buckets. Clancy, you stay here."

Harriet regarded the dog twitching in his sleep. "I don't think he's planning to do anything else."

When they arrived at Miss D's house, Tulla walked her to the front door, holding an umbrella over her head despite the protests issuing from beneath it.

"I'm not made of sugar. I won't melt. Now, Tulla, come next Monday for coffee. About eleven suit? And perhaps I'll have a little surprise." She peered up from under the umbrella, rain splashing her face. "I'll bake that cake for you. And I assure you it'll be a surprise to me, too. I haven't baked anything in years."

EIGHTEEN

TULLA STOPPED AT the Russell on her way back from Harriet's, ran through the rain, and pushed open the heavy front door. It was the most unwelcoming door she'd ever encountered in a hotel. Everything about the Russell was unwelcoming, including the reception clerk who watched her crossing the lobby as if she were trespassing.

"Could you call Leo Harding's room for me, please?"

He chewed on a toothpick. "Checked out. Yesterday."

She wondered if he'd ever swallowed one trying so hard to be cool. "Did he say when he'd be back?"

He smirked and shook his head.

She scurried back to her car and sat thinking as the rain slid down the windows in sheets. *Where does he go in the middle of a murder investigation? This isn't the way it's done on Law & Order. I don't believe this is the way it's done anywhere.* She pulled away from the curb, did a U-turn, and drove back to the police station. A single black-and-white cruiser sat in the parking lot.

Elvie dived for the papers flying off her desk when the wind, rain, and Tulla came through the door.

"Sorry, sorry ..." Tulla scrambled to help her. "Leo's not here, right? I didn't see his car."

"No. Nor his team. Nobody's here, in fact. Norbert went to Orillia with Leo. I don't know why." She smiled. "Yet."

"When are they due back?"

"Not sure. Norbert didn't even know he was going until the last minute. And Leo's like a ghost, drifting in and out. Odd way to run a murder investigation. Or, as we're supposed to call it, 'suspicious death investigation.'"

"My thoughts exactly. If he ever turns up or phones in, could you tell him to clear his voicemail and answer his damn phone. Better still, can you give him a lesson on cellphones, bring him into the twenty-first century?"

Back in her car, Tulla turned the ignition on and hit speed dial on her cell.

Kat's voice answered from the dashboard. "Tulla? You sound as if you're inside a washing machine."

"Might as well be. Your voice is coming through the car audio system. Neat, eh?"

"You phoned to tell me that?"

"*Noooo.* Just checking in."

"We've just ordered pizza. Want to join us?"

"What?" She twisted the volume button.

"Pizza!" Kat yelled. "We ordered pizza. Your favourite, the Popeye Special."

"Tempting, but don't think so. Thanks. Headed for home and a hot bath. I'm soaked, running around in the rain trying to track down Leo. He's flown the coop again."

"He's supposed to be the fox, not a hen. Oh, there's the doorbell. Pizza guy. Hang on a sec. Mel? Run up and get my wallet, please. It's on my bedside table." Her tone went low and harsh. "What are you doing here?"

"Came to get Liam." The voice was loud, slurred, and belligerent.

"I don't think so. You got the notice from the judge? Your visitation rights have been suspended until the next session with the mediator."

"Fuck the judge. I'm taking Liam on a boys-only fishing trip."

"Back off, Shug. You're drunk. And you're not taking Liam anywhere. Get out."

"You going to stop me? Yah, you and who else?"

Another voice, faint. "Me, that's who else. You heard Mum. Get out of here or I'm going to seriously hurt you."

Over the sound of the rain, Tulla could hear scuffling, a muffled yell. "Mel, get back upstairs. Keep Liam up there. Shug, let go of me. I'm calling the police."

"Like hell you are." The phone clattered and went silent.

Tulla threw the car into gear, shouting at the dashboard: "Call 911. Call 911!"

The dashboard replied, "Command not understood. Available commands are 'Call. Directory' ... The car fishtailed out into the street, tires spinning on the wet asphalt, the rain now falling in icy sheets. The wipers whipped back and forth in useless sweeps. Tulla kept her foot down, praying that no one else was dumb enough to be out driving on such a night. As she spun around the corner into Kat's street, the wind caught her broadside, sending the car skidding over the curb and onto the sidewalk. Someone was dumb enough. A truck careened past her, planing like a boat, barely missing her bumper.

She ran up the steps to Kat's door yelling, "*Police!* Open up."

A blurry face peered at her from the side window panel, then the door swung wide. "More cavalry," Kat said, her voice shaking. Behind her, Mel stood clutching a baseball bat. "He's gone. He was plastered. Damn, that man can be scary. But Mel frightened him off. You should've heard her, Tulla."

"I did. Seems she's moved on from Jane Austen to Dashiell Hammett. Then the phone went dead."

"He hit it out of my hand."

Mel suddenly sat down on the bottom stair. "My knees are shaking."

A small voice came from the top of the stairs. "Can I come down now?" Liam peered over the banister. "What are you doing with my bat, Mel? Dad gave that to *me*."

"And thank goodness he did — a full-sized metal baseball bat for a pint-sized eight-year-old," Kat said, scooping him up.

They jumped when the doorbell rang. Tulla peered through the window panel. "Pizza guy."

NINETEEN

NORBERT HAD NEVER been to the OPP's headquarters in Orillia before. He stared at the building in puzzlement. "You sure this is it, Leo? Looks like a prison."

"No, general headquarters is the fancy, much newer building around the corner. We've set up shop here for this operation. Back in the day, this was part of an insane asylum." Leo stood on the sidewalk and gazed up at the barred windows, the crumbling cornices, and a gargoyle at each corner still dribbling water from the recent rain. "The asylum was closed down as a psychiatric facility a few years ago, and most of the inmates were transferred to halfway houses except those deemed not insane anymore. They were just moved out period and now mostly live on the streets. And the new inmates moved in. Us."

He ran up the front steps, peered through a small Plexiglas window, punched the bell, and waved. The desk sergeant in the lobby buzzed them in. "Hey, Harding, meeting's already started. They're in the conference room, arguing from the sound of it. I'm sure your presence will calm them down — not." He pushed a clipboard with the sign-in sheet across the counter. "Who's your friend?"

Leo introduced Norbert. "Wait here, Nob. I'll go ahead and break the ice."

The desk sergeant snorted. "You'll need an axe. Frosty in there. Scrivens is out for blood — yours mostly. Wants you kicked off the team because of the Langtry fiasco. I could hear him ranting a minute ago, even though that door's pretty thick." He turned to Nob. "There's coffee in the lunchroom. Made it myself not two hours ago."

Leo pushed through the door to a sudden hush, pulled a chair out, and sat down. "Morning all."

"You're late," Captain Nemo said, sitting at the head of a long conference table scarred with use. Four detectives sat on either side of the table, all members of Operation Sandbag. Virgil Scrivens was the only one who didn't respond to Leo's greeting.

Nemo, a mild-mannered man, immaculate today in crisp uniform, peered at Leo over half-glasses. "Lucky for you, your shenanigans at the Langtry rally led to the first lead we've had in this case, otherwise you'd be gone."

"You should be, anyway," Scrivens said. "You jeopardized the whole operation." He wasn't mild-mannered. Or immaculate. He had coffee stains on his shirt, and a snow flurry of dandruff fell when he moved his head.

Leo tilted his chair back, hands behind his head massaging his neck, and ignored him. Scrivens had been a formidable enemy ever since Leo had reported him to Internal Affairs for beating up a prostitute. Leo didn't underestimate his vengeance, but for the moment he seemed safe, having gone from the doghouse to alpha dog because of spotting Darla.

"Your friend, Darla Connolly — more than a friend, I hear ..." Scrivens snickered.

Leo sat impassively, maintaining steady eye contact.

Nemo spoke. "We've confirmed she's at Copperton with a *Brother* Ambrose." He held up a file. "We've got more info on him here, and it just gets worse. He's fooled so many church leaders with his act — empathetic, charismatic — that he even has them advising social services in some jurisdictions to send wayward kids to him. He's a classic sexual predator who seems to think he's untouchable. We've got to bring him down."

"Fast," Leo said quietly.

Nemo nodded and continued. "Darla's changed her name to Grace and doesn't look like any of the pictures we have on file from your ... from the old days. Doubt she's had plastic surgery. I don't think any woman would go under the knife to look like she does now. Face like an axe. In the earlier photos, she's quite a looker."

"What did she look like when you 'knew' her, Harding? A babe, was she?"

"Shut up, Scrivens," Nemo said.

One of the detectives held up a hand. "So what's the story? You knew her before?"

Leo nodded.

"How?"

"We're both from Parnell."

Scrivens started to speak, but Nemo cut him off. "We've been watching Ambrose but didn't know Darla was his sidekick until Harding spotted her. Her involvement sheds more light on the nature of their operation. Those two aren't in the business of serving God, that's for certain. We've also been working on getting someone inside."

One of the detectives lifted a finger to identify himself.

Leo leaned forward. "Weasel?"

"Hey, Elbows."

Leo grinned. "Good to see you, man."

"Likewise."

"You guys know each other?" Nemo asked.

"Harding and I played hockey against each other in high school. We all knew not to go into the corners with him. Might come out dead." He reached across the table to shake hands. "Good to be on the same team, Elbows. Safer."

"Okay," Nemo said, "so Detective Gary Burgess, apparently also known as Weasel, grew up in Eganville, about thirty kilometres from Copperton. He knows the area and hasn't been back since he joined the OPP, so the locals know him but not what he does. His family moved away years ago, right, Detective?"

Weasel nodded.

"He moved to Copperton several weeks ago," Nemo continued, "and has made himself known as a drifter. We've given him a new past, including a stint in the slammer, but he's pretending to be born-again — amazing what prison life can do — and has been going to the services at Bluebird. So Weasel here — I like that name — has also let it be known around the pool room crowd that he wouldn't say no to underage sex. Hook baited, fish — small fry, anyway — bit. One of Ambrose's crew approached him at the local bar and said there was a job at Bluebird if he was interested in talking to the chief."

"The chief being Ambrose," Weasel said. "Scary dude. Felt like he could see right through me and my cover story and out the other side. I'm on probation. Not included in anything yet, except to work in the kitchen. The captain has my report on what I've found out so far."

Nemo held up a sheaf of papers and slid it down the table. "Eyes only. These don't leave this room."

"So where do they think you are today, Detective ... Weasel?" Scrivens asked.

"Hey, Detective Dandruff, only my friends can call me that. They think I'm in Copperton sorting out a charge for public drunkenness as well as a dispute with my landlord that I assured the Bluebirds I, and they, didn't want following me into my new life."

"And they bought your story?" Scrivens said derisively.

"Guess I'll find out when I get back."

"Next item," Nemo said. "You all know that Harding is in charge of the investigation in Parnell ..."

"And what a goddamn travesty that is."

That word again. Leo sighed.

"Ah, Scrivens, give it a rest," the man beside him said, shaking his head.

"It's like putting the —"

Leo leaned across the table and spoke very quietly. "If you say 'fox,' I'm going to pop you one, Dandruff. Hear?"

Scrivens made a barking sound.

Nemo ignored him. "Leo, you want someone to take over that assignment? You're going to be pretty much full-time with Operation Sandbag." He consulted his notes. "You have Sergeant Crawford in your unit there. He's a reliable sort, bit of a plod, but he knows the territory now, the locals. What do you think?"

"I'd like to stay on because of the connection with Bluebird." He had the table's full attention. Even Scrivens was listening. "Darla's Dom Connolly's sister."

"Son of a bitch. Nothing in her file about that. You sure?"

"Yeah, I'm sure." Leo's smile was thin. "Grew up with him, too, you know. Two of a kind. When he got out of jail, they lived together for a while in Vancouver. I think she worked for him in the drug trade out there. He was in charge of the Angels' interests in the West. So far we haven't found any other connection between him and Bluebird aside from Darla, but I'm sure there is one. Too much of a coincidence."

Nemo studied him for a minute. "Okay, you'll stay with both investigations. For now. But you'll need a liaison — local force in Parnell, your unit there, and me. You have a reputation for going silent and missing. I need to be able to reach you at all times. Hear me?"

"Got just the man. Knows the patch. In fact, he's here with me. Waiting in the lobby."

Nemo picked up the phone. "Sergeant, there's a guy out there. Send him in, will you?"

There was a knock, and the conference room door opened. Leo tilted his chair back on two legs, hands behind his head. "This is the assistant chief of police, Parnell local force. My go-to man. Norbert Tinsley."

Nob blinked.

TWENTY

THE TEMPERATURE HAD dropped in the night; by midafternoon it was sleeting hard. Tulla crept carefully up the outside steps to Mikhail's apartment just as he stepped through the door, snapping open an umbrella. "We need walkie-talkies like we had when we were kids, since you won't turn on your phone. What is it with you and Leo? Got time for a chat?"

Mikhail looked at his watch. "I have to be at the Manor at four. You could come with me."

His car, like his flat, was spotless — on the inside. The outside not so much. The fenders were rippled with dents and sported an array of colours like paint sample cards. Tulla pulled the seat belt over her shoulder, snapped the buckle, and closed her eyes as he backed out of his parking spot, narrowly missing the car next to him.

When she opened her eyes again, she still couldn't see anything. A solid sheet of water poured down the ice-coated windshield. A car passed them, ploughing through a puddle, and suddenly it was like driving on the bottom of a lake. Mikhail sped up.

"What are you *doing*?" She hit the windshield wiper lever, sending the blades snapping back and forth just off the glass.

Mikhail hunched forward and rubbed the windshield, as if by some sleight of hand he could clear it from the inside. "Ah, there are the gates." He turned left in front of an oncoming car, shot between the stone pillars, sped up the driveway, and braked to a stop in front of the Manor. Tulla rocked against her seat belt and started breathing again.

"The car you cut off?" she said. "It just pulled in beside us. I think the driver wants to have a word."

Mikhail rolled down his window. Paul Skinner stood in the slackening rain, shielding his head with his briefcase. "You're a bloody menace, Novak. You're damn lucky I didn't hit you."

Mikhail nodded genially, as if the lunatic driver on the loose wasn't him.

Paul peered into the car. "Hello, Tulla. We meet again." A smile slid onto his face like partially set Jell-O.

Tulla struggled to keep her mouth from imitating his. She and Kat used to practise his Uriah Heep smile but could never achieve Paul's schizophrenic combination of "You're my new best friend" when it appeared, and "Trust me at your peril" when it vanished. She nodded.

His smile slithered away as he turned and strode to the entrance.

"Is he the Manor's physician now, too?" Tulla asked.

"Replacing his father. Or at least helping him. Old Skinner's not too reliable anymore."

"Never was." Her hand went to her ear. "Remember when Dom hit me with a rock?"

"After you hit him with one?"

"Doc Skinner sewed me up. With no freezing. Bloody sadist."

Mikhail reached into the back seat for his briefcase.

"Wait a sec, Mik. We never did finish talking about Leo the other night. I know you're avoiding the subject but ..."

He got out and stood by the car, stretching his hand palm up. "No time. You could wait for a ride back, but the rain's almost stopped."

"I'll walk. Maybe wetter but safer." She glanced up at the Manor. "Mik, look at your old window. Someone's up there watching us." The curtain swung back as she spoke. "Did you see?"

"Far as I know that floor's only used for storage."

Tulla gazed up at the limestone edifice, a house her great-grandfather had named Ben Nevis. Her mother had called it The Castle. Her father, Warren, had hated the house; Tulla had loved every inch of it. And now it was a home not for a family but family leftovers, a refuge for the oldest and most decrepit of Parnell's population. Her old home was now a holding area for death.

She stood by the car and studied the third-floor window for the watcher. *The first Mrs. Rochester.* The curtain hung motionless, but a movement at the entry caught her eye. Rosalie was just disappearing through the front door, now glass, with a punch button for automatic opening. She hurried after her and stopped dead in the entrance hall. Thirty years later and the walls were covered with the same flocked paper — cream with red vines. The only change was a reception desk angled across the hallway opening into the interior. And the smell. Unmistakably institutional, chemical, the anti-septic overlay of ancient, barely functioning bodies.

The young receptionist watched her curiously. "Are you okay? Are you here to visit someone?"

"Used to live here a long time ago. Just a bit of a shock."

"This was a private house? Cool. You wanna look around?"

"I'm actually looking for Rosie Stevens. I just saw her come in."

"In the coffee room down the hall on your left. Can't miss it."

Tulla stood in the doorway prepared for another wash of memory. Not this time. The room had been Warren's den: a cozy sanctuary lined with bookcases, a worn Turkish rug of reds and deep blues on the floor, a fireplace, a Victorian sofa for afternoon naps, and a claw-foot desk under which Tulla had spent happy hours playing house with her imaginary friends. It now had a vinyl floor, metal tables and chairs, a snack-dispensing machine, and a coffee pot of inky liquid that smelled like burnt rubber.

Rosalie, her back to the door, sat at the farthest table, already deep in her book. She looked over her shoulder, frowning slightly. "Tulla!" She jumped up and gave her a hug. Rosie matched her name — a cap of carroty red hair, reddish-blond skin, and permanently rosy cheeks with a scatter of freckles. And such startlingly blue eyes, so unlike those of Dom and Darla.

"Have you got a minute, Rosie?"

"Sure. My shift doesn't start until four." She looked at her watch. "Oh. It's past that now. Where did the time go?" She shook her head, mystified, finger still marking her place in the book. "No matter. I can be a bit late — one of the perks of being the nurse supervisor here."

Tulla sat opposite her. "I'm sorry about Dom …"

Rosalie held up a hand. "I saw you at the funeral. It was generous of you to come. Can't really say more than that."

Tulla inclined her head. "His death has certainly stirred up this town — so many rumours. Someone told me yesterday that these rumours are being orchestrated."

Rosie grinned. "Would that someone be Harriet Deaver?"

"Of course. And that they're mainly aimed at incriminating Leo Harding."

"The fox-in-charge-of-the-henhouse Leo?"

"I'm worried about him."

"Me, too. He had every reason to hate Bobby … Dom, but so did a lot of people. Seems, though, the pack of louts in this town has chosen him as a scapegoat. My theory is that they're trying to distract the police from the real culprit, if there is one. Leo hasn't even been back to Parnell in years except when he was here to go through his father's things. I had them in my basement ever since he died."

"When was that?"

"He died three, four years ago. I used to keep an eye on him after Celia died. Poor man. He just stopped caring about anything. Too much pain in one life. First, his wife dying so young, then his son getting into … difficulties, then his daughter dying. Too much pain."

"No, I mean when was Leo here?"

"A couple of months ago …?" Her eyes shifted. "And then maybe later … I can't exactly remember." She waved a vague hand. "He went through the boxes, took away some papers and letters, and asked me to get rid of the rest."

"Do you find him changed? More secretive or forgetful?"

"He's always been secretive. I don't know about forgetful. Maybe a bit deaf. I haven't seen him much since he's been back this time. All I can say is he's had a bad time." She glanced at her watch and stood. "I have to go, Tulla. Even a supervisor has to turn up sometime. I'll walk with you."

"Rosie, I only just heard that you testified on Leo's behalf at his appeal against your own sister and brother. That was very brave."

"Well, they were both lying. They've lied all their lives. I used to think that Darla genuinely didn't know the difference between truth and lies. Bobby just didn't care. And neither of them cared how much pain they caused other people. They were like a pair of wolves hunting together."

"Do you ever see Darla?"

Rosalie shook her head. "No interest. I had no idea where she was until Elvie called me yesterday with a 'big secret.'" She laughed. "Everything is a 'big secret' with that girl, at least until she gets hold of it. Nob had just come back from a meeting at OPP headquarters. They think Darla is involved in some religious cult up near Copperton. Seems she's still out there wrecking lives — this time in the name of God. Lucky old God." She squeezed Tulla's arm and turned back down the hall, her rubber-soled shoes squeaking on the vinyl like mice.

TWENTY-ONE

IT SNOWED IN THE NIGHT. Tulla knew even before she opened her eyes because of the cold, clean, knife-sharp smell. She pulled on jeans and a turtleneck and scurried to the kitchen down a slide of snow light reflecting off the hardwood floor. No matter what was going on in her life, new snow, the first real snow of winter, filled her with delight. She'd told Kat it was atavistic, a memory from earliest childhood of the smell and special light pulling her outside no matter the temperature. Kat had told her she was nuts.

Tulla poured her coffee into a travel mug, urged Clancy out the door, and walked along the riverbank. Frost lined the trees, and ice coated the rocks at the water's edge. And for a few moments everything was right in her world.

She and Kat had arranged to go through the Cohen house that afternoon. Kat was waiting at the corner of Main and Brigham. "Hurry up. Light's going, and I've got to get back before dark."

They set off, chins tucked against the cold. "Look at the bridge," Kat said. "It's completely sheeted in ice. How did that happen so fast?"

"It's called winter," Tulla said happily, taking her arm. "Happens every year."

"Don't be so damn cheerful. I'm freezing."

"You're as bad as Clancy. Both whinging over a little cold."

"You mean 'whining,' and I'm not."

"I don't and you are. Whinging means the same thing as whining except more so."

"In what language?"

"Portland language."

"Well, if it means the same thing, why don't you speak our language?"

"*Sheesh!* What's with you, Kat? Why so grumpy?"

"Well, maybe because Shug was on my doorstep again this morning. With a letter from his lawyer saying if I didn't let him see Liam he was going back to court to ask for sole custody. He had some little floozy from the court office with him. I wanted to smash them both."

"How's that possible? I thought —"

"The restraining order was held up somewhere. Apparently, I moved too fast for the wheels of justice that grind exceeding slow." Kat shook from cold, anger, and fear. "Floozy said that if I didn't comply I could be charged with contempt of court, and Shug would get Liam." She bit down on her lower lip and took a deep breath. "So I had to let Liam go with him. He said he was just going to take him to Tim Hortons for lunch and then to a movie at one o'clock — *Frozen*, of course. So who do I see on the way here? Shug on his snow-mobile with Liam. There's hardly any snow and he's out grinding up gravel, and Liam wasn't even wearing a helmet. Neither was he, of course, but no loss if *his* head came clean off. He told me they were doing 'man' stuff together. It was important to counter all the 'girlie' stuff Liam has to do with me. Stupid macho shit."

"Oh, Kat, it will happen. The restraining order will get through eventually. In the meantime, shouldn't you just comply? I mean, maybe you're overreacting. He might be a jerk, but he's not going to hurt his own son. It seems reasonable that he wants to spend time with him."

Kat's voice, cold as steel, plunged into Tulla like a knife. "I can't believe you just said that. Well, yes, I can. You're always so eager to pronounce on things you know eff-all about, wanting everyone to play nice. You make me sick."

Tulla was speechless. She turned away, feeling the shock build to anger. She'd reached the corner when she felt Kat's hand grip her arm.

"Tulla, listen to me!"

Tulla shrugged her hand off and kept walking.

"Listen. You don't know — how could you know? I didn't tell you the other night. I'm sorry I yelled at you. *Listen to me!* Shug's a pedophile."

Tulla stopped dead.

Kat held up a hand. "Let me finish before you ask anything. That's why I'm on screaming tenterhooks every minute Liam's with him. When we were still occupying the same house, I found a stash of child pornography that was —" She shook her head. "When I confronted him — my first mistake — he claimed he was hiding it for a friend who was under surveillance for selling drugs, that he was afraid, the friend was, that if his house was searched the cops would find it and tell his wife. Second mistake, I believed him. He said he'd get rid of it right away. Of course he didn't. Then I found stuff on his computer. Third mistake, I should have reported him to the police, but I couldn't stand the idea of Chief Rockin' Roland knowing about all this, and all I wanted to do was to get the kids away. Fourth mistake, I actually told him I was going to report him. So, of course, then he did get rid of everything. Claimed he'd thrown his computer into the river, so no evidence, or so I thought. What did I know about tracking perverts who visit these websites. I know now."

"Oh, my God, Kat. Liam can't be with him, not even in the daytime."

Kat's laugh was shaky. "Exactly."

"You have to go to the authorities, tell them —"

"They wouldn't believe me. I haven't got a shred of proof. I saw it, but no one else did, as far as I know. And the 'authorities' here? Would they listen? Their computers are probably full of the same stuff."

"But you're right. He could be dangerous, even to his own —"

"Don't say it. Please don't say it." Kat covered her face with mittened hands. "I'm so, so scared. I thought it would be fixed now that Dom's out of the picture, because he was the one who, to quote Shug, 'Had the judge by the balls.' And who knows who else in social services … I can't … I don't know what more to do." She rocked back and forth, sobbing.

Tulla held her tightly, rocking with her. "It's okay, Kat. It's okay."

"No, it's not okay," she whispered. "It's so not okay." She straightened out of Tulla's arms and scrubbed her face with frozen mitts. "I think my eyes have iced shut. I thought salt water didn't freeze. Let's get inside."

Kat pushed the door open and launched a sandstorm of grit along the wooden floors. Oak counters ran along two sides of the front room; the walls behind them were hung with deep, dark, and substantial shelves. It was even colder inside than out.

"Let's leave this for another day, Kat. It's not important, and it's too cold and —"

"No, we're here now. Come on."

They picked their way down the hallway over piles of litter and filthy clothes, paint tins, and a torn sleeping bag. "This is weird," Kat said. "People have been living in here." Upstairs they found stained mattresses and tattered blankets in every room.

Tulla tilted her head, sniffing. "Scented candles. Cinnamon." She pointed to the wax stubs on the floor. "High-class squatters we're dealing with here."

They clattered back downstairs and into the old summer kitchen. "This is what I meant," Kat said. "Through here is the old porch, and this is the shared wall with my back porch. My parents and the Cohens each extended their porches to join across the alley. When they were still friends, it was a communal space. I remember them sitting side by side in their rocking chairs, gossiping, watching the river. But my mother and Mrs. Cohen had a falling out, something to do with Mrs. Cohen saying that though she was a Jew she wasn't a displaced person, like my mother. Didn't go over well. Despite my father's entreaties, Mother had a wall built, cutting the porch in half."

"How wars start," Tulla said.

They went back to the big front room where Tulla turned in a slow circle. "Kat, it's perfect. This space would be for new books. And the smaller rooms would be for used books, each room a different category or subject. History, biography, mysteries and thrillers, a room for kids' books — House of Books. Look, I can't concentrate on this now, but there's a bookstore in Eganville going out of business. I knew the owner when he worked in Toronto, wants to sell up. So I'm thinking Eganville is near Copperton, which is near the religious school or commune or whatever where Rosie said Darla is, as reported by Elvie. So after we see my book guy, we could, you know, for old time's sake, check her out."

"And beat the snot out of her, like she used to do to us?"

TWENTY-TWO

BY SUNDAY, THE SNOW with its bright new promise had frozen into a grey film on the lawns and driveways. As Tulla pulled into the curb in front of Kat's house, a figure swathed in a voluminous fur coat tottered down the path on stiletto-heeled boots. A woollen beret fell over her forehead like an undercooked muffin.

Kat climbed into the passenger seat, took off her Sophia Loren sunglasses, and arranged the skirt of fur around her. "Like my coat? It was Mother's. First time I've ever worn it," she said stroking the fur. "Think Darla will recognize me?"

"She'll certainly notice you. Are you forgetting that this is true hippie-dippie-save-the-seals-stop-global-warming-eat-vegan-no-hunting territory? And this church commune thing is smack in the middle. It's called Bluebird. I Googled it. You'll get swarmed."

"Nah. Everyone will think it's faux."

"Fox? How will that help?"

"Not fox. Faux, as in fake."

Tulla rolled her eyes. "Where's Liam today?"

"At his best friend's house. One of his best friends. He appears to have several, bless him. It's going to be a good week. Shug's away, so I can breathe easy for a few days and pray that the restraining order turns up. I have about fifteen calls into the court office, and I've taken your advice, Tulla, and told my lawyer everything. He didn't actually seem surprised. Said he'd talk to the judge but cautioned me, as I expected, that without proof the judge might discount my story as something I've made up to get sole custody. Enough of that for now. Let's bust out of here, Thelma."

"I'm Louise. You're Thelma."

"How come?"

"Because I'm taller and I'm driving. Now hang on to your muffin. The service is at eleven, according to their website. We'll go on to Eganville after lunch."

"Do you think that's her?" Kat whispered, leaning sideways against Tulla in the pew. "Can't see her face, but she sure doesn't sound like Darla. I think this chick was born and raised in *Deliverance* country. All she needs is a banjo."

"Or a scythe." Tulla held up the service bulletin. "According to this, she's Prophet Grace." She smothered a laugh. "Billed here as 'Amazing Grace.'"

Amazing Grace's floor-length black robe puddled around her feet, her face shadowed by a hood. When she spoke, it was in words polished to opacity, a river of smooth, hammered speech, hypnotic and impenetrable as marble.

"It would be really good ... really good if you took quality *time* to reflect on the gifts Jesus has given you." Her voice had lifted, then dropped like doom, rising up the ladder of words to the dead drop of "time." Then she lifted her face to the congregation.

Tulla squinted, attempting to overlay the possible Darla in front of her on the young Darla she remembered. "I don't think it can be her, Kat," she whispered. "Darla used to be pretty good-looking, even though we never wanted to admit it."

"*Shh, shh!*" A sibilant mist of outrage sprayed the back of their heads, coming from a worshipper kneeling in the pew behind. "You are in the presence of our Lord."

The front two rows were filled with young girls and boys, unnerving in their stillness. Behind the hooded figure, two more rows of youngsters in purple choir gowns swayed to the music that swelled and faded in rhythm with the river of words.

"It *is* her," Tulla said, risking another shower. "That creepy smile. Squinch your eyes and you can see —"

"*Shh!*" A gnarled finger dug into Tulla's shoulder. She turned with a meek smile of apology and tried to sit motionless for the rest of the service.

"And now it is time for your gifts, tithes, and offerings. Please be generous to support our work on God's behalf." Twitching the hood back from her face, Darla revealed lank, shoulder-length hair and a face as sharp as an axe blade. Her smile was no more than a rictus pull of thin lips.

Kat gasped. "Yikes! What's happened to her? That's her smile, but she sure has lost her looks."

Tulla slouched down in the pew, memory washing over her.

She was lying on her back in the mud, just beyond the school playground. Darla sat on her chest, pinning her helpless with bony knees grinding into her upper arms.

"Give in?" Darla snarled through her smile. "Say uncle, you fucking bitch." A loop of spittle hung longer and longer from Darla's mouth. She sucked it back and slurred through a mouthful of saliva, "Say uncle or I'll spit all over ya, fucking bitch."

Fucking bitch? Tulla didn't know what that meant, although she had heard it often enough in the school-yard and had tried it out once at home, with spectacular results.

It was suppertime on the first day of school. "Who's your teacher this year, Tulla?" her mother asked, spooning potato croquettes and a mound of pepper squash the colour of autumn onto a plate. "Pass this to your father."

"Miss Snotgrass."

Her mother's spoon hung in midair.

Bridget giggled.

"Tulla, that's very rude," her mother said. "Her name is Snodgrass. Miss Snodgrass."

"Everyone calls her Snotgrass at school. That fucking bitch Snotgrass."

Bridget's muffled gasp gave Tulla a split-second warning before her mother's anger boiled over her. "Go to your room. Now."

"She doesn't know what she's saying, Sadie," her father said, trying to come to her rescue. "She has no idea what it means."

Bridget crossed her eyes at her as she sidled from the room.

The loop of spit swung over her again, and she flipped her head back and forth, heaving her hips up to dislodge her tormenter. The spittle went straight into her ear.

Another poke into her shoulder brought her back to church. "You can talk now," the voice from the pew behind spoke in a conversational tone. "Service is over."

As Darla led the choir off the dais and down the centre aisle, Tulla and Kat ducked their heads, hands over their faces as if in prayer. Tulla peeked through her fingers as Darla reached the end of their pew to be met with a flat, expressionless stare. She felt as if she'd been punched.

Back in the car, Kat pulled off her coat and flung it onto the back seat with her beret. "Not sure what we just accomplished," she said, combing her hands through her hair. "But it definitely is Darla. She looks pretty rough now, hatchety and hard. But it's her all right. Hope she didn't spot us."

"Oh, she did, she did." Tulla edged the car out onto the sideroad and sped away from the church as if pursued. "She nailed me with a look that said, 'I know exactly who you are.'"

TWENTY-THREE

THE POLICE STATION was quiet, not awake yet. The morning sun slanted through the high windows onto Elvie at her desk as she stared at her computer screen. An agitated Nob appeared in the doorway of the situation room. "Can you raise Leo? Nemo's been trying to reach him. He's steaming. Says he's not picking up his calls."

"Orillia issued him a new cellphone, and he probably doesn't know how to use it."

Leo came through the outside door on a sudden path of sunlight. "Morning all. Who doesn't know how to use what?"

"You and your new phone," Elvie said. "Is it on?"

"It is, I think." Leo dug it out of his back pocket and gazed at the black screen. "Apparently not."

They looked up in unison as the outside door opened again. Shaun inched in backward, balancing a tray of coffee and a box of Timbits.

"Yay!" Elvie said, taking the tray from him. "No question. You're my favourite techie and you obviously have the genes of a fine cop. And Leo needs another phone lesson."

"They told me it's a smartphone," Leo said, handing it to Shaun. "Does everything but make coffee."

"When what you really need is a stupid phone to match its owner," Elvie said.

Shaun glanced back and forth between them.

"It's okay, Shaun. Elvie and I go way back. To when she was still *Elviiiiira* …"

"And you were still shrimp ass."

Leo suppressed a smile. "Not to my face, I wasn't."

"Leo, you gotta call Nemo back fast," Nob said. "I told him you were in the car, probably in a dead zone. That's why you weren't picking up calls. Something's going on at Bluebird, and he's in a tizzy."

Leo's hand froze over the Timbits. "Burgess is on his way here to report. I'll call Nemo." He disappeared into the situation room with Nob.

"What's up?" Shaun asked.

"No idea," Elvie said. "Can you help with that phone? Leo's going to get into real trouble if he keeps missing calls. You know, despite what I said, he's a very smart man. I don't get this problem he has with technology. Seems like it snuck up on him. He's still in the Dark Ages."

"Sure, but what was wrong with the old one?"

"Aside from the owner? For one thing, it would only take three messages and then said the voicemail was full."

"Well, they're idiots," Shaun said. "Got nothing to do with the phone. It's the package he has with the service provider. Same thing's going to happen with this one unless he changes it."

"He'll never change it. HQ will have to deal with it." She watched the outer door swing open for the third time in about as many minutes.

A scrawny, unshaven figure wearing blue jeans hanging from bony hips and an oversized windbreaker strode over to her desk. "Here to see Leo Harding."

"Name?"

"Gary Burgess."

Elvie squinted up at him. "Weasel?"

He grinned. "That would be me. A century ago."

She grinned back and pointed to the closed door behind which Leo's voice rose in a single expletive. "In there."

Weasel passed through into the situation room, hoisted himself up on one of the computer tables, and swung his legs back and forth. "Nice to breathe decent air. Cripes, that place is ugly."

"Give us the details," Leo said. "Nemo's barely coherent."

"Well, Grace the Prophet, she calls herself, the one from here? She's a piece of work that one. Anyway, she recognized two women at the service on Sunday. Seems they all knew each other when they were kids. She's really spooked, thinks they came looking specifically for her. Ambrose thinks they might be undercover cops."

Leo and Nob exchanged glances. "They aren't cops," Leo said. "Think you can convince Ambrose they aren't a threat? Or are you blown? You want to come out?"

"No, I'm good. Cover's still intact. I'll see what I can do with Ambrose, but he's one fearsome son of a bitch. Doesn't listen to anybody except someone he occasionally talks to on the phone, and it ain't God."

"Where does he think you are today? You can't just wander out, right?"

"Nope. Place is a prison. But he sent me on a shopping expedition for the exodus plan. That's really my only news. I told you they seem to have an escape plan in readiness. Escape isn't the right word. It's more like an evacuation plan if a hurricane, i.e., a raid was imminent. Seems they might be moving the departure date forward. Maybe because of those two women. I don't know. Ambrose isn't in any hurry, though. It's a sweet setup for him there — isolated, good buildings, the church front. But he definitely wants to be ready to go fast. I have a list as long as your arm. I think we're going to the Himalayas — sleeping bags, propane heaters, lamps.... Said I wasn't to get anything locally — too suspicious. So here I am about to clean out Canadian Tire." He looked at Leo curiously. "Who are those two women, anyway? Do you know them?"

Leo nodded. "Being a detective, I figured it out. Not too hard, since I know them both and knew this would be just the caper they'd pull. Your report to Nemo on Ambrose's description and Darla's reaction were the clues. They're harmless ... if kept on a leash. I'll right back."

"Bring some doughnuts," Weasel called after him.

"Shaun, I need my phone for a minute." He pushed a speed-dial number and listened, his mouth tightening.

"Bloody voicemail. Tulla? Goddamn it, you two Nancy Drews might have just screwed up our whole operation. This isn't a game. Don't go near that place again."

He tossed the phone back to Shaun, scooped up the remaining Timbits, and returned to the situation room. He wasn't smiling.

TWENTY-FOUR

TULLA'S FIRST INKLING that Leo was unhappy about their visit to Bluebird was the message he left on her phone. The second was when he thumped on her door, unannounced.

"I have a bell, you know," Tulla said after she peered through the security hole and pulled the door open. He pushed past her and down the hallway. "Hey, take your boots off."

"I'm not staying."

"That makes a difference?" She eyed the slushy tracks on the hardwood as she followed him into the kitchen.

He leaned against the counter, arms crossed. "I cannot believe you and Kat went to Copperton. We finally get a lead and you two blunder into the middle of it. You've put one of our undercover agents in danger, you've put yourselves in danger —"

"We just wanted to confirm it really was Darla."

"We knew it was her."

"Then why didn't you arrest her?"

"Because we'd have lost the other players. We haven't got enough evidence that will stand up in court. We're waiting for another —" He stopped speaking and gripped her shoulders, face dark with anger. "Listen to me, Tulla. These people don't fool around. For God's sake, there's already been one murder. We've probably lost Darla because of you. She's good at getting lost."

Tulla jerked away from him, eyes wide. "Hey, you're hurting me!"

He dropped his hands as if scalded. "Ah, Tulla, God …" The anger drained from his face. "You're the last person on earth I would ever hurt." He lifted a tentative hand and cupped her cheek. "I didn't mean to frighten you. It's just that if Darla gets away, if Ambrose and his team escape … she … they have so much to answer for."

"Is this personal? Because of what she did to you?"

He dropped his hand. "This isn't revenge. If you think that —" He shrugged. "Well, I hope you don't, but I can't help what you think. Darla's dangerous. She's hurt people … kids. She's running with a sick bunch." He took her by the shoulders again, carefully, hands barely touching her, as if gentling a startled colt. "Tulla, know that I would never ever hurt you." He studied her face, then kissed her hard on the mouth.

When he left, she watched from her kitchen window as he crossed Memorial Gardens and moved out of sight along the river. Snow was falling again — fat, lazy flakes slapping the pavement and clinging to the dried stalks of coneflowers and frost-blackened marigolds.

"Clancy, come on." She grabbed her coat and mitts, pulled on her boots, and headed out and down the stairs from her deck. At the stone wall marking the division between the tidy garden beds and a field of bracken and blackberry bushes, she unsnapped Clancy's leash and let him run. He knew the way — along the shore path, now under a carpet of wet snow marked only by Leo's footsteps. The river flowed fast toward the gorge and its plunge to the lake below. Ahead of her, Leo climbed an outcropping that hung like a broken bridge over the top of the falls. She called to him over the river's roar, scooped Clancy up, and scrambled up the path to a stone bench perched on the outcropping. Leo sat with his back to her. When she touched his shoulder, he leaped and whirled, gun in hand.

"It's me, Leo, it's me!" she screamed, stumbling backward on the snow-slick rock.

He grabbed her arm. "Jesus, you startled me. I'm sorry."

She clutched Clancy to her chest like a shield. Leo brushed snow off the bench, sat, and pulled her down beside him, holding her close. Clancy, squeezed between them, growled.

"Do you always carry a gun?"

"Only when I might need to shoot someone." It was already out of sight, tucked back into its holster. "Joke, Tulla," he said when he saw her expression. "That was a joke."

She ran her mittened hand over the back of the bench. "Our inscription has nearly worn away. 'All for one, one for all.' I thought that was another Mikhail original." She turned back. "Our 'tell' bench. We couldn't tell lies when we were sitting on it." She looked at him steadily.

He was the first to break eye contact. "What would you like to know?"

"Everything. But I'll settle for what happened with Darla."

He shifted on the bench. "You know what happened. Pretty much everyone knows."

"Only the public story."

"You won't like the personal one." He rubbed his face with a snow-wet hand. "Where to start."

"Try the beginning."

"Yeah, but where's the beginning? The Clod War? Or farther back, maybe the great divide between Valley and Hill Top — where did the enmity begin? Where does any story start?" He leaned forward, put his elbows on his knees, and stared at the ground. "I suppose for me this one started when Celia eloped with Dom. I still think that was an act of pure spite on his part. He bewitched Celia because he could. And I know it's not all about me, but I could never shake the feeling that it was aimed at me."

"You used to talk about that when you visited me in Syracuse that first year."

He smiled slightly. "Those were good weekends. Too bad they ended."

"That's when we lost touch."

"That's when you decided to lose touch."

Tulla remained silent.

"I was holding things together that year — being mature, leaning on you pretty heavily."

"Yes."

"So, anyway, jump forward a few months. I went off the rails, dropped out of college. Did you know that?"

Harriet had told her that before he'd left college he'd come back to Parnell to see her. He had hoped to build a new life, a new family, with Tulla. "But you weren't ready," Harriet had told her. "Leo went into a dark, irrational place then, but he managed to turn himself around. He said rock bottom wasn't a comfortable spot to be. Leo's a very strong man. And then he lost it all again — his freedom and his reputation."

Tulla had been stunned into silence. She had tried to tamp down her guilt at breaking with Leo at a time when she knew he needed her most. Of course, he'd have seen it as yet another betrayal. She thought of herself back then: weak, searching for someone to take care of her. Her mother in Toronto, her father remarried and in the Bahamas, Bridget ... no idea where Bridget had gone. She had no room to take care of someone else.

"Harriet told me," she said to Leo now.

"Drank myself stupid, started having blackouts. I got a job in Sudbury in a nickel mine and ran into Darla there. She was working in the office. We had dinner a couple of times — familiar face from home, even a face I'd never much liked, and vice versa. We had a bit of a fling."

"You mean an affair?"

"A couple of one-night stands."

"That would be an affair."

"Can't remember much about it, except in my drunken logic I figured it was tit for tat. Her brother was screwing my sister, so why shouldn't I screw his."

"God, Leo, that's horrible." She pulled away from him.

"You asked, I'm telling. But no matter the drunken blackouts, I do know one thing — the sex was consensual. She was a willing participant, more willing than me."

"Stop it. Don't try to justify it. This doesn't sound like you at all."

"You didn't know me then, Tulla. Anyway, we parted amicably, I thought."

"But why would she accuse you of … why would she do that?"

"Old enmity?"

Tulla puffed out her lips in disbelief. "A childhood grudge?"

"Mikhail's theory is that the sex might have been consensual, but the parting wasn't."

"A woman scorned?"

"Yes, and a woman in thrall to her brother who's hated me from the get-go."

"But why did he hate you?"

Leo was still for a moment. He lifted his face into the wind. "I think mostly because of you."

"Me? How did I get into the mix?"

"Because of our … friendship, yours and mine. He was jealous. To an insane level."

"How do you know this?"

"Rosie. She told me that where you were concerned he suffered from severe arrested development. Very complicated. Have to ask Dr. Mikhail to explain it. Way back in the mists of time, you put yourself in jeopardy, first by publicly humiliating him in that play you both were in, then again by flattening him in the Clod War, awarding him the dubious distinction of being the only casualty that day. And third —"

"He wasn't the only casualty. I saw a little boy —"

"And third, you took up with me. Rosie thinks you were in his crosshairs. He talked about you the day she took him out to see his new house. At first she thought he was saying he wanted to see you again, invite you to a big housewarming. But when she thought about it, she realized it sounded more like a threat, that he wasn't planning on you having a good time there."

Leo pulled a pack of cigarettes from his shirt pocket, shook one into his mouth, then took it out again. "Darla left Sudbury shortly after our ... fling. No idea where she went. I left, too. Finally got myself straightened out, finished the first part of the police training program, and was in Orillia. So, one evening after classes, I was walking down the hall feeling pretty good for the first time in years when two cops I knew from the force, kind of sheepish, sidled up to me. They said they had a warrant for my arrest. Darla had brought charges against me for rape. They obviously thought the charges were trumped up and would just go away. But they had to act. Woman comes into the station crying rape, they can't ignore it, no matter how long after."

"But how many — three, four years later?"

"There are lots of cases like this — five, ten, twenty years. Some real, some not."

The wind had strengthened, blowing the snow off the rocks in gusts. He pointed his chin at the sky. "It was

November, a day like today, cold, windy, bleak. It's a bit of a blur now. Can't remember exactly. I do recall what I did the next day, though. I drove back here and down to the river to Fortune Beach. And I skipped stones. Had it in mind that if I could skip a stone across to the pier, all of this would go away. No matter how hard I tried, and if you remember, I was a champion stone skipper — they all sank at the first bounce." He stood up and peered into the gorge. The flailing branches seemed to be trying to throw him off the rock. He gazed down at her, eyes dark with pain. "It gets worse. You really want to hear this?"

She patted the bench beside her. "Tell."

Leo squeezed his cheekbones. "She had a child, claimed I was the father. Actually, by then she had two, but only one was of an age that fit." He sat on the edge of the bench and tucked his hands under his thighs. "I went to see her to try to reason with her, and also to see if the kid looked even remotely like me."

"Did he?"

"*She* looked like Celia."

His legs were stretched in front of him, one knee jumping like a piston. He tapped the cigarette on his palm and put it between his lips. When he tried to light a match, it promptly blew out. He lit another and cupped his hands around the tiny flame. Tulla folded her hands around his to keep it alive.

Leo drew smoke deep into his lungs and let it trickle from his nostrils. As he spoke again, she had to lean in to hear him. "When I was released after the appeal,

Mikhail picked me up at the jail. We went back to his apartment. My plan, my burning goal, was to find that little girl." He paused, swallowed. "Mik told me that night that the judge had been lenient with Darla because of the death of her child."

Tulla slid back across the bench and pulled him to her. Clancy, warm between them, stayed quiet. They sat braced against the wind they had known all their lives. It tore at their coats and keened through the trees, howling as if in pain.

At last Leo pulled away, eyes hooded. The hard man was back. "Any more questions? And make it snappy. This stone is freezing my ass off."

Yes, she had one more question: *Did you kill Dom?* But she didn't ask it. "Time to go." She pointed at the dark clouds boiling over the trees.

They scrambled down from the outcropping and back along the riverbank where Clancy took off, barking furiously. Leo peered through the branches. "What the hell is she doing out in this storm? It's Miss D."

When they drew near, she called to them, "Were you up at your bench?"

"You know about our bench?"

"Of course, dear."

"Is there anything you don't know about?" Tulla ducked her face against the ice pellets now stinging her cheeks like buckshot. "Come in with me, Harriet, until this blows over."

The old lady peeked out of her fur-rimmed hood, eyes as bright as a chipmunk's. "I enjoy this weather.

And I'm on a mission. Aggie's taken that photograph down again. Silly woman."

"What photograph?" Tulla asked.

"It's hanging in the library. An old photo of two children. Aggie thinks there's something evil about it, that it's connected somehow to the Fist." She glanced at the furious sky. "Now she'll be all of a twitter." Pulling the hood tightly around her face, Harriet hurried off into the gale.

TWENTY-FIVE

BY THE NEXT EVENING, the wind had dropped, the temperature had risen, and the snow had changed from ice pellets to cold rain again. Sodden leaves carpeted the pavements, but heavy black clouds promised more bad weather.

"Not sure what's in those clouds now," Tulla told Kat when she and Liam arrived for a promised spaghetti dinner, Liam's favourite. "Probably fire and brimstone."

Kat had brought a video so Liam could have a movie dinner while they talked. He unwound his scarf, almost as long as he was, shrugged out of his parka, and kicked off his boots in the entry. "Have you seen this?" He held up a DVD. "*How to Train Your Dragon*. It's really cool."

"It might give us some tips," Kat said.

Tulla set Liam up on her bed with a bowl of potato chips, juice, the remote, and the promise of dinner soon. Then she went into the den with wine and olives and settled in the chair beside Kat. "Houston, we have a problem."

Tulla told Kat about her conversation with Miss Deaver and her non-conversation with Mikhail. "I don't know exactly what's going on with Leo, but something is. Harriet says we don't know him anymore, what he's capable of. Rosie says nothing other than that he's had a bad time and might be a bit deaf, while Mikhail just says nothing. And now Parnell seems to have made Leo the chief suspect in his own murder investigation." She didn't mention their conversation on the bench.

"Leo's deaf?"

"Rosie thinks so. And Harriet says he cocks his head when he's listening." She pointed at Clancy. "Like him. Watch." She snapped her fingers and said the dog's name. He lifted his head and tilted an ear to her. "See the resemblance?"

Kat looked at her sideways. "To you? Yes."

"Funny. So it's up to us to clear Leo and find the real murderer. Ponder on that while I get dinner. Okay if Liam has his in front of the TV?"

"As long as you don't mind spaghetti sauce on your duvet."

When Tulla came in with their plates on a tray, Kat had her head back in the chair, eyes closed. "Are you asleep?" Tulla asked.

"Pondering. Among other things, I'm so sorry for lashing out at you the other day. I was way out of line."

Tulla waved a hand, but the memory still hurt. "Now, about Leo. I think he's hiding something and doing it badly, which isn't Leo's style. He used to be so good at keeping secrets. You didn't even know there *were* secrets.

Now there's a clumsiness about him. Could be real or he could be faking it. At the fitness centre he appeared never to have seen a treadmill before. It was weird, as if he'd fallen into a time warp. And Harriet says we can't be sure what he's capable of after all he's been through, so —"

"So what are you thinking?"

"I'm thinking that it's unbelievable that we're sitting here talking about the possibility of someone we know — and love — being a murderer. I think of the Leo I used to know and believe there's no way he would have killed Dom. He has, or at least had, such a still centre about him, a kind of certainty about right and wrong, sort of like Mik, only quieter. Then in the middle of the night when the horrifications hit — and Harriet, damn her — I think, *What do I know about Leo anymore?* So maybe he did murder Dom. My brain says that, while my heart says absolutely not."

"Well, my heart agrees with your heart. Brains be damned. Except we need our brains to be smart detectives unhampered by sentiment, clear-headed, analytical."

"Like Sherlock Holmes?"

"I was thinking more along the lines of Sue Grafton. More reliable, since her Kinsey Millhone isn't a drug addict. We should start with a list of suspects based on motive, means, and opportunity."

Tulla pointed at the ottoman. "There's a notebook and pen."

Kat drew four columns and labelled them "Suspect," "Motive," "Means," and "Opportunity." She studied them for a minute, then wrote "Leo" in the first column. Under "Motive," she scribbled "Hated Dom."

Tulla shook her head. "We all hated Dom, even his own sister. It has to be a more specific motive."

Kat added, "Hated Dom more than the rest of us did."

Tulla rolled her eyes. "Dom enticed his beloved Celia away, and she died on his watch."

"Yeah, but —"

Tulla held up a forestalling hand. "And Dom lied at Leo's trial."

"Strikes me if Leo didn't kill Dom, he should have." Kat bit the end of the pen. "This is going to be harder than I thought. How do we find out if someone had the means and opportunity? Not just Leo, but for anyone else we come up with?"

"Okay, let's just list suspects and motives."

"Okay, Mikhail." Kat wrote his name under Leo's in the first column. "Motive?" She sucked the pen again, then wrote: "In cahoots with Leo."

"That's not a motive, is it?"

"Could be."

"Okay, so why would Mikhail want Dom dead?"

"Do we know anything that Mikhail wants?"

"He wants to put down all the bad guys," Tulla said. "Dom was first on his list."

"*Whoo!* That's definitely a motive. But was Dom a psychopath?"

"I don't know. That's splitting hairs. He sure was a bad guy."

"Who else?"

Tulla held up a hand and counted off on her fingers. "One or several members of the Hells Angels."

"Motive?"

"Dom double-crossed them? I have no idea."

"Right," Kat said. "I'm not listing them because they are way beyond our meagre detective skills. Besides, they're scary."

"Then there's ..." Tulla paused. "Number three, Thurston."

"Why Thurston?"

"Because he's a foul loud-mouthed little clown look-alike."

"Looking like Chucky the Clown isn't grounds for suspicion. That I hate him now is. So he's on the list. Definitely."

Tulla held up her fingers. "Number four, Snake Skinner."

"Old or young Snake?" Kat asked.

"Both."

"Why?"

"Because old is a bad doctor and has left lots of people with scars." She touched her ear. "And Paul, young Snake, because why else has he come back to Parnell? No one seems to know. Highly suspicious. And because of his Uriah Heep smile."

"All you're doing is throwing up a forest of suspects to hide Leo in."

"Oh, wait. Here's another one with a real motive — Jack."

"Who's Jack?"

"Leo knows him. He was in prison with Dom and apparently crossed him. For his pains, Dom slashed him

in the face. Hence the name Jack. It's not his real name."
Tulla touched her nose.

Kat studied her for a few seconds. "Polanski's movie set in L.A. Got it. Jack Nicholson."

Tulla nodded approvingly.

"So why was he in jail?"

"Kidnapping. College prank gone wrong. Leo says he's one of the good guys. You'd want him on your side."

Kat looked skeptical. "Kidnappers aren't usually the good guys."

"Well, he has good genes. Leo says he's some sort of relation of Harriet's. A cousin's son or something. She was the only one in his family to stand by him when he came out of jail."

Kat rolled her eyes. "So I guess if he's related to Miss D. he's beyond suspicion."

"No one's beyond our suspicion. He's number six. Then there's number seven, Leroy at the fitness centre. Number eight, Tim, the desk clerk at the Russell. And then the clerk at Canadian Tire."

"What clerk?"

"The guy in the candle section. I went there to see if I could find out who'd bought cinnamon candles lately."

Kat laughed. "So did I."

"Any luck?"

"Nope. But I did see the snake tattoo. Asked him if he was allowed to bring it to work. He thought I was serious. He was a rude little twerp with hair like a porcupine."

Kat put the notebook down and picked up her plate. "Good detectives don't just put everyone they don't like on the suspect list. Only bad cops do that. But if creepy is the criterion for suspicion, Shug's at the top of the list, followed by my dishwasher, Frank."

Tulla said slowly, "Does he have a snake tattoo?"

"Yup. Around his scrawny bicep. I think it's a home-made job. The ink keeps running."

"Those three guys — Leroy, Tim, the Canadian Tire guy — all have a snake tattoo, as well. And now your dishwasher. That's a lot of snakes in one town."

Kat sat up. "Shug has one, too. On his thigh."

Tulla shuddered. "His eye? How's that even possible?"

"His *thigh*, Tulla. *Th-igh*. So maybe they're some kind of gang."

"That might have been what Miss D. was talking about when she told me how she wasn't afraid of human snakes."

"But why would she be so mysterious? If she meant there was actually a gang of snake guys, why didn't she just say so?"

"Maybe she thought she had." Tulla sighed. "We're getting nowhere. We have no idea of motives for anyone except Leo. We know Dom had lots of enemies, but we don't know any of them except the childhood ones. And what about alibis? How do we find out stuff like that?"

"Well, Kinsey would pick locks, break into houses, go to the library to do research because she's pre-Google, and then she'd beat the bad guys up. Or shoot them. Between eight-kilometre runs, usually in terrible weather. I suppose we could try that."

"Everything but the running part. She also drinks lots of Chardonnay." Tulla held up her empty glass.

TWENTY-SIX

HARRIET DEAVER'S ship-shaped house anchored the end of Ramsay Avenue behind a row of cheap new townhouses. The line of towering pines around her property stood like sentinels holding back real and imagined attackers. Tulla knew the house well from a tradition that had started in the earliest days of her friendship with Miss D. — weekly tea parties, just the two of them, where she was treated as an equal, where the conversations ranged far and wide and easy about everything under the sun. Except the subjects Miss D. would say had to wait a few years until Tulla was old enough to treat them with justice and understanding. Tulla thought Miss D. was the wisest person in the world. She still thought so despite the growing evidence of "brain slippage," as Miss D. called it.

Harriet's great-great-grandfather had been awarded a section of prime land as befitted his rank in the British Army during the War of 1812. He'd chosen the land rather than passage home because of his determination never to set foot on a ship again, never to go near any body of water bigger than a pond. Then he built a house that looked like a ship as if he still didn't feel safe from the sea. His neighbours called him Noah; their houses were long gone, but his still rode proud, sheltered in its harbour of windbreak pines. It had a second-storey "suicide door" typical of Ontario farmhouses of the day, but that was its only nod to custom. Two non-traditional dormers bracketed the door like eyebrows over the inset windows. They looked down now on Tulla with blank eyes reflecting a sky gone grey with the promise of more snow.

Tulla pushed the bell and studied the stained-glass window set into the upper half of the door. She loved that window. It depicted a shepherd bringing home his sheep at twilight, which upset Aggie because the same illustration could be found carved into many of the gravestones in the Presbyterian cemetery outside town. Miss D. had told Tulla, "Aggie thinks it's morbid and highly unsuitable for a front door. I told her to mind her own beeswax. I think it will help ease the crossing of the bar."

When Tulla stretched out a hand to trace the outline of the shepherd, the door swung inward at her touch. "Harriet?" She peered into the dim hallway. The heavy curtains framing the archway into the living room stirred in the draft.

The house was quiet. All Tulla could hear was the soughing of the wind through the pines, a distant car revving its engine. And all she could smell was burning.

She ran down the hall and wrenched the kitchen door open. Yellow smoke billowed from a pot on the stove, engulfing her in greasy fumes. She grabbed the handle, and with a yelp of pain flung it across the kitchen, yelling in rising panic, "Where are you, Harriet? Answer me! Where are you?" She stumbled over an upturned chair and saw beneath it the old woman gazing at her with sightless eyes, lying silent and still in a scatter of broken china and a pool of blood.

Tulla flung herself down, put her hands on Harriet's face, and smoothed her hair back. "No, no, no. Oh, God, no." She grabbed her by the shoulders, gently shaking her. "Oh, God, no, don't be dead. Please, no." But the old lady's skin was cold, like Portland's when he finally stopped fighting.

Tulla rocked back and forth. "So cold," she whispered, "so cold …" She ran to the living room, tore a curtain down, and dragged it back, tucking it over Miss D. as if she were a sleeping child. And still the woman's milky eyes stared up at her.

Tulla scrabbled for her cellphone and punched the speed dial. "Pick up, Leo, pick up, oh, God, pick up."

He did on the fifth ring. "Leo, come quickly. It's Harriet … she's hurt. She's lying on the floor —"

"Slow down. Is she conscious? Can she speak? Check for a pulse."

Tulla touched Miss D.'s neck. "I can't find a pulse."

"Where are you?"

"In the kitchen. I'm on the floor with her."

"In her house? Or yours? Quick, Tulla, where?"

"Hers. There's blood around her head and —"

"Get out of the house right now, Tulla! Get out *now*!"

"*Noooo*. I'll try CPR. Call for an ambulance."

"Don't hang up. Just get out of the house!"

Tulla struggled to her feet and backed slowly away. The old lady's sightless eyes seemed to follow her every step.

"Talk to me," the cellphone's tinny voice barked into her ear. "Are you out?"

"Yes," she whispered. "I'm on the step."

"Farther, go farther. Go down the street. I'm on my way. Hang up now and phone 911. Don't go back into the house. Do you hear me?"

Tulla shook her head as if he could see her. "I might have missed the pulse, and she's cold, and maybe she's bleeding to death. I'm going back —"

"No, phone now, Tulla. Do it for her. Get the ambulance there as fast as you can. And don't go back in the house. Wait for me." The line went dead.

Leo raced up the street toward her. "Did you call?"

Tulla nodded mutely.

"Stay here." He ran up the flagstone path, digging his gun out from under the back of his jacket as he disappeared through the door. Unmoved, the shepherd continued home with his flock.

When Leo returned, the gun was nowhere in sight and the ambulance was rounding the corner, siren blaring. It slammed to a stop next to Tulla, the doors flew open, and two paramedics jumped out, one running to the back of the vehicle, while the driver asked Tulla, "What's up? This is Miss Deaver's house, isn't it?"

Leo was on his cellphone and held up a finger. The driver turned back to Tulla. "He seems pretty casual. Thought this was an emergency."

"Not anymore," she said dully, turning her face away.

Leo spoke into the phone, his voice low. "Elvie? Track down Roland and Nob. Neither is picking up. Get them over to the ship house. Yeah, the Deaver place, an accident. Call Skinner's office and get old doc over here ASAP. Call me back if there's any problem there. And, Elvie, keep very, very quiet about all this. Don't … ah, never mind. Tell Nob to bring the crime tape, rubber gloves, Ziploc bags." He turned to the driver, whose eyes were wide with excitement. "Miss Deaver is dead. Until we can verify cause of death, her body can't be moved. And don't touch anything else in there. The coroner, Doc Skinner, should be on his way."

"Was she murdered?" the paramedic breathed. "Never had a murder call before. Well, we did bring Connolly in, but sheesh, what's going on in this town?" He glanced at Tulla. "Hey, you're bleeding — your legs."

She looked down blankly.

Leo knelt in front of her. "And your hand's a mess." He gently uncurled her fingers to expose raw flesh.

Tulla shuddered as the pain and the memory kicked in. "I picked up the pot that was smoking."

He led her around to the front of the ambulance and into the passenger seat. "Your knees are shredded. Did you fall?"

She looked at him, eyes full of misery. "I must have knelt in the broken china around —"

"Did you touch anything else besides the pot? Did you turn off the stove?"

"I don't know. I suppose I did if it's off. Why? What difference — oh ..."

A black vintage Cadillac pulled into the curb, gleaming even in the grey light. A tall figure uncoiled from behind the wheel, pulling a leather case from the passenger seat. He paused to rub at a spot on the car's shining flank before strolling to the front of the ambulance. An unlit pipe was clenched between yellow teeth that looked as if they belonged in a horse's mouth.

Tulla turned away as she remembered Miss D.'s description of Dr. Skinner — "a long, mean drink of water," she'd called him, adding, "and try never to shake hands with that man. It's like shaking hands with a tree root."

"So what's going on here? Harding? That you? What are you doing here?"

Leo gestured toward the open front door. "She's in the kitchen."

Dr. Skinner followed him down the hall, coughing and waving his hand in front of his face. "That's bad. That kind of smoke gets in your lungs." He jerked to a stop when he saw Harriet Deaver. "Oh."

The doctor lowered himself to the floor, felt for a pulse, then gently turned her over. His fingers probed the back of her head beneath grey hair matted with blood. "Her skull's crushed. I expect her neck's broken, as well." He turned her gently back and sat on his heels, gazing at her face.

"How?" Leo asked.

Skinner struggled to his feet. "How what?"

"How did she die?"

"I think a smashed skull would do it, don't you?"

Leo looked at him, expressionless.

"Probably slipped on all the grease from the fire. What was she cooking, anyway? Chicken stock's my bet. The grease has coated everything, and she was already unsteady on her pins."

Leo knelt, closed her eyes, touched her cheek once, then stood. "Or someone could have hit her."

"I'll be monitoring the autopsy at the hospital since the death occurred here in Parnell."

"Was she your patient?" Leo asked.

"What difference does that make?" Skinner replied querulously. "I still will be present. I think it's far-fetched to assume she was attacked."

"Perhaps, but I'm calling in the OPP's Criminal Investigation Bureau. Could you make a guess at time of death?"

"Naturally. After all, I *have* been a coroner for forty years." He lowered himself to the floor again, clutching the counter to steady himself, and lifted her blouse to show a wrinkled stomach patchy with liverish purple stains.

Leo caught his arm as he started to turn her over. "Don't move her again."

"Stop interfering, you fool. I'm checking lividity patterns to establish time of death."

"I know what you're doing. And by moving her you're possibly interfering with those patterns. Haven't you got a liver thermometer to establish her core body temperature?"

"I do not …"

"Why do you have to know her temperature? Can't you let her be at peace?" Tulla said tearfully from the doorway.

"Because we can compare her temperature now to normal body temperature. A dead body loses roughly a degree and a half Celsius an hour after death," Leo answered gently.

"Depending on the ambient temperature of the environment," snapped Skinner. "You're the expert now, are you?"

"No, but I do know what happens to someone's blood after death. The heart stops, blood pressure collapses, and blood sinks into the lowest parts of the body. It's called gravity, Doctor. That staining on her stomach means she's been moved since death."

"Indeed, she has. I just turned her over five minutes ago."

"And you know very well that wouldn't have caused what we're seeing here."

Skinner grasped the overturned chair and pulled himself upright. "Since you won't let me do my job properly — and be sure I'll register a complaint about your interference — I won't hazard a guess at time of death." He brushed his sleeves down and adjusted his cuffs. "Her lungs will be an indicator if they contain grease nodules from this smoke." He gestured to the table. "Looks like she was expecting a visitor. Two places set and a cake."

"She was expecting me," Tulla said.

"Interesting." He bared his lips in a smile around his pipe stem.

"You are implying?" Leo said.

A memory engulfed Tulla: she could hear Harriet, only a week ago, cozy and safe in her den, saying, *I believe you mean, what am I implying. Or what have Aggie and I inferred from* ... Now, she shut her eyes against the tears, her cheeks mottled with fury. "You bastard —"

Leo put a restraining hand on her arm.

Suddenly, she was cold, and her teeth chattered from shock with the realization. "Leo, that stockpot was on high." She examined the burnt flesh on her hands. "No one cooks stock on high."

The front door banged open and footsteps thumped down the hall. Roland appeared in the door frame, gun out. Nob jostled him from behind, peering around his shoulder.

"Roland, get Skinner out of here and tape the house," Leo ordered.

The chief lumbered into the kitchen. "Hey, I'm in charge here. This isn't anything to do with Dom, so butt out. What the hell happened, anyway?" He stopped short when he caught sight of the body.

"That's what's happened," Leo said softly.

Skinner stepped forward. "She obviously slipped on the grease and hit her head on the counter." He patted it for emphasis. Leo gripped his arm and propelled him to the door. Skinner shook himself free and picked up his bag. "I'll let the morgue know the body's coming. I'll sign the release right now. You," he said, turning to the paramedic, "can take her."

Leo held up a hand. "She's going nowhere until CIB gets here. I'll wait with the chief until they come. And depending on what they find, I'm suggesting — *Rock's* suggesting — that her body be sent to Ottawa Civic Hospital for autopsy."

Dr. Skinner snapped his bag shut and strode down the hall without another word.

TWENTY-SEVEN

TULLA SNATCHED THE phone up before the second ring. "Dad?" she whispered. "Hang on a minute." Grabbing her dressing gown, she tiptoed down the hall to the kitchen. "Kat's here and I didn't want to wake her. I tried to call you."

"Maureen phoned me, darlin', and Mikhail, and poor Aggie, and a few others. They told me you found her. I'm so sorry. I want you to come down here right away, Tulla. You can't be alone up there."

"Oh, I'm not alone. My place is bulging with people. Kat and the kids are here. Melissa's sleeping on the couch. Liam's pitched a tent in the living room. He's got his Ottawa Senators sleeping bag filled with stuffed animals, a flashlight, a peanut-butter-and-banana sandwich, a hot-water bottle, and Clancy."

Kat stood in the doorway in a long flannel nightgown, hair flying out from her head in frizzy curls. She went to the stove and held up the kettle, pointing to the jar of tea bags on the counter.

Tulla nodded.

"We want you to come down here to us. Kat, too. And the children, of course. I'll get your airline tickets as soon as you say how soon you can all come."

"Wait, Dad, it wouldn't be until … after the funeral."

"That could be weeks, Tulla. There won't be any funeral until the body's released."

"I don't know how it works. Maybe there will be a memorial service before then. I'll phone you as soon as I find out." She swallowed a sob. "Gotta go. Love you, Dad."

She pulled the sleeves of her terry-cloth robe down over her hands and rubbed her face. "Dad's just invited us all down to the Bahamas. Actually, it was less an invitation, more an order."

Kat pushed away from the counter and enveloped Tulla in a hug. "It's so damn sad and bad and horrible that anyone in this town is evil enough to have killed Miss D., a defenceless old woman. Well, physically defenceless. She was so tiny, like a sparrow, but big in spirit."

"And feisty and honourable and fearless. Except for snakes. She was afraid of snakes — the animal kind and not the human variety, she told me."

"She should have been. That's who killed her — the human kind." Kat poured boiling water into the teapot. "Tulla, the kids and I, we can't go to the Bahamas …"

Tulla held up a hand. "Dad's paying for the tickets."

"Oh, no, he's not. But that's not the point. Melissa can't be away because of school, and on top of that she's just started working at Maureen's. And I'm not going anywhere without her."

"We'll figure something out because I'm not going without *you*."

The novelty of the sleepovers began to wear off after three days. Melissa chafed under the constant adult surveillance and early curfews, while Tulla and Kat were exhausted, staying up every night talking and then disturbing each other's sleep when they finally did go to bed. And Liam decided it was time to decamp when Clancy wouldn't let him into the tent.

"Come and stay with us, Tulla," Kat said, rolling up Liam's sleeping bag.

It had been a comfort to have Kat and the kids with her, and the long nights of talk were like old times, a pyjama party of two. But it was past time to get back to normalcy, whatever that was. "Thanks, Kat, but I'm staying put."

"You can't stay alone."

"Of course I can, as long as Dad doesn't find out. And besides, maybe she did just fall."

Kat gave her a level stare. "Like Dom just blew out the window on the tail of a tornado?"

"Maybe everyone's just jumping to conclusions."

They weren't. That same afternoon the preliminary autopsy findings confirmed what everyone in Parnell apparently already knew. The pathologist in Ottawa had wasted no time. Harriet Deaver had died from a blow to the head, but the weapon wasn't a kitchen counter or tile floor. Flakes of iron rust were found in the wound.

Mikhail called her shortly after Kat and the kids left. "I saw the exodus. Thought it would be safe to phone."

"Always safe to phone, Mik."

"Just checking in. I have to go to Orillia, but if you want company, I could be back in a few hours."

"Thanks, Mik, but I'm fine. In fact, a little space is kind of welcome. Let me know when you get back."

"I will. Also wanted to tell you that you were right. There *is* someone living on the third floor at the Manor. They've installed a chair elevator and moved Arn up there by himself. Nobody else is willing to share space with him."

"Can you blame them? Harriet and I were just talking about Arn." She dropped her chin to her chest. Mikhail waited, letting the silence travel down the line. "Does he know about Dom ... and Harriet?"

"Rosalie said he wasn't upset about Dom at all but definitely was about Harriet. When I saw him, he was genuinely grieving. She was his only regular visitor, and he seems to think he's in some way to blame for her death. He's feeling guilty about something. He won't talk to Leo, but he might to you."

Tulla choked. "Me? Why me?"

"Perhaps he doesn't feel as threatened by a woman? He remembers you and certainly knew how close you were to Harriet, which appears to make you a special friend."

She shuddered. "Okay ... if it'll help to find out who killed Miss D."

Tulla was filling a hot-water bottle when the doorbell rang. She pulled the door open to an icy wind and Leo slouching against the door frame.

"You should check before opening your door to a stranger."

"You're not a stranger."

"Did you check?"

She rolled her eyes. "No."

He stepped in and closed the door. "A hot-water bottle? I don't suppose you'd have something else hot, as in whisky, maybe?" At the sound of his voice, Clancy came scrambling out of his tent with a joyous bark.

Tulla hugged the water bottle to her chest. "I was just going to bed, so one drink and then you're on your way."

"Well, not quite." Leo fished into his breast pocket and held up his toothbrush. "I've been tasked — that's Nob-speak — with the security detail."

"This is getting ridiculous. Who 'tasked' you, anyway?"

"Kat. She phoned to say they had moved back home and she didn't think you should be alone. Melissa says your couch is quite comfortable. Clancy and I will bivouac in the living room together."

Tulla headed for the kitchen. "Whisky's in the cupboard over the fridge."

"Join me? You look as if you could do with a drink or three."

"Ah, why not?" She hooked a stool over with her foot and sat at the counter.

Leo turned from the cupboard, holding a bottle. "Where's the sugar?"

"You're putting sugar in Glenfiddich? In that bowl by the stove." Her voice was tight with misery. "Leo, why Miss D.? Why would anyone kill her?"

He put the steaming mugs down on the counter, sat on the stool beside her, and took her hand. "I think she confronted someone with something she knew about them, probably to do with Dom's death, but that's conjecture. We don't know anything for sure except that she did not fall without help."

Tulla stood, straightened her shoulders, and retied the belt of her robe. "Time for bed."

"I think if Harriet were here she'd say, 'Have another drink.'"

She smiled sadly. "I doubt it."

"For sure she would. Such a wise woman. She knew when the times called for special measures." He added water to the kettle, studied it, put it down, poured a healthy measure of Scotch into each mug, and passed one to Tulla.

She sat again. "Okay."

"So talk to me, Tulla. What are you thinking?"

"I'm all talked out. Kat and I pretty much covered the waterfront." Her eyes welled up. "Only thing I can add is that I'd like to kill the person who did this."

"Me, too."

Tulla studied his face. "Harriet told me we didn't know you anymore, that you might be capable of killing."

"Ouch."

She smiled wanly. "Miss D. said you probably weren't, but that we don't know what you've been through, how you might have changed." When he said nothing, she continued. "So help me here, Leo, what *have* you been through? Will you answer my questions, or will you just keep on being an evasive pain in the neck?"

He gave a surprised laugh. "Try me."

"When we were talking at the bench, you never said where you went when you got out of jail."

"To Mikhail's apartment."

"I knew that."

"But perhaps you don't know that Mik is why I got out of jail in the first place."

"He had that much clout?"

"Not sure I'd call it clout." He rubbed the back of his head and rolled his shoulders to release the tension. "Ever heard of Hare PCL-R?"

"Someone we grew up with?"

"Close. It's a test used to assess a possible psychopath. A twenty-point personality checklist. Mikhail was renowned in the OPP, even back then, for going way beyond this test. He used it as a starting point, has a gift for spotting stuff other psychologists miss. A kind of sixth sense. He doesn't need a checklist. So when someone who's that good at his job takes up your case, people tend to listen."

"People thought you were a psychopath?"

"Not me. Maybe Darla, though."

"Where was he at your original trial?"

"He was in England, seconded to Scotland Yard and doing a doctoral thesis. As soon as he heard, he was there for me."

Tulla leaned forward and touched his hands. "Did he know you were doing spider push-ups on a mirror?"

She tented her fingers together and pushed them in and out. "*Cri de cœur*? Remember our code?"

Leo smiled slowly. "He must have. He reviewed every page of the case against me, re-interviewed witnesses, did a criminal profile of me and one of Darla. A detective told me later that his profile of me was the most compelling piece of work he'd ever seen. And Darla's the most chilling. Mik presented new evidence, stuff that had simply been ignored first time around, shredded Dom's testimony by finding witnesses that put him in Vancouver at the time he claimed he'd seen me with Darla in Sudbury. It was a rout. There was a scramble in the provincial justice department to reverse things before the media got hold of another balls-up by the police and the Crown. All records of the charge, the guilty verdict, the appeal, and the exoneration were made to disappear. Supposedly. Nothing disappears anymore in the age of the Internet. And I was told to get on with my life."

"Those are the years I was asking about. What did you do?"

He stood up and stretched. "I finished police training." He paused. "Among other places, I went to what used to be Yugoslavia, to Afghanistan. I went to hell and back, at least I hope I'm back."

Tulla nodded. "Mik told me that much."

"And now I'm going to bed if you'll provide me with a blanket or two." He studied her face. "Unless you'd like to share? Melissa actually said your couch isn't that comfortable ..."

Tulla took a deep breath and looked up at him.

He cupped her chin and kissed her softly on the mouth. "Maybe we could start over, pretend we're back in your dorm in Syracuse." He took her hand.

When Tulla woke the following morning, Leo was gone. She rolled over into the lingering warmth from his body and lay still. Her brain kicked into gear — chastising, warning, scolding. *What the hell are you doing, starting up with Leo again after all these years? Recipe for disaster. What are you thinking? He is damaged goods. You aren't strong enough to take him on … again. He is an infuriating, clamped-down, arrogant, secretive, mixed-up, self-centred loner.* She stretched her arms over her head and smiled.

On the kitchen table, he'd left a note on top of the recipe book Tulla had lent Harriet:

> Coffee's ready. Try not to throw it all over the floor. Clancy and I went out for a short run. Found this on the bench in Miss D.'s entry. Yours since your mother's name is in it? I'll be back tonight. Check I'm not a stranger before opening the door.

TWENTY-EIGHT

ROSALIE MET TULLA and Mikhail in the reception area of the Manor. "I'm so sorry. I have no words about what happened to Miss Deaver."

Tulla nodded, not trusting herself to speak.

"You're meeting Uncle Arn? I saw the note in the appointment book." She handed Tulla a clipboard and pen. "Rock says all visitors have to sign in now. New procedure." She sounded apologetic. "Mikhail, you don't have to because you're considered staff." She smiled at him. "Dr. Mikhail, that's what the residents call him."

Mikhail peered over Tulla's shoulder at the clipboard. "Leo's been in?"

Rosie nodded. "Arn wouldn't talk to him. Neither would my mother. So I bought him a coffee to cheer him up. Although he didn't seem to need much cheering."

Tulla dropped her head low over the clipboard, her cheeks glowing.

"He's in the small interview room," Rosalie said.

Tulla glanced up in alarm. "Leo is?"

"Arn. At least I think he's still there. Half the time we don't know where he is."

"It's the old sewing room on the second floor, Tulla," Mikhail said. "You won't recognize it."

She didn't. Tastefully decorated in maple furniture upholstered in beige on beige, it bore an unfortunate resemblance to a tiny visitation room in a funeral home. A box of tissues sat on the coffee table beside a bouquet of beige flowers. Beige roses and beige freesia and beige lilies. They needed dusting.

Arn, swathed in a purple velour bathrobe, sat hunched forward on a straight-backed chair. His rheumy eyes locked on Tulla like target lasers.

"Hello," she said, struggling to keep her eyes on his face.

"Harriet's dead." He wore a bib that caught the drool as he spoke. His eyes leaked tears; his face devoid of expression. His once-huge shoulders had slipped into folds of flesh like a rumpled shawl. He stretched out a hand, and Tulla forced herself to take it. Lumpy and twisted with arthritis now, those hands were still strong, could still hurt.

"We have coffee at ten thirty. She visits sometimes. And doctors. They visit. Doctors make house calls." He winked. "I have my coffee upstairs."

His hand smoothed the velour back and forth, making it stand up like fur on the back of a cat. He started to hum. The hair on the back of Tulla's neck rose.

"You had coffee with Miss Deaver upstairs?" Mikhail asked.

"With Jaysus." He broke into the cadences of an Alabama preacher. "Jaysus sees the little sparrows fall." His rheumy eyes, narrowed to slits, fixed on Tulla's face. "You were a pretty little thing," he crooned.

Tulla felt her stomach heave.

Arn placed a gnarled finger beside his nose and dipped his head toward her, eyes slyly peeking over his hand, imparting a secret. "I saw him. I told Miss Harriet. Jaysus sees everything. He sees the sparrow fall. He saw Bobby fall." He faltered, losing his place.

Is he for real? Is this just a big fat act? Why am I sitting here listening to this horror, anyway?

"Why are you here?" he asked in a normal tone, as if reading her thoughts.

Tulla jumped. *I can't do this.* She stood up. "I can't stay, just wanted to say —"

His eyes darted from side to side. "She was my friend." Tears started from his eyes again, but this time he seemed sorrowful and frightened. With shocking suddenness he was on his feet. Beckoning imperiously with one hand, holding his robe up with the other, he scooted down the corridor.

They followed him to the bottom of a wide, curving staircase, unaltered since Tulla's time except for the seat fixed to a track running up the risers on one side. Arn was already settled into the chair like a king on his throne, purple robes gathered around him. He pushed the lever into gear and rose slowly up and out of sight.

They reached the third-floor landing to find the chair empty. "How can he move so bloody fast?"

"A skill he's always had, Tulla."

"Not much changed here. Your old apartment, Mikhail." She went to the door and peered in just as a grinding screech echoed down the corridor. "That's the roof ladder, Mik. I'll never forget that sound." They ran toward the noise. "With the place full of lunatics prowling around in the night, that trap door isn't locked?"

The hall ended at a door, open now, revealing the bottom of a metal folding ladder and Arn's robe disappearing from sight. They heard the trap door thumping back onto the roof, letting the light flow in. By the time they scrambled up the steps and out onto the roof, Arn was leaning over the rusty wrought-iron railing, waist-high, that ran in a square around the trap door. Her father had been scornful — a widow's walk so far from the sea. What pretention. Tulla had pointed out that a ship might sink on Crow Lake, which you could see from these heights. Not many ships on Crow Lake, he'd said, unless you count canoes. She gazed around now, remembering the sense of excitement when she and Mikhail climbed up here in secret. It had been forbidden territory, thus one of their favourite haunts.

Arn turned to them. "I saw …"

"What did you see, Arn?" Tulla snapped, suddenly tired of his act. "Harriet is dead, Arn." She was angry at this travesty of a man who seemed to be play-acting at grief, mocking the sorrow and horror of Harriet's murder. "So, you tell us what Miss D. knew."

He leaned over the railing, but not before Tulla caught the fear in his eyes. This part of his act was real. "I didn't see anything, not the sparrow. No, only mah Lord Jaysus, he sees all, he knows all, he knows, and Harriet knows the doctor make house calls …" He twisted and stumbled on his robe, falling to his hands and knees. Glancing at Tulla over his shoulder, he began to hum, rocking back and forth.

Tulla stared at him in revulsion, transported to that sun-dappled copse at the swimming hole, Arn's grotesque body and the small bent leg kicking to get away from him. She ran to the top of the ladder and scrambled down straight into Dr. Skinner, who was standing at the bottom.

He backed away from her. "I wondered why the trap door was open. I was coming to check. You have no business being up there."

Tulla shoved past him, only slowing down in the entrance hall when the pungent odour hit her. Rosalie appeared around the corner, pushing a hospital cart and studying a chart. "How did your … what's wrong, Tulla?"

Tulla leaned against the wall, retching, holding a hand over her nose and mouth, eyes streaming. "Arn …"

"What … what did he do?"

Tulla shook her head. "That smell."

Rosalie pointed at the bin attached to the cart. "Used adult diapers. From the Alzheimer's wing, poor souls. But what happened with Arn?" Rosie helped her to her feet. "You're so pale. It's not just the smell. You look like you've seen a ghost."

"I wish he was. I'm okay, Rosie. But listen, why is that man allowed to wander around? He scooted out of the room and upstairs on that chair thing and onto the roof. Wouldn't it be a good idea to keep that trap door locked?"

"Not again." Rosalie pushed her hair back off her forehead with a crooked elbow. "It *is* kept locked, and the key's down in the office. We have to keep it hanging in an accessible spot because of fire regulations, but how he can get it without being seen is a mystery. We'll have to put a leash on him."

Should have done that years ago, Tulla thought.

TWENTY-NINE

HARRIET DEAVER'S BODY was finally released from the Ottawa hospital mortuary to Bronson's Funeral Home in Parnell. When Tulla phoned to tell her father about the funeral, Brenda answered.

"Your father can't go, Tulla. He has pneumonia. They call it walking pneumonia. He's not bedridden, but he can't fly anywhere. I'm not even letting him come to the phone. You'll have to be his representative."

"How sick is he, Brenda? Should I come down?"

"No, dear, he's not on his deathbed, for goodness' sake. I wouldn't even have mentioned it, but you'd have wondered why he wasn't going to Harriet's funeral. He'll be fine. Don't fret. You have enough on your mind."

Tulla took a deep breath. "Tell him there's to be another service at the interment in the spring, Brenda. Give him my love and tell him I said to do whatever you say."

The Presbyterian church overflowed with flowers and mourners. Miss D. didn't have an honour guard of Hells Angels, but Eddy the Enforcer was there, tears streaming down his face. Hundreds of her former pupils from all over the country were there, too, including three members of Parliament, a Canadian senator, several NHL hockey players, two winners of the Giller Prize, and two repeat offenders for unarmed robbery out on day passes for the occasion. Miss D. had touched many lives. Emotions ran high in the church — grief and sorrow and a tidal swell of rage at her murderer.

Agatha Breeze, alone in the front row, sat ramrod straight, keening quietly. Tulla, Kat, and Mikhail were a few pews behind her, while Leo stood at the back, studying the mourners as they filed in.

"Poor soul," Kat whispered. "Let's go and sit with her."

"Too late." Mikhail tilted his head toward the pair bustling down the middle aisle toward Miss Breeze's pew.

"God, it's the Skinners," Kat said.

Aggie lifted her tear-stained face in defiance and flapped her hands, shooing them away.

"Let's go," Tulla whispered. "She shouldn't be alone."

"Too late again," Mikhail said as they watched Leo dodge out of the way of the retreating Skinners and slide into Miss Breeze's pew. She slumped sideways against him, shoulders shaking, and he slid an arm around her as the organ played the opening chords of Mozart's Requiem.

When the choir filed into the loft behind the pulpit, leaving the middle front seat of the alto section empty, muffled sobs filled the church. The coffin, dark oak like the wainscoting throughout the Deaver house, rested on a gurney, a single spray of white roses across the lid. The service was simple, with readings from the King James Version of the Bible and only one hymn, "Lord of the Dance," a choice that startled a few mourners, but not the ones who knew Miss D. best.

The sole break in tradition was the number of people who spoke, adding their own eulogies to the minister's. Norm Buchanan, now a federal deputy minister in Environment Canada, described Miss Deaver's intervention with his father — a man everyone in town had been afraid of except Harriet. "I was in her grade eight class. My father had beaten me again, but I told Miss D. I'd fallen again. That evening she marched up our steps, and whatever she said to my father, he never struck me, or my mother, again. I believe to this day she saved my life." He pulled an enormous handkerchief from his pocket and wiped his face.

Eddy the Enforcer was next. "I'd like to say Miss D. put me on the straight and narrow. Perhaps some people wouldn't call my path so straight and narrow. Miss D. never judged. But like Norm, I believe she saved my life, too. She … she made me understand I was as worthy of love as anyone else — something I never learned from my parents." He lifted his head and gazed out over the church. "I'm a tough guy. Miss D. gave me the strength to be tough. But this is the toughest I'll ever have to be. To endure losing her … the bastard who took her from us? I hope he fries in hell. I'll try my best to help put him there."

Even the minister nodded in agreement.

Next was Tulla. She walked to the front of the church and stood beside the casket. "Harriet Deaver was a beacon in our lives," she began, her voice low and trembling. She raised her eyes and looked out at the sea of mourners. When she saw Leo tilt his head and cup his hand behind his ear, she stood straighter and raised her voice. "A beacon of kindness, of courage, of intelligence. She was funny, feisty, and brave. She was the best friend any child could ever wish for. She was the best friend any adult could ever wish for."

Tulla turned directly to Aggie. "Her death has left us all bereft, no one more than you, Aggie. You and Harriet, you were the other half of each other. If she were here, she'd be sitting beside you. The two of you would be the Greek chorus, commenting, laughing …" Tulla halted again. "She's here in spirit, Aggie, and in our memories, in all our hearts. 'That bastard,' I quote —" she nodded to Eddy "— has taken her from us physically, but she'll be with us always."

Rubbing her wet cheeks, Tulla continued. "My father, Warren Murphy, was Harriet's closest friend, next to Aggie. Although I think, seeing everyone here, she was the best friend of all of us. She had such a huge heart, room for us all, but my dad was her friend from childhood. He's unable to be here today due to illness. Nothing else would have kept him away." She unfolded a sheet of paper and looked up. "He asked me to read this for him. It's in the way of a letter.

"'Dear Harriet, words cannot express my grief. And I hear you say, "well then, if there are no words, what are you doing speaking?" And as usual, you would be right. So I am leaving the words to one of your favourite poets, and mine, to tell you of our sorrow that you are gone. The poem is "Dirge Without Music," by Edna St. Vincent Millay.'"

Tulla began to read, her voice growing stronger with each verse.

"I am not resigned to the shutting away of
   loving hearts in the hard ground.
So it is, and so it will be, for so it has been,
   time out of mind:
Into the darkness they go, the wise and the
   lovely. Crowned
With lilies and with laurel they go; but I am
   not resigned.

Lovers and thinkers, into the earth with you.
Be one with the dull, the indiscriminate dust.
A fragment of what you felt, of what you knew,
A formula, a phrase remains, — but the best
   is lost.
...
Down, down, down into the darkness of the
   grave
Gently they go, the beautiful, the tender, the
   kind;
Quietly they go, the intelligent, the witty, the
   brave.
I know. But I do not approve. And I am not
   resigned."

The church was silent except for quiet sobbing. And then a single voice cut through the hush, an old voice rusty with tears, shaking with rage. Aggie stood, leaning on Leo. "You said at the beginning of this service, Reverend, that God had called Harriet to her eternal rest. I don't think God had anything to do with this because we all know God loved her. It was the Devil's work. It was the evil in this town. Harriet stood up to that evil, and now she's dead." Aggie sagged like a puppet whose strings had been cut. Leo caught her and lowered her gently back into the pew.

The minister hurried to her side, sat, and took her hand. "I think you're right, Aggie." He bowed his head a moment, then signalled to the pallbearers. Mikhail and Kat moved forward to sit with Aggie as Leo took his place by the coffin opposite Tulla, with Eddy and Norm joining them. Elvie moved into place, blind with tears. The sixth pallbearer walked to the coffin, a tall man in a bespoke woollen coat with a scarred face and sad eyes. They walked slowly, each with a hand on Harriet's casket, guiding it down the centre aisle on the wheeled gurney.

A long, silent procession of mourners filed out behind them. A line of cars escorted the hearse out to the cemetery beyond Crow Lake Road where Harriet would rest in a small mausoleum until the ground thawed. The six pallbearers stood as the coffin was lifted onto a shelf by the cemetery ground staff. There she would lie in the cold grey stone, waiting for spring and her proper interment.

As they turned to go, Leo held back and touched Jack's arm. "You didn't speak at the service."

Jack shook his head. "Harriet did not need me to tell her she was the mother I chose, and I the son she chose. But I have a new mission now."

They hugged in silence.

Tulla stumbled across the frozen ground among the tombstones and stopped before a large stone etched with a landscape — the shepherd bringing his sheep home at the end of the day. She knelt and wept.

THIRTY

KAT HUNG A SIGN on the door of the Klatch: CLOSED. BACK SOON.

"They'll just have to go sip at Tim Hortons," she told Tulla, who hesitated only for a few seconds.

"Gossip?"

"Thought I had you on that one."

"You always think so."

Maureen and Melissa drove her, Tulla, and Liam to the airport, leaving Parnell before dawn. The temperature had plummeted in the night again, making it so unseasonably cold for early December it felt as if winter was there for good. The tires thrummed on the frozen asphalt, and bare trees flashed by in the headlights, white and brittle as a line of skeletons.

They rolled up the ramp to departures and pulled into the curb at the WestJet sign. "What do you think, Melissa? Do we just say, 'Sod it,' and go with them?" Maureen pulled Liam's backpack from the trunk. "Here you go, love."

Mel squatted to hug her brother. "Have fun, kiddo. Watch out for the shar—"

"Melissa!"

"It's okay, Mum," Liam said. "There's only been one shark attack in fifteen years where we're going and that was because the guy was swimming right where a restaurant feeds them every night. He lost a leg. What a dork."

"How do you know that?"

"Googled it."

"Of course you did." Maureen ruffled his hair. "Take care of your mother and Auntie Tulla."

"And you take care of Mel," Kat whispered, giving Maureen a hug. "Keep a close, close eye."

"Won't let her out of my sight."

The plane bumped down the pitted runway and taxied to a stop in front of a small building fronted with palm trees bent almost double in the wind. A cheer went up when the door opened to a blast of moist tropical air.

"Bliss," Kat breathed. "Remind me again why we live in a country with six months of winter." She eyed the blustery sky. "On the other hand, is this still hurricane season?"

"Nope," Tulla said, "but it's often windy here at this time of year. There'll be great surf. We'll have to put Liam on a leash."

Inside the terminal, a calypso band of one welcomed the arriving passengers, and by the time their passports were stamped by a smiling official, their bags were already circling on the conveyor belt.

Kat shook her head in wonderment. "This is so not Pearson."

Liam shot past the customs agents and out the doors into the blazing sun.

"Hello, young man. You travelling alone?"

Liam skidded to a stop.

"Dad!" Tulla bent to hug him. "You promised not to meet us. You're not supposed to be —"

"It's walking pneumonia, darlin'. That means I'm *supposed* to walk." He leaned down to shake Liam's hand and said in a low voice, "I don't want to alarm you, but there seems to be a rather large green turtle on your back."

Liam giggled. "That's Franklin."

"Well, Franklin, I trust you can swim."

"Of course he can," Liam said. "He's a turtle."

"Good. He looks pretty brave, so he'll probably be fine with the lions, too."

Liam's eyes grew round. "You have lions? Real ones?"

"As real as your friend Franklin, but do you know what I don't have?"

Liam shook his head.

"I don't have a single grandson. So perhaps you could call me Grandpa. What do you think?"

Liam looked at Kat uncertainly. She was smiling. "Absolutely okay."

A huge sun hat tied with chiffon stepped out of the shade of the building. The face beneath it had skin of porcelain, pale and smooth, and a smile broad and welcoming.

"Brenda!" Tulla kissed her cheek and knocked her hat askew. After introductions, Brenda led the way to what appeared to be a London taxi parked under a sign that read NO STOPPING. CARS TOWED AT OWNERS' EXPENSE. A tall Bahamian in a blinding white jacket and black trousers with a red stripe stood next to its bumper.

"They have a chauffeur?" Kat said in awe to Tulla.

"No," Tulla whispered. "That's a cop in his dress uniform."

Brenda trotted up to the police officer. "Thank you, David. So good of you to watch the car for us."

"Okay, ma'am." He raised his voice. "Ma'am, this is a no-parking zone. I have to give you a ticket." He handed her a piece of paper and winked.

Brenda took off her hat, winked back, and climbed into the driver's seat.

"What was that all about?" Tulla asked Warren as she loaded their bags into the trunk.

"Brenda has made many very important friends down here, not the least of whom is every cop on parking detail. They all pretend to give her tickets so no one will know she's being given special treatment. And as far as I know, she's never once bribed anyone." He shook his head in admiration. "They just seem to like her."

Tulla smiled at him. "What's not to like?"

Brenda drove sedately down the middle of Grand Bahama Highway, traffic flowing about her like water around a rock.

Kat smoothed the leather seat. "What a car! I'm guessing a 1938 Rolls?"

"You know your cars," Warren said, turning around in his seat. "Limited edition. Well done. It's been completely restored. Took three years. Had to get parts from Britain.

We were told it belonged to the Duke of Windsor, the former King Edward VIII, when he was governor out here."

"For real?" Kat said.

"As real as Franklin and the lions. No idea. But it makes a good story."

Brenda smiled serenely. "Yes, Kat, it's true. Warren is a cynic. He insists on not believing what people down here tell him."

Warren smiled back. "And you believe everything they tell you."

"I do."

He turned to the back seat again. "That's why they all love her here."

Kat gazed out the window. "Can't believe it's December. What are those flowers? The bright pink vines?"

"Bougainvillea," Tulla said. "And those trees with the red berries are poison trees."

"You mean pepper, don't you, dear?" Brenda said.

"That's what I thought. When I was here with Portland, I picked the berries along the fairway at the golf course to grind up for spice. The groundskeepers were horrified, told me they were 'poison' trees. Spread like cancer, they said."

"Did you eat the berries?" Warren asked.

"I did."

"And?"

"Do you mean was I poisoned?"

"Yes."

"Apparently not. I'm still here."

"Ergo, they're not poisonous. Birds eat them, too." He turned to Liam. "That, son, is called scientific reasoning."

Tulla rolled her eyes. "Liam, first thing you should learn about your new grandfather is don't believe everything he says. So don't eat those berries."

"There's another shrub that grows on this island, Liam, with an interesting name."

Brenda turned to glare at him. "Warren!"

He whispered to Liam, "I'll tell you later when there are no women around. It'll be a secret between us men."

Liam beamed.

Brenda turned into the forecourt of a low bungalow on a lane dead-ending at the ocean. A high whitewashed limestone wall enclosed the grounds. Plaster lions sat at intervals along the top, each with a paw raised either in greeting or warning. Liam was enchanted. Kat whispered to Tulla that it looked as if they were swatting flies.

"They do, don't they?" Brenda said, overhearing. "They're from my family's crest and are more impressive on it than on the wall, but I kind of like them. Now, Warren, do not touch those bags. The girls can manage them. Tulla, you and Kat are in the big room at the end of the hall. Liam is right next door."

"In a cupboard under the stairs," Warren said. "That all right with you?"

"I guess so," Liam said doubtfully.

"Did you bring your wand?"

Liam's face cleared. "That's so cool. Like Harry Potter. But I don't have a wand."

"Well, let's go and find one in the garden. They grow on bushes down here, you know."

After a swim, a beach walk, and supper on the patio,

Kat went to put Liam to bed and Tulla helped Brenda in the kitchen.

"Brenda, Dad won't give me a straight answer, so I am asking you. Is he all right?"

Brenda untied her apron and hung it on the back of the door before answering. "He's much better than he was, dear, but tires very easily. Worse than the pneumonia, though, has been Harriet's death and the horror of you finding her. That's flattened him. He can't sleep, he grieves, he frets about you. And somehow he blames himself. Nothing I can say seems to be of any comfort." She lowered the blind on the window over the sink and turned back to Tulla. "He's been frantic with worry about you, and very, very cross with me when I, and our doctor, wouldn't let him go up to the funeral. He'd have gone, anyway, if you hadn't agreed to come to us right after."

"It's as well that he didn't. He'd be even more upset. The OPP investigators, including Leo even though it's technically not his case, think the killer was someone she knew well. No forced entry, and I know she usually kept her door locked. The town's gone into lockdown mode. Everyone suspects everyone else. Logic says the two deaths must be linked, but no one can see it. Dad would have been in the thick of it."

They both jumped when a chair scraped on the patio. "Are you two coming out or are you just going to stay in there gossiping about me?"

Brenda pulled the blind aside and peered out. "I thought you'd gone to bed. What are you doing out there?"

"Eavesdropping, and waiting for someone to bring me a nightcap."

THIRTY-ONE

KAT STOOD IN THE kitchen doorway squinting at her watch, hair squashed flat on one side, eyes puffy with sleep.

Tulla glanced up from her computer. "Before you ask about the silence, Liam's gone to the beach with his new grandparents. Sleep well?"

"Apparently. Twelve solid hours. You doing emails? Could you send one to Melissa?" She peered over Tulla's shoulder at the screen.

"Just did. Asked her to acknowledge same and to phone at suppertime. And I checked the CBC website for anything new on the murders. Nothing." She closed her computer. "Let's go out to the patio. I'll bring breakfast."

They settled side by side on the chaise longues. Kat pulled her nightgown up to the top of her thighs. "I'll expose my cellulite to the sun for just a minute. Don't want to frighten the lions." She leaned her head back against the cushions and inhaled deeply. "It's such a gift to see Liam so happy." She sipped her coffee. "He was giggling like a fool last night when I put him to bed. You know the plant your father was going to tell him about yesterday and Brenda stopped him? Well, he told him later. It's called 'stiff cock.' Liam nearly rolled off the bed laughing. This is just what he needs — a man like your father in his life to teach him that adult males can be decent people, funny, fun to be with, not just scary jerks." She closed her eyes against the sun. "Have we got an agenda today?"

"Yup. Beach, picnic, drinks, dinner, and —"

"The casino where you and I will make our fortunes. Oh, I'm forgetting. You already have one. However, as one of the possible previous owners of Brenda's car said so wisely, 'You never can be too rich or too thin.'" Kat squinted at her legs. "I'll settle for the rich part."

By dinnertime Liam was so blasted by sun, sea, and wind that his head was nodding like a poppy. "Come on, tyke, time for a bath and bed," Kat said.

"Not tired."

"Of course you're not. Nor are you sandy, oily, freckly, tickly." Kat pulled him to his feet and tickled him into whoops of laughter. She swung him up onto her shoulders and galloped out of the room.

"What a joy to have a child in the house," Brenda said. "I'd keep that boy forever."

"I think he's a package deal, darlin'," Warren said. "You'd be keeping Kat, as well."

"No problem there," Brenda said. "You too, Tulla. You must promise to stay until they find who killed Harriet."

"I still don't get why you're so worried about me in all this."

"Everyone knows how close you and Harriet were. Whoever killed her might think she told you something."

Tulla snorted. "That's rubbish. Harriet was close to a lot of people. She didn't tell me a thing unless you count her ramblings about evildoings in Parnell's past, which everyone but me seems to have known about, anyway." She pushed a crumb around her plate with a finger. "I can't get the image of her on the floor out of my head. You know, I think it's the only time I ever saw her lying down. She was always on the move, so full of life …"

Warren's face was suddenly grey with fatigue.

"You'll miss your friend," Tulla said quietly.

"So will you." Warren pulled a handkerchief from his pocket and blew his nose.

Kat met Tulla in the hallway, finger to her lips. "Liam's out like a light. And I talked to Melissa. She said to say hello and tell your dad that Maureen's pining for him."

"Perhaps that message should be iced. Any news?"

"No. Just said all was okay and she was loving it at the Priest Hole. It's a different class of waitressing entirely, she tells me, Miss Snooty Pants. I might have lost an employee. She said I could hire Charlene in her place."

"She's that surly little thing, isn't she? Her parents run the Russell?"

Kat nodded. "Mel's taken her under her wing. New kid at school, apparently having a bad time at home, fighting with her mother and stepfather who, to quote Mel quoting Charlene, is a sadistic brute. Anyway, both my kids are safe and accounted for. Worry quota down a pint, so let's roll."

The cab dropped them at the entrance of the casino where strobe lights criss-crossed the sky as if searching for incoming bombers. Music blasted into the night, and a security guard eyed them with interest as they pushed the door open. "Tulla? That you, baby?"

"Ivor? You're working here now?" She hugged him.

"More fun here than keeping druggies out of the hospital pharmacy. You lookin' *gooood*." He held her by the arms and studied her. "Taller, too. Whatcha been eatin' up there in Canada?"

Kat snorted.

"This is Ivor, Kat. We knew each other when Port was in the Rand Hospital. Used to sit and hold my hand in the cafeteria."

"Set everyone talkin'." Ivor's laugh was a throaty rumble.

They made their way past rows of slot machines, at least half of them with blank screens. A banner draped one wall in dusty folds announcing a slot tournament that had taken place a year before. A few tourists were feeding coins into the slot machines from what looked like yoghurt containers, their faces sweaty and glowing from sunburn and rum.

"Excuse me." Kat stood behind a man wearing a T-shirt that read BEER ON BOARD, an arrow pointing to a low-hanging belly. "Is that your credit card you just put in the slot? Can you just draw money from your bank account straight into the machine?"

Beer on Board turned, almost falling off the stool, and checked her up and down, eyes bleary. "Hey, sweetheart, sit right down." He patted the stool beside him, his full-arm tattoo proclaiming love for his mother. "How about a drink?" He searched around for a waiter. "First time here? You staying at the Sheraton?"

Tulla pulled her away. "That's not a credit card, idiot. It's a player's card. C'mon."

"Hey, what's your hurry? How about we all go over to Rum Runners and do some dancing?" Beer on Board lurched off the stool and attempted a pelvic thrust.

Ivor was suddenly beside them. "Tom, you've had a skinful. Time to quit." He took him by the shoulders and spun him toward the door.

"Just wait a fucking minute. I got money in that machine. You can't —"

"Watch your language! You gotta eat outta that mouth, you know. Time for bed."

"That's just what I been saying." He leaned toward Tulla. "Whaddya think, Legs?"

"Looks like it's going to be a fun night," Kat said.

Tulla led her to the horseshoe bar at the back of the casino where the overhead televisions silently broadcasted *American Idol*.

Kat squinted. "That's Carrie Underwood. Are we in a time warp here?"

"I used to watch that exact same show when I was here with Port. Want to know who wins?"

"Is that the bartender, that big woman in the spike heels? Her legs are even longer than yours."

They turned with their backs to the bar to watch the table action. A smoky voice spoke behind them. "White wine for you, Tulla Murphy. Don't know what your friend be drinkin'. Welcome home, baby."

"Belle! Thank you. This is Katarina from Canada, and she'd like —"

"A big pink drink with an umbrella in it." Kat pointed down the bar. "Please." Belle pulled bottles off the shelf behind her. Kat's eyes widened. "She's just poured enough booze into that blender to fell a horse."

"Saw you talkin' to Tom. You know him from the clinic?"

"Tom?"

"Dude in the stupid T-shirt. Ivor's just put him in a taxi, like every night. Poor baby. He a mess. His wife not doing too good."

"That guy's married?" Kat said. "Apparently, he forgot that little detail tonight."

"He forgets every night. That's why he comes here."

"To forget his wife?"

"Forget she's dyin'."

Tulla sipped her wine. Kat ran her tongue around the salty rim of her glass and watched her.

"Hey, Bar Lady! Could we get some service down here?" A florid-faced man waved his cigar to get Belle's attention. She stared at him without expression and turned back to Tulla and Kat. "I can always tell the people from the clinic, the sick ones and the people with them, wives, husbands, kids — sad. Lousy luck with their health, so they figure they'll catch some luck here." Belle shook her head. "The world or God or somethin' owes them."

Kat sipped a mouthful of pink slush. "Delicious." She jumped off the stool. "This is mine. Belle, what do we owe you?"

Belle waved a hand and strolled away, ignoring Cigar Guy, who was now banging the bar to get her attention.

"Drinks are free if you're gambling," Tulla said. "In reality, drinks are free if Belle decrees they're free. She's like one of those Greek goddesses. Bestows her benevolence on some, her malevolence on others. That guy with the cigar? He'll pay through the nose if he ever does get served."

The casino was getting busier now — sunburnt couples drifting in from long, boozy dinners at the expensive restaurants along the marina boardwalk, groups of young men waving beer bottles and nudging one another as pretty girls in short, tight dresses strutted by, giggling and preening. Some clustered around the roulette wheel, scattering their chips over the felt table like bread crumbs, laughing, drinking, sizing each other up for the night. The serious gamblers headed for the high-stakes blackjack or the no-limit Texas Hold'em tables.

Tulla led Kat to a bank of slot machines with oil wells gushing and an armadillo dancing in a frenzy across the screen. "Wanna be rich?" it screamed. "More rich?"

A waiter appeared behind them holding a tray with one huge strawberry daiquiri and a tumbler of white wine. "Belle's compliments. Good luck."

"Nice to have friends on Mount Olympus, Tulla," Kat said. "A toast — to good luck, good health, and good happiness." She raised her glass and paused. "And to the disappearance of ex-husbands — mine. And success for bookstores — yours. And —" Tulla lifted her glass, but Kat stopped her. "Wait, one more. And to safe kids and good friends."

They clinked glasses and drank.

THIRTY-TWO

"ANOTHER SUNNY DAY in paradise," Kat said, hooking a chair over for a footrest.

Liam came out onto the patio balancing a bowl of cereal topped with strawberries. "Nice bedhead, Mum."

"Think I'll go over to the clinic this morning, say hello to the gang," Tulla said.

Brenda studied her. "Liam, how about you, Mum, and I go to the Rand Nature Centre? We could drop Aunt Tulla off at the clinic and go on to see the flamingos."

"Cool. What about Grandpa?"

"I think he'll rest this morning."

Tulla stared at her, alarmed. "Is he not feeling well again?"

"No, dear, he's fine. Just tired. Don't worry about him. That's my job." She smiled at Tulla to soften the gentle warning: *my turf*. "I'll just make a little picnic for us."

She rose from the table and gathered her silk dressing gown around her. Tulla watched her with admiration.

She really was to the manor born in the best sense of the term. Graceful, kind, exuding a self-confidence that never crowded anyone else out, never overbearing. She rarely revealed the steel beneath the velvet.

"Liam," Brenda said over her shoulder, "what do you call a bunch of flamingos? It's a murder of crows, a mischief of magpies — at least the ones in England."

"A flamboyance of flamingoes?" Warren said from the kitchen doorway. "Good morning all. Liam, have you fed the lions yet? I think I hear them roaring."

Liam scrambled down from his chair. "What's a bunch of lions, Grandpa?"

"A pride."

"Doesn't work. Gotta be something with an *l*."

"Let's see. A line?"

"Nah. Lame."

"A lame of lions?"

Their chatter faded as they walked away down the wall of lions. Tulla put the breakfast dishes on a tray and followed Brenda into the kitchen.

"Leave those, dear. You go and get ready."

"I'll just load the dishwasher. Won't take a minute." Tulla picked up a plate and spoke with her back to Brenda. "Dad told me a nice thing you said when he was in Parnell, Brenda. That when he told you about Dom …"

Brenda waited for her to finish her sentence and finally said gently, "That Dom wasn't his son?"

Tulla nodded. "That you said you were relieved and that if he'd had a 'by-blow …'" She turned to face her. "You wouldn't have minded if it were Leo."

"I did say that." Brenda watched her. "I like him very much."

"He was down here, right? I just wondered why."

Brenda pursed her lips. "Your father didn't tell you?"

Tulla shook her head. "He said something about a drug bust. Didn't make much sense."

"What nonsense. Leo came down to talk to the people at the clinic about when his sister was treated there. You knew she'd been there?"

Tulla nodded.

"And you knew that the clinic director was convinced she didn't have cancer at all?"

Tulla's jaw dropped.

"Apparently, they have a blood test."

"I know about it."

"Well, it didn't find any cancer. I don't begin to understand these things …"

"Their test isn't used in mainstream medicine," Tulla said, "but the clinic relies on its results for treatment guidance. Has done so for years. This is incredible! If she wasn't sick —"

"Leo said she wasn't well when she was here. One of the nurses told him she was weak and could barely eat. Something was wrong, but it wasn't cancer."

"When was he here?"

"A couple of months ago. He came for dinner one night. He told us he had suspicions about how his sister died, that Dom might have had a hand in it."

Tulla was dumbfounded. "He talked openly about that? Leo talking openly about anything personal is amazing, but about Celia? Brenda, that's a huge compliment to you. And to Dad, too. He certainly trusts you both to have ... but what made him suspicious after all these years?"

"He found letters among his father's belongings from Celia to him that he'd never received. She didn't know where he was, had written several times in care of his father, but at that point his father didn't know how to reach him, either. Leo thought she'd just abandoned him. The last letter was from here after the clinic told her she might not have cancer. He showed it to us. It was the saddest thing I've ever read. Heartbreaking. I'll never forget the last lines." Brenda closed her eyes and recited: "'Leo, if I'm dying, my last wish is to see you again. If I'm not dying, it's my first wish. Please, please answer, Leo. I miss you, my little brother. I promised to take care of you forever.'"

Warren stood in the doorway. "Brenda, has anyone ever said you have a —"

"Big mouth? Not and lived to tell about it, Warren. Why didn't you tell Tulla why Leo was here? Is it such a big secret?"

"I think I know, Brenda. If Parnell found out, the rumours — which are bad enough — would get way worse. Yet another motive for Leo killing Dom. Am I right, Dad?"

"You are, darlin'."

Brenda hung up her apron and checked her watch. "Off you go, both of you. Warren, get your book and go lie down on the chaise in the shade. Tulla, your ride's leaving in fifteen minutes."

* * *

The Rolls purred into the clinic parking lot and stopped at the patient entrance. Tulla froze, paralyzed by memories.

Kat touched her arm. "You okay?"

"Fine. I'm fine. See you later. Don't hurry. I'll wait for you on that bench over there."

She watched the car edge out through the gates before pushing open the door into a large, cool room. Chairs lined the walls, with low tables stacked with books and magazines between them. A coffee machine hissed quietly, the aroma of slightly scorched coffee wafted in the air, and the silent, empty space suddenly filled with voices from the past: the laughter, the raucous bets among the patients on how long it would be until one of them was felled by coffee, not cancer.

Tulla swallowed hard, recalling Port's first day here — the fear, the hope, and his complete inability to deal with needles.

"You mean I have to poke these into myself twelve times a day?" he'd asked in disbelief. "I can't do that."

"You can, baby," the nurse had told him, holding up one of the hair-thin needles with its ampoule. "These needles are probably going to save your life."

She just hadn't said for how long.

That first day they opened the door into the waiting room to the sound of laughter. The room was full of patients and their relatives or friends, and it was hard to tell the difference. "It's like a cocktail party," she said to Port.

He raised an eyebrow, or at least where his eyebrow used to be. "Yeah, on the *Titanic*, and these people know about the iceberg."

"Amazing," Portland said to her after a few weeks. "There's old Death sitting right here in the room with us. We know he's there. We know he'll get us, maybe tomorrow or next week. He's in no hurry. He has all the time. We don't. Yet most of us can still yuck it up right in his face."

After three months on the serum, Tulla heard Portland on the phone with his father. "I know 'feeling better' doesn't necessarily mean 'getting better,' Dad, but it sure beats the alternative. I'm walking without a cane, I have much less bone pain, I'm even playing golf again."

They were on the golf course the day the little miracles ended — a humid morning with a gusty wind rattling the stiff palmetto leaves together like bones. Jaunty with his newfound stamina, Portland climbed out of the cart, waggled his club over his ball, and leaped into the air, dancing and slapping at his feet. "Jesus, what the hell!"

By the time Tulla got him into the cart, he was covered with fire ants biting his face, hands, arms, neck, everywhere. The manager was on the forecourt as she skidded to a stop in front of the clubhouse. "Fire ants, is it?" He eyed the tiny welts all over Portland's body. "A shower with carbolic soap will do the trick."

"He's having a reaction. He can't breathe."

"It's okay, not that ba ... bath." Portland struggled to speak with a rapidly swelling tongue.

Tulla swung into the Emergency entrance of the hospital and hit the brakes, the horn, and the curb all at the same time. Ivor was one of the security guards who pulled Portland out and onto a gurney while the triage nurse hustled Tulla inside. "What are we dealin' with here?" she asked, plucking a clipboard off the wall by the entrance.

"Fire ants and now he can't breathe."

"Is he on any medication?"

"He's being treated at the cancer clinic and he's had chemotherapy and —"

The nurse grabbed the phone. "I'll call the clinic. His name?"

"Portland Cole."

"He your husband?"

"No … yeah, sure." It was just easier.

"Well, baby, is he or isn't he? We need someone to sign forms."

Her name was Afrika. People called her "Afrika darling" out of affection for her, Tulla had thought, before she discovered that Darling was the woman's last name. She should have been called Afrika Angel. She saved Portland's life that day, but not his will to live.

Tulla had been completely unprepared for the end game. Afrika had come in to check on Portland's morphine pump, which he was convinced was plugged. The pain was out of control. His eyes pleaded with her.

Afrika spoke softly. "He's slippin' away, baby. He be going soon."

Slippin'. The ultimate euphemism. His head was thrust backward, arms and legs twitching as if caught in an electric current. Afrika took his hand and began to pray quietly. It was just as Port had predicted. Organs shutting down one by one "like the lights going out all over Europe, and I'm Europe," he'd said. His breathing grew more and more ragged, long silences punctuated by a rasping, grating gasp and then the last violent shudder that propelled life from his body as he arched over the bed. It was over.

And now here she was back in this town at this clinic, trying to prevent another kind of death, not with medicine but with the truth. And it looked as if she was having the same kind of success. None.

THIRTY-THREE

LAURIE WALKED THROUGH the doorway as if straight out of the day she'd given Port his lesson on self-injection. "Tulla Murphy, that you?" She took her hands and studied her face. "Not easy, I know. Too many memories for you." Tulla was mute. "Take your time, baby. Take your time. You want to see Dr. Carruthers?"

Tulla nodded.

Laurie reached for the wall phone. "Doctor? Good, you're still there. I have a special visitor for you."

Dr. Carruthers came loping out of his office, gangly as a giraffe, long legs accentuated by trousers belted just below his armpits and riding high on his ankles. "Well, well, my dear girl." He gathered her into a bony hug. "Come in, come in, sit, sit, sit." He ducked back through the door and pulled a chair out in front of a desk the size of a Ping-Pong table completely covered with files and papers. "Was just tidying up." He lowered himself gingerly into his chair as if from a great height. "Have to be careful now — old bones are getting brittle as glass." He stretched out a ridiculously long arm and studied his watch. "I wish I'd known you were on the Island. I have an appointment in a few minutes."

"With a boat?" Tulla had finally found her voice.

"One of the perks of being old and being the boss. May and I are going for a sail this afternoon to Myrtle Quay."

Even only after a few months, he appeared older, his short beard more grizzled, his brown scalp tonsured in grey. He was the heart of the clinic, cheerfully explaining to patients and their families that he really had no idea how the serum worked but what he did know was that it did. Often. Just as often as anything else worked with cancer, and better for particular ones, he said. His confidence was contagious. He had become a friend as well as doctor to Portland. They'd shared a love of sailing, horse racing, and really good martinis. The doctor had flown up to Portland's memorial service, a brave move since half the people there blamed him for Port's death.

Tulla had had to rescue him from one particularly aggressive uncle, edging toward senility and spraying out pompous and misinformed judgments along with gobs of spit. She'd stemmed the flow with a bald-faced lie: Portland hadn't died of cancer, but had been bitten to death by red ants, a deadly strain to be found only in the Bahamas and Africa, where they were known to build bridges across flaming rivers to reach their prey. The man had shuffled off to broadcast the shocking news.

"I won't keep you, just wanted to say hello and ask one quick question," Tulla now said.

"Fire away."

"It's about a patient who was here a while ago. You might not be able to tell me anything because of patient confidentiality, but —"

He held up a hand. "Try me."

"Her name was Celia Connolly. She was diagnosed with breast cancer at a Canadian hospital, but my father just told me this morning that your blood test indicated differently."

"I remember her for exactly that reason, as well as for the fact that her brother was here recently. We did the blood test twice. Neither detected cancer activity, yet her diagnostics from the original treating hospital in Toronto stated stage three breast cancer very clearly. I told her husband we were pretty sure she'd been misdiagnosed. When I told her brother this, he didn't seem surprised. Upset, but not surprised. Didn't say much. I like a man of few words. Means I get to talk more. The brother's a taciturn fellow, isn't he? Full of anger. Obviously adored his sister."

He pulled a few files together and stacked them neatly on top of a nest of others. They promptly slid onto the floor. He frowned at them as if they'd leaped off the desk on their own.

"Did you give Leo her records?"

Dr. Carruthers seemed sheepish. "Well, the bits and pieces we could find. We had a researcher here who pulled the record room apart, was doing some kind of statistical analysis of results of our treatment over the past twenty years. He gave up. He said he felt like Sisyphus tackling the mountains of records in the storage area. When he discovered there were more in the basement — mouldy, you can imagine — he said he felt like Hercules trying to clean the Augean stables. He certainly knew a lot about mythology … for a scientist. Anyway, we have everything almost back in order now."

Tulla glanced at the mess of files spread across his desk. "You found the missing bits?"

He nodded. "They'll be in the files now unless Tina pulled them when that doctor got in touch with us from Toronto, asking for Celia's records." He peered at Tulla. "Did I tell you about him?"

Tulla shook her head.

He tapped his forehead. "Needs an oil change. He said there had been a problem with the lab at the hospital where she'd been diagnosed — biopsy results over a period of months mixed up or something, letters sent out to all the patients involved to come back in for re-testing. It might be that Celia was one of these patients, which could explain why our test didn't find any cancer. We didn't know about any of this when Celia was here. I'll ask Tina to get the file." He pulled the phone across the desk, sending more files skittering to the floor, punched in a single number, and listened. "Who's that? Oh, I was calling Tina. Isn't this her intercom? What's her number then. Four? Rightyo, thanks." He punched out the extension again. "Tina? Oh, Eustace — the lab? Sorry." He slammed the phone down, went to the door, and yelled down the hall, *"Tina!"*

A voice floated back. "Dr. C., use yo' damn phone." A petite woman with a mop of curls and an uncanny resemblance to the singer Tina Turner appeared in the doorway, hands on hips. She glared up at him, then grinned at Tulla. "Welcome home, baby." She turned back to Dr. C. "What yo' want?"

"Would you be good enough to get Celia Connolly's file for us?"

Tina was already out the door, her spike heels clicking on the linoleum.

Dr. C. propped his feet on the desk. "Ask her about Celia's husband. She took a real scunner to him."

Tina returned with the file and a tray with coffee, milk, sugar, and a plate of enormous doughnuts.

"Get yo' feet off the desk," she said, handing him the file.

Dr. C. paged through it. "Here. The diagnostics from Princess Amelia Women's Hospital in Toronto. I was right. Stage three breast cancer, with metastases to liver and bones. Recommended treatment — bilateral mastectomy, chemotherapy, cisplatin cocktail, radiation followed by five-year course of an aromatase inhibiter ..." He flipped through the file. "Nothing about that happening, though. And no records of baseline studies — bone scans, MRIs, ultrasounds to establish extent of metastases. Yet the pathology report indicates mets. Curiouser and curiouser. Could those results still be misfiled?"

"I don't think we ever had them," Tina said. "But the researcher who had been digging around in our records found this in another file." She pulled out a sheet of paper and handed it to him.

Dr. Carruthers read through it quickly. "This is the last patient family conference. The meeting was recorded by Freedom Bethel — that's Tina's real name, Tulla. Attendees were patient's husband, Dominique Connolly, and a friend of the patient, whose name isn't given, just referred to here as X. The patient, Celia Connolly, wasn't in attendance." He looked up. "I don't remember any X. Do you, Tina?"

She shook her head.

"The report says I asked why the patient wasn't there. Her husband said she wasn't feeling well enough. I explained that the reason for the meeting was that we were still waiting for the patient's follow-up records from Toronto." Dr. Carruthers tapped the paper. "There we are. We never received those records. Let's see. We told the husband that no cancer was detected in two of our blood tests. Therefore, we weren't able to begin treatment. The person identified as X replied that our tests were a sham, and the husband concurred. I then recommended that the patient should go to Florida for further testing in Miami. The husband objected, saying that would be too expensive for a Canadian, that their medical insurance wouldn't cover it.

"Then I said that the patient should go back to Canada for diagnosis verification and that I hoped our clinic tests were right and the patient had been misdiagnosed. The husband asked if that was the case why was she so sick; X said it was because she had cancer. The husband then said he would take the patient back to Princess Amelia Women's Hospital with my letter. I told him I wanted to talk to the patient personally about our blood test results. The husband said no, that he didn't want to get her hopes up only to be dashed again. The meeting ended at ten thirty a.m."

"Did you tell Celia about this, Dr. C.?" Tulla asked.

"I did," Tina said. "I met her walking alone on the beach the next day. At first she couldn't take it in. She said that if she really didn't have cancer, she would never give up control of her life again. I thought she was talking about giving in to the disease, giving up. But these notes … I don't think that was it at all. Her husband seemed more like her keeper than her supporter."

"He didn't take her back to Canada," Tulla said. "The bastard took her to Mexico to a back-alley setup in Tijuana. That's where she died."

Dr. Carruthers was stricken. "Oh, I'm so sorry about that. Did you know, Tina?"

"No, I didn't. But I'm not surprised about her husband doing that. Handsome on the outside; beneath the surface, pure pitch."

"Did she seem afraid of him?" Tulla asked.

Tina thought for a moment. "Not afraid, but she was weak, no will of her own. She was sick, but not from cancer."

"She used to be so strong," Tulla said. "She pretty much raised her brother after their mother died of breast cancer. And then, God help her, she married Dom." Tulla got to her feet. "You'd better scoot, Dr. C., or May will be sailing without you. Leo hasn't seen these conference notes, has he?"

"No. The researcher only just found them."

"I could take a copy to him, unless, of course …"

"Patient confidentiality? Fiddlesticks. All yours." Dr. Carruthers unfolded from the chair like a dragonfly emerging from its pupa. He touched her shoulder and loped out the door.

Tulla sat on the bench in the shade of a bougainvillea, its arched branches dripping with crimson blossoms. Bees buzzed in the heat, and a single bird screeched at intervals like a cranky screen door. She lifted her head at the sound of the Rolls's throaty growl.

"A flap of flamingos!" Liam yelled from his window. "A flash of flamingos, a fan of flamingos."

"Who started this?" Kat groaned.

A short while later, when they turned through the gate of lions, Warren was waiting on the front step. Liam jumped out of the car and ran to him. "Grandpa, you should have come with us. There were a zillion flamingos and —"

Warren ruffled his hair. "Next time, son. Now you'd better go and wash up because lunch is nearly ready."

Brenda looked surprised. "You made lunch?"

When Liam was out of earshot, he said, "Leo phoned. There's been another murder."

"Oh my God, no. Who?"

"Arn. He was pushed off the roof of the Manor."

Kat and Tulla stood stunned. Brenda was beside Warren in an instant. "Come inside."

After lunch, which no one ate except Liam, Tulla phoned Leo, who for once answered before her call was flipped to voicemail. "Dad just told us about Arn."

"Yeah. Poor bastard."

She paced, the cord on the wall-mounted phone keeping her on a short leash. "This cannot be happening." She straddled a kitchen chair, resting her chin on her forearm along the back, phone pressed against her ear. "It wasn't an accident? That he'd tried to fly to 'Jaysus' or something?"

"He was pushed. The ground maintenance crew found him early yesterday morning and had the sense not to touch anything, but Roland didn't. The fool let the paramedics load up the body, so unfortunately any evidence is messed up, both around the body and on the gravel roof. If he'd just fallen against the railing, it might have bent, but the base screws on the uprights wouldn't have pulled out. Which they did. I've got forensics doing a sweep now."

"What's going on in that town?" Tulla had wound the telephone cord so tight around her wrist that her fingers had swelled into fat white sausages. She imagined his shrug at the other end of the phone line.

"You and Kat been behaving yourselves down there?"

Bite the bullet. "I've been to the cancer clinic."

"Why?" His voice was stony.

She jumped up and started to pace again. "To see Dr. Carruthers. He was so good to Portland and —"

"Why?"

"He gave me copies of the stuff from Celia's records that were missing when you were here."

"Just like that? Out of the blue?"

"Did you know someone else was with Dom and Celia when they were here?"

274

"Who?"

"No one knows. His name isn't in the notes, and no one can remember him. Oh, I've just thought of …" The phone jerked out of her hand as she reached the end of the cord, swung in an arc, and crashed against the wall.

"Dropped the phone. Listen, Leo, I know —"

"Tulla, leave it. It's history. Stop meddling. Got it?" The line went dead.

Brenda and Warren took Liam for a swim, and Kat and Tulla sat on the patio and pretended to read. Glancing up from her book, Kat said, "It's time."

"For what?"

"For you to tell me the real reason you went to the clinic without me. You're such a terrible liar. Brenda knew you were lying, too. Seeing the old gang, indeed." She bent the corner of the page she was on and closed the book, ignoring Tulla's frown. "It's a crap book, anyway. A dog ear isn't going to make it any worse."

"It's still a book." Tulla leaned back, arms behind her head, and studied the sky, cloudless above but with the usual afternoon pile of storm clouds over the western sea. "Funny how those clouds build up every day and threaten to blow us off the map, but they rarely do. Exactly opposite to the storms at home that come boiling out of nowhere and wreak havoc." She rolled her head toward Kat. "You knew that Dom brought Celia here for treatment."

"I didn't know that. Why here?"

"Apparently, she refused to have anything to do with surgery, chemo, or radiation because of her mother's experience — the disfigurement, the pain and sickness, loss of hair, all for nothing. She died anyway. So Celia went looking for another route."

"Did Leo tell you this?"

"God, no. Harriet did. Celia had helped bathe her mother toward the end and saw the terrible burns from the radiation. And the mastectomy scars, which in those days were pretty ugly. Slash, poison, and burn — I can understand why someone would turn away from it all and search for another option. Like Portland, but Celia didn't go the traditional route first. Not even surgery, according to her medical records. So they came here. That was the story, anyway.

"Dad let slip that Leo was here a few weeks ago. He went all shifty-eyed when I asked why, claimed it was police work. I knew he was lying, but I couldn't figure out why it was such a big secret. I know now." She swung her legs over the side of the chaise and leaned forward, elbows on her knees, chin in hands. She spoke very quietly, as if someone other than Kat might be listening. "Leo thought Dom was responsible for Celia's death, and he came to ask questions at the clinic."

"But didn't she die of cancer like her mother?"

"Logical thinking. Family history being a major risk factor, no one questioned it. Why would they? Except Leo. Dad didn't want anyone back home to know Leo had been here, let alone why."

"Because it gives him an even stronger motive for killing Dom."

"Right. So I figured the clinic people could tell me something that would convince Leo she died a natural death, if cancer can be called natural. Then there would be one less motive for Parnell to pin on him. But my plan backfired. Dr. Carruthers doesn't think Celia ever had breast cancer, that it was a misdiagnosis."

"So if she didn't have cancer, what did she die of?"

"Dom. Death by Dom."

Kat grimaced. "This is looking worse and worse for Leo."

"Kat, Leo is *not* a murderer. And if he did kill Dom, it would have been an accident, and if it wasn't, it wouldn't count as murder if it turned out that Dom killed his sister."

"Are you hearing what you're saying, Tulla?"

"Yes," she said miserably. "But look, there's absolutely no way he killed Miss D. I was there when he arrived and saw her on the floor. He's not that good an actor."

"How do you know? You haven't seen him for decades. People do change, you know."

"That's what Harriet said. You're both wrong. So shut up."

Kat held up both palms to fend her off. "I'm being devil's advocate, dummy. Of course, I don't believe he murdered Miss D." They stared at each other. "But if he did kill Dom, that means there are two murderers in Parnell. Or maybe three. Because someone pushed Arn."

THIRTY-FOUR

AN HOUR DOWN THE coast was a favourite beach of Brenda's — miles of soft white sand lined by the sea-scoured remnants of a stand of mangroves twisted like skeletons by a hurricane years before. She said it was like picnicking in a forest of Giacometti sculptures. For the two days after her visit to the clinic, Tulla was so quiet and withdrawn that Brenda decreed a picnic was in order. "Take your mind off things," she said.

"Things being Leo," Kat added.

When he saw her preparations, Warren asked Brenda what army was joining them for lunch.

"Talk to Melissa this morning?" Tulla asked as they gathered up bathing suits, towels, sunscreen, chairs, goggles, flippers, masks, and bocce balls.

"Had a text," Kat said. "All's well. She's loving it at Maureen's restaurant. Claims it has a classier clientele than the Klatch. Can you imagine anything classier than the Moose People?" Kat picked up Liam's soggy, sandy bathing suit and gave it a shake. "Did I hear you talking to Leo this morning? Just asking. I'm always curious when someone takes their telephone calls in a cupboard."

"I couldn't hear properly in the bedroom."

It took three trips to get all their essentials from the car park four hundred metres through the mangrove marsh to the beach. Liam hurled himself into the sea like a puppy let off his leash. Tulla ran out after him, grabbed his hands, and swung him high over the gentle surf. His laughter floated back on the breeze.

"That's it," Kat said. "We're never going home. Melissa's just going to have to come here for the rest of her life."

They packed up a little before sunset and trudged fully laden back to the car. Except for Brenda, who led them through the mangroves, empty-handed and cool. Liam slept all the way home.

The phone was ringing as Warren unlocked the front door. Tulla dropped her armful of soggy towels and dashed for it, but it had already switched over to voicemail. There were several messages, the first from Mikhail. "Tulla, please phone me when you get in."

Uh-oh. Wonder what Clancy's done now. She hit the button for the next message. "Hi. Maureen here. Kat, need to talk to you. Phone me as soon as you can before you talk to anyone else, but don't fret."

Tulla froze and glanced over her shoulder to see if Kat had heard, but she was still outside trying to extract Liam from the car without waking him. Tulla took the phone off speaker and pressed the receiver to her ear but could barely hear the next message. It was low-pitched, as if the caller had covered the mouthpiece. "Do you know where Melissa is? Is my daughter with her? Please call this number. Don't phone the hotel. Please don't phone the hotel. Oh, God!" And the message ended.

Replaying it, Tulla strained to make out the voice as Kat came by, Liam draped over her shoulder like a rag doll. "Who is it?" she whispered.

Tulla held up a finger and shook her head. As she played the message a third time, her cellphone rang in her purse. She scrambled for it and checked the screen. "Leo, what's going on? What's happening? Where's Melissa?"

"You've heard from Maureen?"

"And Mikhail and a complete stranger — all voice messages. We've just come in."

"Does Kat know?"

"Know what?" Tulla asked, her voice rising. "She's here now. I'm putting you on speakerphone."

"Kat? Listen, Melissa's gone off somewhere, possibly with Charlene, the kid who works in the Russell coffee shop. Maureen had a text message from her saying she was okay, not to tell you, that you'd just worry. Thing is, now she's not answering her cell or texts. Thought you might have some idea where they could be."

Kat slid down the wall to the floor and looked up at Tulla with huge eyes. "Oh, God, oh, God, no."

Leo's voice over the speakerphone sounded tinny and unconvincing. "Mel left a note for Maureen apologizing for missing her shift and that she'd repay her for the food from the restaurant fridge. Seems evident that she planned this disappearance, that she knows what she's doing. I didn't want to tell you until we knew more but was afraid you'd hear from someone else and think the worst."

"This *is* the worst. I'm coming home."

"Would she have taken your car?" Leo asked.

"She doesn't have her licence yet." Kat's voice was barely under control. "The car's in the garage."

"Okay, listen, put me on with Tulla again."

"I'm here, Leo."

"Am I still on speaker?"

Tulla punched the button. "No."

"Kat's car is gone. She should come as soon as possible, obviously, because there would be no way to keep her there. But is there any way you and Liam can stay down there?"

In the hallway, Kat was rocking back and forth on the floor, face down on her knees. "No way I'm letting Kat go by herself, but I'm sure Brenda and Dad will keep Liam. If Kat will leave him, which I doubt."

"Tell her it's the safest plan. When kids start to go missing — it sounds as if Charlene ran away and Melissa's gone with her, probably in her help mode. Whatever, she's put herself in danger, too. I've just pulled in to the Russell." Tulla heard brakes squeal and a car door slam. "Going to talk to Charlene's mother."

"That's who must have left that other message. I got it wrong. This scary voice asked if we knew where Melissa was, if she was with her daughter. Didn't say her name or Charlene's. I thought it was someone threatening Kat, asking if she knew where *her* daughter was."

"Call me when you know what flight you'll be on." The phone disconnected.

Tulla ran down the hallway and slid down beside Kat. "Listen, you and I will go back as soon as we can get a flight. But Leo says Liam should stay here."

Kat raised a face wet with tears. "*No!* I'm not letting him out of my sight."

Tulla put an arm around her shoulders and pulled her tight. "Listen, Kat, I know you're terrified, but Leo says this will be the safest thing for Liam. He didn't mean Liam in particular would be in danger, but that it would be better if you didn't have to worry about him, too."

Kat continued to rock, her arms clutched across her stomach. "I can't do this, Tulla. I can't stand it. Since Mel was born, and then doubled when Liam was born, I've been so frightened that I wouldn't be able to protect them." She grabbed Tulla's arm. "Phone Leo back now. Tell him to find Shug. He might just pull a stunt like this."

"Mum?" Liam stood in the hall rubbing his eyes.

Kat scrambled to her feet and scooped him up.

"Why are you crying?"

"Salt water. Should have worn my swim goggles."

Brenda had the car at the front door early the following morning to take Tulla and Kat to the airport. She had called in some markers, as she put it, to get seats for them on the return leg of the WestJet round trip from

Ottawa via Montreal. Warren was taking Liam on the glass-bottom boat trip that afternoon.

"Will there be sharks?"

"You bet," Warren said, "and octopuses and giant stingrays. They come right up to the glass looking for little boys to sting."

"Warren!" Brenda said.

He took Liam's hand and dropped his voice in a conspiratorial whisper. "We'll buy a special lunch in the marketplace. What does Franklin like to eat?"

"Ice cream."

"Okay. What else?"

"Jelly beans from that shop with the big tubes of candy in the window."

"I think that probably covers the five food groups." He stood on tiptoe to kiss Tulla's cheek. "Keep safe, darlin'." He hugged her hard. "And, Kat, Melissa will be fine."

Liam scrambled into Kat's arms and buried his face in her neck. "I want to go with you."

Kat squeezed him so tight he whimpered. "I'll phone you every night, and you can tell me if Grandpa's behaving himself."

THIRTY-FIVE

LEO STRODE UP to the till. "Afternoon, ma'am. Charlene off today?"

The woman didn't look up. "She doesn't work here anymore."

"Sorry to hear it. How come?"

"You should know," she burst out, slamming the drawer shut. "You're one of them, aren't you?"

"One of whom? Where is she?"

"You tell me." She stared defiantly, eyes flooding with tears.

Leo pulled his badge out of his back pocket and flipped it open. "Ma'am, I'm a police officer and —"

"I *know* who you are. You think I'd go to the police? They'd be the last people I'd go to in this town." Suddenly, she crumpled forward, her ample bosom spreading like a pillow over the counter.

"Come around here and sit." He steered her to a table, went over to the coffee shop door and flipped the sign to CLOSED. Then he pulled paper napkins from the dispenser and handed them to her as he sat opposite. Her hands shredded them like two frantic animals making a nest.

"Ms. … I'm sorry. I don't know your name."

Her fingers rolled the paper into soggy pellets.

"Ma'am, I know Charlene has disappeared. You have to help me here because she might be in danger."

Her hands jerked, and the pellets scattered across the tabletop and onto the floor. "We can't talk here. He might come back and see us."

She tried to stand, but Leo gripped her wrist. "Sit."

She collapsed back onto the chair. "She left … three nights ago. Neil said she was fine, that I wasn't to contact anybody, especially the police. I don't know many people in this town and —"

"Neil? Your husband?"

"He's the manager here. Charlene's stepfather. I should never have married …"

"And he told you not to worry about her? Did you and she have a fight? Did she have a fight with him? Could she be staying with a friend and not have told you?"

"No, we didn't have a fight, or not more than usual. She only started at the high school here this year. She doesn't have any friends that I know of except that girl Melissa. Her mother owns —"

"I know Melissa. You phoned her mother today, didn't you? In the Bahamas?"

"The Bahamas? I didn't realize. The Koffee Klatch is closed and the machine there gave a number to call in case of emergencies." She looked up at him with sudden hope. "Is she there with Melissa and her mother?"

"No. And Melissa isn't there, either."

She deflated like a balloon. "I knew they were planning something …" She dug into the pocket of her apron and pushed a cellphone across the table with a trembling hand. "This is Charlene's. Neil doesn't know I got it for her. Said she didn't need one. It's a pay-as-you-go." She paused, took a big breath, closed her eyes for a second, then continued. "When she didn't come home, I went looking for something — a note — and I found this. She never goes anywhere without it. I checked her text messages." She paused again, embarrassed. "I've done that before to try to keep track of her, but she usually deletes them right away. But there are messages to and from Melissa, I think."

Leo studied the dark screen and handed it back to her. "Show me."

She punched some keys and gave it back. Leo read the texts:

> Getting worse. He a pig. Have to get outta here
> Ur mother help
> No, useless. She scared 2
> Can u get to my place
> Now
> ASAP. If he stops u say ur helping at Priest Hole
> Ill try

Leo looked up. "Is there a date somewhere on these?" She pointed.

He pocketed the phone. "Let's go talk to Neil."

"*No!* He'll kill me if he knows I've talked to anyone. No, please." She grabbed his arm as he stood up.

"Ms. … look, what's your name. Tell me now."

"Leach," she whispered. "Lena Leach."

"Ms. Leach, do you want to find your daughter?"

She nodded wordlessly.

"Then let's start with your husband."

"He'll think I called you. That's why I yelled at you when you came in." She gave a furtive glance around. "I thought he might have come back, might have seen you come in."

"Where is he and how do I reach you directly? Do you have a cellphone?"

"Yes, but I can't find it." She clapped a hand over her mouth. "Oh, no. Neil might have it. I thought he didn't know I had one, but he must have found it. No one knows the number except Charlene. If she's trying to reach me, he'll answer it."

"Unless she's with him. Give me the number." He handed her his notebook and a pen.

Lena moaned. "Oh, please, God, he hasn't taken her to that place."

"What place?"

"Charlene said he was involved in something bad at a place called — it's a bird's name …"

"Bluebird?"

"That's it. She wanted me to tell someone. I didn't know who to go to. Neil has a lot of friends in this town, and I didn't know who I could trust." She hung her head. "I should've done something. The day after Charlene disappeared I heard him tell someone on the phone that he'd meet them at that Bluebird place, that he'd have another delivery. Two for the price of one, he said."

Leo jerked his head up.

"And that this would earn them brownie points with the new guy. I don't know what he was delivering. Maybe drugs. I don't know." She jumped to her feet. "Please go. He could come in any minute." She ran across the café and peered through the glass into the lobby. "Tim didn't see you come in, did he?"

"No idea, but since I'm staying here he'd hardly be suspicious."

"Yes, he would. He's Neil's spy."

"Ms. Leach, call me immediately if you hear from Charlene." He peered at his cellphone. "My number should show in here somewhere. The phone's new."

She took it from him and pointed at the screen.

"Oh, it's the same number as my old phone." He scribbled it on a corner of a napkin and handed it to her. "Call me anytime, day or night. If you hear anything, if you see anything, if you need help with your husband, anything." He flipped the sign back to OPEN and strode out through the lobby.

THIRTY-SIX

THE CANDLES GAVE OFF a lovely cinnamon smell but not much heat. Even so, the girls, cocooned in their sleeping bags like a pair of monks, huddled over them as if they were little campfires.

"Stop kvetching," Melissa said.

"What's kvetching?"

"Whining, moaning, complaining, generally being a pain in the butt."

"Well, I'm freezing."

"Me, too."

"And starving."

"Oh, Char, get a grip! Starving is when you live in Africa during a seven-year famine. We ate a few hours ago."

Charlene sniffed. "It was cold and horrible."

"Well, tough. It was too risky to put on the lights and the stove."

"And I'm scared."

"There you have a point. But consider the alternative — you could be in the hands of your ugly stepfather, being dragged off to God knows where."

The candle flames danced in the draft from the plywood-covered windows, casting shadows across the ceiling.

"Can't you turn your flashlight on?" Charlene whispered.

"The batteries are dying, and besides, someone might see the light from outside." She pulled her sleeping bag up to her chin and gazed into the flames. This would be their third night in the empty, freezing house, which had definitely not been her plan. She'd thought it would be straightforward: she'd collect Charlene and drive straight to Mikhail's or Maureen's. No way would they go to the police station — Charlene had put paid to that idea, saying, "Neil's a friend of the chief of police. I heard him on the phone talking about that Bluebird place. He was furious when he saw I was listening, and hit me in the face."

Mel had tried in vain to track Leo down. Not only was he not answering his phone but his voice mail was full. Then Mikhail. He seemed to have vanished, too, his phone giving her the same frustrating response every time she rang: "The party you are trying to reach is not available." Maureen's phone ditto. The restaurant phone had a message saying the place was closed for the week and wasn't taking reservations.

"Where the hell is everybody?" Mel now asked out loud. "God, I wish Mum and Aunt Tulla were here. What about your mother, Char?"

Char stared at her in alarm. "*No!* She'd probably turn us over to Neil. She's that afraid of him. What about your stepfather?"

"Are you nuts? I wouldn't ask that guy for help if I was drowning. He's scum. And he's not my stepfather. No way."

Char spoke hesitantly. "Has he ever … touched you?"

"You mean hit me?"

"Well, that, or … you know."

"Never. Never. Never. I'd kill him. Or Mum would."

"Couldn't we just go to anyone's house? They'd take us in."

Melissa was quiet for a long time, watching the candles as if they held the answer. "I don't think that's a good idea," she said finally. "It's as if Parnell is under siege. These murders have made everyone so suspicious of one another. I don't think they'd even answer the door. And if someone did, with our luck, it would be someone who'd say, '*Tsk, tsk*, you have to go to the police,' or worse, they'd be one of the bad guys. One of your father's —"

"Stepfather."

"Stepfather's gang."

After their first bone-chilling night in the empty house, they had tried to go to the Priest Hole where it was warm and no one would be suspicious if the lights were on. They'd set out after dark, taking back streets, driving slowly, hearts thumping.

"A car has just turned onto the road behind us," Char whispered.

Melissa doused the headlights, sped up, took the next corner too fast, and slid off the road into a snow-filled lane. She kept her foot down, ploughing the car as far as she could to get it out of sight. It came to rest quite gently against a pine tree whose branches shed their weight of snow over the car like a mantle. The engine coughed and died.

They sat in the sudden silence, listening to the engine tick, straining to hear if the car had followed them. After what seemed an eternity, they climbed out and surveyed the damage. "This baby isn't going anywhere anytime soon," Mel whispered, shining her flashlight on a pool of fluid staining the snow around the front of the car. "Do you think that's gasoline?"

"Or maybe from the radiator. I don't know."

"Oh, boy, Mum's going to be so pissed."

"I think that might be the least of our worries," Charlene said, her voice shaking. "Now what?"

"We go back."

It took them over an hour, avoiding the main streets, hiding every time a car came by. The houses they passed were all in darkness, like fortresses in lockdown for the night. No succor there.

Now it was their third night, and Mel suddenly exploded. *"Stop snivelling!"*

Charlene began to wail. "I'm not snivelling. I'm sniffing. The cold's making my nose run. I can't stand this. We can't stay here. We're going to freeze to death."

Mel struggled to her feet. "Okay, we'll hide in the Klatch for the rest of tonight, but we can't put any lights on. Frank has a key, so he could turn up anytime. Besides, they'll be watching the Klatch like hawks."

"Why can't we go to your house?"

"Same reason. They'll be watching it. They probably keep searching it. Come on."

They scooped up their sleeping bags, put out the candles, and crept down the hallway by the light of Melissa's fading flashlight. "One good thing, Char. If they notice Mum's car is gone, maybe they'll think we got out of Parnell."

When they reached the trap door, Mel put her finger to her lips, handed Char her sleeping bag, and pocketed her flashlight. She eased the trap door up and a sliver of light knifed down the stairs.

"Char, did we leave a light …?" The trap door flew up and a hand grabbed her hair. "Nice of you to join us, girls. We've been waiting."

"Char, go back! Go back!" Mel screamed, fighting against the hand hauling her through the opening.

"Get the other one!" the voice ordered.

Frank scrambled down the steps and re-emerged dragging Char. He flung her down and swore. "She bit me, the little bitch."

Neil hauled Char to her feet. "You've caused me a lot of bother, Charlene." He hit her across the face. "You know I don't like to be disobeyed."

He hit her again, and Melissa flew at him. Frank caught her around the waist, restraining her. Neil's attention didn't waver from Char, who had fallen to the floor, blood flowing from her nose and a cut on her cheek. He pulled her to her feet and swung again just as Melissa drove an elbow into Frank's soft gut, leaped across the kitchen, spun, and kicked Neil in the groin. When he buckled in pain, she aimed another kick at his head, missing by a hair. He grabbed her foot and twisted her off balance. She fell hard, her head bouncing off the side of the stove. The fight was over.

THIRTY-SEVEN

KAT AND TULLA HAD their phones on before the plane rolled to a stop at the gate. "No messages," Kat said, her voice panicky. "You?"

"One from Leo to say that Nob will pick us up." They pushed past other passengers. "Sorry, sorry, an emergency," Tulla muttered all the way off the plane and to the front of the immigration line, ignoring the dirty looks cast their way. They ran down the escalator and pulled their carry-on bags through the crowd toward Nob, who was waiting next to the baggage carousel.

"C'mon, c'mon, no time to wait for your bags." He strode toward the exit doors.

"Don't have any," Tulla said, but he was already halfway across the atrium. They ran to keep up, struggling into their coats. "Wait, Nob, wait. Have the girls been found?"

He turned and looked at them blankly. "What girls? *Come on!*" Sweat beaded on his forehead despite the cold.

Tulla caught his arm. "Nob, are you all right? What is it?"

Kat caught his other arm. "What do you mean 'what girls?' Aren't you looking for Melissa and Charlene? Aren't the police searching? What's going on?"

"What's going on is there's been another murder —"

"We know about that," Tulla interrupted. "Leo said someone pushed Arn off the roof."

"He was shot." Nob's voice rose to a shout. "He was shot." People around them stared.

"Arn was shot?"

"*No!* Not Arn. The chief."

"Roland? Oh, my God. Leo didn't say —"

"Leo doesn't know. Elvie found him an hour ago when she came on shift. She radioed me. In his office. C'mon, I gotta get back. Move it."

They stumbled through the revolving door into a blast of freezing wind and ran to the cruiser parked half on the sidewalk, lights flashing. When the car door resisted Nob's shaky attempts to pull it open, he smashed his fist into it in frustration. Tulla grabbed his arm. "You're in no condition. I'll drive."

"Get in the back," he said, jerking the door loose. "I'm driving."

"Like hell you are." Kat snatched the keys from his hand. "I haven't come all this way just to be killed before I can find Melissa. Get in!" She propelled him around the car and into the passenger side. "Put your seat belt on." She handed the keys to Tulla and jumped into the back. "Go."

The radio squawked static. Nob had to translate. All hell had broken loose. Word was already out that an officer was down. The RCMP and OPP detachments from across the province were mobilizing. There was talk of a manhunt. Elvie had already alerted the CIB, and a forensics squad was on its way. An anonymous voice in the ether suggested that the unit should rent an office in Parnell.

"Is Elvie alone there? Has anyone arrived to help? Where's Leo?"

Nob leaned forward and switched bands. "Elvie? It's Norbert. Has anyone arrived from other units? Ten-four."

Kat pushed her face against the mesh between the front and back seats to hear better. "Not from other units," Elvie said. "The paramedics are here. But there's nothing they can do for the chief. They're just keeping me company. I phoned Dr. Skinner. He's on his way. Where are you?" Even through the static they could hear her voice quavering. Elvie, afraid of nothing, was frightened.

"On my way back. Tulla and Kat are with me."

Tulla took the microphone from Nob and spoke into it. "Elvie, it's Tulla. Have you heard from Leo?"

No response, just static.

Nob grabbed the microphone back. "You have to push the button. Just drive. I'll hold it."

Tulla repeated her question. Still static.

"Say ten-four or over because she won't know to talk."

"Oh, Elvie? Ten-four."

"No, he's not answering his phone and I don't know where he is. Over."

"Okay, just a sec and I'll put Norbert back on."

She looked quickly over at him and then back to the road. "This is important. Tell Elvie to keep the para-medics with her, and when Skinner comes, they mustn't let him into the chief's office."

"I can't tell her that. I don't have that authority."

"Yes, you do. Think about it, Nob. You're in charge now. You're next in line in the Parnell force." She didn't add, *The only one in line.* "Tell her the medics will help her with Skinner. There's no love lost there, and Skinner *will* give her a very hard time."

"But he's the coroner, Tulla. He has to see the body … the crime scene. We can't keep him out."

"Please trust me, Nob. I saw what he did at Harriet's. He's either starting to lose it or was mucking things up on purpose, probably to antagonize Leo. You have to make sure that doesn't happen here. Tell Elvie to seal the office until either the CIB detectives or forensics arrive."

Nob switched the mike on. "Elvie? Don't let Skinner into the chief's office. I'll explain later. That's an order. Ten-four."

"Copy that. Over." They could hear the doubt in her voice.

"The medics will help you deal with Skinner. They can seal the office. The crime scene tape is in the broom closet. Okay, Elvie? Ten-four."

"I can handle Skinner, Norbert. Don't worry about that. I'm okay. You? Over."

"Yeah, I'm okay. You be careful, Elvie. Hear me? Ten-four."

"Copy that. You drive carefully. Roger and out."

They made it back to the outskirts of Parnell in under three hours. Tulla drove fast and focused, watching for patches of black ice that glinted in the headlights every few miles. Cold gripped the car in a fist of darkness, the silence inside the car broken only by the clinking of belt hardware when Nob shifted position. Tulla kept an eye on Kat in the rearview mirror, watching her rock back and forth against her seat belt. The body language of both passengers screamed for her to go faster.

In the east a huge winter moon appeared over the trees. *Maybe it's a good omen*, Tulla thought, and wrenched her mind back to the road to keep the panic at bay.

At the Parnell exit she pulled off onto the shoulder and unclipped her seat belt. "You all right to drive, Nob?"

They switched sides, Nob hit the flashers and siren, spun the wheels sending out a shower of icy gravel, and raced into town. Kat yelled from the back seat, "Drop me at home, Nob, before you go to the station. I'm on Bell at the corner of —"

"I know where you live." Nob slowed for an intersection and then accelerated through and down Main Street, around the corner, and rocked to a stop in front of Kat's house. He punched a button on the dash, and the back door swung open.

"Go with Nob, Tulla. I'll come to the station as soon as I've checked the house and the Klatch and Maureen's." She climbed out of the car and ran up the walk, dragging her case over the snowy ruts.

"Wait!" Tulla yelled after her. "You haven't got a car. Get mine and I'll wait for you at the station."

Kat turned. "What do you mean I haven't got a car? It's in the —"

"No, it isn't." She tossed her car keys to Kat, and Nob slammed the car into drive. Tulla put her hand on his arm. "Wait until we see she's okay."

Kat fumbled with the lock and ran into the house, leaving the door wide open behind her. A minute later she reappeared, shook her head once, and disappeared back inside.

They heard raised voices as soon as they jumped out of the car in front of the police station. "Oh, boy, Skinner must be going nuts." Tulla broke into a run.

"That's not Skinner. That's Elvie's voice. She's in trouble." Nob sprinted past her and wrenched the door open.

Tulla peered over his shoulder. "It's okay, Nob. Elvie's not the one in trouble."

Elvie stood with her back to the chief's office door, which was draped with crime tape, staring down at Thurston, who was spitting with fury and stamping his tiny booted feet in a dance of frustration. "You stupid dyke!" he screamed, his squeaky voice rising higher with every word. "Get out of my way! You have no authority. I have every right to go in there."

Elvie towered over him, almost two metres of solid contempt if you counted the modified mohawk gelled to a point at her forehead, her arms folded, eyes snapping. "I've already told you that no one's going in there until the forensics people get here." She smiled at Nob as he lumbered toward her. "I'm fine, Norbert. I can handle this twerp. Piece of cake after Dr. Skinner. The medics had to practically carry him out. But I'm so glad to see you." She stepped around Thurston and hugged Nob in an embrace that would have winded a lesser man. Tears streamed down her face.

Nob patted her back awkwardly, his head level with her shoulder. "It's going to be fine, Elvie. It's going to be all right." He was weeping, too. Tulla watched them in amazement, clinging to each other in a bubble of mutual comfort. They must have really liked the guy.

Thurston's voice burst the momentary calm. "When you two freaks are through blubbering, one of you open that door *now*."

"No," Nob said with a quiet dignity Tulla had never heard before. The same way she'd never seen him run so fast as when he thought Elvie was in trouble.

"You're fired! As of this second, you're fired. Give me your badge. And give me the fucking key."

"Know what, Thurston? I don't care if you are the mayor. I wouldn't care if you were the prime minister. I'm not giving you the key and I'm not giving you my badge. I'm in charge and I'm telling you to leave."

Thurston gaped at him. "You'll be under arrest by the end of the day, you dumb jerk." He pushed past Tulla and stormed through the door.

"Way to go, Nob," Tulla said. "But you'll have to watch your back now."

"I'll watch his back," Elvie said.

At that moment Tulla got it. It wasn't that the two of them loved the chief; it was that they loved each other.

She left them and went outside to wait for Kat. The forecourt was lit like a prison yard, with dirty snow eddying across it in the wind. Along the street the big maples swayed and cracked. What was happening in this town? Something or someone was out of control. She'd been horrified, wary, unbelieving, but now fear hit her hard, triggered, she realized, by Thurston. It wasn't his clown-like face or spitting rage that had gotten to her; it was his terror. She'd never seen that before, and now she was frightened for them all. For herself, for Kat, for Melissa, for Charlene, and for Leo. For everyone caught in the web of horror tightening over Parnell. Where was Leo? And Mikhail? She pulled out her phone, but her hands were too cold even to hit the speed-dial key. She went back inside, stomping her feet to warm them and to warn Nob and Elvie that she was there.

THIRTY-EIGHT

ELVIE WAS AT her desk, while Nob had pulled up a chair opposite and sat with his elbows on his knees, head in hands. He looked up, his face grey.

"He's just seen the chief," Elvie said.

"I'm all right — bit of a shock."

Tulla's phone rang in her hand. She read the screen. "Kat?"

"Your car started. No problem. Nobody was at Maureen's. The restaurant is closed. I want to check the Cohen house. Maybe they're hiding. I just phoned Mose. He's had a security camera installed and the locks changed and left the new keys at the police station. See you in five."

Tulla turned to Elvie. "Could I borrow the keys for the Cohen house?"

Elvie seemed dazed. "They're here somewhere." She rummaged through the drawers in her desk. "Why do you want them?"

"Kat thinks the girls might be there."

"What girls?"

"Melissa and a girl called Charlene are missing. We thought the police were looking for them. But you didn't know about any of that, did you?"

Elvie shook her head. Tulla could feel her anger rising. *Why isn't every cop in the province looking for them?*

"I guess I can give them to you," Elvie said doubtfully.

"I'm buying the building, Elvie."

"Don't."

"Don't what?"

"Don't buy it. That's a bad house, bad space. It's been empty for years for a reason. Some people think it's haunted. They claim they've heard voices crying —"

"I know squatters have been using it, but I doubt ghosts need sleeping bags and candles."

"Well, don't let Thurston know. Ghosts or not, he doesn't want that building sold."

"Why not?"

"I don't know. There have been offers, but he's managed to screw up the deals every time. He'll do the same thing to you." She pulled out another drawer, then slapped her forehead, narrowly missing the gelled coif. "Mr. Cohen asked me to have copies made. I gave the master to my father. He hangs around here a lot, drives me buggy, so I send him on errands, make them up half the time just to get rid of him. That was before —" She gestured toward the chief's office. "I forgot about it. Can it wait until tomorrow?"

"No. I can go out to your house as soon as Kat gets here."

"He's not there. He'll be in church. Heaven's Way, down on Barber."

The door banged open, making them all jump. "Just me," Kat said. "The forensics truck just pulled in." She stared at the door criss-crossed with yellow tape and averted her eyes.

Elvie scribbled a note and handed it to Tulla. "My father can be a pain in the ass sometimes. You might need this to convince him to hand the keys over. And take this." She reached into a cupboard behind her desk and pulled out a police-issue flashlight the size and heft of a baseball bat. "Though I don't suppose it'll be much use against evil spirits."

Tulla got into the driver's seat and tossed Kat her phone. "Try Leo again — speed dial two."

"No answer. And surprise, surprise, his voicemail's full. What's wrong with that guy?"

"Try Mikhail on three."

Kat listened, then shook her head. "Turned off."

The church, a suburban bungalow with a watch-tower tacked on one end, had a yard light that shone on cars parked like a tattered skirt around the building. A rent-a-sign peppered its message in red letters into the night: PREPARE TO MEET THY MAKER.

Tulla angled into a no-parking area directly in front of the entrance.

"No parking there, ladies, or God will strike you down." A figure bundled in a plaid hunting jacket and fur hat watched them from the step. A cigarette glowed like a cat's eye in his beard.

"Just here for a minute to look for someone," Tulla said.

He shrugged. "Service has started."

Tulla checked her watch. "What time will it be over?"

"Who knows? They could go on whoopin' and hollerin' all night." He spat past the cigarette. It wobbled but stayed in place. So did the spittle hanging from his beard like an icicle.

They pulled open the door to an explosion of music, a wave of gospel, twanging guitars, and voices stretching like barbed wire over the high notes.

"Do you know what Elvie's father even looks like?" Kat said into Tulla's ear. "He's going to be hard to find in this crowd." An elderly usher, bent almost double, hobbled up to them holding out programs. "Yer late, but it ain't never too late to meet yer Lord. Follow." He turned and started a slow shuffle down the aisle.

Tulla grasped his sleeve. "We didn't come for the service, sir. We're just looking for someone. His name is —"

The man snatched the programs back from them and shuffled away.

Tulla touched the shoulder of a large woman swaying in the back row. "Excuse me, ma'am." The rotund face that turned toward her glistened with faith and perspiration. "Could you tell me which is Elmer Paterson?" Half the congregation wore toques pulled over their ears, and they all had their faces tilted to the roof in song.

"Elmer? He the long drink of water playin' the banjo."

"When will they finish?"

A wizened face peered around the woman's shoulder. "We're on eighteen and countin'."

"You sit down here with us," the large woman said. "You're both welcome in the Lord's house." She scrunched her tiny husband along the pew and pulled Tulla down beside her with a grip of iron.

The congregation sang, "I'm standing on the rock, the rock of ages." As the hymn swelled, its harmonies fractured on the high and low notes and soared confidently through the choruses as the banjo twanged on.

"What do we do now?" Kat asked, jittering with panic. "Every minute we waste —"

Tulla put her hand over Kat's. "Sing," she instructed. "Just sing." She began to hum the tunes that floated up out of long-buried memories. Even the words started surfacing: "I'm longing for that glorious day when Jesus will come back …" She listened to herself in amazement. So did Kat.

Finally, the choir, then the congregation, and last of all, Elmer's banjo plinked to a stop.

Kat and Tulla were smothered in the upholstered embrace of their neighbour. "Wait here." She returned with Elmer in tow. "These young ladies are lookin' for you, Elmer. Whatcha been up to?" She poked him in the ribs.

His sly grin disappeared when Kat grabbed his arm. "Mr. Paterson, we need the keys for the Cohen house."

"What for?" he said belligerently. Kat wasn't playing by the rules, the slow tacking up to the subject required by all rural inhabitants of the county.

Tulla intervened. "Hello, Mr. Paterson. You might not remember me. I'm Tulla Murphy, Warren's daughter? We used to live on —"

"Brigham Avenue." He sized her up. "You look like your mother. I remember her from way back. Quite a looker."

Tulla held out Elvie's note. "There's a bit of an emergency and we do need the keys."

He looked up from the paper. "She don't say nothing about no emergency."

Kat jumped in. "Pipes have burst."

He squinted at her. "If you can't get in, how'd you know?"

"Water's running out under the door."

Their large new friend had been following the conversation, her head swinging back and forth as if she were watching a tennis match. Her gaze lingered on Kat for a moment. She stuck her face into Elmer's and barked, "Give them the keys, you ol' fool! Can't you see they're in need. This one's —" she pointed at Kat "— about done in and it's none of your business why. Call yourself a God-fearin' man?" She snorted. "They've had the courtesy to wait until the end of the service for you. You should have the courtesy to keep them no longer."

Elmer blinked, dug into his pocket, pulled out a small brown envelope, and dropped it into Kat's outstretched hand.

Kat turned and hugged the large woman. "Thank you."

"Go now. And God be with you and help you through your trouble."

THIRTY-NINE

THE HOUSE WAS A FORTRESS. New plywood had been nailed over all the windows, a new lock and deadbolt had been installed on the front and back doors, a sensor light lit up the front steps when they approached, and the eye of the security camera stared down at them.

Tulla unlocked the door, and Kat pushed past her, through the front room, and down the hall. "Mel?" Her voice echoed off the bare walls. She played the flashlight beam into the kitchen at the end of the hall. Nothing. The floors were scrubbed clean, the litter and filth gone.

They ran upstairs to the first bedroom. "People have been in here again," Kat said, shining the light around. "The stuff's gone, but I can smell the candles."

"There, in the corner!" Tulla said, pointing at the stubs on the floor. "But how did they get in? No one could have the key. There's only the master and we've got it."

They checked the other two bedrooms. Nobody. Nothing. A tree branch scraped the plywood window covering in the wind. Tulla checked the bathroom. "This has been cleaned, too. There's a box here, though." She pulled open the flaps. "Just crumpled newspapers and some metal rods." She pulled one out. "Looks like part of a tripod stand. And there's a camera here, too."

"C'mon, they aren't hiding in a cardboard box. Only room left is the storage room. I know they aren't here, though. If they were, they'd have answered." Kat's voice broke.

They hurried downstairs into what had been the old porch, closed in now, a sheet of plywood nailed over the back entrance. In the flashlight's beam, Tulla saw a gleam of metal in the floor. "Is that a trap door?"

"Root cellar. We have one, too. No way in or out of it except up through the trap." Kat knelt on the floor and flashed the light on the handle recessed into the pine boards. "Probably rusted shut."

"If the girls were here, how the hell did they get in?" Tulla asked, peering over her shoulder. "Are you sure that can't be opened?"

"In ours there used to be a little button thing to release the catch from either side, probably long gone, though. It was to make sure that if the trap door fell shut when someone was down there, they could get out." Kat slid a finger under the crescent handle. "Hey, the knob's still here! It just clicked."

Tulla sprang to help her wrestle the trap upright, letting it crash back onto the floor with a thump that shook the house.

"If it's the same as ours, there should be steps," Kat said, beaming the light into the hole. "There they are."

She backed away from the opening, her eyes huge. "I can't —" she whispered.

Tulla took the flashlight, backed down the ladder steps, and shone it around the space. Water dripped from the century-old board walls that held back the earth. The smell of decay was as thick as mist. "Nothing here, Kat." She aimed the light up the ladder to guide her down.

"Cul-de-sac," Kat said. "Another one."

"Maybe not." Tulla played the light on one wall. "There's no handle or anything, but doesn't that look as if there used to be a door or opening there?" She felt all along the edges but found nothing.

"Ours has the same thing," Kat said. "When I was a kid, I used to wonder if it opened into another world, like Narnia. Never managed to find a way to get it open. Mother told me it would be a disappointment, anyway, because it opened into earth. Like a grave, she said. One of the few times I ever heard Dad speak sharply to her, 'Let her dream, Sophie. Let her dream.'" She ran her hand over the earthen frame. "Well, I've dreamt and it's a nightmare. Let's get out of here."

On the front steps, they stood uncertainly in the blue glare of the sensor light. "What now?" Kat asked, despair in her voice. "Where do we look now?"

Tulla directed the light down the alleyway between the Cohen building and the Koffee Klatch. "Kat," she said slowly, "have you got your keys to the Klatch?"

Kat pulled them from her pocket. "I've already checked there. First place I went after home."

"C'mon," Tulla said. "Maybe, just maybe …" She unlocked the café door and flicked on the lights. "Where's the root cellar?"

"Old porch, now storage room," Kat said. "The trap door to it is under shelving where we keep all the canned stuff." She led the way through the kitchen to a narrow door half hidden by a commercial freezer. "See, this is the same deal as next door — a porch made into a storage room, so no windows." She edged through the door. "The trap's under those — hey, those shelves were full when I left. Why would anyone steal a bunch of cans?"

"No one did." Tulla pointed at the corner where gallon-sized cans and jars were stacked. "Just moved them to get at the trap door." Her voice rose in excitement. "There must be a way to get into the Cohen house from here, and Mel found it."

Kat attacked the shelving unit, tipping it into the towers of cans and jars, which rained down like bombs, clanging off one another, exploding when they hit the floor. Ketchup arched over the wall like a spray of blood.

Tulla knelt on the floor, feeling for the catch in the trap door. "I can't see. My eyes are full of ketchup." She rubbed her face with the inside of her elbow. "Where's the handle?"

Kat thumped down beside her. "Here. Same as next door. My hands are covered with oil. I can't get a grip."

Tulla fumbled for the button. She heard the release click and pulled the door free of the floor. It came silently. "Someone's oiled the hinges," she said, puffing.

Kat laughed hysterically. "Maybe we just did." They scrambled down the ladder and shone the flashlight around the plank walls. "There's the same door outline," Kat breathed. "It must open somehow." She gave it a kick. "Open, you bugger! Open, damn you!"

They ran their hands down both seams and banged at the rotting boards. "Okay, maybe if we both push together," Tulla said. Kat put the flashlight down, and they turned with their backs to the door and pushed until their knees buckled and they slid to the floor, gasping. "We need a pry bar. Have you got any tools here?"

"Only a hammer, a couple of screwdrivers, and the big kitchen knives."

Tulla jumped up. "I'm going to get those metal bars from next door. They might work. Back in a sec." She returned with two long rods. "I flattened the ends to make a chisel."

"How?"

"Slammed the door on them." She gave one to Kat. "And I found …"

"C'mon, c'mon." Kat squatted in front of the wall and traced the outline with the flashlight.

"Near the floor." Tulla pointed. "There's something."

Kat trained the light down. "Just a knothole. Wait, there's a ring inside it. I can get my finger through it." She grabbed it and pulled. The wood panel shifted out from the bottom.

"The hinges are on top," Kat whispered. "It's not a grave. My mother was so wrong. It's a tunnel." The earthen opening before them was shored up with old axe-hewn beams. "Oh, God, that's Mel's sleeping bag." She fell to her hands and knees and crawled forward across bedrock, dank and creviced. "The wall of the Cohen root cellar is right ahead of me." Her voice was muffled.

Tulla crawled up beside her. "There's the door outline. We missed the doohickey thing at the bottom." They pushed the panel where it met the floor, and it swung up without a sound.

"This must mean Mel and Charlene are hiding. Don't you think so? That they haven't been kidnapped?" Kat tucked her shaking hands into her armpits. They were back in the storeroom staring at the mess. "But where are they now, Tulla? *Where are they?*"

FORTY

CROWD CONTROL BARRIERS cordoned off the police station, overkill to keep the handful of gawkers at a distance. Kat and Tulla edged past them and rushed into the station, followed by a security cop yelling at them to stop. Elvie was at her desk; Nob stood at the open door to the chief's office talking to a group of uniformed OPP officers. They both waved the security cop away.

"They're undercover ... with us," Elvie snapped.

Tulla handed the keys to her. "Your dad was fine. No problems. One more thing. Could you put out a broadcast to find a car?"

"An all-points bulletin? Whose car?"

"Mine," Kat said.

Leo came out of Roland's office peeling off rubber gloves and tossing them into the wastebasket behind Elvie's chair. "Done already."

"God, Leo, where have you been? Have you heard anything?"

"No, Kat, but the whole province is now on the lookout for your car."

She stared at him and held out her hands, palms upward. "Leo, explain. Just explain. No more hints. *Just tell us what's happening!*"

The group with Nob went silent and stared at Kat.

"Fresh coffee in the kitchen," Leo said, taking Kat's arm and leading her and Tulla down the hallway to a small room housing a photocopy machine, a tiny fridge, a table, four metal chairs, a coffee pot, and a box of Tim Hortons doughnuts. "Sit," he told them, holding up the coffee pot. When they shook their heads, he filled a mug and sat at the table with them.

"Here's what we know. The church at Bluebird, where you saw Darla, is a front for a human-smuggling operation. They've been snatching kids for years. It's been under surveillance for several months, but we've had to go slow. The guy in charge, he goes by one name — Ambrose. His real name is Lyall Kelly, but I guess that didn't have a classy enough ring to it. He's a very convincing, empathetic church leader. He's also a sexual predator, as was his father before him. Darla's completely in his thrall. We're pretty sure Neil is a sort of outreach officer, to use the lingo. Most churches reach out to a community.

"Bluebird has perverted outreach into a trolling exercise, scooping up vulnerable kids. Some stay in the commune, usually the pretty young ones. The older kids are shipped out virtually into bondage — sex slaves, work slaves as domestics being paid very little, made to do all the work in a house as well as care for the children, not allowed to talk to anyone, only sometimes allowed to attend a 'church' affiliated with Bluebird. Some kids end up in sweatshops or as farm labourers. It's a network that stretches all over the continent. Bluebird's only one of the collection points."

Kat gripped the table so hard the metal edges cut into her palms. "Are you saying Mel's there? Oh, my God, please not —"

"Kat, the kids are *not* at Bluebird. Charlene was on her way, though. She thought her stepfather was up to something that involved that place, but Lena, her mother, was too afraid to act. Neil kept her on a tight leash made up of equal parts physical, psychological, and verbal abuse. Kept her isolated — she's from out west somewhere, grew up on a farm, not well-educated, no family here. Neil grew up around here, so he has the connections. When Charlene disappeared, Lena was frantic, but so terrified of him she didn't tell anyone. He told her she'd never see her daughter alive if she went to the police or anyone else."

Kat covered her face and whispered through her fingers, "Now what?" Her voice was despairing. Tulla pulled her chair closer and hugged her close.

"When did you eat last?" Leo asked.

She shook her head dismissively.

"It's after eight. First thing, you both have to eat, then sleep. In the morning, things will look better. By then maybe your car will be found. We've put a tracer on Mel's cellphone, as well."

Tulla spoke for the first time. "Why the hell has it taken so long to start searching for them?"

He regarded her steadily. "Didn't want local cops in on it. There's been months of surveillance on the whole network, not just Bluebird but several other links in the chain province-wide. We've also been working with the Sûreté du Québec. We have an inside man at Bluebird now. You know this, Tulla. The raid's imminent, but we're pretty sure there are some bent cops involved. That's the only way we can figure the network managed to operate for so long. If word got out that two girls were missing, one with obvious connections to Bluebird, and that there was a police search, the place would be empty in a hot second." He turned to Kat. "I know that sounds cold and calculating —"

"It doesn't sound like it is," she spat at him. "*It is!* This is my daughter you're talking about."

"But I have a lot of faith in Mel. She's resourceful, she's brave and smart —"

"And her life's in jeopardy because of this delay." Kat stood, knocking her chair over with a crash. "But how would you know. You've never had a kid disappear on you."

Before Tulla could speak, Leo stopped her with a brief sideways slice of a hand. "We'll find her, Kat."

Kat turned away from him. "Tulla, are you coming?"

"Right behind you. I'll just tell Leo about the Cohen house."

Kat stomped from the room.

"Leo, I'm so sorry about that. She doesn't know —"

"What about the Cohen house?"

"We're sure the girls have been hiding there."

"Not possible. Shaun checked the security camera videos. Nobody's gone in or out of that house in the past week."

"They didn't use the front door. They couldn't because of the new locks. But we found Mel's sleeping bag in the passage."

"Back up. What passage?"

"Between the house and the Klatch. It's the only way in." She described the trap doors into the root cellars, the panels into the connecting tunnel.

Leo stood as suddenly as Kat had. "It must have been a holding station right under our noses in the centre of town. That's where the snake tattoo crew brought the kids until they could be transported to Bluebird and other places. Who else besides Kat has keys to the Klatch?"

"Mel does. So do Charlene and the kitchen help guy who put out the garbage and recycling while we were away."

"His name?"

"Frank somebody. All I know about him is that he has a snake tattoo ..." Tulla recalled joking with Kat in her den about the snake tattoo gang in town ... so long ago now. A lifetime.

"He's probably one of the 'collection' team." Leo slammed the table with his fist. "They've all disappeared. The desk clerk at the Russell, Leroy —"

"A guy who works at Canadian Tire."

"Didn't know about him. He'll be gone, too. The one at the Klatch probably caught the girls if they were going back and forth between the Cohen place and the café."

Tulla covered her mouth, her eyes stricken.

"Goddamn it! Okay. I need a recent photo. Head-and-shoulders school picture or something of Mel. I already have one of Charlene from her mother. We'll put out an amber alert right away." He ran down the hall, yelling for Elvie to get Orillia on the line.

Tulla raced after him. "Leo, wait! Shug Bassett has a snake tattoo, too."

FORTY-ONE

KAT SAT SLUMPED AND shivering in the passenger seat. Tulla got behind the wheel, turned on the engine, and took her hand. "We're going to your place, Kat. Leo needs a photo of Mel. He's putting out an amber alert on the girls."

Kat sat up. "Don't they only do that when a child's been abducted? What did he tell you? What are you not telling me?"

"He's using every option to trace them, Kat. This is one of them." She clapped a hand to her forehead. "I forgot to tell him — I'll be right back."

She jumped out of the car and dashed back into the police station, colliding with Leo as he came out of the situation room. "Leo, I found something in the Cohen house — a box with bits of a tripod in it."

"Not now, Tulla, I have to go."

"And there was a video camera."

He stopped short. "It's still there?"

"I think so. It's in a box in the bathroom."

"Did you touch it?"

"Probably. I was digging around to find the rods. Oh, no, my fingerprints again." Her voice was a whisper. "Are you saying this is a crime scene? That someone has been murdered here? Oh God, Leo, no."

He steadied her, hands gentle on her shoulders. "I don't know yet, Tulla. Say nothing to Kat. I'll send someone for the camera. It could tell us —"

"Don't say it." She turned and ran back out to the car. "Okay, Kat, let's go. You're staying at my place tonight."

"No, I'm not. I'm staying at home in case Mel comes back. Let me borrow your car. I'll drop you at home and take a photo over to the police station." Tulla opened her mouth to argue, but Kat held up a hand. "I'm doing this, Tulla. Don't fight me on it. You can stay at my place if you want. I'll come back and get you."

After Kat dropped her off, Tulla let herself into her condo and rolled her suitcase into the entry. "Clancy? I'm home."

Silence. Even in the few days she'd been away, dust had gathered on the surfaces. She called again, then hurried down to the kitchen. No Clancy, but a note was propped against the coffee machine. "Tulla. Had to go out of town. My stepfather ill. Agatha Breeze has Clancy. She offered. M."

Tulla sat down, suddenly overwhelmed with exhaustion. Should she eat something? Her mind started to drift. She cradled her head on her arms on the counter.

The doorbell woke her — an especially loud chime that tolled in the kitchen, bedroom, and den. Kat was standing over her. "Tulla? I've been ringing and ringing. Are you all right?"

"Yeah. Fell asleep for a minute, I guess."

"Jeez, Tulla, now's not the time to leave your door unlocked. In fact, it wasn't even closed. I could've been anyone. And how come Clancy didn't bark?"

"He's not here. Mikhail left him with Aggie. He had to go out of town. His stepfather's ill."

"Doesn't his stepfather live in England?"

"I thought he did. Maybe he's gone there. Have you eaten anything?"

"Not hungry. Let's go."

"Wait! I should call Aggie."

"She doesn't know you're back. So it can wait. Don't even unpack. Just bring your bag and get your winter gear. It's getting colder by the minute."

Leo pulled up a chair beside Elvie. "Tell me some good news, my friend."

She touched his arm. "You need sleep, Leo. You look terrible."

"Headache," he muttered. "A headache the size of the Ritz." He rubbed the back of his neck. "Where are we on the amber alert?"

"The crawls are already on all local TV stations in Ontario and Quebec. I've sent the girls' photos and descriptions to HQ. Kat came in with Mel's a while ago. Poor woman. She's —"

Leo nodded glumly. "I know."

She studied his face. "This is bad, isn't it, Leo? The girls aren't in hiding, are they? Someone's got them. Can I do anything? I want to help. Sitting at this desk doing nothing is driving me nuts."

"There is something. You've got the keys for the Cohen house?"

She dug into her desk drawer and held up the small brown envelope.

"Tulla said there was a box in the bathroom with some camera equipment in it. It could be evidence. See if you can find it, bag the camera and tripod pieces, label place and time —"

"I know how to collect evidence, Leo." She stood up, went to the broom cupboard, and pulled out gloves, evidence bags, and crime scene tape. Her eyes shone. "Are you going to swear me in as a deputy?"

"Not necessary. One more thing, Elvie. When Shaun gets here, tell him to check the security camera footage from the Cohen house as far back as it goes."

Elvie had her coat on and the police-issue flashlight in her hand. "Already done. He's recorded all activity since the camera was installed. He hasn't much else to do. The file is on the desk he uses in there." She nodded toward the situation room.

"Then get him to run Frank whatever-his-name-is through the usual websites. See if he has a police record. And the guy at Canadian Tire."

"They have names?"

"Tell him to practise his detective skills. The clue is a snake tattoo. We've got what we need on Leroy. Oh, and Shug Bassett. See if Shaun can get any hits on him."

Leo was leaving Mikhail's apartment when his cellphone rang.

"It's me, Elvie. Reporting in." Her voice brimmed with excitement. "I'm back with the evidence."

"Good. Lock it in the broom cupboard. I'm on my way."

"Okay. I don't think he's going to like it, though."

"He?"

"Yeah," she chortled. "He. When I got there, I found the kitchen guy from the Klatch. He was climbing down a ladder into the old root cellar, carrying a box. So I arrested him for tampering with evidence. Citizen's arrest, since you wouldn't deputize me. I had to subdue him a little because he resisted. That's a criminal offence, right, resisting me even though I'm not really a cop?"

"Resisting you is a criminal offence, period. Where is he now?"

"Locked in the car. He's got a bit of a headache. That was *soooo* much fun."

"Bring him inside before he freezes. Well done, Officer Elvira. You're retroactively deputized."

When he arrived at the station, Leo found Frank sitting on the floor in the situation room handcuffed to the radiator. Elvie and Nob were on chairs facing him. "He's not freezing anymore," Elvie said. "He's quite toasty."

Leo patted her shoulder. "Hello, Frank. Comfortable?"

"I want a lawyer! That bitch hit me with her flashlight. I wasn't doin' nothin'."

Nob rose to his feet and leaned over him. "Take that back."

"What back? You can't keep me here. This is police abuse."

"I'm not a policeman," Elvie said cheerfully. "At least I wasn't when I hit you."

Nob nudged Frank with his size-fourteen boot. "Apologize or I'm going to kick you into next week. And I *am* a policeman."

Leo intervened, grinning slightly. "Now, Frank, I'm sure you have all sorts of things to tell us." He turned to Nob. "I need Shaun to set up the microphone and recorder. And could you take off the handcuffs? I think Frank would be happier sitting in a chair. And perhaps you could rustle up some coffee?" He winked at Nob.

Nob looked confused, then suddenly winked back, smiling broadly, and pulled the cuff key off his belt. "Right. Come on, Elvie."

Leo shut the door behind them and pulled a chair out for Frank across the interview table from him.

"Sit. We'll just have a little chat while we're waiting."

"I ain't sayin' a fuckin' word. I want a lawyer."

"Ah, for God's sake." Leo reached across the table and grabbed Frank's collar, twisting it hard against his throat. "Demonstration of the term 'collar,' as in I'll keep twisting until your eyes pop out or until you knock on the table that you're ready to talk." Frank scrabbled frantically, his face mottled. Leo twisted harder. "Slow learner, Frank."

Frank hit the table with his fist. Leo let go and leaned back. "Now, this shouldn't be too difficult for you. I know you're bottom of the totem pole, so I won't ask you any tough questions. First one, where are the girls?"

Frank rubbed his throat. "W-what —"

"Don't even think it, Frank. Do ... not ... say ... what ... girls."

Frank tried to dodge, but Leo's reach was lightning-fast. Almost as swiftly, Frank thumped the table again. When Leo let him go a second time, he leaned over the table, gasping for breath. "Neil."

"Neil what?"

"Took ... took them to Bluebird."

The door opened, and Nob appeared with two mugs of coffee, took one look, put the mugs on the table, and quickly backed out.

"Details," Leo said.

Ten minutes later Leo went to the door. Shaun and Nob were grouped around Elvie's desk. All three glanced up at him, round-eyed.

"Ah, Shaun, the canary's singing. I'm ready for that mike and recorder. It's important to follow the rules in police work. Remember that."

No one said a word.

FORTY-TWO

TULLA FITFULLY SLEPT in Mel's room. Kat didn't sleep at all. Tulla heard her prowling the house and waited for her to come back upstairs. Finally, she took a blanket off the bed and went to the kitchen. Kat was sitting at the table, still shaking, hands curled around a mug of tea, face grey with fatigue. Tulla draped the blanket around her shoulders.

"Have you got anything to help you sleep, Kat? Even a couple of Aspirin? You're going to collapse. And then what use will you be to Mel when they find her?"

Kat's eyes were leaden. "There's some Tylenol in the cabinet in my bathroom. Top shelf. Key's in my shoe shelf — the red running shoe. I keep it locked because of Liam, who's been known to make a ladder out of the vanity drawers and climb to the ceiling."

"No surprise there. Have you talked to him?"

"Yes. He's fine. Loved the stingrays. Wants to bring one home for Mel as a pet. Says he'd only choose a little one that would fit in the bathtub." She swallowed a sob.

They both went back to bed, each in their own bubble of fear and worry. Tulla's mind raced, trying to make sense of the horror that had taken over their lives — the murders, the girls' disappearance, the vanishing act of the snake crew ... and underlying it all was the bass note of dread and burgeoning certainty. *Ah, Leo, who are you now?* She turned over for the umpteenth time and buried her face in the pillow.

Dawn had arrived with no sun, just a slow greying in the east. Tulla stood at the kitchen window watching the snow swirl in mini-tornados across the yard littered with twigs and small branches brought down by the wind.

"I'm up," Kat said from the doorway.

"I've made coffee and porridge."

"Yuck!"

"Sit down and eat."

"How can you eat porridge without milk?"

"I found some in the freezer and thawed it."

"How do you eat porridge period?"

"With a spoon. Get it down you, because I have a plan."

"Thank God someone has." Kat straightened. "What?"

"We go to Bluebird."

"But Leo said they weren't there. I was hard on him yesterday, but he was right about us not screwing things up ... again, which is what we might do if we go there."

Tulla put down her spoon. "Kat, you had every right to be hard on him. Do you remember when we were playing detective — God, it seems so long ago — and we agreed he had the strongest motive to kill Dom? Our brains said that, but our hearts said, 'No way!'" Her voice trembled. "Kat, there's something wrong with the way he's behaving. He's not doing his job properly — vanishing all the time, so distracted by his own issues, whatever they are. I think it might be revenge." She covered her face with her hands, and tears seeped through her fingers.

Kat moved the chair she was sitting on next to Tulla and pulled her hands from her face. "You've never stopped loving him, have you?"

Tulla bit her lip. "No ..."

"Hang on to that. Trust him. He's the same Leo you've always loved."

"There's something I haven't told you, Kat."

"What?"

"He and Darla had a daughter."

Kat stared at her in disbelief. "Leo and Darla? Is that a joke? They have a daughter?"

"Had a daughter. She died. Leo thinks from neglect, from abuse at the hands of Dom and Darla."

"Oh, my God!"

"I think he's blinded by his own pain, guilt, and rage. I think his perspective is so skewed that he might be missing stuff or maybe missing it on purpose. I don't know anymore. Anyway, even if they're sure the girls aren't there, we might see something or talk to someone who — Kat, I don't know what else to suggest. I think you might just go crazy sitting here waiting for news. Me, too. We have to do something."

Kat smiled wanly. "Have I ever told you how much I love you, Tulla? Let's go."

They were on the road by nine, driving north toward a bank of heavy clouds bulging with menace. At Copperton they left the highway and drove down the main street wreathed with exhaust from cars in the angled parking spots. It was too cold for drivers to risk turning their engines off while they did their errands. The Bluebird complex came into view about sixteen kilometres north of town on a rutted and snow-packed sideroad. Tulla turned into the parking lot and stopped. It was quiet, no cars, a drift of snow across the church steps unmarked by footprints.

"Go around the back," Kat whispered.

Tulla nosed the car around the corner of the church. "Look, the gates are open into the complex. Cars have been up here this morning." She pointed at the tire tracks carved into the unploughed driveway.

Kat rubbed a circle clear on the frosted side window and peered through. "Look at that sculpture. Guess those must be bluebirds on the guy's hands. St. Francis maybe."

"We can't drive in there — too conspicuous." Tulla reversed and drove back to the front of the church. "Besides, we'd probably get stuck. Let's just walk a little way up the drive and see if anyone's around."

"And if there is?"

"We wing it. But who'd be out in this cold?"

"Us, apparently."

Kat and Tulla buttoned up their coats, wound scarves around their necks, and pulled on mitts and hats. "Let's do it," Kat said. They pushed open the doors at the same time, and the wind howled through the car like a living thing. They staggered, gasping, into the lee of the church.

"This is turning into a seriously flawed plan," Tulla said. "It's just too cold."

"May I help you, ladies?" a voice asked, seemingly coming from the church eaves above them. It was warm and mellifluous and cut into the cold like hot caramel through ice cream. "Come into the church out of the wind."

The tallest man Tulla had ever seen stood behind them, arms spread out to shepherd them through a small door in the back wall of the building. For a crazy second she thought the sculpture had come to life. Short of bolting back to the car, they had no choice. Inside the church, it wasn't much warmer, but the air was still and redolent with the comforting scent of candles.

The man wore a long black woollen coat, unbuttoned, over a turtleneck sweater, a scarf artfully tossed over his shoulder. Cold apparently didn't affect him. He smiled at them, and it was as if the sun had come out. His face was sculpted, bronzed by no natural sun, but it was his eyes that riveted, deep brown and piercing. Tulla had always thought brown eyes belonged in spaniels, supplicating and friendly. These weren't spaniel's eyes, though. The only apparent flaw in his classic looks was a too-long neck partially camouflaged by the scarf.

"You're the statue," Kat whispered. "You must be Francis."

He smiled. "I'm Brother Ambrose."

Tulla stifled a gasp.

"Then you should be carrying a beehive," Kat said, laughing nervously, "and speak in honeyed tones."

"You certainly know your saints, ma'am. And may I know your name?"

"Uh, Joan ..."

"Another saint," Ambrose said, eyes sweeping her face like warm sunlight.

"But I stay away from fires." Kat's flirtatious laugh warbled up the scale.

"And may I ask your last name, fireless, fearless Joan?"

"Sundae."

Ambrose arched a perfect eyebrow.

"Spelt *S-u-n-d-a-e*. Not the way you were thinking." Her laugh was getting shriller.

Ambrose swivelled his head like a periscope toward Tulla. "And your name, ma'am?"

Before she could speak, Kat said, "And this is my friend, Lois. Lois Laine."

The eyebrow arched higher.

"Spelt *L-a-i-n-e*, French for wool." Tulla had found her tongue again and listened to it babble.

"Well, Ms. Sundae and Ms. Laine," he said, speaking Tulla's new name with flawless French intonation, "I feel certain you're not out sightseeing on this cold and frosty morning, so I can only repeat my offer of assistance in whatever your quest."

"You're right, Brother Ambrose," Kat said hesitantly, as if embarrassed, not nearly wordless with fright. "You've caught us out. I guess we're trespassing, right?"

Tulla held her breath. *Where is Kat going with this?*

"Not at all," Ambrose said. "God's kingdom is never private property."

"Well, the truth is," Kat continued, and Tulla watched in amazement as she wrung her hands and tears filled her eyes, "I have a … son. He's very troubled. I'm at my wit's end, and someone told me about Bluebird, that you help wayward boys here, and I thought maybe I, maybe he …" She stumbled to a stop, rubbed her eyes with her scarf, and continued in a low voice. "I feel so ashamed. I've done my best for him, but he just stopped listening to me. He started to steal things — money from my purse — and then I discovered he was smoking marijuana." Her voice had risen in disgust. "And running with a bad bunch of boys and —"

"Joan, don't upset yourself," Tulla said, interrupting the litany of wrongdoing, almost convinced by Kat's performance that she did have a delinquent son. "He's not that bad a boy, really. He only needs guidance."

"And your husband?" Ambrose asked Kat.

"He left us," Kat said, her voice wobbling. "That's when my son started to act out. That's what the social worker called it."

"So you are on your own with this burden," Ambrose said in caramel tones. "You are right to turn to God for guidance. We've helped many troubled children — girls and boys — at Bluebird. We offer a safe, loving space for them to live and be taught in the ways of Christ."

"There are girls here, too?" Kat asked in alarm. "Oh, maybe that wouldn't be good for my boy. You see, girls are part of his problem."

"Where is your son now?" Ambrose asked.

"Reform school, or whatever fancy term they use now. And I'm afraid he'll just learn worse things there. But what are the living arrangements at Bluebird? Are the dorms coed? Could we perhaps have a tour?"

Too far, too far, Kat, Tulla thought.

"I'm afraid that isn't possible today." Ambrose's voice oozed with regret. "As you probably noticed, the gates to the commune are open today. Normally, they're only open on a Sunday morning, for the safety of the children, you understand. But we're in the midst of transporting items to a new branch of Bluebird. It's an exciting time for us, but things are in upheaval at the moment. Why don't you leave me your address, Joan, and telephone number, and I'll get in touch with you when the dust has settled?"

Kat pretended indecision, casting a glance at Tulla for help.

"Perhaps Joan could contact you, Brother Ambrose?" Tulla finally found her voice. "Since … Clem's in reform school, she doesn't have to make any decisions right now. How long does he have to stay there, K— Joan?"

"Six months more. And I wouldn't want his father to find out I've been inquiring about Bluebird."

"I thought you said he was no longer with you." Ambrose's tone was perceptibly colder.

"He isn't. I mean, he doesn't live with me, but he comes by the house sometimes, and he'd be very angry if —" She dropped her voice. "He's very anti-religious."

"Perhaps that's one of your son's problems," Ambrose said. "You take your time. I'll be here, and with God's guidance, together we can help Clem." He fished into his pocket and held out a card. As Kat reached for it, he pulled it back, laughing slightly. "But, of course, this will be out of date after this week. Do give me your coordinates and I'll be sure to reach you."

"We'd better go, Joan, before it starts to snow," Tulla said. "She's in the telephone book, Brother Ambrose. It's not a big town."

"And that would be what town?"

"Pembroke," Kat said.

"Arnprior," Tulla said.

Ambrose studied them, eyes narrowed. "Well, ladies, which is it?"

Kat grabbed Tulla's arm and squeezed hard. "Pembroke. I've lived there all my life. Everyone knows me. And Clem. My friend's a bit deaf. She misheard."

Tulla pointed to her ear, nodding like a fool. "Yes, I'm sorry. I thought you asked …"

Ambrose watched her, lips compressed in a thin line.

"I thought you asked where Clem was going to school. He's in —"

Ambrose turned away, took Kat's elbow, and ushered her to the door. "You should both go now before the weather worsens. Let me see you to your car to make sure it starts in this cold."

It did. Tulla revved the engine to prove it, and Ambrose stood back in the wind, coat streaming behind him like a cape. "God be with you," he called, lifting his arms in benison. His head jerked at the sound of a car coming down the lane from the commune. He stepped in front of it and waved the driver to stop. As Tulla pulled out onto the sideroad, she watched Ambrose in the rearview mirror. He was gesticulating in anything but benign blessing.

Tulla drove fast, as if her car were the getaway vehicle in a heist. After a few kilometres, she pulled off onto the frozen shoulder and skidded to a stop.

"What's wrong?" Kat asked in alarm.

"Nothing. I'm shaking so hard I can't steer properly."

"Do you think we got away with it?"

"Lois? Lois Laine? Do you think he's never heard of Superman? And Sundae, spelt *a-e*? Where did that come from?"

Kat hiccupped. "I have no idea. I was so scared that my tongue kind of detached from my brain. But Clem? I'd never call any son of mine Clem. I nearly asked who Clem was." The car exploded with hysterical laughter, and as quickly, Kat was sobbing. "Mel might be in there. She might be an item that's being transported. Oh, God, Tulla, we have to tell Leo they're moving."

Tulla pointed to her phone in the console. "Hit two." She pulled back onto the road, checking the mirror for cars following them. No cars, but a snow squall was barrelling down the highway as if giving chase.

Leo's voice filled the car. "Where are you?"

"On the road with Kat. You're on speakerphone. Leo, you aren't going to like this, but no matter. We've been to Bluebird …"

"*Jeesus!* What is wrong with you two?"

"What is wrong with us, Leo, is that my daughter's missing, and I'd like to get her back!" Kat shouted at the dashboard.

Tulla thumped the steering wheel. "Both of you shut up and listen. Leo, they're clearing out of there. Ambrose caught us snooping around the church. We never got into the commune itself. He made sure of that. He talked about being in upheaval, that they were moving to a new site. Did you know they were moving today?"

They heard Leo take a deep breath. "Weasel hasn't reported in. This … this isn't good. Have to go."

"Wait, Leo!" Tulla cried. "Don't hang up. There's something else. A car came down from the complex as we were leaving. It was Mikhail's car."

Kat stared at her in horror.

The dashboard was silent for too long, then Leo asked, "Are you sure?"

"Yes, I'd know his car anywhere."

"Was he driving it?"

"Couldn't see. But Ambrose stopped whoever it was. When we left, he seemed to be telling him to go back. Is he your inside man? I don't understand, because he left me a note saying that —"

"You two get out of there *now*!" Leo said, cutting her off. "Get back to Parnell and stay there." The dashboard emitted a dial tone.

FORTY-THREE

SNOW SWIRLED AROUND Mikhail's car, peppering his face when he cracked open the window.

"Are you thinking of leaving us?" Ambrose leaned in toward the opening, his hand curled around the top edge of the glass.

"Have to get to Ottawa before this turns into a blizzard."

"I don't think so." Ambrose slapped his hand against the car roof. "You were there in my office when I said no one was to leave, remember?" He thumped the metal again. "Everyone has to help in the transfer. And we need your car, especially in this storm. Drive me back to the commune."

He moved with surprising speed around the front bumper and into the passenger seat. "I was freezing my ass off out there." Gone were the mellow, soothing tones of Brother Ambrose. "And turn down the fucking music. Are you deaf?"

Mikhail put the car in gear and drove slowly into the church parking lot. "You're not fond of Gregorian chants?"

"Not at that decibel. Where are you going? I told you to go back to the commune."

"I'm turning around," Mikhail said mildly. "I don't want to risk getting stuck. This car's an automatic, so if we get stuck, we stay stuck. It's very powerful, but it needs care to stay on the road. Pulls a bit to the left. Have to watch that."

"God, you're such an old lady, Novak. This boat of a car could drive across those fields without a problem. It's like a bloody snowplough with that grille." Ambrose turned and looked into the back seat. "Were you a Boy Scout? Is that your problem? I see you're prepared for a spell in a snowdrift." Suddenly, he snarled, "Pull the lead out. Park at the back entrance to the dorms. And ditch all those blankets. We can fit four kids in the back seat alone. Move it! I have to shift the transfer forward. Those two women snooping around were the same ones at the service. Undercover cops for sure but remarkably bad at their jobs."

"What women?"

"Shut up and drive." He leaned forward and punched the radio off.

Mikhail drove back up the lane and backed in between two unmarked vans parked behind the back building. "You go ahead. I'll just stow these blankets." He fiddled with the blankets until Ambrose slammed the door.

"Stay down, stay put," he said softly, lips barely moving. "Wait a couple of minutes until Ambrose and I are inside. Crawl into the front seat. Keys are in the ignition, Mel. You drive. You can do it. Try not to spin the wheels in the deep snow going out. If the gate's been closed, drive through it. This car's pretty much a tank. Turn right at the road, not through the town. There's another entrance to the 417 about eight kilometres up. Keep your speed down on the highway and watch for black ice." While he was talking, he dumped a file out of his briefcase and shoved it under the blankets with the girls. "Get this to Leo." He pushed the door open against the wind and was gone.

Charlene whimpered. Mel shushed her, waited a minute, then cautiously poked her head up. Snow swirled around the windows that were already frosting over again. "C'mon." She slithered into the driver's seat and studied the dashboard. "I can do this," she muttered. "How hard can it be?"

Charlene landed beside her and slid out of sight. "Can you reach the pedals?"

"Barely." Mel hunkered forward, turned the key, found the shift, and threw the car into gear. It lurched backward, wheels spinning. "Yikes! I meant to go forward."

Charlene squealed and covered her face.

Mel put the car into drive, easing down on the accelerator with one foot, braking with her other foot. The car jerked down the lane like a jackrabbit. "Is there anyone following us? I can't see a thing in the mirrors."

Charlene scrambled back up and peered over her shoulder. "Nothing. Only snow."

"Okay, we're good. I'm going to go faster. Hang on."

Charlene slid down in the seat, cradling her head in her arms.

"Don't do that," Mel snapped at her. "You have to be the lookout. And you have to get the defroster and heater working or we're in trouble."

"You mean more trouble." Charlene fiddled with buttons and dials on the dashboard. A blast of choir music filled the car. "Sorry, sorry, wrong button."

The car shot out between the gates, around the church, and out onto the sideroad. Wind whipped across the fields, blowing snow sideways, and the car drifted in a slow skid toward the opposite ditch. Charlene screamed. Mel fought with the wheel, and the car straightened itself like a large, clumsy animal. She took a shuddering breath. "Ice. Gotta watch for ice."

Cocooned in the big car, they couldn't hear the opening salvos of the gale, but in the open areas they felt it buffeting the car. They were silent, both hunched forward, eyes straining. Every few minutes Charlene checked for pursuers. "I don't think there's anyone after us. They'd have to be on our bumper for me to see them, anyway." She turned back. "If we see a place, a restaurant or something, shouldn't we stop and phone someone?"

"I'm scared to. They'll know by now we're missing and that Mikhail's car is gone. Oh, geez, what's going to happen to Mikhail when they find out he gave us his car?" Mel's foot eased up on the accelerator.

"What are you doing?" Charlene cried, voice rising in panic. "We can't go back. He could say we stole it, that he didn't even know we were there. Drive. Let's just get to Parnell and then decide what to do."

"I guess we have to. Okay, watch for the entrance to the highway."

There was silence in the car then except for the wind and the steady thrum of tires on the road. Charlene sat up suddenly. "I've just thought of something. Why was he there in the first place?"

"Who?"

"That Mikhail guy. Is he one of them?"

"How could you even think that?" Mel said. "He helped us escape."

Another few miles passed.

"I don't know why he was there, Char," Mel finally said hardly above a whisper. "I can't bear to even think he's one of them."

"Well, you were the one who said we can't trust anyone."

FORTY-FOUR

THE BLUEBIRD COMPOUND consisted of two cinder-block buildings joined by a covered walkway — ugly, utilitarian, a startling contrast to the pretty stone church in front of it. It crouched low in the snow, the high, narrow windows like slit eyes. The front building housed the official entrance, with a side alcove for meetings with outsiders, rarely used since they were discouraged from visiting. Occasionally, a distraught parent arrived in search of a missing child. They were met with courtesy, as long as they didn't try to venture beyond the pastel walls of the pleasant entrance, which was simply furnished with comfortable armchairs, boxes of tissues on the side tables, and a large cross hanging on one wall.

Beyond the locked door into the rest of the compound, all pretense at civility vanished. A narrow hallway with a scuffed linoleum floor ran the length of the building, its doors set into unpainted walls at intervals, and today as cold inside as out. The second building housed a cafeteria and two dormitories, ten bunk beds in each. Doors marked WASHROOMS — MALE and WASHROOMS — FEMALE led to showers, toilets, and sinks grouped around two central changing rooms, each with a one-way window set into a wall shared with an observation room. One-way windows also opened into the cafeteria and hallway. There were no secrets in this building. The narrow windows high under the eaves allowed daylight in, but no possibility of letting anything out. Or anybody.

Snow had already started to drift in through the door Ambrose had left ajar. Mikhail ducked into the cafeteria kitchen after him, closed the blinds on the outside window, picked up the coffee pot, and peered at it. "I wonder how old this is. No matter, I'll make some new."

Ambrose watched him. "What's with the blinds?"

"Agoraphobia." Mikhail rubbed his arms as if the closed blinds would keep out the open spaces as well as the cold. He smiled as if making a joke.

"You're a mystery to me, Novak, an enigma of giant proportions. One minute I trust you, the next ..." He shook his head. "I can't read you at all."

"What's to read? I'm here, aren't I? Do you want coffee or not? Apparently, it's going to be a long, cold drive."

Ambrose leaned against the counter and crossed his arms. "Yeah, sure. By the way, where the hell are Shug and his gang? They were supposed to have the food packed up." He continued to study Mikhail, who had his back to him and was carefully measuring the coffee into the filter basket. "You're really not happy in your work here, are you?"

"My work?" Mikhail's voice was uninflected.

"Oh, for Christ's sake, don't be coy. You knew what it was all about before you signed on. You're a bleeding heart where the kids are concerned. You try to hide it, and you're very good at hiding what you think and feel, I give you that, but not good enough. I've had Shug watching you in case you did something stupid. I was convinced you were a liability and might need to be disposed of. But then I found out you might not be so squeamish about some other things. So maybe you're not the enemy, after all. Or even if you are, I now have something to keep you in line." His smile was that of a cobra before striking.

Mikhail filled the pot with water, poured it into the machine, and pushed the button before he turned to face Ambrose — and waited.

Ambrose smiled again. "Aren't you going to ask me what?"

"I think you'll probably tell me."

"You killed Connolly, didn't you?"

Mikhail raised an eyebrow. "Why would I kill Connolly?"

"Darla says you and your cop friend have had it in for him for years."

Mikhail shook his head. "That's quite a leap."

"Not so much. Shug's been talking to people in Parnell. The old coroner, sources at that old people's home."

"His mother?"

"Shug's mother?"

"Connolly's. She lives there."

Ambrose shrugged. "And the mayor. He thinks you and the cop set it up together. How did you do it?"

"Do what?"

Ambrose moved fast, pushing his face into Mikhail's. His voice was no longer affable. "Don't play games with me. Did you?"

Mikhail didn't flinch or answer.

"Word is he died of an accidental heroin overdose, but word also has it that he wasn't a user." Ambrose waited.

"Well, I guess he must have had help then."

"From you?"

Mikhail turned his back to check the coffee maker.

"Why'd you do it?"

The coffee machine wheezed and beeped. Mikhail poured a mug and cupped it to warm his hands before answering. "Connolly was simply a waste of skin."

Ambrose barked with laughter. "Reason enough, I guess. But the old lady? You do her, too?" His eyes raked Mikhail's face, searching for the tell. What he saw was fury boiling up as quickly as a summer storm. And as quickly vanishing, leaving his face expressionless. Mikhail started for the door.

"What about my coffee?" Like a snake recoiling into his basket, Ambrose stood down, no longer in attack mode.

"Get it yourself." Mikhail cocked his head, listening. All he could hear was the wind.

FORTY-FIVE

THE BLIZZARD HAD snuffed the daylight early, and the headlights on the big car beamed an endless tunnel through the snow-filled dark. Now that they were on the four-lane highway, an occasional car swept past them, making Mel veer to the side of the road each time.

"I see lights," Charlene said. "Is that Parnell?"

Mel kept her eyes on the road. "Parnell's at least three hours from here, more the speed we're driving. So don't start with the 'Are we there yet?' stuff. I don't even know where 'there' is at this point. I wish Mum were home."

"You already said that."

"Did I?"

"About a million times."

Mel stole a quick glance at Charlene, who was staring woodenly through the windshield. "Try to sleep," she said. "It's going to be a long ride."

"It already is."

"You know what, Charlene? I'm beginning to wonder why I ever risked my neck for you. You can be such a flipping pain."

A long time later Charlene whispered, "Sorry. I'd like to wish my mother was here, too. But I don't know who she'd choose — me or Neil. If your stepfather did something like this, you know for sure who your mother would choose."

"Oh, yes, me. No question. And he isn't my stepfather. Not anymore. Not really ever." She pulled herself forward with the steering wheel. "Did you see him back there? He was in one of those rooms when they brought us in down that hallway."

"Did he see you? Wouldn't he have tried to help …?" Charlene's voice trailed off. "I guess not."

"You guess right. He must be part of the setup. Doesn't surprise me," Mel said, her voice wobbling.

Snow streamed past the car as if they were going through it at Mach speed. When a light appeared in the distance, a glimmer in the endless dark, Charlene gazed hopefully at Mel, who just shook her head.

The minutes passed with excruciating slowness, turning into hours. Charlene sounded resigned when she pointed out more lights in the distance. "Parnell?"

"Might be. I think that's the light on top of the water tower. Yell when you see the exit. It's getting really slippery."

"There it is! We're going to miss it!"

"Too fast. I'm going too fast!" The car hit the shoulder, shot down the exit ramp, through the curve, over the embankment, and slammed nose first into a barrier of snow carved by the funnelling wind. The engine went silent.

Charlene whimpered.

"Are you all right?" Mel asked.

"My face hurts."

"Did you hit it again?"

"I didn't hit it the first time. This time the dashboard did. You okay?"

"I think so."

"Nice driving. You're getting good at burying cars in snow."

"Shut up."

"Now what?"

"Well, we can't just sit here waiting for someone to find us. It might be the wrong someone."

"Aside from the fact that we'd freeze to death first because no one could see us way down here so far off the road."

Mel released her seat belt and tried to open the door. It wouldn't budge against the snow. "Can you get yours open?"

"No, but I think I can get the window down. Lucky it's not electronic. This car is really from the Dark Ages."

"It got us this far. Wait." She pulled the blankets from the back seat and handed one to Charlene. "Do you think that's the right time," she said, pointing at the clock on the dashboard. "Can it be eight already? Did you notice if it was working before?"

"It was, but it's slow. I've been watching the minute hand jerk around for hours. Not working at all now, though. It's way past eight."

"I think we have to find the closest house now. We don't have any other option. But if it's really late, they for sure won't let us in."

"Is there a gas station around here?"

"No idea. And Tim Hortons is at the other exit, but the Priest Hole is at least at this end of town. It'll be a hike, but I know where the key is. If we don't get lost, we'll be fine. If we see anything sooner — a house with lights on or something — we'll chance it."

Charlene struggled with the window, pushing against the glass at the same time as she wound the handle. It scraped and stuck three-quarters of the way down, but the opening was big enough for her to crawl through. She fell into the snow and rolled down the drift, the blanket tangled around her. Mel followed. It was quiet at the bottom of the embankment and very cold. They floundered up the steep slope and into the wind that hit them like a fist.

FORTY-SIX

IT WAS LEO'S THIRD visit to Mikhail's apartment. Each time it seemed emptier, the silence thicker, the only sound his footsteps from room to room. It was as if no one had ever lived here, that no one ever would. Each time he came he searched for evidence that Mikhail had been back, knowing he hadn't been. His own footprints were the only ones on the snow-covered steps up to the front door. Inside, nothing had changed since his last visit. No furniture shifted, the counters still spotless but now no longer shiny. A sheen of dust lay over everything. Leo wondered how dust had collected from this snow-filled world. But there it was, like a thin shroud in the snow light from the window.

He stepped outside onto the stairs, pulling the door shut behind him. What now? The raid on Bluebird had netted nothing. The SWAT teams had burst through the doors of an empty building. The dormitories were in disarray, bedding and clothing strewn about. Pots of soup sat still warm on the stoves, filing cabinets in the office gaped open and empty. No kids, no young women, no tattooed staff, no Ambrose, no Darla, no Weasel, and no Mikhail.

The waiting was getting to him. He was missing something, and the longer he missed it, the more he was convinced Tulla was still in danger. Not from Dom's murderer, but from Harriet's. There had to be two. Highly unlikely, but how else to explain his fears? His head ached. He swayed at the top of the steps, for a few seconds not sure where he was. He stood still, eyes closed until the moment passed. He knew how to deal with them now, but it was worrying. The spells were getting worse again. He let his head fall slowly forward, stretching the neck muscles, forcing his shoulders down until the dizziness passed. Finally, he moved, picking his way down the stairs to his car. When he turned the key in the ignition, the defroster blasted on, startling him. He watched the windshield slowly clear, like his brain. *An internal defroster*, he thought. *That's what I need. Might work better than drugs.*

At the police station Shaun had emptied the jail cell to accommodate Frank, setting up the computers in Chief Roland's office now that the forensic crew had finished up. Nob and Elvie were sitting at her desk when Leo arrived.

"Any good news from anywhere?" Leo asked.

Elvie shook her head. "Nothing. I sent Shaun home. He wanted to sleep here to keep an eye on Frank."

"How did he make out with the snake crew?"

"He found some info on Shug. The guy has an old arrest for possession of child pornography. The case was thrown out for lack of evidence."

"Local judge?"

"Shaun thinks so. He hasn't tracked down the guy from Canadian Tire yet, Tim at the Russell has no record, and Frank does — a domestic assault case, bar fights, drugs, but no jail time."

"Yet," Leo corrected.

"And two guys from your unit who set things up here — Evans and Burton, never did get their first names — are over at the Manor finishing up the questioning about Arn. It's taking forever, Evans said, because the patients aren't the most reliable witnesses. Some talk about events that happened fifty years ago, and most of the staff are reluctant to say anything at all. Why don't you go back to the hotel and rest, Leo? You look like the wrath of God. I'll phone you if anything happens."

Leo shook his head. "I'll go over to the Manor, Elvie, and see how things are going."

A sign was taped to the closed coffee room door at the Manor: IN USE. COFFEE MACHINE AT RECEPTION. Leo gave a quick knock and went in. Sergeants Evans and Burton sat at a table going over a list of names. "Did you bring coffee?" Evans asked without looking up. "It's been a long day."

Leo pulled back a chair and sat, tilting against the wall, hands behind his head, massaging his neck. "Any joy?"

"Nah," Evans said. "Waste of time, really. We have one more staff member to see. The nurse supervisor …" He consulted his list. "Rosalie Stevens. But we've interviewed everyone else who was here the night that guy died, except for the Alzheimer's gang. They're in a locked wing and couldn't have seen anything, and wouldn't remember if they had." He glanced up at Leo. "However, from what the PSWs tell us, the inmates wander around this place at will."

"I don't think we're supposed to call them inmates," Leo said. "Who or what are PSWs?"

"Patient support workers. Most of them are Filipinos — very nervous, very hard to understand. In fact, one of them couldn't speak English at all."

"You think?" Burton said. "That good-looking one? I was watching her. She understood everything you said."

"How do you know?" Evans asked.

"Watched her eyes. She understood all right, but I think she's scared to get involved."

"Did you get anything at all?" Leo asked impatiently.

"One guy, name of —" Evans consulted his notes again "— Peter Pahulu. Says he heard some banging from the roof. He was sleeping in the third-floor bedroom for whichever PSW is on the night shift. The bells in the patients' rooms ring there as well as at the nursing stations. He said it was pretty windy. In fact, several of them mentioned that and figured it was just the wind blowing something around. He actually said,

I quote, 'This house has voices. When wind comes from over the river, it cries ... the house was crying that night.'"

"Did he hear screams and moans?" Leo asked.

"Someone heard screams?"

"When the wind blows hard from across the river, this house sounds like an insane asylum."

"It is an insane asylum," Evans said.

"It groans and shrieks, at least the eavestroughs do." He dropped his voice. "And in the night the cistern in the basement ticks. It crouches down there waiting to spring —"

"What the hell are you talking about?"

Leo grinned. "I spent a lot of time in this house as a kid. It was a private home then, belonged to the family of a friend. What else have you got? Have you talked to the Skinners?"

"Not yet," Evans said. "They're a difficult pair. You might have to pull rank, especially with the old guy. He's one patronizing son of a bitch. The son's quite friendly, just hard to pin down. And there's another doctor." He checked the list again. "Mikhail Novak, the psychologist who used to work for the OPP, not really on staff, apparently, but here a lot. Haven't managed to reach him yet. Then there's the three kitchen staff and the maintenance staff — a married couple. We've talked to them all. And the patients who still have their wits about them. One old fellow claimed he heard someone running down the stairs in the middle of the night. When I asked if it could have been a staff member coming down in response to a patient's bell, he was contemptuous. 'They don't run,' he said. Bit of a racist, I'd say."

Leo stretched. "Okay, you guys knock it off for the day. I'll interview Stevens. I think I saw her in reception when I came in. Ask her to come here on your way out, will you? And I'll track down the Skinners."

"And the psychiatrist?"

"Psychologist." Leo paused. "Yeah, sure."

Evans and Burton stood and gathered up their papers. "Think I might ask that woman at the station if she'll type up our notes," Evans said. "She's a knockout."

"The really tall one with the mohawk?" Burton asked.

"Is there another?"

"Not like her."

A minute after they left there was a quiet knock on the door. It was Rosalie, standing in the hall shaking like an aspen. She had her hands tucked inside the sleeves of her scrubs, clutching her elbows to quell the trembling.

"Rosie. Come here." He took her arm and steered her to a chair.

"I waited until you were alone." Tears poured down her cheeks.

Evans stuck his head around the open door. "Can't find the Stevens woman. She's not at — oh, sorry."

Rosie turned her face away.

"The victim, Arnold Connolly, was her uncle."

"Sorry, ma'am. Sorry for your troubles." Evans closed the door.

Leo went over to the door, locked it, sat opposite Rosie, and gently pulled her hands toward him over the table.

She tugged a hand back and rummaged in her purse for a tissue. "It's about Arn." Her sobbing slowed. "This is so hard. I was so selfish. I put Maddie at risk."

Leo knew Rosalie's daughter only vaguely. "Rosie, back up. Start from the beginning. Did something happen to Maddie?"

"No, well, yes, but not … it could have been worse. And I knew. Mikhail didn't have to tell me. I already knew Arn was bad to the core. I always made excuses for him. It wasn't his fault. He was born that way. But Mikhail told me that night that he'd come to believe that eventually it doesn't matter why a person does bad things, but it does matter how much pain and hurt he causes others. Mikhail said Arn would never stop on his own. Pity or excuses would never change him. Not even his blessed Jesus could stop him because of the sick, twisted notion he had about Jesus. He wasn't his saviour. He was his partner in whatever Arn did."

"When did you and Mikhail talk?"

"The night Arn —" She bit her lip.

"The night Arn died?" Leo kept his voice conversational, without urgency.

Rosalie nodded. "I had Maddie at the Manor with me after school that day. I often have her here in the late afternoons if I'm on shift. The thing is, Leo, I don't need to. Stan would collect her every day. Everyone says he's lazy and selfish, especially after his accident, but that's not true. He's in pain much of the time. It's changed him. But he adores Maddie. He'd do anything for her."

"Rosie, what happened to Maddie?"

She kept her head bent, her voice a whisper. "I knew it was a risk with Arn wandering around, but I never left her on her own for more than a minute, and there was always one of the staff around. She was colouring in here. I had just gotten her some juice and we were chatting, or at least she was a mile a minute, telling me ..." Her voice faltered. "But all of a sudden the call bells went crazy from the Alzheimer's wing. A PSW had left the TV on and one of those wretched talk shows — you know, where everyone yells and accuses each other of awful things. They're usually all members of the same family — cheating husbands, incest, bottom-of-the-barrel stuff. The dementia patients often get confused and think it's their own family and start yelling and fighting, too. We've banned the shows, but sometimes the PSWs forget. By the time I got there, a brawl had erupted in the common room. I had to go and quell the riot. All it took was to turn the TV off and ... and ..."

Leo waited as she circled and sidled up to what she didn't want to describe.

"I'd only been gone a few minutes, but when I got back, Maddie wasn't here. I found her in the interview room." She looked up finally and her eyes were desolate. "With Arn. He was sitting, holding her between his knees, crooning and stroking her hair. Oh, God, Leo, she looked so frightened. I'll never forget her face, confused and scared, and she was standing quite still ..." Tears poured down her cheeks again. "Her eyes were huge, her little face, it broke my heart. My heart keeps breaking. She trusted me to protect her and I did the opposite. I exposed her to that pervert. I'm so ashamed, feel so guilty. I should never —" Rosie stopped speaking. Her whole body shook.

"Did Mikhail see this, too?"

"No, I told him later. I took Maddie home, tried to be calm, to play everything down, not overreact, not frighten her more. After supper I left her with Stan and came back here, and Mikhail was just coming out of the Skinners' office. He said he'd been looking for a file he needed for one of his research subjects. Said he was going to be away for a few days. He asked me not to mention to anyone that I'd seen him because it would just rile old Skinner. I told him then what had happened with Arn." She covered her mouth. "Oh, I broke my promise to him."

"It's okay, Rosie. Mikhail won't mind you telling me. The thing is, you arrived in time to stop Arn. That's the main thing. Right, Rosie? Arn didn't do anything else, did he?"

"He started to undo her blouse," she said, her voice rising in anguish. "I think, I hope, I pray that Maddie is fine, but I also know somewhere, sometime, this will suddenly surface for her. She'll remember the fear, the revulsion she felt but didn't understand, and she'll remember how her trust was shattered. I know this because it happened to me."

Leo cradled her hands, caressing her palms with his thumbs in a circular motion to pull her back from the horror she was reliving. Her hands were wet with tears. A flash of memory pierced him. "Round and round the garden like a teddy bear ..." It was his mother's voice, his mother's hands cradling his. "One step, two step …" His mother's thumbs circling his palms, then her fingers walking up his arm, and he was already wriggling and giggling in anticipation of the tickle. "Tickle him under there," but in this memory she didn't tickle him. She pulled him to her as if she were drowning. He was five years old again, and his hands were slick with her tears. "Celia will always be there for you, my love. Your sister will be your mother and take care of you, and you must take care of her. Promise me, my little lion." And he remembered nodding, terrified by his mother's grief.

It was his mother's pain he thought of now, knowing she wouldn't be able to protect him from all the badness in the world she had to leave. Like Rosie realizing she couldn't protect her daughter from the eventual memory of the evil of Arn's touch.

His hands jerked convulsively, squeezing Rosie's hands so tight she flinched. She touched his cheek, and the memory fractured.

"Rosie, I've been such a fool. A meddling idiot. I'm so sorry."

"Leo, listen —"

He pressed his finger to her lips. "No, you listen, Rosie, and promise — a promise that you will not break — to say nothing of this to anyone. Promise me."

"I can't."

"You can and must to protect Maddie and — you aren't on shift now, are you?"

"No."

"Is Stan picking Maddie up today?"

"Yes, he's taking her to ballet class."

"We have a minute more to talk then. Let me just say this, Rosie. You are guilty of one thing and nothing else. You are guilty of being the best mother there is, that's all. I know that. Mikhail knows that. That's why he … why we are here for you. You're a courageous woman, always have been. You've survived a family that's nothing but —"

"I don't think of them as my family anymore, especially now."

"Good. You, Mikhail, and I can be each other's family then because we don't have one, either. You and I are sort of, anyway. You're my sister-in-law, right?"

"Not quite, Leo. I was Celia's sister-in-law."

"Close enough. And Mikhail and I —"

"You've been like brothers since you were children. And Kat and Tulla were like sisters to both of you. You four were a family all on your own."

Leo's smile was decidedly lopsided. "I don't really think of Tulla as a sister." For the first time Rosie smiled, a very small wobbly one. "Tulla can be your sister, though, and in good families everyone has one another's backs, as Miss D. used to say."

FORTY-SEVEN

LEO FOLLOWED ROSIE home in the police cruiser. While he waited for her to go inside, he radioed the station and asked Elvie to patch him through to Orillia. "Nemo there?" He waited, drumming his fingers on the steering wheel. "Captain? Harding here. I need to talk to whoever's in charge of the investigation into Arnold Connolly's death. Tell me it's not Scrivens."

"Nope. I am. He's second-in-command. What's up?"

"I screwed up. You can call off the dogs, especially Scrivens. I was wrong about Arn, Captain. It was an accident. Been over the roof again. *Mea culpa.*"

Nemo sighed. "So what did you find?"

"Clearly, Connolly fell against the railing, which gave way. No evidence anyone tampered with it. Wood was rotten, screws were rusty, pulled out of the footings as if they were butter. No indication anyone else was there at the time. Forensics matched footprints, but they were all staff. I was overzealous, I guess."

"You, Harding? Never."

"Forensic prelims pointed to an accident, but I got a bee in my bonnet. Forgot that deaths happen, right? And they don't all have to be murders. Even in this town."

"I need a report from you, Harding, and from forensics. It was a team from Smiths Falls, but I haven't heard from them yet."

"Copy that, Captain. Thanks." He clicked off the radio, did a U-turn, and drove fast across town, skidding to a stop at the curb in front of the Skinner house. He checked his watch: 7:39. There was still time. Skinner held evening hours until eight o'clock twice a week, a holdover from his old practice when he was the only doctor in town. The office was an addition built onto the side of the Skinner family house, an imposing red-brick pile with gingerbread trim and a deep veranda encircling it like a skirt. The broad back lawn swept to the river, now iced and glinting in the street lights on the bridge upstream. The cold was deepening. Leo wrenched the office door open against the wind trying to snatch it from his grasp. He stumbled into the foyer narrowly missing Paul, who was on his way out.

"Harding. What brings you here on such a night?"

"It's nippy out there." Leo unbuttoned his jacket.

"I wouldn't take that off if I were you. It's probably colder in here than out. Pipes froze last night and the furnace gave up the ghost. I just came in to cancel appointments. Is this a professional visit?" Paul's smile slid onto his face and stuck.

"I'm not here for medical attention, if it's yours. And I'm not here to arrest anyone, if it's mine. I was looking for your father."

Paul's smile slid away, but his tone remained affable. "He's inside locking up the files. Not sure he'll have time to see you. He's not happy about —"

"Yeah, well, that's what I wanted to speak to him about. I've come to eat crow. I made a mistake about the autopsy results on Arn's death. He was right."

"Oh, boy, that's a message he should hear himself. And I'll want to witness it. Come in, come in." His smile slid back, brighter than Jell-O. He opened the door into the inner office. "Dad, someone to see you."

"Not seeing anyone. Too damn cold in here. If it's serious, tell 'em to go to Emergency."

"You'll want to see this one." He ushered Leo through the door.

Dr. Skinner glanced up. "You! Get out of here, you interfering —"

Paul put his hand on his father's arm. "Harding's come to — wait for it — apologize."

"For what? Being an asshole?"

"I suppose you could say that."

"I *am* saying that."

"Dad, listen to the man."

"Dr. Skinner," Leo said, "you were right about Arn's death. I misread the 'crime' scene. It was an accident, just as you said. The bruises on his arms were made when he fell against the railing. I've checked the roof again and found several spots where the railing was rusted through, ready to give way with any pressure at all. I managed to snap part of it just by leaning on it. And Arn weighed a lot more than I do. Likely he fell against it, probably tripped on that robe he always wore. It was long and trailing."

Paul grinned at his father. "So you're vindicated, Dad."

"I told you from the beginning it was an accident. But, oh, no, Mr. Know-It-All wouldn't accept it. Just like he wouldn't listen to me about Harriet. I know those idiots from Ottawa said someone hit her, but they're wrong. Just as you were wrong about Arn, Harding. Always sticking your oar in and screwing things up."

Leo put on a suitably chastened face. "I've talked to the OPP detective in Orillia who's in charge of the investigation. Under the circumstances, he's decided that the body doesn't need to be sent to Ottawa. Your coroner's report stands. I'm sorry, sir. I jumped the gun. I couldn't accept that after two murders in this town in a matter of weeks, Arn's death was an accident and not another killing." He straightened his shoulders. "So, again, I apologize for interfering." He held out his hand.

Doc Skinner glared at it as if Leo were offering him a fish. He bared his teeth in a yellow grin. "Apology accepted. Now get out."

FORTY-EIGHT

"MUM?"

"Liam, is that you?" Kat pushed the phone hard against her ear. "What's wrong, hon? I can't hear you."

"Mum, it's me." And then a torrent of sobbing.

"Mel? Oh, God, where are you? Are you all right? Has someone got you? Mel, stop crying. Tell me."

The sobbing grew louder, then a woman's voice came on the line. "Kat —"

"What are you doing with my daughter?" Kat screamed into the phone. "Don't hurt her."

"Kat, listen to me! She's —"

"Who are you? Put Mel back on the line."

"*Kat!* Would you ever listen? She's fine. It's Maureen. The girls are here at the restaurant with me. They're safe."

"You're at the Klatch?"

"No, my restaurant. The Priest Hole."

"She's really fine? I'm coming." Kat flung the phone down, yelling up the stairs as she grabbed her jacket,

"Tulla, Mel's safe! She and Charlene are at Maureen's. Come quick!"

When Tulla and Kat flew through the door of the restaurant, the girls were wrapped in blankets and sitting at a table. Mugs of hot chocolate steamed in front of them. Mel jumped up, tripped on her blanket, and fell into Kat's arms. "Mum, I thought you were still in the Bahamas." She burst into tears. So did Kat. They swayed together, oblivious to the world.

Maureen pushed backward through the door from the kitchen carrying a platter of pancakes, eggs, and bacon and a plate piled high with toast. She grinned. "A treat for me to announce the good news, Kat, but I didn't expect to be accused of abduction." She put down the food hurriedly as Kat grabbed her. "Maureen, yours was the best telephone call I've ever had, probably ever will have."

"For sure. Next call about Mel will be from the police saying she's drunk and disorderly again at the school dance."

Kat turned and wrapped her arms around Mel again. "Okay, by me, Mellie. Any time you want to get drunk and disorderly at a school dance it's all right with me. Just, for God's sake, don't get kidnapped again."

"Mum, you gotta stop hugging me."

"Right, it's Charlene's turn." She leaned down to embrace the youngster, and for the first time focused on her face. "Oh, love, what happened to you?"

"Her bastard of a stepfather hit her, that's what happened," Melissa said.

Charlene's eye was puffed closed, her cheekbone gashed, and her mouth still scabbed with blood. "Then the dashboard," she whispered.

"You poor tyke," Kat said softly, cupping the side of her face.

"I'm okay, really," Charlene murmured, her voice breaking.

"Does your mother know you're safe?"

Charlene shook her head. "I'm afraid to phone her at the hotel in case my stepfather's there. And I took her cellphone by mistake, so I can't call it. It was dead, anyway. She never kept it charged."

"So's mine," Mel said. "Neil killed it. He took it away from me, smashed it, and threw it out the car window."

"I tried to call Leo, but his voicemail's full," Maureen said.

"Yeah, we know!" Kat and Melissa said at the same time.

"So I left a message with Elvie that the girls are here," Maureen said. "Now who's hungry?"

Tulla watched Kat and Mel with such joy that she could hardly speak. "Welcome back, you two." She stepped forward and hugged both girls.

Kat sat opposite Mel, scanning her face. "Did he hit you, too?"

"Well, sort of, but only after I kicked him in the balls," she said. "Though I was aiming for his kidney."

Kat gazed at her with shining eyes. "That's my girl."

"She was amazing," Charlene said. "She was like Cameron Diaz in *Charlie's Angels*. Just flew into the air and nailed him."

Mel picked up the story. "But when he could talk again, he said that if I didn't do what he told me to, he'd just keep beating Charlene. And then when he finished with her, he'd start on me." Her voice faltered. "He really likes hurting people. You could tell."

"You won't have to worry anymore about Neil, Charlene," Kat said. "He'll be arrested for sure. Phone your mother now. No more beatings, no more fear."

"Use my phone, dear," Maureen said. "Come in here where you can talk." She led Charlene into the kitchen and came back with a pot of coffee.

"Now, Mel, from the beginning," Kat said. "Tell us what happened."

"Let her eat first, Kat. These kids are starving. I'll tell you what happened at my end." She reached for mugs from the Welsh dresser and a bottle of Scotch from the cupboard beneath, holding it up. "Anyone?"

Kat and Tulla both nodded. So did Mel. Maureen winked at her. She poured the coffee with a generous splash of Scotch into three mugs, a smaller one into a fourth for Mel, pulled another chair over to the table, and sat.

"So this is how I knew they were here, or at least someone was here. The alarm system is hooked into my smartphone, and a very *smart* phone it is, too. It beeped at me earlier this evening to say the front-door alarm had been disarmed, which made no sense. I just blamed faulty technology. Then it beeped again to say it was reset, but the internal sensors had been disarmed. I've had a couple of false alarms in the past month, and both times, before I could stop them, the fire truck and

Nob arrived at the door, issuing dire warnings of fines if it happened again unless the place was really burning down or full of burglars." She stopped and turned her head toward the kitchen. "Do you think that little girl is all right?"

"Yes. I can hear her talking to her mother, between hiccups. Poor kid." Tulla tilted her chair back and peered through the door.

Maureen continued. "So I drove over to find out what was going on." She smiled and pointed at Mel. "And this was what was going on. Except I didn't know right away. I had to disarm the door alarm again, but just as my smarty-pants phone told me, the internal sensors had indeed been switched off at the panel, which made me a tad wary. Especially when —" she paused for effect "— I could hear breathing, obviously the ghost some people claim to hear, especially after they've had drink taken. Scared the bejesus out of me." She sipped her coffee and sighed happily. "It seemed obvious to me at that crazy moment that I was hearing Glendinning in the priest hole, but it was also fairly obvious, even in my paralyzed state, that Glendinning wouldn't have known how to disarm the alarm system. So I thought to myself, *Who knows the code for this alarm?*" She reached over and ruffled Mel's hair. "These two were packed in the priest hole like baby birds in a nest."

Mel waved a forkful of pancake and syrup. "We were so scared. We thought it was someone from Bluebird who'd followed us." She giggled. "Then we heard, 'Ready or not, you must be caught.'"

"And they came tumbling into the fireplace like a pair of chimney sweeps," Maureen added, gazing fondly at Mel. "A pair of hungry, frozen, scared sweeps."

Kat squeaked and grabbed Mel's hand.

"But wait, how did you get back to Parnell?" Kat asked. "Did you get a lift or what?"

Maureen laughed. "This is the best part. Mel drove."

"Oh, no. Drove what?"

"Mikhail's car," Mel said, her words tumbling over themselves. "I was so scared. That car's a monster. I couldn't see, and it kept trying to steer into the ditch, and a car pulled out behind us and we thought it was from Bluebird, and so I had to go faster and —"

Tulla turned to Kat. "That might have been us after we left Bluebird, when we pulled off onto the shoulder —"

"To have hysterics. Mel, how in the world did you manage to do that? The road was terrible … and how did you get Mik's car, anyway?"

"He gave it to us, he —" Suddenly Mel slapped a hand to her mouth. "Hey, where's Liam? Oh, my God, Mum, tell me you didn't leave him with Shug? He was at Bluebird. He works for that scary dude that runs the place, Ambrose."

"Don't worry, Mel," Kat said. "Liam's in the Bahamas with Tulla's father and lovely stepmother. Did Shug see you?"

"I think so, but he pretended not to. He was talking to Neil. Two of the creeps there were dragging us down a hall, and I saw him through a doorway. I only got a glimpse because Char and I were shoved into a room not much bigger than a cupboard — no windows, no furniture, just a bare floor, with candle stubs and an old blanket." Mel started to shake. "It was cold, like the Cohen place."

This time it was Tulla who gathered Mel up in a hug. "You were hiding there, weren't you? Your mother and I found the way through to the Klatch."

Mel gave her a high-five. "Hey, good for you. Not easy to find. But unfortunately someone else did, too. That loser, Frank? He must have noticed the shelves had been moved. We couldn't put them back over the trap door obviously when we returned to the Cohen house. They were waiting for us when we came through to get some food. That's when Neil beat up Charlene, and Frank just watched him. Then he grabbed me when I tried to stop Neil. It was ugly."

Tulla held her tightly, eyes closed, willing the scene out of her head. Charlene stood in the kitchen doorway, her smile tentative. "My mother's on her way over. Is that okay?"

"Of course," Maureen said, getting to her feet. "We'll have a party."

They all looked up as a blast of cold air hit them. "A private party, or is everyone invited?" Leo stood in the entry, stamping snow off his boots, unwinding a frozen scarf.

FORTY-NINE

"WELCOME BACK, KID." Leo strode to the table, put his hand on Mel's head, and touched Charlene's shoulder. He bent and studied her face. "Neil?"

She nodded.

"He won't do that again. He left Bluebird before the raid but was arrested last night at the Montreal airport. Unfortunately for him, his flight to Chicago was delayed by the storm."

"What about the other guys?" Tulla asked. "Did you get them all?"

Leo pulled a chair over from another table and sat down. "Are there any refreshments at this party? It's been a long day." He tilted his chair back against the wall, his hands behind his head.

"Are you off duty?" Maureen asked.

"Always."

She filled a mug with coffee and added a generous shot of Scotch.

He nodded his thanks and took a long sip. "The raid was pretty much a disaster — no one's fault. The storm really slowed the SWAT teams getting up there. The roads were a mess, and our guys were driving way too fast. Had to stop twice to get a couple of cowboys back on the road. When we told the crew from Smiths Falls what the raid was about, they were a little overzealous. They wanted to nail the Bluebird gang first and ask questions later. We got one of the Bluebird vans, in the ditch, about sixty-five kilometres north of Eganville." He lifted his eyes to Kat. "Nine kids and Shug."

Kat put her hand to her mouth and said nothing.

"They were pretty cold, but Shug lit candles in the car, and they had blankets. The other guy with them was Tim from the Russell. He and Shug had a fight. It seems Shug tried to call 911. Said he was going to give himself up. Tim grabbed his phone and smashed it before the call went through, then abandoned ship. We found Tim about three kilometres from the van, but not until this morning. Dead. Hypothermia."

Tulla watched Kat. "So Shug does have a spark of humanity. Your brief and shining instinct was right."

Kat returned Tulla's look and crossed her eyes. "Where's Shug now?"

"Jail," Leo answered. "Says he'd had enough. Wanted out but was afraid of Ambrose."

"Sure." Kat's voice was flat. "And the others?"

"There were two other vans according to Frank, your kitchen guy."

"Where did you find him?"

Leo grinned. "I didn't. Elvie did. She collared him trying to hide the camera stuff you spotted, Tulla. Apparently, she whacked him over the head with her flashlight. Claims he resisted arrest."

"And Darla?" Tulla asked.

"Long gone."

"Spooked by us?" Kat asked.

Leo shrugged. "Rat leaving the sinking ship. The rest got through the net, but we're fairly certain they haven't made it into the States. The border's on high alert, but Ambrose obviously has an unmanned crossing somewhere. However, in this weather they won't be able to use it. All the back roads will be plugged. My guess is they're hunkered down somewhere waiting for the weather to clear."

"And Mikhail?" Tulla asked.

Leo's eyes were steady on her face. "No sign of him or his car."

Mel and Charlene exchanged glances, then Mel said in a small voice, "We know where his car is."

"So, Parnelli Jones, tell Leo about your insanely brave drive from Bluebird," Kat said proudly.

Leo listened, his face impassive as Mel described their trip through the blizzard, afraid to stop anywhere. "I took the exit too fast and we ploughed into a big ditch. The car buried its nose in a drift and kind of sighed and died. You can't see it from the highway."

"That's truly impressive, Mel," Leo said. "Have you ever tried to drive that car, Tulla?"

"No. I find it hard enough to drive *in* it."

"*I* can't even drive that car," Leo said. "It has a death wish and keeps trying to veer off the road."

"Mikhail told us that when we were hiding under the blankets," Mel said. "He was pretending to talk to Ambrose but was really giving me instructions."

"There's an all-points bulletin out on Mikhail's car," Leo said. "I'll call this in from the cruiser."

Tulla stood up. "I'll come out with you, Leo. I've got groceries in the car. Maureen, would you be insulted if I brought in a couple of frozen pizzas to have now? And a box of white wine? Would that be allowed in the Priest Hole?"

"Absolutely. I'll get glasses."

Leo waited for Tulla at the door. He looked at her running shoes in the entry. "You can't wear those. They're soaked."

"My boots are in the car."

"Is it locked? I'll get them and the food."

"Not locked." She lowered her voice. "Leo, why was Mikhail at Bluebird?"

"I don't know."

"He wasn't your undercover man?"

Leo shook his head. "No, that was a detective. We had to pull him out fast. He was pretty sure Ambrose was onto him and was just playing him along. We got word to him just in time, and he made it to Eganville. He knows the area, all the back roads."

Tulla picked up his scarf and wound it around his neck. "Mikhail, of all people, could not be mixed up with that crowd. A person can't change that much. And you know him. You agree, don't you? He risked his life to rescue Mel and Charlene. He's a good man, Leo." *And you are, too, Leo. Please, God, you are, too.*

Leo covered her hand holding the scarf at his throat. "He's been in some dark places, Tulla."

"That's what he said about you."

Leo shrugged. "Different places. His childhood was one of them, his work with psychopaths another, his despair when he lost faith in the ultimate goodness of human nature. He's been fighting his demons all his life. I don't know whether he's still winning." He pulled the door open, tucked his head down, and stepped into the roaring wind.

Tulla sat on the bench in the stone entry and waited for him. "What about Arn?" she asked as soon as he returned.

"I made a mistake there," Leo said shortly. "Jumped the gun. It was an accident. He fell against the railing on the roof and it gave way."

Tulla scrutinized him closely. "What made you change your mind?"

"It was pretty obvious after I saw the railing. And I guess I just *wanted* someone to have pushed the old bastard."

"And Dom? I suppose now the verdict is that he just died in his sleep?"

"You could say that. He died of a heroin overdose. Had enough in his bloodstream to kill a horse."

"That's odd. Eddy the Enforcer told Harriet that Dom never used drugs. He ran the operation but didn't even touch marijuana."

Leo's eyes lit up. "That's Jack's informant … of course."

"Eddy told her it was a power strategy, that he'd launched the rumour himself.

"I can see how that could have given him the advantage over his enemies who thought they could capitalize on his weakness and muscle in on his territory," Leo said slowly. "Except, of course, there was no weakness. The Angels' kingpins must have liked how he protected their turf. Which would be why they turned out in such numbers at his funeral. Attendance was probably mandatory."

Leo studied her for a long moment. "The autopsy showed needle tracks on both —" He stopped abruptly. "Of course it did. Look, I have to go to the station."

"Okay. And I'm going home tonight."

"No, you are not." He put his hand on the door handle. "Tulla, your dad's convinced that Harriet was killed to keep her mouth shut. I am, too. He's adamant that Miss D. told you something, or someone thinks she did."

"There's nothing, Leo. We've been over and over that."

"Listen to me. You're still in danger. Not from Dom's murderer but from Harriet's murderer."

She stared at him in astonishment. "What are you saying? A minute ago you weren't even sure he was murdered. Now you're saying he was, even though the autopsy says otherwise. That means you're saying that if he was murdered, the person who killed him isn't the same person who killed Harriet, that there are two murderers on the loose. Unbelievable."

Leo rubbed the back of his neck. "Just trust me."

"What are you not telling me?"

"I'm not telling you what I don't know. I don't know who killed Harriet, but whoever did wanted to keep her quiet. What about the recipe book I found at Miss D.'s? Have you checked through it?"

"For what?"

"I don't know. Anything that's not a recipe. Where is it?"

"With my other cookbooks over the fridge at home."

"I'll get it. Give me your keys. I'll check Mikhail's place while I'm there. Keep some pizza for me."

She stood in the entry, hugging herself for warmth and comfort. Mel was safe, the Bluebird operation was smashed, at least for the moment, and most of the snake tattoo guys were in custody. The police seemed certain they'd catch up with Ambrose, so why wasn't she more elated? She gazed at the door Leo had just pulled shut behind him. *Who are you, Leo. Who are you now?*

Wind and snow tore into the restaurant half an hour later, announcing Leo's return. "Total whiteout now. No one's going anywhere tonight." He handed Tulla the recipe book and went over to the fireplace to warm his hands. "They found Mikhail's car, Mel, just where you put it. Said that it was a neat bit of parking. When I told them how you managed to keep it on the road all the way from Bluebird, they were impressed. When I told them you were barely over a metre tall, couldn't see over the steering wheel, couldn't reach the pedals, and were only fifteen and driving without a licence, they wanted to arrest you."

Mel's eyes widened.

He grinned at her. "Just kidding."

Tulla leafed through the recipe book as she ate, wiping her fingers on her jeans every once in a while. "Nothing here except recipes and a whack of Post-its." She turned the book on its end and shook it. Nothing. "There goes that theory, Leo."

"Humour me. And if not me, your dad. Stay with Kat and Mel."

Tulla sighed. "Okay."

Mel fist-pumped the air. "Dope."

"Nope?" Tulla asked. "You don't want me to stay?"

Mel grinned. "I said *dope*. Means *cool*."

FIFTY

THE BLIZZARD HAD blown itself out by morning, and the town lay under a thick mantle of snow. Tulla stood in Kat's living room window, eyeing the white bump in the street out front.

"My car," she said, pointing.

"I love snow, don't you?" Kat said, standing beside her.

"You hate snow."

"Not today. Today I love everything. Here's your coffee. Looks like Christmas out there. Didn't actually notice that yesterday. The street decorations are all up. All we need is Bing Crosby and Danny Kaye."

"*Are* Bing …"

"Who?" Mel was behind them, pulling the sleeves of her pyjama fleece down over her hands.

"I bet it's on Turner Classic Movies this week," Tulla said.

"What will be on what?" Mel asked.

"You've never seen *White Christmas*?"

Mel shook her head and yawned.

"You're in for a treat. Check the TV listings. Anyone got a plan for today?"

"Nothing, *nada*, *rien*," Kat said happily.

"I was going to go over to the library and get Clancy, but my car's obviously going nowhere before spring."

"The library won't be open," Kat said. "Nothing will be open. We're snowbound. And do I care? I do not. Mel's safe and happy here with us, Liam's safe and happy with Brenda and your dad, and Shug's not safe and happy but thawing out in a jail cell where he'll remain a good while if there's justice in this world."

Tulla clapped her forehead. "I forgot to phone Dad last night. He'll be frantic."

"It's okay. I phoned Liam and gave them the news. All's well there. They asked if I wanted to bring Mel down when I go back for him. I'm thinking that's a good plan. You'll come, right? Leo obviously still thinks you'd be safer out of Parnell."

"Leo's paranoid."

"Well, things really haven't changed. Mel's safe, but that hasn't made everything else go away. There are too many bodies. On top of that, Mikhail's disappeared."

"Oh, no," Mel groaned. "Mikhail put something under the blankets in the back of his car when he got out with Ambrose. He told us to make sure it got to Leo. I totally forgot."

Tulla picked up her phone. "I'll leave a message with Elvie."

For the next two days they went nowhere, saw no one, and had one brief call from Leo. "Elvie gave me your message about the file in Mikhail's car. I'm on my way to Smiths Falls now. The car was taken straight to the impound yard there. Pretty sure no one's even looked inside. Talk later."

The blinding white world beyond their door lay empty and still. And very, very cold. In the wake of the storm, temperatures had plummeted, breaking records and freezing pipes, car batteries, and people. The lake ice boomed and cracked, and trees, brittle with frost, snapped like gunshots. Nothing moved. Even the roar of gossip had been reduced to a whisper by all the downed telephone and hydro lines.

"Want me to make a drizzle cake?" Tulla asked on the second afternoon of their hibernation.

Kat glanced up from her book. "You? Sure. But I think you should own up to your subterfuge. I knew you weren't baking all that stuff." She stretched. "Phyllis at the bakery told me what you were up to."

Mel uncurled from her chair. "I'll help. I'm going stir-crazy."

Tulla went to the kitchen and leafed through her mother's recipe book. "Right, Mel, we need flour, butter, eggs, and —" She stopped. "Oh, jeez, there's a white Post-it stuck on the bottom of the drizzle cake recipe. I missed it."

Mel peered over her shoulder. "No wonder. The book's full of them."

"It's a note Harriet wrote to herself. She'd started to write herself reminders because she was getting so forgetful." Tulla squinted. "The writing's miniscule. 'Bake for Monday. Tell Tulla about other photo. NB. House calls.'"

Tulla looked up. "She told Leo and me about a photo that Aggie keeps taking down. I wonder if she means that one and forgot she'd mentioned it? And what's 'house calls' mean? I'll phone Aggie right now. This is weird."

When Tulla returned to the kitchen, Mel was pulling the mixer down off the shelf and Kat was rifling through the fridge. "Did you get her?" Kat asked.

"On her cell. The land line's down. She's not opening the library today. She doesn't think Clancy should go outside in this cold, and she won't leave him at home alone."

Kat laughed. "Seriously?"

"I'm pretty sure that's what she said. I'll go over tomorrow evening to pick him up ... if I can get my car out. Aggie said she doesn't know about another photo, only the one of the boys hanging on the back wall. Harriet told her she couldn't get rid of it, that it had historical significance. Aggie thinks if she had, Harriet would be alive today. And she doesn't have any idea what 'house calls' means."

"Who's the photo of?"

"She doesn't know. I'll look at it tomorrow and then she's going to burn it."

Next day Kat and Mel worked at the Klatch to get ready for reopening, arriving home exhausted by late afternoon.

"Tulla managed to get her car dug out," Kat commented as she unlocked the door.

"But she's staying here, right?" Mel said.

Kat nodded. "Which means Clancy is, too. She's collecting him from Aggie tonight."

Maureen phoned Kat a few minutes later to say she was keeping the Priest Hole closed for at least another week. "No one's interested in gourmet dining right now," she said. "Everyone wants to go to the Klatch."

"What, the Klatch isn't gourmet?" Kat said.

Maureen chortled. "In a word, yes. But aside from food, the Klatch serves gossip, so who needs gourmet. You're going to be very busy, so you'll need Mel. Leo said that Charlene and her mother are leaving town and going back out west."

"You talked to Leo? We can't reach him. Where is he?"

"Not sure. He phoned me to find out if I'd heard from Mikhail. Which I haven't. You?"

"No. I'll tell Tulla you've at least talked to him. She's been trying to reach him."

Kat hung up and called Tulla. A faint ringing came from upstairs. She cocked an ear — Tulla's phone.

When Tulla got to the library, last on her to-do list, the ground floor of the town hall was in darkness except for a shaft of light streaming through the glass doors of the library and down the stairs from the second floor. Agatha was behind the checkout desk stacking books to go back on the shelves. When she saw Tulla, she bent over and said to the floor, "Clancy, Mummy's here."

Tulla winced. Clancy shot around the end of the counter, his feet scrabbling on the hardwood floor, and yelped a greeting. Tulla crouched to rub his ears.

Aggie beamed at him. "He's been very good, haven't you, darling? You can come and stay with me anytime." She sounded wistful.

Elvie emerged from the stacks carrying an armload of books. "The rest can wait until tomorrow, Auntie. Let's close up now or we'll be late. Hey, Tulla! The station's swarming with cops, so I came over to take Aunt Agatha to her bridge club."

"Elvie, dear, I have to keep the library open for at least another hour. Besides, I don't want to go to bridge. Harriet was always my partner."

"You have to go, Auntie." Elvie's voice was kind but firm. "She'd want you to."

"No, she wouldn't. She'd want me to stay home and be miserable and grieve and —" Her voice broke. "And besides, people have been phoning about getting books out."

"I'll stay, Aggie," Tulla said. "I know the drill. Remember, I used to work here when I was in high school and it can't have changed that much."

"Of course it has," Agatha said indignantly. "I have a computer now."

Elvie held up a hand. "I'll get your stuff." A couple of minutes later she came out of the office with Aggie's coat, boots, purse, and a key ring.

Aggie took the keys from her and turned to Tulla. "This big one is for the outside door, the Yale is for the library door, and you'll have to set the alarm. Oh, dear, I shouldn't be going."

"Put your boots on, Auntie. Say goodbye to the dog and let's go. Tulla, all you do to set the alarm is push the green button. You have a minute to leave then. Not too complicated."

"Wait! I told Tulla I'd show her a photograph."

"I'll find it, Aggie," Tulla assured her. "If not, I'll come back another time. Off you go."

FIFTY-ONE

TULLA MADE HER WAY down the stacks, checking titles and sliding the books into their allotted spaces, finishing up in the reference section. A chest-high shelf along the back wall held the big dictionaries. Probably no one consulted these anymore; Google had made them obsolete. But for Tulla it was like seeing old friends that had helped her through her high school years.

The wall above the shelf was hung with the overflow of town photos from the lobby, sepia pictures recording events from Parnell's past — group shots of lumberjacks leaning on their crosscut saws, a newspaper account of the violent storm that had wedged the *Farewell Belle* between two islands, hurling passengers onto the shore and one baby into the trees. And there was the photo way off to the side by itself. It was hauntingly beautiful. Two boys stood in shallow water, mirror images in profile to the camera, facing each other and bending over a toy sailboat. One was dark-haired, one blond, but that was all she could make out. Their faces were in shadow, bodies in dark silhouette against the sunlit water. The sandy bottom on which they stood, rippled like ribs.

She lifted it down to check the back for names. Nothing written but something was sticking out of the paper backing. She pulled it out and held it toward the light — a black-and-white group photo, a bit blurry, creased where it had been folded. It looked as if it had been taken at a picnic. The faces were familiar.

She looked down as Clancy pushed against her knee, and growled. It sounded to her like distant thunder. "What do you hear, Clancy?" She peered down the dimly lit aisle toward the lights in the lobby. "It's like a tomb in here. Nothing emptier than a library after hours at night."

"Not so empty," a voice spoke out of the shadows. "I thought I'd find you back here, Tulla Murphy. Meddling as usual." Dr. Skinner stood at the end of the row of shelves, smiling at her, his yellow horse's teeth glinting in the fluorescent overheads from the lobby. "I saw you from the roof, but I didn't see you come out. I had planned to visit Aggie." He looked slyly at her. "She's as bad a busy-body as Harriet was. But then I saw her leave with that freak, Elvie. So I said to myself, 'What's that girl doing in the library by herself?' Up to no good, was what I thought."

Clancy growled louder, hackles rising.

"You saw me from a roof?"

"Your old house, Tulla Murphy. I call it Arn's roof now. He saw lots from there, too, things he shouldn't have. Crazy old Arn. No one ever listened to him except Harriet."

Tulla's hands shook as she tried to fold and stuff the hidden photo into the back pocket of her jeans. She backed up against the dictionary shelf, suddenly very afraid of this old man whose younger face had looked out of the photo at her, a hand resting on his son's scrawny shoulder. He was smiling in the photo just as he was now. His son was not.

He moved toward her, one hand in his parka pocket, the other stretched toward her. She froze.

"What have you got there?" He grabbed her arm as fast as an adder striking.

"Nothing. Just this picture." She held out the framed photo of the boys.

He let go of her and took the photo, studying it for a long time. "Aggie usually keeps this hidden — stupid, suspicious old woman. Do you know who they are?"

Tulla shook her head, backing slowly away from him.

Skinner touched the figures in the picture. "Cain and Abel, that's who they are." He pointed at the dark-haired one. "That one's Abel. He's dead now." He pointed at the blond one. "That's Cain. He killed him. Which makes me Adam, I guess." He laughed. "Doesn't matter now because no one knows. No one alive, I mean. Except you." He tapped his mouth. "And I suppose Aggie. That complicates things." His hand shook.

"Dr. Skinner, I don't know anything about these boys. I was looking to see if their names were on the back, but there's nothing there."

"Don't lie, girl. Harriet told you. And Arn told her what he saw. He tried to tell everyone, but Harriet was the only one who figured it out."

"Harriet didn't tell me anything, she —"

"And what else are you trying to hide?" He pulled her arm from behind her back and grabbed the crumpled photo out of her hand. "Let's just have a little look." He unfolded it, stepped over to the table, and spread it flat. He went still. "So that's where she hid it. I've searched for this for years. My erstwhile wife told me she'd take it to the police if it didn't stop. Not that it matters now."

Tulla was transfixed at the change in his face, now suddenly awash with grief. Tears ran down his long, hollow cheeks.

"God forgive me," he whispered, spreading his hands on the photo, one spatulate finger over his son's face. "I can't undo what happened. All I can do is try to fix —" He inhaled deeply, then continued in a strangely conversational tone. "So, missy, you still claim Harriet didn't tell you anything? How then did you know where to look for this?" He patted the photo.

"I didn't know … it was tucked into the back of the other picture."

He seized her with one hand and pulled a hypodermic needle out of his pocket with the other. Launched by Tulla's scream, Clancy attacked, sinking his teeth deep into Skinner's leg. With a howl of pain, the old man kicked the dog into a somersault down between the bookshelves.

Rage replaced her fear, and in one swift movement Tulla grabbed a dictionary off the reference table and swung it with both hands. Skinner folded to the floor without a sound.

"Oh, jeez," she breathed, dropping to her knees beside him.

"Dad, are you in here?" Paul appeared at the far end of the aisle. "Dad!" He limped toward them at startling speed, crouched awkwardly, and felt for the old man's pulse. "What did you do to him?"

"He attacked me."

"This old man?" His father whimpered softly. "It's okay, Dad. You're going to be all right. Don't try to move."

"That old man came at me with a hypodermic needle with God knows what in it. Paul, he's dangerous. He meant to kill me."

Paul looked around. "I don't see any needle. You're lying."

"It's under him."

"Dad, can you hear me? We're going to get you out of here to the hospital. Just stay quiet." He folded his scarf into a square and slid it gently under his father's head. "I'm going to phone for an ambulance now, Dad." He shrugged out of his jacket and tucked it over his father.

"He *is* going to be okay, right?" Tulla gazed down at the old man who looked as harmless as an empty coat now.

Paul stood and punched a number into his phone. "He'd better be, for your sake."

Tulla grabbed the photo from the table, scooped up Clancy, and didn't stop running until she was in her car.

Tulla, Kat, and Mel sat at Kat's kitchen table, Mel and Kat with hot chocolate and Tulla with a glass of Scotch cupped in her shaking hands.

Kat was agog. "What did you hit him with?"

"The *Random House Dictionary*."

"The unabridged one? God, you're lucky you didn't kill him."

"He's lucky, you mean," Mel said, wide-eyed.

"I was so scared. And he kicked Clancy."

"Well, of course, you had every right to brain the guy then," Kat said.

Tulla gazed down at her glass. "I've got to stop drinking so much whisky."

Kat rolled her eyes. "Two nights in a week. Road to perdition. But I'd say that's the least of your problems. What happens if Paul files assault charges?"

Tulla glared at her. "You weren't listening. He attacked me. And Clancy."

Kat leaned back in her chair. "Okay, but Paul will get rid of the hypodermic needle obviously, and who's going to believe you were afraid of that bag of old bones."

"Kat, have you looked at that bag of old bones's hands? They're monster claws. He has a grip like a leg trap. But what is it that I apparently know that's so dangerous to him? I don't know if it was the photo of the boys or this one that set him off." She dug into her back pocket and unfolded the picnic group photo. "This must be the other photo Harriet meant in her note."

Kat studied the picture closely. "That's Dr. Skinner … and Paul. That one looks like Mikhail, so that must be his mother."

Tulla squinted. "Must be. Even though she was a horror, she sure was beautiful, wasn't she? And that woman beside old Doc Skinner? She's a beauty, too. Looks Eurasian or something." They gazed in silence.

"You know who that is?" Kat asked. "It's Opal."

Tulla exhaled. "For sure."

"And that's Dom in front of her, beside Paul," Kat said. "The boys all look about nine or ten. And, of course, that's Arn. And isn't that Celia?"

Tulla took the picture and tilted it up to the light. "It's hard to tell because she's half cut off in the photo. And you can see she's holding a kid in front of her. You can just see his shoulder, so it must be Leo. There are a couple of other kids I don't recognize."

Mel came around, leaned over Kat's shoulder, and pointed. "Bet that's Shug."

"Oh, my God, it is!" Kat said. "So what's this group, anyway? And who took it?"

"Celia's in the photo," Tulla said. "Celia who in those days never went anywhere without her best friend. That's who took it."

"Bridget."

"Who's Bridget?" Mel asked.

"My older sister. She left Parnell before you were born. She and Leo's sister, Celia, were inseparable when they were growing up, then Celia left —"

"She eloped with Dom," Kat interjected, "the guy who was killed in the storm — a very big mistake. And then she died. Everyone assumed of breast cancer, except Leo, who thought —"

Tulla stopped her with a glare. "Ancient history now."

"Leo thought what?" Mel asked.

"That Dom had killed her," Kat said.

"Did he?" Mel's eyes were like saucers.

"*No!*"

Mel studied her. "Are you sure?"

Tulla said nothing.

"So it's not history," Mel said. "Then what's the big deal with that photo?"

Silence.

Mel grinned. "You look like a pair of sphinxes. Don't worry. I'll soon find out, since this town sucks at keeping secrets. But the biggest mystery of all is why you guys still live here."

The sphinxes continued mum. Later, Kat told Tulla, "Probably because we didn't know the answer ourselves."

FIFTY-TWO

CLANCY AWAKENED THEM the following morning barking in the front hall. Kat pulled open the door to Leo standing on the doorstep, stamping his feet and blowing on his hands. "Coffee on?"

"Shut the door. It's freezing." She went into the kitchen and pushed the button on the coffee machine. "Where have you been, Leo, and why don't you do something about your voicemail? We needed you last night. Big ruckus."

"I heard." He pulled out a chair and sat. Clancy scrambled over and put his paws on Leo's knee, a crazy grin splitting his face.

"What did you hear?" Tulla asked, standing in the doorway and tying the sash of her bathrobe.

Leo turned to her. "That you beat up a defenceless old man in the library."

Tulla snorted.

"I guess there might be another side to that story."

"Thank you."

"So tell me yours."

Tulla did. When she showed him the group photo, his face closed down. "Do you remember that day?" she asked.

He shook his head and placed a finger on Celia in the picture. "She's smiling. Hard to believe in that crowd." His eyes were stony. "See those adults? You've probably guessed by now that they were all pedophiles — the bloody lot. Opal was the worst. They destroyed the lives of a lot of kids."

Tulla swallowed. "Was ... were Celia ...?"

"No, Celia was old enough to avoid being a victim, and she protected me from them. Just as Bridget protected you. We were lucky to have those two. I suspect that when they were younger they protected each other. I don't know how come they're in this group. I assume Bridget took the photo if Celia's in it. I suppose there were times when —" He squinted at the picture. "Look, you can just see figures in the background, and that's the old town dock. It must have been taken at a church picnic or something where they would've been on their best behaviour. Look at the smirk on Skinner's face."

"And the fear on Paul's." Tulla touched Leo's clenched hand. "Have you always known about this?"

"I'd hear stuff. You must have, too. Then after Dom died, your father told me more about this group because he suspected it was somehow connected to his murder. Then when Harriet died he was certain. That's why he's been so worried about you. He thinks Harriet got wind of what was going on at Bluebird, maybe from that biker ex-student of hers."

"Eddy."

"And she figured some of the players were from Parnell. The new crop, as she called them. The kids who'd been sexually assaulted by these ones." He stabbed a finger at Opal, Arn, and Skinner in the photo.

Kat put coffee mugs in front of them and sat. "Like my soon-to-be-ex-husband."

"And Paul and Dom and —" Tulla stopped.

"And?" Leo's face was expressionless.

"Mikhail. He didn't seem to have a protector."

"What about his mother?" Leo asked.

Tulla's eyes flashed. "Are you kidding? She'd have fed him to the lions to protect herself. Have you found him yet?"

"No, but we've caught Ambrose and a second van of people. They were headed for a border crossing at Akwesasne, not the official one. This one is un-manned. People drift back and forth across it all the time. A sharp-eyed toll-booth attendant at the bridge in Cornwall got suspicious of an unmarked van full of people so close to the border and called it in."

"So," Tulla asked, "is Ambrose talking?"

"Yes, he talked, but nothing you could believe. He denied all knowledge of any human-smuggling ring. Claimed he was only moving his charges to the new site, was just trying to serve God."

Kat gagged.

"So who *did* he mention?"

"Mikhail."

Tulla stole a glance at Kat, whose eyes were locked on her coffee mug as if something were swimming in it.

"Who else?" Tulla asked.

Leo smiled thinly. "Thurston. Which might explain the mayor's panic at not being able to get into Roland's office. Roland knew about the operation but had been blackmailed into silence. Thurston threatened that if he ratted on them Roland would go down, too. He'd kept quiet about it too long to come out lily-white. If he turned in the rest of them, he was turning in himself. After Harriet was killed, Roland decided he couldn't keep silent any longer. He had a file on the Bluebird operation as well as reports on what was going on at the Cohen house. Neil and Thurston were in charge of that part of it."

"How do you know all this? From Thurston?" Kat asked.

"No. He wasn't there when we swept the place. We'll pick him up. Can't see Thurston leaving Parnell. I'm guessing he still thinks of it as his personal fiefdom, that somehow he's safe within its borders."

"So who?"

"From Roland."

"What? When? Couldn't you have raided the place earlier then?" Kat was gearing up for an attack.

Leo held up a hand. "He didn't tell me in person. I found a file he'd left locked in his filing cabinet. That's what Thurston was trying to get hold of after Roland killed himself."

Kat looked at him in disbelief.

Tulla cocked her head. "After Roland what?"

"Roland killed himself, Tulla. He committed suicide."

Tulla had heard him the first time; she had understood the words but not the meaning. Her brain had dropped the portcullis, buying her time to put the two together. She covered her mouth with her hand, her eyes filling with misery.

"Forensics found the gun. It had fallen under his desk. They tested it back at the forensics lab in Ottawa and lifted his prints off it. They also found a note underneath his body. It was an apology to Parnell."

Tulla bowed her head. "That is so sad. Another victim of this town."

"Kat, tell Mel thanks for me," Leo said. "Mikhail's file was still in the car — a meticulous dossier of the main Bluebird players. He was studying them just as he used to do for the OPP. Most of them come off as your run-of-the-mill scumbags, a couple were convicted pedophiles, including Neil, but Ambrose and Darla are the most interesting. They're in a league of their own. Ambrose will be put away for life as a dangerous offender if anyone in the justice system actually reads Mikhail's profile. Same for Darla." Leo rubbed his face as if trying to wipe away memories. "She was right in the thick of it, like her mother before her." He rolled his shoulders and massaged the back of his neck.

Tulla watched Leo drag himself back to the present and asked, "What did Mikhail say about Ambrose?"

"The classic predator — a subspecies in humanity that needs people to pick on and does everything possible to keep them within striking distance simply for the pleasure of striking. It's a damning portrayal. He notes that individuals in this 'predatory subgroup,' as he calls them, are most often found in positions of authority, say, as priests or church leaders, doctors, cops, judges ..."

"Sounds like Parnell's finest," Kat said.

"He even commented on the prevalence of predators in his own profession — psychologists, mental health workers, who rarely get caught because they're so credible that no one believes their critics. If confronted with exposure, they become highly dangerous. Mikhail cites several cases where the person who tries to out them ends up dead."

Leo pulled a crumpled sheet of paper from his pocket and smoothed it out. "I copied this from his notes. It looks like a kind of aside to himself. He says, 'Confronting a professional predator is harder than taking on a criminal. They are so much smarter and so supremely confident in their own ability to quash their enemies. As a result, the worst of them often never get caught.'" He folded the paper and shoved it back into his pocket.

Tulla studied Leo's face but said nothing.

"Is Mik safe, Leo?" Kat asked. "Do you think they figured out what he was doing?"

"I don't know." Leo drained his coffee mug and stood. "Gotta go." He caught Tulla's eye and tilted his head toward the door.

In the entry, he lifted his parka off the hook, took an envelope from the pocket, and handed it to her. "This was in the file, addressed to me."

Leo, things haven't gone according to plan, so I am going to try to send this file to you via Melissa if I can extract her and Charlene successfully. I trust they'll make it home safe. "Home safe" has a nice ring to it, doesn't it? Wish I could say the same for the rest of us.

I am going away for a spell, provided I make it out of Bluebird in one piece. Don't worry about me turning up in Parnell anytime soon, so loyalties will remain unstrained. Just remember, he had true evil in him, born or bred in the bone, I never could fathom which. I suppose that could be said for us all. Whether evil or good, there's always a primary site.

— Mikhail

Tulla shook her head in bewilderment. "What does he mean? Who has evil in him? Ambrose?"

"Dom." Leo shrugged into his parka, pulled Tulla into a hug, and spoke into her hair. "Mikhail's a good man, Tulla, and whatever he's done, he's still my friend."

"Mine, too," she whispered as the realization hit her. "Whatever he's done, mine, too."

When she returned to the kitchen, Kat regarded her quizzically. "What was that about?"

Tulla walked to the window, her back to Kat. "The sky's so bleak. More snow coming."

Kat waited.

"There was a letter in the file that Mikhail wrote to Leo. It was as if it was written in code that Leo seemed to understand." She stretched the skin over her cheekbones with thumb and forefinger. "I think he was saying that he killed Dom." She turned from the window, and her eyes were like the sky. "I think he was saying that he'll never come back to Parnell because it would test loyalties. I think he meant that Leo would have to arrest him."

"Mikhail couldn't have killed Dom," Kat said flatly. "Because, listen to me, that would mean he also killed Miss D., as well, and that is, that is …" She threw herself back in the chair and glared at Tulla.

"Inconceivable. Of course it is. To Leo, too. That's why he's holding on to the theory of two murderers. Or that Dom wasn't murdered at all. But if Dom wasn't murdered, why was Harriet killed and why did Skinner attack me?"

"That question hurts my brain." Kat groaned, clutching her head with both hands. "We have to assume Dom was murdered, or we get nowhere with anything else. So whoever killed Dom also killed Harriet to keep her quiet, and Skinner is either that person or is protecting that person, and went after you because he thought Harriet told you what she knew."

"No, because he'd have known that she'd have told Aggie … oh, but I bet Aggie was his first target. He said he was watching the library from the roof, so he must have been looking for her. Then I arrived, Aggie and Elvie left, and I was still in —"

"What?"

"Skinner said Arn had seen something from the roof and tried to tell people, but no one understood except Harriet. He said he knew Arn told me, too. Now I know when that must have been. Skinner was on the ladder when I came down from the roof when Mik and I followed Arn up there. He must have heard the whole conversation."

"What did Arn say?"

Tulla screwed up her face in thought. "More blather about *Jaysus*, something about the doctor making house calls."

"Do you think that's what Harriet was referring to in her Post-it note? Maybe Arn saw Doc Skinner's car in front of her house. Everyone knows that car."

"He couldn't have. When we were kids, we could see her house from up there, but not anymore. There's a row of townhouses in front of her house now. Besides, Arn saw something before she was killed and told her."

She stopped suddenly, remembering what Rosie had said.

"Ah, Kat, there's something else. Everyone at the Manor calls Mikhail doctor, as well. And everyone knows his car, too."

Kat closed her eyes. "We need to do another chart. In the meantime you're staying here."

"Nope. I'm going home." She hugged Kat. "The important thing is that Mel is safe. The rest will all come clear eventually."

FIFTY-THREE

TULLA PARKED AT THE grocery store and was reaching for her purse when someone tapped on the window. Clancy burst into joyous barking.

"Hear you're going home," Leo said when she swung the door open.

"Kat phoned you, right?"

Leo nodded. "Followed you here. Got time for breakfast?"

"Where? The Klatch isn't open yet."

"The drive-through at Tim Hortons. We can have a picnic in your car and keep Clancy company."

After they got their coffee and food, they unwrapped their breakfast sandwiches and peeled the lids off their cups, while Clancy wiggled between the seats, looking hopeful.

"Thanks for breakfast, Leo, but I'm still going home." She paused. "Of course, if you're worried that I shouldn't stay alone, you could come, too."

"I could, especially since the Russell is seriously under-staffed these days. In fact, it's closed. But this morning I have to go to Orillia for a debriefing on the raid. I'll be back tonight, though."

She smiled. "Clancy will be delighted."

They sat in silence, sipping their coffees.

"I have a question," Tulla finally said.

Leo gave an exaggerated sigh.

"Rosie says you're deaf."

"Yes."

"Since when?"

"Couple of years."

"Did it come on suddenly?"

"You might say that. An IED in Afghanistan. There were four of us — military police — in a Jeep, right in the middle of Kabul." He focused on something way beyond the car windows. "I play it down. Lets my bosses pretend it's not there, otherwise they'd have to pull me from active duty and put me behind a desk."

"So we just shout at you?"

"That helps. Harriet noticed it. Said I looked like Clancy when I was trying to hear." He cocked his head and studied her. "You know Clancy lip-reads, right?"

"It's called speech reading now. I've noticed you doing that. But here's the thing, Leo, you're not deaf. So why are you pretending to be?"

His nostrils flared. "I'm not —"

"Shouting rarely helps. A truly deaf person knows that. Okay, maybe under some circumstances. But more important is that people enunciate their words.

They don't turn away from you when they speak and they don't put their hands over their mouths. I've watched you, Leo. You have no problem with any of those things. You can hear when there's loud ambient noise, you can pick up a whispered conversation across the room … your hearing is acute."

"Hearing loss can take all sorts of forms. You can't know what's going on in my ears … my brain."

"Well, I sort of can." She lifted her hair and turned her head to show him the curved device behind her ear, a translucent tube running into a skin-coloured mould in her ear.

Leo leaned forward, all bluster gone. "I've never noticed that —"

"Not surprising. I don't normally point it out to people. And I also have an in-canal aid I wear sometimes. It's tiny, virtually invisible, though not as powerful as this one. But it serves its purpose, especially at times when I prefer not to draw attention to my … disability. This behind-the-ear aid can be distracting for me as well as for other people." She struggled not to smile as she saw the comprehension dawn on Leo's face.

"I am getting better at fooling people, especially since I don't wear an aid in my other ear — not enough hearing to boost. That ear is mainly for decoration. So I do know what goes on in a deaf person's head. Not yours, though, Leo, because you're faking it." She let the curtain of hair fall back.

"When …?" He pointed at her ear.

"Did it start? Ironic to think now. It was Dom, still Bobby then. Remember after the Clod War he used to stalk me, throw rocks at me? Well, one afternoon he knocked me off my bike with a rock that cut my ear. Doc Skinner sewed it up badly, and ever since then, you probably wouldn't remember, I was prone to ear infections. A few years ago, when I lived in Saratoga, I developed a whopper of an infection in the mastoid bone and had surgery, which uncovered a mess. My hearing was compromised, and this is the result." She pointed at her right ear. "Then a couple of years ago my good ear packed it in."

"Just out of the blue?"

She nodded.

"Pretty much. Sudden inexplicable deafness is quite common, it turns out. The first time, it was like radio static. The crackling had gone by morning, but about two weeks later I woke up with no hearing at all, not even static, just a humming, one of the many versions of tinnitus, in that ear. So I have about fifty percent hearing in one ear, the other nothing. I kind of went through the five stages of grief." She counted them off on her fingers. "Denial, anger, bargaining, depression, and acceptance. I skipped bargaining, doubled up on depression, and replaced denial with self-pity. So that's my story. What's yours? Why are you pretending to be deaf?"

He made a show of facing her directly, enunciating his words. "I fake it because it's a cover for some other things going on."

"Like not knowing what a treadmill is? Not being able to figure out your phone?"

He shrugged. "Not the time for going into all that, Tulla, but I'm really sorry if I've offended you by moving in on your turf."

"Oh, for God's sake," she snapped. "You think I own deafness? I'm glad to share with anyone who isn't a fraud."

He held up an appeasing hand.

"You're good at deflection, Harding. Yeah, I hate being deaf, but hey, there are so many worse things. You know, it was Harriet who jolted me out of the self-pity stage. I was listing off all the things I missed — nuances in speech, the subject or direction of a conversation with more than one person, movie and TV dialogue, a joke everyone but me heard and laughed at, music … everything sounds out of tune now. All *blah, blah, blah*. So Miss D. told me to stop wallowing, that everyone has some cross to bear. I was flummoxed because I thought she'd said everyone had a 'cross-eyed bear.'" She blinked back tears, remembering Harriet's voice.

Leo took a Tim Hortons napkin and blotted her cheeks. "Miss D. knew I wasn't deaf but played along when I told her what I was doing. She got a kick out of being my ally in deception. Tulla, I have to go now or I'll miss the debriefing. I'll see you tonight. In the meantime, keep your damn door locked. And answer only to me."

FIFTY-FOUR

ELVIE LOOKED UP at the light streaming from the library window and shook her head. Shielding her mohawk — pink today — she pushed the car door open and ran up the steps through the wind stinging her face. "Auntie, are you still here?"

Aggie stood at the window. "Quick, Elvie, it's the Fist. I knew it was coming." She clutched a photograph against her chest.

"You can see the knuckles," Elvie whispered. "I've never actually seen it before." The clouds writhed and spread as the wind rose to a scream. "It's as if those damn gargoyles are howling. Come away from the window, Auntie. It's not safe." She led Aggie back to her chair behind the checkout desk. "How did you know it was coming? I've never heard of the Fist hitting in the winter before. The Weather Channel said it was going to be clear and cold here, that the blizzard was staying north of us."

"I just knew …" Aggie held out the photograph of the two boys standing in the water. The glass had splintered from top to bottom through the little sailboat that lay broken between their crouched figures.

"Did it fall off the wall?"

"No." Aggie was calm. "When I knew the storm was coming, I went to take it down. I'd left it up because Harriet always told me I was just being a superstitious old woman, so I thought I'd let her have the last word on something." She touched the broken glass. "I found it like this on the wall. It hadn't fallen. Unless someone else hung it back up." Her voice faltered. "It's a message from Harriet. I think she was telling me I was right, after all." She pulled the photo out through the broken pane and ripped it in two. "I should've done this years ago. It might have stopped the evil. It might have saved her."

Darkness had fallen by the time Tulla got home. It seemed a lifetime since she'd left, not counting the brief nap at her kitchen counter before rushing back out with Kat. She unlocked her front door, and Clancy shot past her into the dark hallway, his claws clattering on the hardwood.

"Are we good? No mad stabbers?" When she flicked on the kitchen light, Clancy already had his rock. He looked up and grinned. Home safe.

It took her three trips to unload her car, staggering up the front steps against the wind, piling groceries and suitcase just inside the entry. Before she closed the door, she stood on the step and gazed at the sky. In the east, the black roof of the world hung with stars blazing in the cold. In the west, it was another story. As she watched, an angry tower of swirling cloud obliterated the stars. The Fist, a force beyond imagining, loomed over the town, about to strike.

A reddish light dancing on the snow caught her eye. Lightning? How could it be at this time of year? She scanned the front of the building and saw the glow through the curtains in Mikhail's apartment. Her heart leaped. The fireplace in his living room! She took the steps two at a time and banged on the door. "Mik? It's me."

"Come in. Door's open."

She kicked her boots off in the entry and raced to the living room where she could see the back of his head over the top of the armchair facing the fireplace. "You're here. Thank God —"

He rose and faced her, nearly stilling her heart.

"Paul?"

"Hello, Tulla."

He pulled the matching chair over beside his. "Sit by the fire. You must be cold."

"What are you doing here? Where's Mikhail?"

"I have no idea, but I didn't come to see him. I've been waiting for you."

"Me? Why?"

"You know very well why. Dad told me how you wheedled the truth out of him in the library."

She backed away. "Truth about what? I don't —"

"I told you to sit." He grabbed her arm and twisted her into the chair. Never taking his eyes off her face, he showed her the hypodermic needle in his other hand. "Recognize this?"

Tulla laughed nervously. "Déjà vu all over again. Paul, I don't know what you think your father told me. I have no idea. I did find a group photo taken years ago. You and he were in it, but so were a lot of other people — Leo, Mikhail, Celia ..."

Paul waved a dismissive hand. "He told me, but that isn't the problem. What was going on then turns out not to be the big secret he thought it was. Besides, I was just a boy. I had no control over what was happening then." His gaze shifted to the fire, to the past. She threw herself out of the chair but not fast enough. He flung her down and held the needle close to her face. "Bad idea," he snarled.

She pressed back against the upholstered headrest. "I still have no —"

He hit her across the ear. "Do *not* say that again."

She reeled with pain, blood poured down her neck, and her terror grew as she saw his pleasure at hurting her.

"You know I never liked you much, but that didn't stop me from lusting after you. You were such a bitch. I often daydreamed about taking you down a peg or two."

Paul's smile was no longer the Jell-O one from his Uriah Heep days; it was now the smile of a killer. His blow had smashed her hearing aid, driving shards of plastic into the bone behind her ear and the mould deep into the ear canal.

"Did I hurt you? I knew you wore one of those. You keep it hidden. You're so vain, Tulla Murphy, cloaking your … defect behind your lovely thick hair … like a curtain." He brushed her hair back and pulled her hand away from her torn ear. His smile was sardonic. "But, really, Tulla, did you think you were fooling anybody? Well, maybe some people, but not me." He stared down at her. "The one flaw in your perfection, right, Tulla Murphy? Like my leg, my one flaw." His voice had dipped into a whine of self-pity. "But you can hide your flaw, can't you? Your weakness. Your 'impairment.'" He touched his leg, never taking his eyes off her. "I can't hide mine. Is that why you wouldn't have anything to do with me when we were young? You certainly had no time for me, and still don't. You could hardly bring yourself to speak to me when we saw you at the market." His eyes were cold as marbles.

Tulla put her hand back to her ear to staunch the flow of blood. Her eyes welled from the pain.

"It hurts, does it? Your own fault. You shouldn't have tried to get away." He studied her, detached as a scientist observing a specimen pinned to a board. "Must be hard to depend on something so fragile in order to hear."

He shot his hand out and flicked the smashed casing behind her ear. She tried to smother a yelp of agony and pressed back into the chair.

"I hope you can still hear me, though. Can you? Because I want you to know how you're going to leave your cozy, self-satisfied life. It would be too bad if you miss the last words you'll ever hear, or not hear, I mean." He grinned.

Tulla pretended not to understand, but as long as she could see his mouth, read his speech and body language, she could understand what he was saying as clearly as if she could hear every syllable.

"It's your own doing, you know, that I have to kill you. If you hadn't tricked my father into telling you that the boys in that picture were me and Dom …"

Tulla tried to hide her gasp with a cough. "He didn't tell me that. He said they were Cain and Abel."

"Exactly. And that made my father Adam. He was quite proud of his little joke."

"But you and Dom aren't brothers."

"Well, as I found out only recently, we are. We share a father. Opal was kind enough to divulge this information to Dad the night before Dom's funeral." He studied her slyly. "Apparently, there was more than one candidate for the position, as it were." He chuckled. "Including your esteemed father. But Dad beat out all comers." This time he laughed loudly.

"Are you saying you killed Dom?"

"Of course I'm saying that. Cain did kill Abel, correct? Don't pretend again you hadn't figured that out, or I'll have to end this friendly fireside chat prematurely." He held the needle up to the light and depressed the plunger slightly. A spurt of fluid shot out the end. "Know what's in this, Tulla? It's SUX. You nearly being a doctor, I'm sure you've heard of it."

She stared at the needle.

He enunciated clearly, almost shouting. "I want you to hear this, Tulla Murphy. It's important. SUX, short for succinylcholine, is completely undetectable after a few hours. It'll paralyze your muscles and you won't be able to breathe. Of course, you won't be found here. You'll be discovered in the snow. I was going to wait for you in your apartment, but those forensic scientists, they're way too good at finding DNA when there's any suspicion of how you died. So I waited for you here, and you bounded straight into my trap — all unsuspecting, not hearing my voice clearly, so sure it would be Mikhail's."

He looked at her expectantly as if waiting for her to comment on what a great plan he'd hatched. When she didn't speak, he continued. "So you'll be found outside." He glanced at the window. "Deeply buried in the snow, it now appears. And your demise will be attributed to a weak heart, a conclusion influenced by the local coroner's report." His smile slid wide across his face. "Perhaps he'll find evidence of a heart murmur from childhood. He can be very creative. And with all the stress you've endured in the past little while, no wonder your poor heart gave up."

FIFTY-FIVE

LEO WAS SO EXHAUSTED he could hardly focus on the five men at the conference room table. Nemo was getting testier by the minute, Evans and Burton were not making eye contact with anyone, Nob was growing more and more agitated, and Scrivens was beaming with triumph. What was supposed to be a debriefing on the Bluebird raid was turning into an inquisition, with Scrivens the inquisitor and Leo the inquisitee, if there was such a word.

"I don't have time for this, Scrivens," Leo finally said. "I'm leaving for Parnell while I still can get through, so make your case or shut up."

Scrivens leaned back in his chair, baring a shirt front covered with mustard stains from lunch. He picked his teeth slowly, tooth by tooth, staring at Leo. With a sudden movement he rocked forward and stacked a sheaf of papers in front of him. Aligning the corners precisely with slow, deliberate care, he spoke.

"These are internal memos about your behaviour as well as witness statements putting you in Parnell the day Connolly died. You have motives coming out of every orifice, and there have been complaints that you screwed around with the final autopsy report." He read from the top sheet. "'Detective Harding muddied the investigation by delaying the final report. His repeated and unexplained absences amount to a deriliction of duty and —" He glared at Leo when a phone rang. "Harding, that's your damn cell. Turn it off!"

Leo checked the screen, jumped to his feet, and hurried into the hallway. "Mik? Where the hell are you?" His face went still. "I missed it entirely. I'm not in Parnell, either. I'm in Orillia. The whole team's here." He rubbed his forehead. "How could I have been so blind? I'll try to raise Elvie and see if she can get help in town."

Scrivens burst through the doorway, followed by Nemo. "For Christ's sake, Scrivens, he's not going to make a run for it."

Making a play for Leo's phone, Scrivens growled, "Wanna share?"

Leo punched him in the throat.

"Jesus, Harding …" Nemo seized Leo's arm.

Scrivens sagged against the wall, gasping for breath.

Leo held up his phone. "That was Mikhail Novak. He's a psychologist —"

"I know who Novak is," Nemo said wearily.

Leo started for the entrance. "He says the person who killed Connolly and Harriet Deaver is probably about to kill again. It's a pattern. The guy's a psychopath. And the woman Mikhail thinks is his next target is in Parnell with no protection. God, how could I have missed —"

"Who is it?" Nemo interrupted. "Can Novak do anything?"

"He's stuck at O'Hare Airport in Chicago. Nothing's flying. There's not a single officer in Parnell. I have to get back right now."

"You're going nowhere, you bastard," Scrivens rasped, pushing himself away from the wall.

Leo whirled. "One more word from you and I'll pop you for real."

Nemo didn't hesitate. "Go. Take Evans and your man, Tinsley. And report in, damn it!"

The OPP desk sergeant held up a hand, pushing his headphone hard against his ear. "Just getting a report. There's a big pileup at the Arnprior exit. A semi jackknifed and flipped over and then a snowplough drove straight into it. Both north and south lanes are blocked, vehicles all over the place. Nothing and nobody can get through."

Leo closed his eyes briefly. "Number for the Parnell cop shop, quick." He held his phone up.

The sergeant shook his head. "We just lost the cell tower. I'll try to raise them on the radio."

"There's a small airport just south of Parnell."

"Nothing's flying, Harding. Have you looked outside?"

"What about the search-and-rescue helicopter? They'll fly in anything."

"Not in this they won't."

"Goddamn it!" Leo took a deep breath. "Okay, does your satellite phone work?"

"Patchy, drifts in and out ..."

Leo shoved his phone across the counter, screen lit. "See if you can reach this number."

The sergeant shook his head. "I doubt it will."

"Don't doubt, just dial!"

"You don't dial a satellite phone, you —"

Leo leaned over, grabbed the man's collar, and twisted. The sergeant pulled away in alarm. "Okay, I'm on it."

FIFTY-SIX

TULLA TRIED TO THINK straight, to quell her terror. *I've got to keep him talking. Make him shout. Someone might hear or notice the lights from the window and investigate.* She knew the Parnell rumour mill, in its collective mind, had already ground Mikhail's disappearance into an admission of guilt for the murders and the smuggling ring at Bluebird. He'd been raked over the ashes at the reopening of the Klatch after the blizzard that had buried the town. Someone would be delighted to catch him.

"Did it bother you, Paul, to find out you'd killed your own brother?"

He laughed. "Not at all. It was his own fault. He tried to blackmail me into helping deal with his third wife. She's a very brave — or stupid — woman. She wouldn't back down and demanded a huge divorce settlement. He was furious that anyone would stand up to him. But even if I'd known he was my brother —" he curled his lip "— I wasn't about to play. Oh, no, too much to lose now. He shouldn't have pushed me. We'd been as close as brothers, though, from way back. We had a special bond from the day of the Clod War. Bobby always thought you'd seen something. Funny, when I think of him back then, he's always Bobby, not Dom. Still a little bit innocent until that day. Do you remember?"

Suddenly the light dawned.

"It was you and Dom, you beat that little boy to death."

"Not entirely accurate. He didn't die until a few weeks later. My father examined him. Threatened his grandmother that if she told anyone, he'd swear she'd beaten him, which terrified her."

"She was my mother's best friend," Tulla said. *Delay, delay.* "Remember her? Ida Larson?"

Paul nodded. "She was the biggest busybody in Parnell until my father put the fear of — I was going to say 'God,' but perhaps more accurate would be —"

"The Devil," Tulla whispered.

Paul gazed at her without expression and continued. "Dad told her to get the kid back to his parents, get him out of town. We didn't actually mean to kill him, but my father put it right."

The logs in the fireplace had burned down to embers. There was no chance anyone would see a light now. Tulla turned her head slowly, carefully. The fireplace poker hung well out of reach, the stack of spotless firewood equally unreachable. There was nothing else, every surface bare.

"Too bad Novak's such a tidy little housekeeper," Paul said, watching her with obvious amusement. "No handy weapon lying around. And your stalling isn't going to help you, either. Your knight in shining armour's in Orillia, ostensibly for a debriefing on the Bluebird raid, but my source there, a bent cop who has it in for Harding, tells me Leo's there for questioning in the homicide of Dominique Connolly."

She closed her eyes in despair.

He walked backward to the window, never taking his eyes off her. "I'll just close these completely now, make sure we don't get any visitors."

He took a quick peek out the window. "Not a sinner in sight out there, as my useless mother used to say. And she was one of the worst. An enabler, for sure. She knew what was going on and never did a thing." He pulled the curtains tightly shut with one hand, the other holding the needle loosely by his side. "The sinners are all inside tonight." He returned to his chair. "A couple in this very room. You were pretty cruel in high school. No time for anyone else but your own little circle." He pulled his withered leg up over his knee and straightened the crease in his well-pressed trousers. "Open your eyes, Tulla Murphy. I want you to hear me. These little things come back to haunt us. I never forget. Or forgive." He nodded. "I have a long memory."

She shook her head slightly, the stab of pain stopping her. "I don't know what you're saying. Speak louder."

He shouted, "I never forgive or forget! That's enough for you to know!"

"Then what do you remember about that group in the picnic photo?" she asked, keeping her voice low and expressionless. "You were abused, weren't you? You look so frightened in that picture. Who hurt you, Paul? Arn? We all knew to keep away from him, but maybe he caught you." She was stopped cold by the memory of that little sandy foot so long ago, and looked down at his leg, bent at an awkward angle even when he was sitting.

"Bobby and I tried to protect each other. I didn't have a sister to take care of me like you and Leo did." There was bitterness in his voice now. "And my mother sure didn't."

"But you had your father …" Her eyes widened. "I get it now. No one protected you from him."

The room exploded with his rage. He leaped, his face livid, and hit her hard across the face.

Through the blood pouring from her cut mouth, she choked out words. "You'd get clemency. You were created by those terrible sins against you, by your own father."

He pulled her out of the chair. "Bye-bye, Tulla Murphy," he whispered.

She felt the needle plunge into her arm. Her head hit the brass fender of the fireplace as she fell and the freezing darkness rushed in.

FIFTY-SEVEN

KAT AND MEL sat at the kitchen table, reading their books, drinking tea, and polishing off the lemon drizzle cake.

"Snowing again," Kat said contentedly, pulling aside the kitchen blind. "And that wind's brutal."

Mel jerked her head up. "I hear a phone." Hers lay silent on the table in front of her. "Must mean we have service again."

Kat dug hers out of her pocket. "Not mine." She cocked her head. "There it is again." She stood and searched the counter. "Tulla's." She peered at the screen. "She needs to wear it around her neck like Rosie does."

Mel's fingers flew over the keyboard on Kat's phone. "Yay, we've got Internet! No, we don't. Yes, we do. It's like driving through dead zones."

Tulla's phone gave a short ring, then nothing, another … and nothing.

Kat handed it to Mel. "Do you know her security

code? It sounds as if someone's really trying to reach her. It might be her mother's nursing home."

Mel tapped the keyboard. "One, two, three, four … nope. Zero, zero, zero, zero … nope. Four, three, two, one … bingo. I'm in."

"How did you do that?"

"The three most common codes."

"Fits. Tulla's not big on security, for sure. Half the time she doesn't even lock her door. Last week she didn't even close it. I found her asleep at the kitchen counter."

Mel eyed the screen, puzzled. "Seems to be a bunch of texts, but those were phone calls." She read aloud. "'Audio poor quality. Cannot record. To listen to your voicemail message click on the attachment.' What's that mean?"

"Her phone calls come in as texts as well as voice in case she can't hear the message. Can you get at them?"

Mel put the phone on speaker and hit the audio attachment on the first message. They leaned forward, straining to hear through the static and roaring.

"That sounds like Leo," Kat said. "What's he saying?"

Mel played it again. "Sounds like 'stay.' Something about Paul. Does he mean that Skinner guy?"

"No idea. Play the next one."

A voice buried in the static. No words at all this time.

"I think it's Leo again," Kat said. "Is there another one?"

Mel nodded and clicked on the next attachment. "This one doesn't sound like Leo. Wait, I hear a name." She played the message again. "It sounds like 'Jack.' Any idea who —"

"The guy with the scar," Kat said, standing. "We'd better go over —"

Tulla's phone rang again and Kat grabbed it. Static, then the voice clear, the message chilling: "… he's going to try and kill you."

"Mik, is that you?" Kat yelled. "Where are you? Who's going to kill — you're breaking up …"

"Tul … get help … Elvie …"

Kat ran to the door. "Mel, call 911. It's patched through Elvie sometimes. Tell her to get someone, anyone, to the Mill condos."

"You phone, I'll drive," Mel said as they raced down the snow-filled path to Kat's rental car. Mel drove fast, the tires juddering in and out of ruts. The car fishtailed the length of Tulla's street and slammed sideways into the snowbank at the entrance to the parking lot.

Kat was out of the car and sprinting before Mel turned off the ignition. The door to Tulla's apartment stood open, snow sifting down the hall. "Tulla? Tulla? *Please* be here."

Frenzied barking from behind the closed kitchen door answered Kat. She jerked it open, and Clancy shot past her, down the hall, and up the outside stairs. She dashed after him and banged on Mikhail's door. "Tulla? Are you there? Is Paul there? The police are here. They're coming up the stairs now. Unlock the door!" She pulled at the handle, kicking at the door.

Mel pushed her mother aside. "Key," she said, and smashed the lock with the fireplace poker. Two direct blows and the door swung open. Tulla's body lay crumpled on the floor, blood pooling around her head, a tarp spread under her.

FIFTY-EIGHT

MUFFLED FOOTSTEPS. Faint voices in the distance. Tulla could feel the needle in her arm. *Have to get it out, get it out before the stuff reaches my heart. SUX. That's what he said. Untraceable. Where is he?* She struggled to lift her hand, but it was pulled back, held down. She tried to scream, but her voice was only a raspy whisper.

"She's waking up," someone said. "She's trying to pull out the IV."

Pull out ivy? No! IV … intravenous. Oh, God, no one will know what was in it. "Get it out, get it out!" she screamed, a raspy whisper again. "It's SUX!"

"What did she say? It sucks?" A figure in white gripped her arm, warm hands, soothing touch. "You're in the hospital, Tulla. You're safe. Lie back now. Lie still. You're safe."

"Rosie?"

Rosalie's face was close to hers. "You've had a bad time, but you're going to be fine." She could see Rosie's mouth forming the reassuring words.

Someone was crying — loud, gulping sobs. And she could feel wetness on her face.

Tulla squinted into the blurry figure leaning over her. "It's me. It's Kat. Welcome back."

"Where have I been?" Tulla whispered.

"To hell and back, Tul."

"Mum saved you." Mel this time, her voice high and loud with pride. "She flew through the door and nailed him with your fireplace poker."

"Which Mel brought from your fake fireplace, Tulla, after she parked my car in a snowdrift again."

"Did you kill him?" Tulla whispered. "Is Paul dead?"

"Not quite."

"Okay, everybody out," Rosalie said, shooing them to the door. "I don't know who let you all in, anyway. Tulla, when I get the IV back into your arm, don't touch it again. Hear me? Ah, no, you probably don't. Wait! I'm going to prop you up a bit."

She eased Tulla against the pillows and gently looped what appeared to be a rigid stethoscope, like a large hook, around her neck. From its end hung a small rectangular audio receiver with a wire trailing from it. Rosie pronounced her words clearly. "Your audiologist says this might work. He uses it for testing hearing aids with his clients, but he's rigged it so you don't need the aid or mould anywhere near your ear. Just this." She held up the hair-thin wire. "I'm going to feed it into your ear canal. When you can hear what I'm saying, lift a finger. Did you get that?"

Tulla lifted a finger.

"Okay, here we go." As she carefully threaded the probe into Tulla's ear, trying to avoid the still-open cuts and abrasions, she recited in a normal tone, "'Along the line of smoky hills, the crimson forest stands …'"

Slowly, the wire went deeper. Tulla winced when it brushed against the wound and bruising deep inside the canal, but she remained motionless and silent.

Rosie's voice grew quieter as she concentrated on her task. "'The crimson forest stands. And all the day …' Can't remember the rest. 'And all the day —'"

"'The blue-jay calls throughout the autumn lands,'" Tulla whispered, holding up a shaky finger. "'Indian Summer,' my favourite poem." She could hear Rosie's voice, she could hear footsteps in the hall, she could hear the beeping and clicking of the machines. She could hear life. Tulla touched the wire running from the receiver into her smashed ear. "I'm back online. Thank you, Rosie."

Rosalie squeezed her hand and picked up the call button looped to the bedframe. "We're going to do another brain scan to make sure all's well. You've given us a bad scare, Tulla Murphy. You've been in a coma for almost three days. That's where you've been." She held up three fingers. "Not supposed to tell you, but you did ask. I'll be back to get you soon."

Leo peered around the doorway the minute Rosalie left. "Hi."

Tulla squinted at him as he crossed the floor. She patted the edge of the bed. "Leo …"

"*Shh!* Rosie the Riveter doesn't know I'm here."

"Leo, how come I'm still alive? He ... Paul said that stuff in the needle would kill me and leave no trace."

"You're still alive because the cavalry arrived just in time." He leaned over her, eyes bright, smile broad, granite gone. "It went like this. Kat and Melissa were the first responders, along with your grandfather, who apparently with great forethought made the poker Kat decked Paul with. Then Elvie and Shaun, the techie, arrived with the fire trucks. But before any of this, Mikhail —"

"Mikhail? He's safe?" Tulla tried to pull herself up from the pillows.

"Sit back. He is. He was the one who figured out it was Paul who killed Dom and Harriet."

"How?"

"You told him."

"Me? I didn't know it was Paul until he told me himself."

"You told Mikhail that Paul had been the person with Dom and Celia in the Bahamas."

"I tried to tell you, but you wouldn't listen, so I —"

"Yes, well, more fool me. Mik figured that meant Paul had probably been with them in Tijuana, and he wondered why. What was the connection between Dom and Paul and why the secrecy? He was just starting to investigate and discovered that the medical centre there had recently been closed down by the authorities and the staff had scattered. Some were in jail, others merely had vanished. But he tracked down a nurse who said she'd talk to him, but only in person. Since he was embedded in the Bluebird setup, he couldn't go to Tijuana, but didn't think there was any urgency. He was only pursuing it to indulge a paranoid friend." Leo pointed at himself, raised both eyebrows, and grinned at her. "As some wise person once said, 'Strange how paranoia can link up with reality now and then.' Me again."

Tulla gave a tiny wave of dismissal and an even tinier lopsided smile. Both caught Leo's heart. He rubbed a finger back and forth across his mouth, buying time to find his voice again. "Then the whole Bluebird thing blew up. Mik escaped and wanted to go away, anyway, so he flew to Tijuana and interviewed the nurse, who told him there had been a doctor with Celia and her husband the night Celia died. They spent some time in her room alone. Some of the nursing staff were sure the intravenous drip had been tampered with, but they were afraid to tell anyone because the police were already investigating the centre."

"Oh, Leo …"

"Mikhail said it was suddenly so plain that he couldn't believe he'd missed it — a classic profile apparent even when Paul was a youngster. The charm, the mood swings, the lack of empathy, remorse, or guilt, the belief that anything that happened was someone else's fault, bearing grudges for a lifetime." He touched her hand gently. "Not to mention, the need to control. He's a psychopath. Made or born, who knows? Mikhail basically says, 'Who cares?' He would've continued to kill. His father knew about both murders and was trying to cover for him. As coroner, he persuaded the young and very new pathologist who did the autopsy — bullied I guess is a better word — that the needle marks Paul added to Dom's arms went back years, indicating Dom was an addict and hadn't been murdered by anyone.

"He messed up the crime scene in Harriet's kitchen. That was why he was so enraged when I insisted her body go to Ottawa. He was going to take care of Aggie because he was certain Harriet had told her what she knew. Then you came into his sights. He was losing it, trying so hard to keep suspicion away from Paul, because he blamed himself for what his son had become — a stone-cold killer."

Tulla inhaled shakily. "Yes …"

"As soon as the pieces fell into place, Mikhail tried to get back here, attempted to reach you, me, the OPP team, Elvie, Kat … anyone."

"Where were you? AWOL again?"

"Not fair, Tulla," Rosie said, steering a gurney into the room. "He risked his life to get back to you."

"I was caught in Orillia by the storm. Remember that? And my instruction not to open the door to anyone but me?"

"No. I don't remember any of that." She smiled at him. "So how did you get here?"

"He actually persuaded someone to fly him here right through the Fist," Rosalie said.

"It was Jack who did the persuading. He found a helicopter and a pilot and said this guy owed him a favour — I suspect he might have threatened to kneecap him — and told the hospital in Orillia to clear their pad, that it was a matter of life and death. Which it was — yours. They thought he was bringing in a patient, but the helicopter was coming in to get Nob, Evans, and me. Jack also got someone at that little airport near Parnell to put the lights on and clear a spot. When we got near Parnell, Nob spotted the Fist. We could actually see the cloud shape, like knuckles over the town. Jack had warned the pilot but had assured him it would be piece of cake for someone who'd flown missions into the siege of Sarajevo. When we finally landed, the pilot said he'd take Sarajevo anytime. Me, too. It was one scary ride." Leo smiled slightly. "Since Kat had already knocked him unconscious it was a fairly easy arrest."

"Leo, Tulla's exhausted," Rosalie said. "Now go. She's getting a scan and then rest."

FIFTY-NINE

WHEN TULLA WAS ALLOWED visitors again, her father was the first through the door. "Darlin', I blame myself. I don't know why I hadn't guessed." He kissed her cheek. "Brenda says that the minute you can travel you're coming down to us. She's actually here with me in Parnell. Can you imagine that? We brought Liam."

Tulla smiled at him. "I'll come, Dad. Boy, will I come. And you can't take the blame. There's none left. Kat says this wouldn't have happened if she'd insisted I stay on with her. Mikhail sent a note with flowers to say it's his fault. I have no idea why."

Mikhail stood in the doorway. "Because disappearing after the raid focused suspicion on me and away from the real culprits."

Tulla held out her arms. He moved forward and hugged her longer than he had ever done before.

"Actually, it was my fault," Leo said, coming into the room behind Mik.

"This is turning into a French farce," Tulla said.

Leo shook hands with Warren, touched Mikhail's shoulder, and sat on the bed next to Tulla. "How are you, kid?'

"Peachy. So how come it's your fault?"

"I didn't want to be left out."

Tulla relaxed against the pillows and beamed at all of them.

When the others left, Leo handed her a file. "When you feel up to it, could you read this? It's part of Paul's statement. Check that it's an accurate record of what happened in Mikhail's apartment, as much as you can remember." He contemplated her pale face, the heavy bandage around her head. "You're tired."

He stood, but Tulla reached out to him. "Leo, why did you say it was your fault Paul wasn't caught earlier? I know you weren't joking when you said that."

He sat back down. "Three reasons. First, because I kept having to leave Parnell in the middle of the investigation."

"Why?"

"That accident in Kabul that burst my eardrum? What I didn't tell you was that the driver and the other two were killed. I went through the windshield and ended up with a broken neck, a fractured skull, and amnesia. The three or four years before the accident are mostly a blank, and I have selective amnesia over several years before that. So that and collateral damage from such a severe concussion aren't great if you want to be a cop. Actually, not great if you want to be anything."

"That's what you've been trying to hide with your fake deafness?"

He nodded. "Badly, as it turns out. I was deaf for a while, but my hearing came back. No one in the lower ranks knew the extent of my injuries. I wanted to keep it that way. If guys like Scrivens knew, I shudder to think."

"Scrivens?"

He waved a hand. "A scumbag cop of no importance. Only way I could persuade the brass — those who knew — to keep me in the force was to take part in a clinical trial looking at the treatment for retrograde and selective amnesia. Which is why I kept disappearing. I had to fulfill the requirements of the study or take long-term medical leave which, translated, means getting booted off the force."

"Why didn't you tell me before when we talked in the car?"

Leo spread his hands.

"It's a disability, not a weakness, Leo." When she was met with silence, she asked, "And the other reasons?"

"Mikhail and I have to share the next one. We were fools to have suspected each other."

"You suspected each other?"

"He went away because he thought I'd killed Dom. That's what he meant in his note about testing loyalties. If he came back, would he turn me in or cover for me because of our friendship? And I thought he meant he'd killed Dom and he'd be testing my loyalty if he returned because I'd have to arrest him or cover for him."

Tulla started to shake her head and winced. "That's crazy. Where were your brains?"

"Think about it. We both hated Dom. Me for personal reasons, Mikhail for more general ones. He was an evil-doer, and Mikhail could no longer condone such evil. And the last one, if I'd killed Dom, Paul wouldn't have had to, wouldn't have murdered Miss D. and nearly you."

"That's —"

"Crazy? No, Tulla, because I found out enough at the clinic in the Bahamas and then that horrific setup in Tijuana to confirm my suspicions, at least enough for me to act. I was positive Dom had killed Celia. I didn't know about Paul being there, but it wouldn't have mattered, anyway. I was determined to take Dom out. It was revenge, but —" He shrugged. "So I was biding my time. Paul just beat me to it. By the way, how did you find out it was Paul with Dom and Celia at the clinic?"

"Two things. A doctor from Princess Amelia Women's Hospital recently wrote to the clinic requesting Celia's records. He said there had been mistakes made in the hospital's pathology lab and there was an inquiry. This made no sense. Not about the screw-up in the lab, which explains Celia's misdiagnosis, but no sense that a doctor would be trying to get Celia's records from the clinic after all this time — in fact, for any reason at all. The hospital knew she'd been misdiagnosed. Anyway, I tried to find this doctor — Graydon Smith — on the Internet, but there was no such guy.

"However, I did discover a bunch of stuff about Paul, for instance, that he was under suspicion for altering patient records. According to an old colleague of mine from my Princess Amelia Hospital days, the deal was that if Paul left quietly, the hospital wouldn't press charges. She also said there had been a rumour that he'd been accused of sexual assault by one of his patients. The authorities really didn't want that to surface. Then I talked to a friend who worked at the casino bar in the Bahamas. She remembered him and described him to a T. That's when I thought he might be this mysterious doctor and wondered why he was asking for Celia's records, but I figured I was connecting dots that weren't there, and then Mel went missing and —"

Leo pointed at the file. "Paul was Graydon Smith. After he found out I'd been to the clinic, he got nervous and embarked on some serious cover-up. In his statement to us, he says Dom was happy to rid himself of Celia because he wanted to replace her with someone new. So the two of them exploited the misdiagnosis by the hospital in Toronto and encouraged her to seek alternative medicine, first, in the Bahamas, and then even better in that horrific place in Tijuana. I believe him when he says that she wasn't hard to persuade, given our mother's experience. He claimed that she believed she could cure cancer with yoga and green tea. God, he's an unfeeling bastard."

He took a deep breath before continuing. "Hard to believe, but Dom came to him again for help in disposing his current wife who foolishly threatened to reveal his human trafficking involvement if she didn't get the settlement she wanted out of their divorce. When Paul refused, Dom went ballistic, promising dire consequences. He would incriminate him in Celia's death, reveal his connections to the Bluebird set-up, all without implicating himself somehow ..."

Tulla held up a hand. "Wait. Did you say Bluebird?"

"Yeah. Paul took over the leadership there after he killed Dom, but he's been involved for several years. There was no way Skinner would let Dom have that kind of power over him, so he arranged to meet him at his Crow's Nest house. They had a couple of drinks, he slipped Rohypnol into Dom's Scotch, and when he passed out, injected him with an overdose of heroin."

Tulla closed her eyes, then asked, "And what does he say about Miss D.?"

"That she knew too much about how Dom died and had to go. We were right about the motive, just didn't know whose. He says she summoned him to her house — he sure didn't like that — and told him Arn had seen his father's car heading to Dom's place the night of the Fist, although he hadn't known Paul was at the wheel ..."

"Of course," Tulla whispered, "Crow Lake Road. I forgot we could see it from our roof. That explains what he meant with 'the doctor makes house calls.'"

Leo nodded. "Apparently, Miss D. also let him know that her friend Eddy, the Hells Angel enforcer, told her that Dom never took drugs. Then she signed her own death warrant by telling Paul that she had every intention of letting the authorities know all this. So Paul killed her and staged her death to seem like an accident. He even cranked up the heat under the chicken bones she had simmering for stock, trusting they would boil dry, start a fire, and burn the house down before her body was discovered. He was particularly proud of this ploy, even though it didn't work."

Leo took a sheet of paper from the file and held it up. "This is from Mikhail's notes on the transcript of Paul's interrogation. He mentions one of the dichotomies of a psychopath's reasoning: he's very clever and wants everyone to know it. The temptation to boast about what he's done fights with the need to keep quiet. When he's caught, it all comes spilling out. Paul wanted everyone to know how smart he was. His lawyer was having a fit trying to shut him up. He incriminated himself at every turn. That, and how none of it was his fault. Always someone else's. Dom's for threatening to blackmail him, Harriet's for threatening to tell on him, yours for worming the Cain and Abel story out of his father ..."

Crepe-soled shoes squeaked up the corridor, and Rosalie came through the door wheeling the meds trolley. As she passed Leo, she put her hand on his shoulder. He covered it with his and smiled at her. Then she handed Tulla two pills in a little cup. "Can I trust you to take these on your own, or do I have to stand over you."

"Are they painkillers?"

Rosalie nodded.

"Only two?" Tulla tipped them into her mouth.

After Rosie left, Tulla reached for her cup of water. "She's very fond of you, isn't she?"

"And I her," Leo said. "She's had a bad time."

Tulla waited, but he said nothing more.

"Okay. I understand everything you've told me so far, but what I totally don't get is how could you and Mikhail ever have suspected each other of killing Miss D."

"We didn't. As it turns out, we both thought old Doc Skinner had gone to persuade her to keep quiet about the old days and his role. Neither one of us suspected Paul. We both thought that maybe the old man had grabbed Harriet, she'd fallen against the edge of the old wood stove in her kitchen, and hadn't been hit with the iron frying pan. Obviously, we were dead wrong. Then Paul's father spilled the beans to you in the library, so now you had to be silenced."

Tulla leaned back on the pillows. "What an entanglement! It seems we all secretly suspected one another. Kat and I thought you'd murdered Dom, but we didn't care. You believed Mikhail had murdered him, and you didn't care. Mikhail was sure you were the murderer, but he didn't care. I even thought for maybe five seconds that Kat had killed Dom, and I didn't care. Note that none of us suspected one another of killing Harriet, so I guess our moral compasses aren't completely fried." Her eyelids fluttered, then snapped open. "What about Arn? Did Paul kill him or did his father?"

"No one killed him. He fell."

"No, he didn't." Rosie stood in the doorway. "Tell her, Leo."

"He fell."

"I pushed him."

Tulla's eyes widened.

"When I saw him with Maddie, I snapped," Rosie said. "I took her home and went back to the Manor later that night with some tools. That's when I saw Mikhail and we talked. After he left, I went up to the roof and loosened the screws in the footings of the railing. Then I took Arn up. I did it for all the kids he'd caught as well as for Maddie and myself. But I have to go to the authorities now."

Tulla felt tears trickling down her cheeks. "Oh, God, Rosie. *No!* You had the courage to take on evil face to face and not wait for the system to deal with him."

"And Rosalie Stevens, I'm the *authority* here. I'm still a cop ... for the moment. If you try to confess, Mikhail will lie and say he killed Arn. Then you'd be guilty of letting an innocent man go to jail." Leo smiled slightly. "It's all about guilt, you know."

"Apparently," Tulla said, her voice fading. "Oh, wait, before I forget. I have a plan."

"Not now, Tulla," Rosie said. "Sleep."

"I've been thinking." Her words were slurred. "This town doesn't need a bookstore. It's got Aggie and her library. So I'm going to turn the Cohen house into a shelter for troubled kids. But first I'm going to gut it. Personally. Me and Kat. I mean, Kat and I. With pick-axes." Her voice was fading. "We'll knock holes in the walls to let the evil out, like that skyscraper in Hong Kong that has a huge hole in it to let dragons fly through. We'll let the evil fly right through and away down the valley ..." Her voice was barely a whisper now.

"I'll help," Leo said.

"If you can take time off from being a cop."

"I'll have time because I'm quitting. I'm not fit to be a cop yet. I realize it now. So I'm going on an odyssey."

"You're going after Darla?" Tulla asked.

"No, I'm going after my daughter."

"But you said —"

Leo touched her lips. "*Shhh!* Mikhail's been tracking Darla now that we know all her aliases and record in the States. He's just told me that her child did die, but it wasn't the little girl I met. It was the baby, a much younger child. Of spinal meningitis."

Tulla tried to sit up. He pushed her gently back onto the pillows. "Want company?" she whispered. "I'm always up for a good odyssey."

ACKNOWLEDGEMENTS

THIS BOOK WAS LONG IN THE WRITING. My friends and family can attest to that. Over the lengthy gestation period, so many people have been my supporters, guides, believers, readers, and critics — the good kind.

Kirk Howard, founder, president/publisher, and now publisher emeritus of Dundurn Press, took a flyer on my first book, *That Other Place*, despite its hybrid nature and unknown author. I am forever grateful for that, and for his continued support. Also at Dundurn, Kathryn Lane, editorial director, and Jenny McWha, assistant project editor, for their help and encouragement and for ensuring that this book stayed on track; and Shari Rutherford, whose superb proofreading provided the final safety net.

Hilary McMahon at Westwood Creative Agency critiqued my first "open-door" draft, which became my road map for all the many versions that followed. This is the draft you finally summon the courage to show to another human being; it's often the point when the book you thought you had written turns into the one you have barely begun.

A good editor has the skills and tact to shape and improve a book while always respecting the author's voice and story; has an ear for good writing; knows when to hold fast, when to give in; spots inaccuracies, inconsistencies, inconsequentialities; and saves the author serious embarrassment by catching her really egregious mistakes. I was blessed with two such editors whose many "saves" included a geriatric pregnancy of such length it would have astounded the medical world, and a roadside bomb in Afghanistan — an "IUD" — whose explosion would have certainly baffled the military one.

Dianne Perrier did the first copy-edit pass, pulling lots of weeds. Also a crackerjack researcher, she provided additional facts to enrich some historical sections of the book.

Michael Carroll, meticulous, thorough, and apparently able to operate without sleep, did the in-depth pass — copy and substantive — immersing himself in the text to the point I believe he came to know my characters almost better than I do, and also the twisty parts of the plot. And I'm betting he didn't miss a clue salted throughout the story.

Friends and family — both directly and indirectly — who have helped me bring this book to fruition, I thank you.

Directly: Matt Williams (in-family publishing navigator), Sam Williams, Erin Cunningham, Erinn Somerville, Nancy Lee, Roger White, Pat Hood, Helen Meubus, and my granddaughter, Ruby Williams, for her clever concept for an alternate cover.

Indirectly: My other grandkids: Kieran, Abram, and Louis; Loranne Sackmann, Joe Fisher, and their tribe; Keith Sackmann and his; and Allen Sackmann and Cindy Charters. My brothers, Seaton Findlay and Chris (Mobe) Findlay, for our tiny book club, so exclusive we only read one another's manuscripts. And Joan and Sue, who hold reader memberships. My special group of old friends, Andrea Spry, Margaret Ault, Liz Barnes, Sheila Rorke, and Martha Clark: since our high school years together one of our strongest bonds has been the books we've shared, discussed, and discovered for one another.

And once again, I thank my husband, Allen Sackmann, for pretty much everything. He is a devil's advocate, a sounding board, a stirrer of ideas, a bringer of logic and laughter, and an enabler of the best kind.

Mystery and Crime Fiction from Dundurn Press

Birder Murder Mysteries
by Steve Burrows
(BIRDING, BRITISH COASTAL TOWN
MYSTERIES)
A Siege of Bitterns
A Pitying of Doves
A Cast of Falcons
A Shimmer of Hummingbirds
A Tiding of Magpies
A Dance of Cranes

Amanda Doucette Mysteries
by Barbara Fradkin
(PTSD, CROSS-CANADA TOUR)
Fire in the Stars
The Trickster's Lullaby
Prisoners of Hope

B.C. Blues Crime Novels
by R.M. Greenaway
(BRITISH COLUMBIA, POLICE
PROCEDURAL)
Cold Girl
Undertow
Creep
Flights and Falls

Stonechild & Rouleau Mysteries
by Brenda Chapman
(FIRST NATIONS, KINGSTON,
POLICE PROCEDURAL)
Cold Mourning
Butterfly Kills
Tumbled Graves
Shallow End
Bleeding Darkness
Coming soon: *Turning Secrets*

Jack Palace Series
by A.G. Pasquella
(NOIR, TORONTO, MOB)
Yard Dog

Jenny Willson Mysteries
by Dave Butler
(NATIONAL PARKS, ANIMAL PROTECTION)
Full Curl
No Place for Wolverines

Falls Mysteries
by J.E. Barnard
(RURAL ALBERTA, FEMALE SLEUTH)
When the Flood Falls
Coming soon: *Where the Ice Falls*

Foreign Affairs Mysteries
by Nick Wilkshire
(GLOBAL CRIME FICTION, HUMOUR)
Escape to Havana
The Moscow Code
Remember Tokyo

Dan Sharp Mysteries
by Jeffrey Round
(LGBTQ, TORONTO)
Lake on the Mountain
Pumpkin Eater
The Jade Butterfly
After the Horses
The God Game
Shadow Puppet

Max O'Brien Mysteries
by Mario Bolduc
(TRANSLATION, POLITICAL THRILLER,
CON MAN)
The Kashmir Trap
The Roma Plot
The Tanzania Conspiracy

Cullen and Cobb Mysteries
by David A. Poulsen
(CALGARY, PRIVATE INVESTIGATORS,
ORGANIZED CRIME)
Serpents Rising
Dead Air
Last Song Sung
Coming soon: *None So Deadly*

Strange Things Done
by Elle Wild
(YUKON, DARK THRILLER)

Salvage
by Stephen Maher
(NOVA SCOTIA, FAST-PACED THRILLER)

Crang Mysteries
by Jack Batten
(HUMOUR, TORONTO)
Crang Plays the Ace
Straight No Chaser
Riviera Blues
Blood Count
Take Five
Keeper of the Flame
Booking In

Jack Taggart Mysteries
by Don Easton
(UNDERCOVER OPERATIONS)
Loose Ends
Above Ground
Angel in the Full Moon
Samurai Code
Dead Ends
Birds of a Feather
Corporate Asset
The Benefactor
Art and Murder
A Delicate Matter
Subverting Justice
An Element of Risk

Meg Harris Mysteries
by R.J. Harlick
(CANADIAN WILDERNESS FICTION,
FIRST NATIONS)
Death's Golden Whisper
Red Ice for a Shroud
The River Runs Orange
Arctic Blue Death
A Green Place for Dying
Silver Totem of Shame
A Cold White Fear
Purple Palette for Murder

Thaddeus Lewis Mysteries
by Janet Kellough
(PRE-CONFEDERATION CANADA)
On the Head of a Pin
Sowing Poison
47 Sorrows
The Burying Ground
Wishful Seeing

Cordi O'Callaghan Mysteries
by Suzanne F. Kingsmill
(ZOOLOGY, MENTAL ILLNESS)
Forever Dead
Innocent Murderer
Dying for Murder
Crazy Dead

Endgame
by Jeffrey Round
(MODERN RE-TELLING OF AGATHA
CHRISTIE, PUNK ROCK)

Inspector Green Mysteries
by Barbara Fradkin
(OTTAWA, POLICE PROCEDURAL)
Do or Die
Once Upon a Time
Mist Walker
Fifth Son
Honour Among Men
Dream Chasers
This Thing of Darkness
Beautiful Lie the Dead
The Whisper of Legends
None So Blind

Border City Blues
by Michael Januska
(PROHIBITION-ERA WINDSOR)
Maiden Lane
Riverside Drive
Prospect Avenue

Cornwall and Redfern Mysteries
by Gloria Ferris
(DARKLY COMIC, RURAL ONTARIO)
Corpse Flower
Shroud of Roses